Vida Blue

Susie Perez Fernandez

21 tales

Vida Blue

Copyright © 2018 Susie Perez Fernandez

ISBN: 978-1732263-9-01

www.21talesmedia.com

1 2 3 4 5 6 7 8 9 10

To all those kindhearted ladies who are
tough chicks in disguise…your cape is on the way.

"Its scenic vistas, art history, and incredible food and drink have long made Italy a destination for romance-seekers, foodies, and adventurers. But Positano, located just south of Naples along the Amalfi Coast, is a true jewel to visit. When you travel to Positano, the first thing you'll notice is the breathtaking natural beauty of this part of Italy: high craggy cliffs rise like curtains from the azure sea below."

— *Travel and Leisure*

TABLE OF CONTENTS

Acknowledgments

It has taken me ten years to finalize this story. It has evolved, as I have evolved through the years, and I humbly believe this is the best version. I am thankful for all those family members and friends who stood by me, cheered, and encouraged me on this journey.

Always one to promote and nourish my dreams, my love, Eddy . . . the reason for writing this book, the love of my life. I was able to write this little novel because of your immense love.

An honorable mention and thank you to the city of Positano for inspiring me. I only hope I did you justice in describing your beauty, your citizens, and life on the Amalfi Coast. God has truly blessed this beautiful region of Italy.

Included in Vida Blue is also my love for India. From childhood you have always inspired me. The culture, people, food, customs, and faith are humbly included in the story to make it richer for the reader. Accept this mention not as a token but out of extreme respect and admiration for your country.

I must thank my parents, Delfina and Frank. I am me, after all, because of them. They exemplified love; therefore, I can love in return without bias or conditions.

This book would not exist if it weren't for the guidance, hard work, sweat, and tears (literal and figurative) of my editor, Susan Hughes. You are one special lady! Thank you for believing in me and my story even when I did not. Thank you for taking care of the integrity of my characters, who I fondly refer to as my children.

If love does not make you happy, it was never love.

CHAPTER ONE

Don't go into that building, Santos. It's just the supplies warehouse. The words reverberated through his head as he pulled the car to a stop outside the complex of a dilapidated metal structure in the middle of the hot, dusty desert outside Campeche, Mexico. Why is it that when someone tells you not to do something, you seem compelled to do the opposite?

Santos could not escape the nagging feeling that something was terribly wrong. His business partners were up to something; he was certain of it. It was that gut feeling, among other things, that led him to this place in the middle of nowhere, more determined than ever to discover what was going on, to prove once and for all that there was more to this business partnership than just fine Mexican tequila. There had to be evidence inside that warehouse—if he could get inside and find it.

"You can't sit here all day, Santos," he grumbled to himself as the car's idling engine strained against the brutal Mexican heat. Storm clouds brewed ominously on the horizon, and a southerly wind whipped at the vehicle, tossing dust against the windshield. If he was going to show the agents any proof of his suspicions . . . *It's now or never.*

As Santos turned off the engine and stepped from the vehicle, the desert heat nearly took his breath away. He shielded his eyes from the sun and sand as he looked about. No sign of life as far as the eye could see. It was a Sunday, after all. No big surprise that he was alone. He took a step toward the building and was stopped in his tracks by the vibration in his shirt pocket. He pulled out his phone and glanced at the screen. *Ari.*

"Hey, love. How are you?" he whispered, relieved to hear a friendly voice but knowing full well that she could always detect a lie.

"Where are you? I thought you were at the airport. Did you miss your flight again? Santos, you promised!"

Santos paced near the car, unwilling to get any closer to the building until he could give the place his full attention. "Yes, my love . . . well, the weather is not great here, and there are more storms coming. I decided to wait it out and take the next flight. I know how much you worry."

He hated to lie to her, but telling her the truth would only make her frantic. He couldn't do that to her. Ari was and always would be the love of his life. He'd give his own life to protect her and would do anything in his power to make her happy.

"Ari, listen. I've been thinking about the house in Positano lately. Actually, I've been thinking about it a lot, much more so than in the past few years, and . . . well, I need to—"

"Positano? You haven't mentioned that in ages and—"

Santos nervously combed his hand through his hair, searching for the right words. "I want to go away with you to Italy sooner than we had planned."

For a moment, all of his troubles, doubts, and gut feelings about what waited in the warehouse seemed to disappear. Ari was his life, and no matter what happened with his business, they had a beautiful future ahead of them.

"When you get home . . . I'll finally feel at home," Ari said sweetly into the receiver.

This gave Santos the strength he needed to move forward with his mission. He promised to get home early to celebrate and then ended the call and headed for the warehouse just as the first raindrops spattered from the sky. The storm had arrived, but Santos had no time to think about its significance, to consider it an omen of what might lie ahead. Had he done so, he might have returned to the car and driven back the way he came, never looking back.

Within minutes, he had the outer door pried open, only to be greeted by a thick concrete wall and a massive metal door, its key pad blinking, the security system armed. No code, no time. Now what? Santos had promised the agents that he would bring them something definite today, some real proof of his suspicions. Time was definitely not on his side. Possible code combinations ran through his head, but as his finger hovered above the key pad, only one number hammered at him: eighty-seven, the number of the home he and Ari planned to buy in Positano. It was as if the cosmos was sending him a message, and he had no choice but to go with it. He punched in the numbers three times, but the pad lit up red. "Damn it!" He tried another combination. Wrong again.

Suddenly the ground shook as a bolt of lightning struck nearby, followed immediately by thunder so loud he could feel it beneath his feet. Santos dropped to the concrete floor, fearing the worst. But the worst turned out to be better than he could have imagined; in fact, it was exactly what he needed. The lightning struck the electrical box wired to the cluster of warehouses, and without electrical current to secure the door, it finally opened.

Santos slipped into the warehouse, giving his eyes time to adjust to the gloomy darkness. Inside, he found no barrels, nor did he smell the musky odor of bourbon—used, according to their plant manager, to give tequila that aged, reposado taste—that would have accompanied the oak barrels they'd purchased in France to store the tequila. Instead, the space was stacked ceiling-high with crates. Santos wiped the sweat from his forehead, his mind focused on getting what he'd come for and getting back home to Ari. With the aid of a crowbar he found in a far corner, he carefully pried open one of the crates. There, Santos found the proof he had been searching for. His partners were dealing in something much more sinister than tequila.

Evidence in hand, Santos sprinted back to his car—an impressive feat, given the weight of the box he carried. The rain and wind would make driving to the meeting point difficult, but nothing could stop him from reaching the agents as planned. Santos took to the road, angry and driving much faster than was safe. Within minutes, he caught sight of the flashing lights on the vehicle behind him as they cut through the pounding rain and sliced across his dashboard. Santos found it odd than anyone else would be on the road, given the intensity of the storm and the two-hour distance between his current location and the nearest town. He slowed down and pulled the car to the side of the road, windshield wipers pounding almost as quickly as his heart. He squinted at the approaching vehicle as it passed and pulled to a stop at a sharp angle in front of him.

"Shit," Santos muttered. "Green Valley."

Things were about to get much worse. Ari would have to wait a bit longer.

***

Avinash Batra flipped off the office light and locked the door behind him, annoyed that the business meeting took longer than expected. He headed for the pub, still impeccably dressed in the chic, black, Italian designer suit and starched grey shirt he'd put on early that morning. As he approached the pub, likely to be filled with other businessmen eager for a quick midday drink, Avinash, a Mumbai native, ran a quick hand through his jet-black hair and smoothed his mustache and goatee, though it really wasn't necessary; there's never a single strand out of place. Avinash, president of World Bank, is known as London's leading playboy, a man with outstanding table and bedside manners. It's a reputation he worked hard to maintain.

He swung the heavy pub door open and held it for a young woman on his heels. He flashed a smile that reached all the way to his eyes and ended with a wink. She returned the flirtatious grin and flipped her hair over her shoulder as she hurried inside and disappeared into the crowded shadows. A scoundrel and yet chivalrous and compassionate, Avinash enjoyed helping the less fortunate. He swaggered to the bar with a palpable confidence, an air envied by those around him. It had been a busy morning. Time for one quick drink. Alone.

A well-known skirt chaser, Avinash was attracted to intelligent and witty women. He loved the play on words and was a sucker for skillful conversation and comedic banter laced with flirtatious, sexual undertones. Avinash was good at everything—sports, cooking, business, investments—with one exception: he had not managed to find a compatible partner who shared all his interests. The dinner planned for tonight with Anjali, his business partner Sam Waters, and Lola, his new twenty-six-year-old conquest, might provide just the entertainment he needed. Just thinking about it excited him. He downed his drink and returned to the office with a smile on his face.

"Is everything ready for dinner tonight, Anjali?" he asked as he passed his assistant's desk and headed for his office. "I'm making a delightful pasta dish and—"

"Who are you bringing tonight to torture me? I can see it in your eyes. You're just chomping at the bit, aren't you?" she said, shuffling papers on her desk as if she had real work to do. "Why do you waste your time with these girls? I just don't understand it, Avinash!"

"Oh, come on, Anjali. Why do you get so uncomfortable at these gatherings?" he said as he settled at his desk, his chin cupped in one hand. "Surely you enjoy meeting my new . . . friends." Anjali approached and planted both palms in the middle of his expensive, polished cherrywood desk.

"Seriously, why do you date these girls? It's all a dark, Machiavellian game to you. It's totally unfair to you and the girl, you know? Why do you bother cooking and inviting them to your place, making them feel all secure, like there's a real relationship going on? And wipe that raised eyebrow off your forehead!"

Avinash leaned back in his chair, listening, amused by her incessant and predictable tirade. "What raised eyebrow?"

"The one that says *pussy* on it!" she said, pushing back from his desk in a huff. "I know what you're thinking. Don't act all innocent and confused with me."

"Oh, come on! Seriously, Anjali? This is my life. How long have you known me? I've always been this way. I enjoy the now, the present, and I laugh at all these serious matters you take to heart. I don't care what people think. I appreciate your concern, but—"

"But what?" she said, gesturing wildly with her hands, close to unraveling.

"But . . . butt out. Truly! Just come over tonight, smile your little smile, enjoy the conversation, and forget about everything that troubles you. Can you do that?" he said, quite certain that she indeed could not. "I promise you can lecture me about my meaningless life tomorrow. *Theek Hai?*"

"All right, but I know there is someone out there for you."

He smiled, victorious once again, chuckling as she turned on her heels and fled from his office.

***

That evening in the Chelsea neighborhood of London, at the prestigious Hyde Park Building where the last flat sold for thirty-five million pounds, Avinash brought Sam a Scotch and water. The waitstaff set the table, while the delicious dinner Avinash prepared warmed in the high-tech kitchen.

Lola, the conquest, sat cross-legged on the cognac-colored leather sofa across from Avinash and Sam, her foot *tap-tapping* against the mahogany cocktail table as if in sync with her heart as Anjali admired the million-dollar view from the living room's floor-to-ceiling windows. Avinash flashed Lola a wary smile, his eyes glued to her leg as he tried to focus on Sam's words. It was an awkward few moments, and he began to wonder whether Lola would be worth the extra effort.

When Sam pulled the table away from Lola's twitching foot, she stilled, sat up straight, and turned her attention to the artwork on the wall, wondering aloud if it was African in origin.

"Ahh no, actually, they are from India. Original pieces from several artists. Do you like them?"

Before Lola could reply, Anjali crossed the room and made herself comfortable on the sofa with the gentlemen, one eyebrow raised at Avinash.

"So, Sam, I sent Ms. Ariadne Cordero, the client who is buying the home in Italy, an email with all the instructions today. She must be so excited, starting a new life and all."

Avinash smiled, knowing full well that Anjali was infuriated at Lola's presence, if not her ignorance. He looked over at Sam with curiosity.

"This client of yours . . . she's American and she wants to move to Italy? Is she looking for a house or a man?"

"Actually, she wants to move to Italy to forget a man," Sam said with a nervous chuckle. "Ms. Cordero is a well-traveled woman and should have no problem adapting, but I expect it may not be the best move for a young, beautiful woman her age, especially considering her reasons."

"Well, I think it takes courage to do what she's doing — moving to another country, forgetting the past and starting over. I admire her and hope to meet her soon," Anjali said. She looked at Avinash with feigned innocence before firing the first shot at Lola. "I think she would be an interesting person for you to meet, Avinash. She's smart, loves to travel, enjoys food and fine art . . . all the things you admire in a woman. What do you think, Sam?"

Sam, dumbfounded, opened his mouth as if to speak but no words came out. With a twinkle in his eyes, Avinash took a sip of his Scotch and came to Sam's rescue.

"I never say no to a new client of our bank. Set it up, Anjali. Let's give Ms. Cordero the red-carpet treatment." With disaster averted, at least for the time being, Avinash extended his hand to Lola and asked her to accompany him to the balcony.

"You went too far, Anjali. The poor girl didn't know what to do with herself," Sam whispered once they were out of earshot. "Ms. Cordero will not accept an outing with Avinash. She's much more intuitive than you think. She'll know what you're up to."

"Oh hush, Sam. If Ms. Cordero is as smart and sophisticated as you say she is, she will accept the outing and be fascinated with Avinash. He's a very appealing chap, and she's no fool. If her husband left her, as you say, she will want to forget him. Meeting Avinash would be the best thing for her right now, and honestly, Sam, Avinash needs some stability. Don't you spoil my plans by telling him what I'm up to, or I'll kick your English bum back to Sussex. Do you hear me?"

Sam nodded, speechless once again.

***

In Rome, the evening was winding down, the busy back streets of the Piazza Farnese all but deserted. As the shop owner put away the last pieces of merchandise, Marcelo pestered the attendant for some missing pieces to an old chandelier he'd been restoring. He was told the vitreria shop down the street had what he was looking for, but they were closed. He would have to come back tomorrow.

Marcelo, worn out, headed to the café, ready to end the day with vermouth and a smoke. He settled at the bar and lit up a cigarette. Marcelo had been smoking since he was seventeen, a bad habit he'd picked up from a friend. He knew he should have quit long ago but couldn't figure out why he ought to at this point in his life. He gazed at the crowd, faceless in the smoky haze, and remembered a time when he had plenty of friends and was surrounded by the crème de la crème of Italy. Memories. Those bygone days still disturbed him from time to time, but he tried to forget. Vermouth helped. He ordered another one.

Marcelo, from a humble family of meager means, was born near Pisa and grew up near Cinque Terre, where he spent his summers cleaning the yachts of the rich and famous in Portofino. It was there Marcelo became an avid dreamer and learned much about how the rich dealt with their money. He landed in Naples in 1973 at the age of twenty-five, eager and ready to start his new life. After a couple of odd jobs, he met Signore Carlo Batalli, a well-known underground gambler and alleged mafia leader who needed someone to help refurbish his new villa, The Castellammare, near Sorrento. He also enlisted Marcelo's help in divorcing his wife, an almost impossible act in Italy at the time. Marcelo signed on for a meager salary, but he knew Batalli would be a stepping stone into a whole new world, one he could lustfully taste. Indeed, Carlo Batalli was so well-connected that within a matter of months, Marcelo was named head of the villa remodeling efforts and later became the manager of the gambling tables—a sure shot into the rich and famous world he longed for.

Marcelo, incredibly handsome and blessed with a natural wit and street smarts, quickly made wealthy friends and met beautiful women. To help Batalli secure the divorce from his wife, Marcelo seduced her and had a friend take pictures of them in bed. The next day, the papers announced the scandalous infidelity, and Signora Batalli had no other choice than to flee and grant Batalli the divorce he wanted—albeit with a generous monthly stipend to keep her quiet regarding his underground gambling business.

In this high class society, the older signoras wanted Marcelo for nothing more than a good time, but later he became as endearing as a son to many of them. They dressed him in the finest clothes, pampered him, and bestowed upon Marcelo all their money to use as he pleased, just as long as he visited and entertained them with his stories and his time.

By his late-twenties, thanks to Batalli and Marcelo's own innate wits, he had everything a man could want: wealth, women, connections, and the youth needed to take him places—those places where deals were spun just like those of the wealthy men on their yachts off the Bay of Portofino. So many opportunities awaited. Where would life lead him now? Perhaps up Viale Pasitea?

Raucous laughter and boisterous cheers from a group at a nearby table snapped Marcelo from his reverie. He downed the last drop of vermouth and signaled the cameriere for the check. He dropped a couple Euros on the table and made his way outside, weaving around an elderly couple walking hand in hand as he disappeared into the darkness.

***

Ari waited nervously in the British Airways VIP lounge at LAX. She'd decided to fly first class this time; after all, money was no longer an issue, considering the fortune she and Santos had built. She ordered a glass of wine at the bar and found an empty couch in the corner, doing her best to remain invisible. Chewing on the inside of her cheek—an annoying habit she'd acquired, thanks to Santos—Ari wiped her sweaty palms on the cocktail napkin and looked up to survey the room. There weren't many travelers in the lounge, which suited her just fine. With a sigh of relief and a cool sip of Chardonnay, Ari grabbed a magazine from a corner table and settled in.

"Excuse me. Are you saving this seat for someone, Miss . . .?"

The voice was dreadfully close to her, and Ari made a conscious, but unsuccessful, effort not to slosh her drink all over herself as she looked up into the deep brown eyes of a handsome Arabic man. She'd seen him earlier at a table near the bar, half hidden behind his newspaper. Ari, tall and fair, her hair reddish-brown with blonde tones, had the ability to confuse anyone who tried to guess her nationality. Many people said she looked French; some had compared her fair complexion and big eyes to Lady Diana, but no one ever thought she was of Spanish descent. Ari dressed well, always classy and in fashion. Her hazel eyes with specks of green turned a shade darker when she was nervous or about to engage in sexual activity.

"No, I'm by myself." She smiled up at the mysterious man and scooted to the far end of the couch.

"My name is Akash Ramkissoon, but my friends call me Kash. Are you on your way to London?" Before she could reply, he said, "Wait. I'm sorry. Don't answer that. These days, someone of my nationality could get arrested for asking the wrong questions at an airport."

Ari laughed. "Yes, and I might be mistaken for someone who could fly beneath the radar, so to speak. I look like the perfect accomplice. I guess we're a doomed pair."

"Indeed!" he said as he settled next to her on the couch and tucked a massive leather briefcase near his feet.

Ari fidgeted, struggling with the idea that this gorgeous Lawrence of Arabia, his accent a charming mix of Indian and British, might be on her flight to London. Even more alarming was the fact that she felt no sense of danger in his presence. Instead, a powerful magnetic undercurrent seemed to ripple between them.

"I'm Ariadne Cordero, but my friends call me Ari," she said as she reached out to shake his hand. "Nice to meet you."

The handsome stranger returned the polite gesture but held onto her hand a bit longer than usual. They chatted, tidbits of somewhat hesitant conversation that soon became comfortable banter. By coincidence, or fate, perhaps, they'd be taking the same flight to London, and Kash had no problem getting the gate agent to seat them together in first class. They spent hours talking about everything, from their childhoods to cultures, travel, business, politics, and love.

Kash, a charming Punjabi who left his country young and grew up in the suburbs of London, was now a powerful diamond magnate based in Australia. Even more interesting to Ari was the way he managed to get into her psyche. She never opened up to strangers, and after everything that happened with Santos, she was even more reluctant to do so. Somehow Kash managed to make her comfortable enough to let her guard down. *Careful, Ari,* she thought as the flight attendants lowered the lights and they all settled in for the overnight flight.

As they made the descent into Heathrow, Kash handed Ari his business card. "My private number is on the back. Call me anytime. I'd love to show you London."

Ari smiled graciously. "Maybe we could meet for dinner. I have a busy week ahead. I have a meeting scheduled this afternoon with the realtor and several transactions to handle with World Bank regarding my loan."

"World Bank? I used to know some people there. It's been a long time though."

As the plane came to a stop, Ari unbuckled her seatbelt and unfolded herself from the seat. As she reached up to retrieve her bag from the overhead compartment, Kash stepped behind her, his body pressed against hers as he pulled the bag down for her. He stood dangerously close, his face mere inches from hers, and Ari sensed he would kiss her if she turned her head his direction. Distracted and suddenly unsure of herself, she thanked him, took her bag, and hurried from the plane.

Kash caught up with her and they headed to customs. Once they were through, he reminded her that he had a car waiting.

"Can I give you a lift somewhere?" he asked, one hand at the small of her back as he guided her from the airport.

Ari's nervousness returned with a vengeance. "There's supposed to be a car waiting for me outside, but thank you," she said, praying Anjali had arranged for her transportation as promised.

As they neared the door, Kash pulled her aside. "I really like you, Ari. You're a beautiful breath of fresh air. Promise you'll call when you have a few hours to spare. I'd love to see you again."

She smiled and placed a gentle kiss on Kash's cheek. "I will. I promise."

Just outside, amid a long line of serious-faced drivers, Ari spotted a tall gentleman in a black suit and mirrored sunglasses, her name emblazoned across the sign he held. She smiled at him and waved, and he acknowledged her with a slight dip of his head. Kash squeezed Ari's shoulder one last time and handed her bag to the driver.

"I'll see you soon. Good luck," he said, walking away as the driver ushered Ari into the waiting vehicle.

The valet at the Four Seasons grabbed Ari's bag and escorted her to the front desk. The receptionist greeted her with genuine warmth and quickly checked her into her suite.

Ari couldn't hide her confusion. "A suite? But I'm certain I didn't—"

"Yes, Ms. Cordero. An upgrade courtesy of World Bank of London. You'll be pleased with your room, I assure you," the young woman said.

Ari thanked her and took the key without further question. I hope this good fortune continues, she thought as she headed for the elevator. She reached her room, opened the door, and stepped into the opulent, mirrored entryway. Before she could explore further, her cell phone rang.

"Is that you, Ariadne? This is Sam. Are you in London already?"

Ari put a finger to her free ear, straining to hear him through the background noise. "Yes, yes. Hello, Sam. I'm at the hotel. I just got to my room. Thank you for the upgrade. What a lovely gesture. I had a great trip over."

"Brilliant! And you're welcome. I'm sure you're ready to unwind a bit, but I just received word from the owner of the home in Positano. They're ready to negotiate on the price. Seems like your deposit to hold the home as a good faith gesture years ago was a good move. You've arrived just in time to celebrate. Congratulations!"

Ari couldn't believe what she was hearing. "Are you sure? The house on Viale Pasitea, the one I liked so much with the open terrace over the ocean and the bougainvilleas hanging everywhere? That house? Oh my God, that's amazing!"

"Yes indeed, the very same house. You're fortunate. Several people had their eye on that house, including the original builder, but in the end our tactic worked. They're negotiating their offer on Monday in Naples. It should take two to three weeks to process, and then it's all yours. We should celebrate tonight, if you're up to it."

"Absolutely! But it'll be my treat, Sam. You've been my guardian angel through all of this. I couldn't have done it without you. I . . ." She stopped, her voice cracking, and tried to compose herself. *This is all happening so fast!*

Sam, always the diplomat, picked up the slack. "Very well, then. We'll pick you up tonight at eight. Will that work for you?"

"Eight sounds perfect. I'll be ready."

She ended the call and plopped down on the bed, fatigue taking over as she made a mental list of the things she needed to do before dinner. A short nap and a long, hot bath, for sure. After that, who knows? Ari kicked off her shoes and settled back on the bed, letting the silky comforter envelope her. As she drifted off to sleep, she recalled Sam's words: "We'll pick you up at eight." *We?* Sleep overtook her before she could give it more thought.

***

Two days before Ari's arrival in London, an angry Marcelo Donati appeared at the Naples courthouse to learn that his house, the one he'd built years ago for Lucia, his former bride-to-be, had been sold. He'd put a bid on it a week ago and never heard back. Though he'd been delighted to finally find the glass piece he needed for the chandelier, the trip to Rome had exhausted him. And this latest news sent him into a tailspin. Despite telling off the courthouse clerk using Italian expletives that would have his mother rolling over in her grave, God rest her soul, it was no use. He'd been outbid by an American, and the final documents were being negotiated on Monday in Naples.

Marcelo slumped on the bench in the long, worn-out hallway that had probably seen its share of injustices during

Mussolini's era. He ran his long fingers through his salt-and-pepper hair and lit a cigarette. He could not have imagined this blow a month ago. The house at 87 Viale Pasitea had sat lifeless for over sixteen years. The gossip along the Amalfi Coast was that no one wanted to touch the home after the heartbreak that tore apart the relationship between gambler and playboy Marcelo Donati and model Lucia Ferretti. Even today, people still talked about it, though Marcelo had managed to skirt the issue in some towns along the coast. But not in Positano. Marcelo and Lucia had been deeply in love, the couple of the century, beautiful in every way and often compared to Rainier and Princess Grace. They appeared on magazine covers worldwide and graced the pages of all the gossip magazines in Italy. Would they get married? Was Lucia pregnant? Did Marcelo gamble away all his money? Was the mafia after him? Story after story, all hypothetical and none ever proven one way or the other. Only Marcelo and Lucia knew the truth about their storybook romance, and they fought hard to keep their privacy intact.

It was in the midst of this maddening period of time that Marcelo decided to build a house for his beloved Lucia. The home on Viale Pasitea was constructed high on the mountain and had no visible backyard, only a massive stone terrace that hovered over the cliff above the Mediterranean Sea. Nothing but azure sea and sky, as far as the eye could see. As the song says, on a clear day, you could almost see forever.

The paparazzi, their speedboats peppering the blue waters along the coastline, tried hard and often to capture a clear shot, but a moneymaking photo was hard to secure, given the villa's layout and the way the mountain seemed to envelop it. The place was a virtual fortress, private in every way, just as Marcelo and Lucia had planned.

In fact, it was the home's isolation that had attracted Marcelo in the first place. He bought the dilapidated home that originally stood there for next to nothing and hired an army of highly skilled workers to remodel it quickly. At the suggestion of a friend who worked in a bank in Naples, Marcelo made use of a stash of floor tiles left over from the construction of a casino in Havana. Somehow, they'd been shipped to Naples via freighter when Fidel Castro took over Cuba in 1959 and had been stored in the bank's basement. Dozens of crates of porcelain terrazzo just sitting there, no one certain to whom they really belonged. With his friend's blessing—and without asking for further permission, which was not his style—Marcelo hired a semi, arranged the necessary and fraudulent government papers for transfer, and had the tiles loaded and brought over to the new home.

The project involved the best masonry workers, roofers, plasterers, and glass experts in the country. The home became Marcelo's baby, as he worked to ensure everything was to Lucia's liking. Marcelo took every detail into consideration—the lighting, the way the sun's rays would slant into each room. There was nothing left to chance. Nothing, that is, except their relationship.

Marcelo put so much into the home that their relationship began to fray and crumble, much like the rubble scattered along Viale Pasitea when he'd had the old house gutted. On a late summer evening in August, Marcelo asked Lucia to come to the home and inspect the masterpiece, the love nest he'd created for her. He could not have imagined what Lucia would say when she saw the home or the drama that would unfold there. But in his heart he knew it was a labor of love—a love that remained to this day, tucked away in the remains of that home at 87 Viale Pasitea.

Marcelo walked out of the courthouse defeated, but he hadn't thrown in the towel completely. Not yet. Surely there was a way to get his house back, even if he had to con his way into it. He needed a plan, a way to get the American to sell the home back to him. The more he considered it, the more encouraged he became. Marcelo had revenge in his sights, and if the American woman became a pawn in his game, so be it. He was ready, feeling secure again, and eager to fire the opening round in the war to save his home on Viale Pasitea.

Chapter Two

After a quick nap, Ari shuffled through the bank loan documents that Sam had left at the front desk for her. She was still too groggy from the flight to concentrate on numbers. A drink and a hot meal would be great right now, but she had plans with Sam for the evening, and according to the clock on the nightstand, she had just enough time to take a quick shower and reapply her makeup.

It was early March in London, and though spring had begun a week ago, you couldn't really tell it from the dip in temperatures. Ari decided to go with a dark grey pantsuit, a silver blouse with a plunging neckline, and sexy pumps. Though Sam and Ari were only business acquaintances and friends, it was still a celebration after all. The outfit hugged her five-foot-eight frame well, and she wore her hair down, blonde highlights sparkling through the long, thick waves that cascaded past her shoulders. She thought of calling Kash just to say hello, but that would seem too desperate. She'd wait a day or two if he didn't call her first.

The call from the concierge announcing the arrival of her ride came at seven forty. The same driver who had picked her up from the airport was waiting, and she thought that odd since she was only having dinner with Sam. Then again, he had mentioned the possibility that others might be included. Still, she was surprised when she slid into the back seat to find a beautiful Indian woman waiting for her, a blinding, flawless smile from ear to ear.

"Ms. Cordero! So nice to meet you. I'm Anjali from World Bank." Sam, seated on Anjali's far side, gave Ari a quick wave.

"How nice to finally meet you," Ari said as she leaned in and lightly kissed both of them on the cheek. She noticed the surprise on their faces and couldn't suppress her laughter. "Oh, sorry, guys. I'm Spanish and we kiss everybody we meet. Guess I better curtail that habit while I'm here."

"It's quite all right, Ari. I more than expected you to do that, since you always send love and kisses when you text me," Sam remarked, putting a clever spin on the situation to ease their nerves.

"Anjali, what a pleasant surprise to see you tonight. I didn't expect to meet you until Monday, but I'm happy you came. Is Mr. Batra also expected at this dinner?" Ari had done her homework before arriving in London and she knew about Batra and his salacious lifestyle. From that point on, she was right to be suspicious about the man's involvement in the whole matter; from supplying the driver to the suite upgrade. He probably planned the celebration they were about to have too.

"Well, you know how bankers are . . . always busy with their clients. He may show up just to say hello, if he can get away. You never know with his schedule. I swear the man never really sleeps," Anjali said.

Ari smiled, more cynical than amused. "Roaming the streets looking for fresh prey?" Anjali coughed nervously, and Sam covered a grin with his hand. He knew Ari was no sucker.

"Well, once you meet him you'll know what I'm talking about. He is quite the bachelor, but he enjoys meeting people, especially if they're also his clients."

They stuck to small talk for the duration of the twenty-minute ride to the restaurant, with Anjali leading the conversation most of the time. While Ari spoke with Sam she noticed Anjali's eyes on her, examining her face, scanning her clothing and looking pleased. At one point Ari thought the woman might be attracted to her, but perhaps it was just a cultural thing, or maybe she was wearing the wrong garment or too much perfume. Either way, Ari found Anjali quite entertaining and soon felt herself beginning to relax.

They arrived at the restaurant, and while the driver waited for the vehicles in front of them to unload patrons, Ari's phone vibrated in her purse. *Who could that be?* she thought. She pulled the phone from her chic black clutch and glanced at the caller ID. *Kash!* Her heart nearly jumped out of her chest. She looked up to find Anjali's eyes on her, a curious look on her face.

"Hello? Hang on for a second," she said into the phone as she jumped from the car and hurried into the restaurant.

"Kash? Is that you? Can you hear me?" There was a lot of noise and commotion in the waiting area. Apparently this new restaurant, Morocco, was the talk of the town, and everybody who was somebody was there that night.

"Hello. Yes, I can hear you. Where are you? It's very noisy," Kash replied.

Anjali and Sam followed on Ari's heels as she tried to move through the crowded lobby. "I'm at a new restaurant. There are a lot of people here tonight. I'm with Anjali and Sam, my friend from World Bank. Remember we spoke about him? The offer I made on the house in Positano was accepted, so we're here to celebrate. Can you hear me, Kash?" Ari yelled into the phone.

As they reached the hostess desk, the noise level increased. Ari signaled to Anjali and Sam that she was going to step back outside to finish up the call. They nodded and she pushed her way back through the crowd.

"I'm sorry, Kash. Can you hear me better now?"

"Yes, dear, much better. It's highly unusual that a banker would be taking you out to dinner over the purchase of a home. Must be a very expensive property."

"It's definitely not your average house. Should I be worried?" Ari asked.

"Oh, no. I remember Anjali, and she is a dear. And Sam . . . well, he's harmless. Is Avinash Batra there with you?"

"No, I haven't met him yet," Ari replied.

"He's quite the scoundrel and has a reputation in London. Don't talk to him about your personal life—just business. And don't tell him about me. Take my word for it; we have our history. He's an honest man and all, but he can wrap you in his tentacles and take you for a ride. I'm just trying to look out for you."

24

Ari knew of Batra's reputation, but Kash's soft, sexy voice distracted and somehow comforted her. Before she could put together a coherent sentence, he continued. "When can I see you, Ari? I miss you."

"Um . . . how about tomorrow? Maybe a late lunch? I'm a bit jet-lagged, and I don't know how late I'll be tonight."

"Sounds perfect, Ari. May I pick you up about two o'clock? And dress casually."

"All right, then. See you at two, Kash. Have a good evening."

"Yes, love, you too," Kash said as he ended the call.

Love? It's a bit soon for that, she thought as she headed back into the restaurant. Before she could think more about it, a server approached her. Anjali and Sam had already been seated, so Ari was ushered through the restaurant to join them. As they made their way, she took a moment to admire the setting and was quickly caught up in the exotic ambience. The lighting was perfect, with lamps from Morocco, India, and Malaysia scattered about. Soft music played, a cross between Buddha Bar and Cafe Mar, and the sweet, intoxicating scent of incense wafted on the breeze left behind by busy waitstaff. The place was packed. Everywhere Ari looked she saw beautiful, sexy people—all ages and nationalities represented.

They approached a massive wooden door, much like the gate to some ancient temple. The door opened and Ari stepped inside and through a sheer, white curtain that billowed in the space between the door and the dimly lit private dining area. She squinted hard, straining to see through the misty fog of incense and smoke from what appeared to be hundreds of twinkling candles. Once her vision cleared, Ari spied dark wooden floors and a low, rectangular table. The other guests were seated around it on beautiful, multicolored pillows. Anjali looked right at home, but Sam seemed uncomfortable, tugging at his dinner jacket and squirming about like an unruly child. There was one vacant pillow next to the third guest, a mysterious-looking Indian gentleman so dashing and handsome that it had to be Mr. Avinash Batra.

The tall, elegant man got to his feet, flashing a brilliant smile as he moved toward Ari. "Ms. Cordero," he said as he grabbed her elbow with one strong, well-manicured hand and shook her hand with the other. "It's so nice to finally meet you. I'm Avinash Batra." He smiled with his eyes, as if she was born to know who he was.

For the first time in her life, Ari was speechless as she gazed into his eyes, those eyes that seemed to smile. She didn't dare kiss him as she normally would greet new people; it would spell danger. In his cobalt-blue shirt, half-tucked into pewter-grey dress trousers and a Hermès belt, he dressed to kill. The smile was intoxicating, and Ari was momentarily caught up in it. Batra took her coat and slowly lowered her onto the pillow. She could see him scanning her from head to toe, and Avinash, the scoundrel, seemed to like what he saw. Finally, Ari spoke as she stared up into his eyes.

"Please call me Ari. I'm pleased to meet you, Mr. Batra. I must say I've never had this much fussing-over in my life. I can honestly admit that . . . well, I kind of love it."

Everyone laughed and Avinash smiled again with his eyes, not taking them away from hers for one moment. The server came to the table, and Avinash touched Ari's arm as if to ask permission to look away from her momentarily in order to speak. He quickly ordered a round of drinks for everyone and what she assumed to be appetizers, though Ari could not make out what he was saying in rapid-fire Hindi. No one questioned what he was ordering or why. He was the king at his table, and they were his loyal subjects. His rendition of the menu was fascinating as he went over each item in detail, explaining what was good to try and why. This was followed by the ordering of specific drinks that matched each food item and a detailed description of how each would taste in her mouth. Avinash Batra was so smooth and cool that you would swear he and the devil were related. Without ever taking his eyes off Ari, Avinash ruled the evening but never spoke too much. He just asked the questions and listened intently as the others scrambled to answer him.

Every time he brushed his hand over Ari's, she felt a shock and a pleasure that she hadn't felt since Santos was in her life. During the course of the evening, they sampled a variety of unusual dishes, and Ari was eager and willing to try them all. Quick-witted and smart, she kept up with the conversation, no matter what topic he threw at her, laughed at the occasional quip or jab, and enjoyed herself immensely. All the while, Avinash watched her, and Ari was quite certain he was fascinated.

The evening progressed, and the hours seemed to pass like minutes as Ari and Avinash got to know each other better, much to the exclusion of Anjali and Sam.

"Do stay and have one last drink with us," Avinash said as Sam began his goodbyes. "The evening is on me." Sam and Anjali declined, thanking him for his generosity, and

Ari quickly detected a hint of smug satisfaction on Avinash's face.

Once they were alone, Avinash signaled to the waiter, requesting that he take a drink order up to the terrace for them. He helped Ari off the pillow and her knees buckled —either from sitting crossed-legged for hours or drinking too much, neither of which was a good idea after a long flight. She fell into Avinash's arms for a moment to get her balance, and he held her close. With one arm around her waist, he grabbed her clutch and coat and hurried her through the crowded restaurant and up the stairs.

They finally reached the rooftop terrace. Ari shivered in the cool night air, despite her coat and the alcohol pulsing through her, Avinash pulled her closer, positioning the two of them beneath a portable outdoor heater. She felt much better in his arms, though he seemed to enjoy taking advantage of her unsteadiness. *The scoundrel*, she thought as she snuggled closer. The cool night breeze licked at her feet as the heater's warmth wrapped around her. She closed her eyes and took a deep breath, absorbing the sounds of the city below and the soft tango mix playing softly in the background. *Could this evening be more magical?*

"What are you doing tomorrow?" he asked, interrupting her thoughts.

"Oh, I was going to just relax tomorrow. You know . . . the flight, the time change. I'm a little out of sorts." Ari nervously sipped her cocktail and avoided his gaze, knowing her eyes would give her away.

"Nonsense. Being tired . . . it's all in your mind. I'm a pretty decent cook, and I can have my driver pick you up. We can spend a relaxing day at my home. No pressure, Ari.

I really enjoyed talking with you tonight. You know, I wasn't going to come to meet you, but I'm glad I did. What can I say? You're enchanting, Ms. Cordero. I must be careful not to let you get under my skin." He smiled again, and Ari seemed to melt.

Just then the second round of drinks arrived—a blend of chocolate, tequila, and some exotic spices she couldn't make out. It tasted sexy somehow, and as she took another sip it hit her. Everything about this evening—the food, the drinks, the deserted terrace—was carefully woven by Avinash to bring her into his web.

She suddenly realized there was too much tequila, too much food, and way too much flirting, coupled with fighting the intense attraction she had toward him from minute one of their meeting. The trip to the terrace would just be the game point for Mr. Avinash Batra.

"I would love to, Avinash. Really. But I promised a friend I would have a late lunch, and I can't turn it down."

"You mean you have more friends in London besides Sam and me? That would have to be a world record. Where did you ever find the time?" he quipped.

Ari smiled but insisted. "It's getting really late. I'm tired. Can the waiter call a taxi, please?"

"That won't be necessary. My driver can take you back to the hotel," Avinash said, pulling his phone from his pocket to make the call.

He escorted Ari from the terrace and down to the curb, where a long Mercedes sedan awaited. They settled into the plush leather, with Avinash seated facing her. He looked at her, smiling, as if she were a piece of cake he'd like to nibble on. Ari felt a sudden compulsion to thank him for such a wonderful night. She hadn't felt so needed, pampered, or tipsy in an awfully long time, and she needed to let him know how she felt.

As the car pulled out into the street, she leaned forward in her seat and placed her hands on his knees to steady herself. It probably wasn't the smartest thing to do, but the drinks were talking, and she was feeling no pain. She felt Avinash tighten up at her touch, his gaze shifting from her eyes to her breasts, unsupported and threatening to spill from her sexy top as she leaned toward him. As the driver made a sharp turn, he gripped her by the elbows to keep her from toppling over.

"You're truly an amazing man, Mr. Batra. I admire you and everything you've accomplished. You're an example of what a man can do when he has the will. I look up to people like you. I want to be more like that in my life. You know . . . not afraid of anything. I had an amazing dinner and the most intellectual conversation I've had with a man in a long, long time. Thank you so much."

The car came to a stop, and Ari leaned in closer and lightly kissed Avinash on the cheek. Her lips brushed his stubble, and she could feel his hot breath on her neck. She took a deep breath to settle her pounding heart. *He still smells wonderful,* she thought, quickly pulling herself away from him.

Avinash stared at her, his mouth open as if to speak and a perplexed look on his face. Before he could say anything, Ari smiled and exited the car, heading into the hotel without a backward glance.

***

The usual overcast and gloomy Sunday morning in London didn't keep Anjali Mukerji from getting up happy, realizing that perhaps her plan for Avinash and Ari was beginning to reap its fruits. She decided to send a text to Avinash, though it was barely nine in the morning.

"Avi-ji, how was it last nite? Deep in talkie-talk? Ur thoughts?"

There was no quick answer. Anjali figured he was still sleeping, though he rarely slept late on any day. As she was preparing her tea and getting ready to meet a friend for some shopping, Avinash finally texted her in return.

"Best nite. True keeper. Thank U!"

Anjali was shocked. *A keeper?* Anjali could not figure out what to do next.

***

Ari awoke, groggy and unrefreshed after tossing and turning for most of the night. *Big surprise*, she thought, given all the food and alcohol on top of jet lag. Then she thought of Avinash and smiled. Ari kept seeing his stunned face when she told him what she felt. *Was it inappropriate, even if it was from the heart?* Perhaps no one ever really told him that they admired him. Perhaps he's been called a scoundrel so often that he believes it. Whatever it was, she couldn't get him off her mind.

Ari decided a good massage at the hotel spa would help her out of her slump. She dialed the spa extension and made an appointment for a Swedish massage at eleven thirty. That would give her time for a jog around the area first. She wasn't hungry, but she headed down to the hotel restaurant for some coffee and Greek yogurt, enough to hold her until lunch with Kash.

After her run, Ari took a quick shower and dressed for lunch. She checked her phone to find a missed call and listened to the voicemail.

"Good afternoon, Ari. This is Avinash. I couldn't stop thinking about what you said last night. It truly touched me. I'm sorry I didn't know how to react. I was still trying to take it all in, trying to take all of you in, Ari. Let's get together on Monday after your meetings at the bank. I want to show you a nice place outside London that you'll love, if you're up to it. Have a relaxing Sunday. Namaste, Ari."

Her heart racing, Ari tossed the phone on the bed and wiped her sweaty palms on the towel. What an unexpected effect this man seemed to have on her! Not even Kash, with his suave manner and kind voice, gave her the feelings that Avinash did after just one evening. Was this just nervous sexual upheaval, or was it something else? Maybe she was unfairly comparing Avinash to Santos for some reason. Whatever it was, she certainly didn't need it at this time in her life, now that Positano loomed closer than ever. But the attraction she felt to Avinash was undeniable. It was palpable, and she was as attracted to his mind and intelligence as she was to his body.

So much for that massage, Ari thought as she tried to shake off the tension Avinash's voicemail had renewed in her. *I've got to calm down before I meet with Kash. He's going to notice something is wrong.* She checked the time and headed to the bathroom to put on her makeup.

They had lunch at an outdoor café near Hyde Park. Ari enjoyed people-watching as Kash ordered their meal.

"Do you want coffee or tea, Ari?"

Surely Avinash would know what I wanted without asking me, she thought.

"Ari?"

"Coffee is fine, Kash," she said, her tone a bit sharper than she intended.

"Is there something wrong?" he asked once the waiter moved out of earshot. "You seem distracted." He patted her hand and smiled.

"Oh, no, sorry. It's not you. I haven't slept well for a couple of days, and I'm getting grumpy." She smiled sweetly and squeezed his fingers.

During the pleasant Sunday lunch, the sun finally peeked through the clouds, and they spent what seemed like hours in pleasant conversation. Kash was easy to talk to, as if they'd known each other for years instead of just a few days.

Kash excused himself to the men's room, and Ari checked her phone to find a text from Anjali. She asked how the evening went and wanted to know if Ari was free that night to visit her home. Ari decided to call her.

"Hey, Anjali, how are you? We had a great time last night. I would love to see you. Shall I bring dinner to you?"

"Brilliant, Ari. Yes, it's best you bring dinner. I can't cook a thing. I can make drinks though! I'll send you my contact information. Come whenever. I'll be here."

As Ari ended the call, she saw Kash trying to escape a conversation with an older woman who looked like she was questioning him about something. Kash excused himself and walked briskly over to the table. Ari saw the woman squint at him, and she decided not to ask Kash who she was or what she wanted. Kash mentioned that he'd paid the bill inside and rushed Ari from the café without even asking if she was finished. She did her best to keep up with him as they crossed the busy street and hurried into the parking garage.

He was quiet but Ari did not inquire. When they arrived at his car—a black, late-model Alfa Romeo—Kash opened the door for Ari, smiled, and slowly leaned in to kiss her. She was surprised but accepted the kiss and pulled him in closer to her. He breathed heavily, as if the kiss relieved his troubled soul, and put his arms around her waist. Once their lips unlocked, Ari smiled without saying a word, backed into the passenger seat, and waited for him to close the door.

The ride to the hotel was uneventful and quiet. Kash pulled the car to the curb and reached out to squeeze her hand. "Thank you for today," he said, the only words he'd uttered since they'd left the café. For the second time in as many meetings, Ari felt a mysterious undercurrent from Kash. Before she could comment, the hotel doorman appeared and helped Ari from the vehicle. She smiled back at Kash without a word and hurried inside.

Later, Ari called a taxi, and after making a quick stop at a nearby grocery store, she arrived at Anjali's apartment late that afternoon, finally relaxed from all the craziness of the last few days. They got along famously, just as Ari knew they would. Anjali had a drier, British sense of humor and Ari a sharp, but cute, wit. They occasionally went from tears to laughter as Anjali delivered a darker side of her life in India, including stories of the love of her life, why she left years ago, and how she met Avinash Batra—all intriguing subjects to Ari, though it was Avinash she wanted to know more about.

According to Anjali, Pranav Chopra was studying to be an industrial engineer, and the two of them quickly fell in love. Her parents, however, had a different candidate in mind, an older and extremely well-off gentleman who owned the movie studio where her family had been overseeing the production of Bollywood films for over twenty years. The love between Anjali and Pranav became so intense that they decided to run off to London and escape everything.

Sounds like a simple plan, Ari thought. "What happened?"

"It's really sad, *dosti*. When our plans were uncovered, Pranav's family sent him to Dubai to finish his studies, and my parents shipped me off to London to study under the tutelage of a family friend. The friend was none other than the father of Avinash, Subash Batra, a wealthy man who'd apparently had his eyes on me since I was young."

Anjali explained that Avinash's mother died of cancer when he was just a boy, and his father sent Avinash and his sister away to live with his mother's family. Later, the wealthy elder Batra met the Mukerjee's at a party and saw Anjali. That's when he decided to set a large dowry for her, expecting to get his wife when she turned twenty years of age. With Pranav in Dubai, Anjali learned of this plot and panicked. She tried to escape to a friend's home in New York, but she was stopped at the airport by Batra's henchmen and sent to live like a prisoner in his home.

"It was torture!" she said, tears pooling in her eyes at the memory. "I hated him and could only think of my love in Dubai."

Ari put her hand on Anjali's shoulder to comfort her. She couldn't believe such things happened in the twenty-first century. "What happened next? How did you get away from him?"

"It was Avinash who somehow found out what his father was up to and forcibly entered the home, fighting and kicking all the security guards on his way in. He was enraged, and he grabbed me by the arm and led me out of the house. You realize I had no idea what Avinash looked like. I wasn't sure who this man was, taking me by force out of the home, but one thing was clear—he was out for justice. So I trusted he was doing the right thing. Once he placed me safely in his car, he reentered the home in search of his father. They had a major blowout; I could hear them fighting even from the car. I covered my ears, expecting to hear gunshots at any moment.

"Finally, Avinash exited the house, still furious, and his father yelled all types of obscenities from the entryway. He told Avinash he would disinherit him and take away all the funding for his studies. Avinash didn't care; he didn't even acknowledge anything he said. He drove me away from there, and he's been taking care of me ever since. We moved to London, and he worked odd jobs to finish his studies while I went to the university with my scholarship transfer from Mumbai. Avinash met a friend in the university whose uncle was a prominent banker. The friend introduced them, and he helped Avinash work his way up to a management position at the bank."

Anjali went on to say that when the banker, Mr. Dutta, passed away, he left much of his fortune to Avinash. Mr. Dutta had no children of his own, so Avinash became the bank's majority shareholder, and none of the other board members questioned the decision. He was the best choice to lead the bank, and they all knew it.

"Everything Avinash has today he's worked hard for, and everything that I am I owe to Avinash. He saved my life, Ari."

Ari was touched by the story. *You never really know what's behind a person's smile until you dig a little*, she thought as she wiped a stray tear from her cheek. "Well . . . I think it's time for one of your special drinks, Anjali."

Ari took Anjali's hand and they got up from the sofa and headed for the kitchen, eager to put the horrible story behind them—a story they never spoke of again.

Anjali and Ari spent the rest of the evening talking and listening to music. Ari cooked a fabulous Tuscan soup— without the beef, just in case it would be offensive to her new Indian friend—and accompanied it with crusty bread and a wonderful Piedmonte wine. Around eight o'clock, the intercom to Anjali's apartment buzzed. Ari thought it odd for a Sunday evening, and Anjali hadn't mentioned she was expecting anyone.

Anjali went to the door, and Ari got up to get more wine from the kitchen. When she returned, she couldn't believe who was standing there. It was, in fact, Avinash in all his sweaty glory. He'd apparently swung by the apartment unannounced, still dressed in his polo clothes. No one should have to endure the sight of Avinash Batra in a white polo shirt, snug riding pants, and boots, but Ari was glad she was there to take it all in. He smiled at Ari and walked over to greet her.

"So this is who you abandoned me for today?" He wrapped his arms around her and pulled her close.

Ari, a bit astounded, looked over Avinash's shoulder at Anjali, who flitted about the apartment as if she didn't know what to do with herself. *Calm down, friend,* she thought as she caught Anjali's eye, one eyebrow cocked in warning. She took Avinash by the hand and led him to the sofa.

"So how was your polo match? Are you hungry?" Ari asked.

Avinash propped his feet up on the cocktail table and turned his muscular torso toward Ari. "It was a tight match, but our team managed to score the winning point at the end. And yes,"—he leaned into Ari—"I'm very hungry. What's to eat, Anjali?" He smiled like a Cheshire cat, knowing full well Anjali couldn't even boil water.

"Well, it just so happens that Ms. Cordero is quite the chef and has made dinner tonight. I think there is still some warming in the kitchen. Shall I bring—"

Before she could finish, Ari bounced off the sofa, almost losing her balance. "It's okay. I'll serve it up for him. Quick, Anji, get Avinash something to drink." Ari stared her down, and Anjali got the message as Ari headed toward the kitchen, trying her best to appear she was in control.

Once inside, Ari pulled a bowl from the cabinet and rinsed the ladle she'd used earlier when preparing dinner. In her haste, it slipped from her fingers and crashed to the floor with a clatter. "Dammit!" she whispered as she bent down to pick it up. "Get a grip, Ari." Suddenly, a pair of muddied, brown, size ten riding boots appeared in front of her.

***

That same evening in Positano, Marcelo arrived on the last ferry from Sorrento. It was a chilly, misty night. He decided to visit his old friend Lorraine who still lived near the city, just a short walk up past the church and onto the main road, Viale Pasitea.

When they first met years before, Lorraine Newly was a reporter for the *London Times* who visited Capri and was part of the young jet-set that took over the island in the seventies. Between London, Ibiza, and Capri, Lorraine befriended many famous and not-so-famous people. Among them was Marcelo Donati. He had not seen Lorraine for at least twenty years. Occasionally they would see each other in Naples and have a drink, relive the past decades, and Lorraine had always felt a sense of sorrow for not being one of those people who stood by in support of the famous couple, Marcelo and Lucia. During this time she met her husband and became pregnant with their first child, Pippa. Had she known what was happening with her friends, she would surely have assisted in some way, but ironically for the "latest news" reporter, she found out on the pages of Italy's paparazzo magazines. When she tried to reach out, neither Marcelo nor Lucia was living in Positano.

When Lorraine moved back to Positano in 2002 after her husband passed away, she accepted a concierge position at one of the luxury hotels and then became the most sought-after wedding planner on the Amalfi Coast. On her way out of Positano heading toward Sorrento, Lorraine would pass the famous couple's home and get a sense of the emptiness and sorrow that remained there, a past that remained raw even to this day.

The knock on the door at ten thirty in the evening was not uncommon. Lorraine's door was always open, and her friends entered when they pleased; she was always happy to entertain them. As she looked through the peephole, Lorraine didn't recognize the man at the door but opened it anyway. Standing there before her was a worn and tattered man in his early-sixties, with beautiful grey eyes and peppered hair. The stubble on his face added an air of elegance, but she still could not tell who it was.

"Ciao, Lorraine," Marcelo said in his deep, raspy, unmistakable voice.

Lorraine stood there frozen for a moment, trying not to choke up. She motioned him inside without uttering a sound and closed the door behind them.

He smiled at her. "*Cosa? Non ti ricordi de me?*"

"Of course I remember you, Marcelo. How could I forget?" She hugged her old friend as she led him into the living area of her flat overlooking the coastline. "How long has it been?"

As they caught up with each other over trivial matters, Marcelo told Lorraine his reason for seeing her. He needed her help; he needed to get something back that belonged to him. Lorraine listened intently.

The proposition was simple—he wanted to get his home back. Lorraine couldn't understand his motivation. "What is the purpose of getting back a structure if what you loved the most is no longer part of it?" she asked him.

"Don't worry about those details," he said. "There is an American woman who has bought the home. It needs a lot of repair, and she will be looking for someone local to repair it, no?" Lorraine nodded. "*Bene*, then I want you to get friendly with the woman, suggest a couple of contractors but introduce her to me. I will do the rest."

"You want to repair the house for this woman, but how will that get you the home, Marcelo?"

"You leave it to me. All I need is your . . . how do you say . . . *raccomandazione. Capire?* Can you do this for me?"

Lorraine couldn't say no to a recommendation, but she was worried that he would end up getting into serious trouble, or, worse, the American would find out about his story and wonder what he was doing in her home. Either way it spelled disaster, but she knew Marcelo was determined and so she agreed. The small town of Positano was in for some of the biggest gossip since 1978.

***

Lorraine asked if he had a place to stay, and when she offered her second bedroom to him, Marcelo accepted. Besides, Lorraine's warm apartment was much better than wandering the streets of Positano on a chilly March night. Knowing his plan could work, Marcelo fell asleep quickly and slept like a baby for the first time in a long time.

The next morning, he decided to get a coffee in town and left Lorraine a note that he would return soon. He walked past the cathedral and ordered at a café, downing his coffee quickly and moving on. He didn't want anyone to recognize him, though it had been years since he stepped foot in Positano. Up the street, past the vendor stands, their crates of large, brilliant-yellow lemons on display, and people bustling about as they set up their shops, Marcelo transported himself back to a time when he couldn't even walk down the narrow streets without a grandmother hugging him, a *ragazzo* pitching a soccer ball at him, or women swooning at the sight of him. *Those bygone days that will never return*, he thought.

Marcelo then decided to walk up Viale Pasitea to the home. There was a crisp coolness to the breeze and it was a bit foggy, but he could find the house blindfolded. The sight of freshly caught fish and the aroma of warm, baked bread filled the narrow streets as the townspeople bustled about, setting up their stands and preparing for the day ahead. Past several shops and carports overhanging the perilous mountain range, Marcelo found the home. Standing before him was a sorry display of cracked paint and broken windows, with a touch of graffiti for good measure. The masterpiece home was no more. He cursed at the way the house had been treated as he entered the rusted gate and walked toward the patio of the home. He found the windows boarded up, and entry through the front of the house was nearly impossible. *What does this American woman want with this house, this town, and the life in this city?* he thought. None of it made any sense at all. Marcelo tried to picture the woman in his mind as he pried a board from one of the side windows and entered what used to be a small studio. It smelled musty, and there were spiderwebs everywhere. Within a matter of hours, Marcelo wrote down a lengthy repair and supply list that would put him ahead of the game, allowing him to give the crazy American a contractor quote before anyone else. He would make sure she couldn't refuse him by getting all the bulk items at cost and with no markup. Sure, he would be losing some money up front, and it was inevitable, but it would get him in the door and in her good graces in a snap. Time was a factor.

He'd have to move quickly if his plan had any chance of working.

***

Avinash and Ari spent some time talking in Anjali's kitchen while he devoured his meal. She could tell Avinash enjoyed life to the fullest—even the way he dunked his bread in the soup and took it to his mouth showed her he took nothing for granted. Avinash was a man who savored every drop and did the same in life. They talked about polo as she poured more of the 2002 Piedmonte into his glass. The good girl in Ari wanted to help Anjali out with the domestic duties by washing all the dishes; the bad girl in her just wanted to stare into Avinash's eyes—eyes that pulled her in like a full moon tide. He turned the barstool to face her and motioned her to come closer. She put the kitchen towel down and slowly walked over to him, stopping close enough to see into those deep, brown eyes.

"Avinash, what do you think about my move to Positano?" she asked and then almost bit her tongue at the audacity of the question.

"The question is not fair," he said in a serious tone. Ari took a step back and studied him. "You have not told me much about your past, not a great deal of anything about you that was of any true significance. How can I tell you what I honestly think if you don't trust me?"

"Well, I've just met you, Avinash." Ari slowly moved into the space between his thighs, which were open like a Venus flytrap, and spoke in the most honest and flirtatious tone she could find. "However, if I told you everything . . . and I mean *everything* . . . would you tell me then? Would you tell me if I'm doing the right thing, Avinash? Because

43

though I'm dreadfully sure about it, I so want to know what you think."

Avinash put his hands on her waist and brought her in a little closer. She could feel his breath on her face, but he kept her at a taunting distance. "I want you to tell me everything when you're ready, but certainly not here and not someplace where you can't have my undivided attention. Though I must admit, Ms. Cordero, that when I'm around you, I really can't concentrate on anything else."

He got up from the barstool, walked over to the kitchen door, and made Ari a proposition she could not refuse. "Sam tells me you have a love for Indian music and customs. Splendid, then! I have a cousin who is marrying in a couple of weeks just outside London. I would love for you to attend the wedding as my guest. Our weddings can be traditional and ceremonial. We can sneak away, and you can tell me everything then. You'll be in a good frame of mind; the energy is always favorable at weddings. Will you attend with me?"

Ari was thrilled at the thought of attending an Indian-Punjabi wedding. She had been to one in Chicago with a friend, but it was a very disappointing and Americanized version of an Indian wedding, with a mild splattering of Indian customs here and there. She was all for seeing the real thing, and with Avinash as her guide and companion, the evening would surely be memorable. Just then, Anjali burst through the door and announced that she thought it was a great idea. "We'll all have so much fun!" she said as she hugged Ari and Avinash.

"Anjali, you're always listening behind doors," Avinash said, his brow furrowed. "It's such a nasty habit, you know?" Anjali frowned and looked to Ari for rescue, but she was still on a high from receiving the wedding invitation and didn't notice.

"You haven't answered me, Ari. What do you say?" Avinash asked.

"Yes, yes of course. I'm so honored. Are you sure it will be okay for me to attend?"

"Okay? He's paying for most of the wedding, dear. He can invite whomever he wants," Anjali interjected.

"It's settled then. I'll have Anjali take you shopping for proper wedding attire. You two always have so much to talk about. Remember, you promised to tell me everything. I'm holding you to your word, Ari."

"Yes, yes absolutely!" she said with an enthusiastic nod. He kissed her on the cheek and left for the evening, saying he had imposed too much.

As Avinash walked out of Anjali's apartment that night, Ari had second thoughts. The idea of pouring her soul out to him was a little scary and perhaps presumptuous. *Why did I have to ask him such a question? Was I flirting with him, or do I really want to hear his answer?* Anjali couldn't help but ask what the promise part was about. When Ari told Anjali it was something about the house purchase, she didn't buy it. What would surely become common knowledge soon was that the infamous Avinash Batra had invited an American client to a family wedding, and the gossip would be interesting for the next few weeks, especially at London's World Bank.

CHAPTER THREE

I t was not the usual Monday morning at World Bank. For starters, Sam Waters got the news that the closing on the house at 87 Viale Pasitea would be delayed due to several issues, one of them being that someone had broken into the house overnight, and the local *polizia* had reported it to the home's current owner in Milan. With all this going on, Sam was not in the best mood as he walked into Anjali's office to let her in on the news.

In the meantime, the loan office was getting ready for Ari's early morning meeting, and they weren't sure what the delay was in Italy. Avinash was just finishing his shower after hitting the gym when he got the call from Anjali. He promised he would be there soon and asked Anjali and Sam not to break the news to Ari just yet until he found out what the problem was. He was sure there was more to it than just a break-in.

***

Ari drug herself out of bed and into the shower. It had been after three a.m. when she finally returned to her hotel, and she'd barely fallen asleep when the alarm sounded. Her head ached and she didn't feel up to making important decisions today—especially decisions related to money and mortgages. She wished Avinash would just take care of everything like he said he would and give her the best option.

Ari slipped on a beautiful cobalt-blue trench coat dress that tied around her tiny waist and a pair of bone-colored pumps. For good luck she wore an Indian bracelet that she loved. Topping it off with a simple pair of earrings and her Prada bag, she looked elegant and appeared ready for business.

Sam was horrible at lying, so he left that department to Anjali. Ari was told there was a slight delay in the paperwork, but that those sorts of things were quite normal. "We're working on it right now," Anjali said, "so if you'd like to come into my office and have a cup of tea or coffee, we should hear something soon."

Ari looked over at Sam for a reading and he glanced away, an apprehensive look on his face. Ari followed Anjali and locked her arm through hers. "What's going on, Anj?"

"Don't worry," she whispered. "Avinash is handling it, and Sam is having a subdued English meltdown right now." They laughed as they headed down the hall toward the small kitchen. "So, Miss Spanish She-devil, what did you think of last night? Avi-ji is inviting you to the family wedding, and you are supposed to confess some deep, dark secret to him?"

"Anjali, you're horrible. I'm excited about the wedding, but the secret part was a flirtatious, backfired question that went wrong. I mean, the invitation is wonderful, but what I need to say to him . . . well, I'm not sure I want to tell him everything about myself just yet. It's not the right time. Am I making any sense?"

"Oh, dearest, a little eating, drinking, dancing at the wedding and he will forget what you promised. Seriously, Ari, Avinash will remember every word. You're doomed."

***

"Is Ari here?" Avinash asked as Sam stepped into his office.

"Yes, yes. She's outside. I'm not sure what to tell her. Thank God Anjali is keeping her busy."

While Sam filled him on the delays of the house closing, Avinash walked to the door and asked Sam to follow. There at Anjali's desk, Ari sat crossed-legged and looking quite smashing. Avinash gave her a hug and asked Anjali to get the bank in Italy on the phone.

"Come with me, my dear." He took Ari by the hand and led her to his office. "It may take me a couple calls, Ari," he said as she settled on a comfortable white-leather sofa with a beautiful view of the Thames. "So if it gets boring, please tell me."

Avinash made call after call, catching Ari's eyes on him from time to time. When he finally hung up, he pushed back from the desk and crossed the room to sit next to her. He put his hand on her shoulder, frowning as he got right to the point.

"Ari, you need to tell me everything about Mr. Santos Echegui."

"What do you mean? What does Santos have to do with any of this, Avinash? I don't like this questioning at all," she huffed.

"I see this subject makes you uncomfortable, but without a lot of personal details right now, I specifically need to know why he went to prison. This information is affecting your home purchase. Both you and Mr. Echegui are listed on the deed of the home; therefore, any information regarding either of you that is left out can be interpreted as fraudulent. Do you understand?"

Ari and Santos had signed the offer and deed on the home almost four years before and placed a sizeable deposit to hold the home. Since Santos left, everything had stopped, and the owner of the home was kind enough to wait for them to settle things.

Ari's heart pounded in her chest as the familiar flush spread up her neck and across her face. Every time she opened her mouth to speak, she stopped, unable to put together a coherent sentence. Instead, she wiped her sweaty palms on her sleeves, nibbled the inside of her cheek, and shook her head in disbelief. Avinash got up from the sofa and brought her some cold water from the bar. After she took a sip, he took the glass from her hand and placed it on the coffee table. Avinash moved in close to Ari and cupped her hands in his.

"Ari, look at me. Please, dear, you don't have to be embarrassed. If you want to close on this home, you need to tell me everything. I can't help you if you don't help me."

Ari looked up at him as his intense brown eyes locked in on hers. Impeccably groomed and sharp-looking in his dark blue suit and crisp white shirt, her eyes were drawn to a simple red string tied around his wrist. *Well, at least somebody's wish is still coming true*, she thought as she scrambled up from the sofa.

"Ari, please don't go," Avinash said, a firm grip on her arm.

He seemed so sincere, but she was truly heartbroken. Her dream had a huge roadblock, and the worse part of it all was that Santos had been framed and shouldn't have gone to jail in the first place. The injustice of it all hit her hard this Monday morning; it was way more than she could handle. She shook herself free of his grasp and made a desperate dash out of the office.

***

Avinash hung up the phone just as a bewildered-looking Sam rushed into the office.

"What's going on?" Sam asked, shutting the door behind him. "I just saw —"

"Yes, I know. She's gone. I need you to hold off on negotiations regarding the house she's trying to purchase."

"Yes, of course. No problem, Avinash, but how can I help?"

"You can help me by locating Ms. Cordero. Also, have Security get me all available information on businessman Santos Echegui." Avinash gathered his things and headed for the door. "And one more thing, Sam," he said over his shoulder. "I need to know why he was imprisoned. This is to be kept completely confidential. No leaks. Airtight. Understand?" Sam nodded as he followed Avinash from the office and headed down to Security.

Avinash hurried toward the bank elevators, jabbing at the DOWN button just as Anjali appeared in the hallway. "Hey, Avinash!" she said as the elevator door slipped open. "Where are you going?"

"I'm off to find Ari. If she contacts you, let me know immediately." He stepped into the elevator, and the door closed behind him.

***

Within the hour, Sam had been briefed on the Echegui case from a contact in the district of Los Angeles County, California. He called Avinash and asked that they meet somewhere. They agreed upon a local pub, and when Sam arrived, Avinash had already taken in a pint, his tie hanging at half-mast. He motioned for Sam to join him and ordered two more pints while Sam took his seat.

"What do you have there?" Avinash said, his eyes on the file Sam held in his hand.

"Have you found Ari? Anjali and I are worried, Avinash. Ari is sold on this dream of hers; it will be devastating if it doesn't happen."

"Well, I know that, Sam," Avinash snapped at him. "And no, I haven't found her. I went to her hotel, but she hadn't returned. I'm not too sure this dream of Ari's is in her best interest. All I know is it was a plan that she and her ex hatched together, and though he's no longer in the picture, she's still holding onto this promise and wants to see it happen. But are we helping her fulfill a dream, or are we contributing to her mental and emotional breakdown? I just don't see clearly why we should invest in this deal, do you, Sam?"

Sam smiled. "Well, old friend, from a business standpoint, I agree it looks like a bad investment, but from a personal point of view—the one that is keeping you in a pub at one in the afternoon taking in two pints before lunch—I think you are personally invested in Ms. Cordero. Therefore, your business objective is worth bullocks!"

The waiter arrived with the pints and put them down on the table. Avinash stared Sam down, wanting to slug him but knowing full well he was right. Sam continued.

"Aside from what's in this file, you have more than a business interest in Ari. I'm sure part of you would like to see her fulfill this dream, but the other part would prefer she didn't leave. So you're torn and you're probably thinking, 'I can help like a businessman without wanting anything in return and let her go, or I can fight like hell to keep her here in London.' It's your call, Avinash. What's it going to be?"

Before Avinash could reply, his phone buzzed on the table. It was Anjali, and he was grateful for the interruption.

"Avinash, I haven't heard from Ari, but Security said she took a taxi that was heading toward London's theatre district. Does that help? I'm so worried! Dammit, Avinash! For God's sake, what's going on? Don't keep me in the dark!"

"I'll explain later. I promise, Anjali. I have a plan. *Shukriya!*" He thanked her and ended the call.

Avinash grabbed the file from Sam and scanned over the briefing. He understood from the documents that Mr. Echegui, a Portuguese businessman who had moved to the US in the eighties, had been framed and was used as a scapegoat in a business investment that had gone terribly wrong. The case took a turn for the worse when the crooked investors suddenly left the US before being indicted, leaving Echegui holding the bag and all fingers pointing at him after they found shipments of drugs and firearms instead of tequila inside the barrels being sent abroad. During the long trial, Echegui was convicted by a jury of his peers and was given a reduced sentence of eight months for agreeing to help authorities capture a fugitive who they believed was dangerous. The report also mentioned the fugitive was wanted in numerous countries by Interpol and several investigative authorities. Soon after, Echegui was cleared of all charges. He retired from the business world and led a fairly quiet life. An *LA Times* news article clipping inside the files showed that all charges were subsequently dropped. The article concluded with, "Currently, Mr. Santos Echegui is planning to retire and buy a home on Italy's Amalfi Coast with his wife, Ariadne."

Avinash stuffed the documents back in the folder and said with a smile, "Sam, I'm going to fight like hell. How's that, old man?" He handed Sam the file. "Get rid of it. This information never surfaced, understood?" The two men raised their pints, clinking them together to seal the deal before downing the last few drops.

Time to find Miss Ari Cordero, Avinash thought as he paid the tab and left the pub.

***

Ari sat in a quaint French café off Piccadilly Square, upset, disappointed, and overwhelmed by a sense of loss. The life she wanted in Positano was taking a turn in another direction, much like the winding road that leads you through the beautiful Amalfi landscape. With each turn of events, Italy's breathtaking sunsets moved a little further from her grasp. It was ironic to her that her namesake, *Ariadne,* was the Greek mythological daughter of King Minos of Crete who aided Theseus in his escape from the

Cretan labyrinth after killing the Minotaur. It would seem that her life was always, in some shape or form, a labyrinth that she managed—through luck or conscious effort—to navigate her way out of. But this time, the events in her life were taking a toll on her, and Ari was tired and worn. This latest news hit her hard in a split second, perhaps a reaction to repressing her true feelings for so long. The love of her life, Santos, was gone, and she was alone. And now her dream home had eluded her again.

Aside from the constant memories of Santos, there was Avinash Batra, someone she'd just met and for some reason could not stop thinking about even for a nanosecond. *What should I do?* Ari pondered over and over again as she ordered another café au lait. Her life had always been hectic and busy, with never a dull moment. Her father, a Spanish naval officer, and her mother, a beautiful woman born in Madrid of Italian parents, met in Madrid. It was a whirlwind love affair that had no support from either side. Ari's grandparents, the Cordero Pradas, were a rich and powerful family that bought and sold expensive art pieces. Ari fondly remembered traveling with them to distant lands as a child, as they searched for the most exquisite art pieces—from Prague to Switzerland, Germany, and England.

When she was eleven, her mother allowed her to travel with her grandparents as far as the Orient and India. While in India on one of the art searches, Ari became dreadfully ill with a fever that kept her in a hospital bed for two months. She was so ill that the hospital ward assigned her a personal nurse. She felt loved and pampered by all the medical staff, but Devyani, a young woman from Mumbai, was her favorite. She grew so close to her that Ari didn't want to leave her side. Devyani was the nurturing mother that Ari never had, whose singing, story reading, and life lessons helped a sick little girl recover. Ari told her grandparents she wanted to stay with Devyani, but they obviously refused. Her grandmother understood how Ari could feel closer to Devyani than she ever did to her own mother, a disciplined and caring woman who was not big on love and demonstrations of affection.

Ari had no idea at the time that her parents were separating. Later, she found out it was due to her father's infidelities. At the time when Ari needed her mother the most, she was more concerned with her husband's dalliances than her daughter's needs. Ari recalled the day she was to take the train in Calcutta and leave India. Devyani gave her a gift to remember their beautiful friendship. It was a delicate, handmade Indian bracelet and a porcelain vase with an intricately carved elephant on its lid. Devyani explained that the elephant held many mystical and magical powers. If she kept it close, it would hold the most precious things she could think of, and those precious things would, in turn, bring her the love of her life. Devyani also said the vase would bring her back to the things she loved most. Ari's torn soul wept for Devyani's love as the train pulled away from the station. Even today, the vase and the necklace were treasures she held close to her heart.

Later, during her college years, Ari was sent to the US to study, and she made many wonderful memories in Boston. She had the ability to attract all kinds of people with her humor and giving personality, and she blossomed into a tall, beautiful woman who turned heads and had all the male instructors in a battle for her attentions. Her upbringing didn't permit her to get into too much trouble. She had never smoked, experienced an illegal substance, or even touched a firearm. Heck, she didn't even have a tattoo! *How boring*, she thought, but she was proud that such temptations, though sometimes pressured by peers, were not things she gave much thought to—especially now, with so many trials and tribulations under her belt.

Her cell phone vibrated again, disrupting her heavy thoughts, but she didn't want to look; in fact, she hadn't checked it for hours. She decided to take a look just in case it was a call from Italy, but it was Kash. Ari didn't have the strength to listen to his apology or any excuses for his behavior the other day. Besides, she was thinking of someone else, Avinash Batra, and wishing the call had been from him instead. She'd run away from him in haste, and though her heart was broken, she realized— several hours and three lattes later—that he was truly trying to help her.

Ari paid her bill and left the café. She couldn't remember where Avinash lived, but she knew it was the Hyde Park flats, and any taxi driver could find it. She flagged down a cab, and the driver sped off in that direction. It was almost four thirty in the afternoon when she entered the building, much too early for Avinash to be home from work. *Good God*, she thought, *I should have headed toward his office.*

She introduced herself to the security guard, and he asked her to be seated. Ari heard him make a call and tell the person on the line that a Ms. Cordero was sitting in reception. Within minutes, Avinash rushed into the lobby, concern creasing his forehead and clouding his eyes.

"Are you okay?" he asked as he put both hands to her shoulders and then hugged her.

His embrace felt like the medicine she needed, and Ari held onto him, returning the tight embrace. Avinash waved to the security guard and thanked him and led Ari to the elevator. As they waited for the private lift, Avinash held onto Ari and stroked her hair. He didn't reproach or scold her; he simply held her close. They entered the elevator, and Ari wanted to say something meaningful, intelligent, well thought out, but the words wouldn't come. He pulled her closer, and Ari could feel he was excited as she moved her hips against him. With one finger, Avinash opened the front of her trenchcoat dress, studied her breasts and pressed them together. "This is unfinished business from the other night when you taunted me with them," he said while keeping his eyes focused on her breasts.

The elevator reached his flat, and they paid no attention as the doors opened and closed. Avinash pushed the button to hold the elevator in place, and they continued to consume each other, their hunger fueled by passionate kisses and caresses. Ari could hardly breathe but it didn't matter. She would inhale his hot, panting breath, use it to survive if she needed to.

Avinash pinned Ari against the elevator doors, his hands cupping her bottom, pressing her up so she could feel him completely. Suddenly, Ari felt the urgent need to catch her breath. She put her hands on his chest and held him at arm's length, and though her mind told her to say, "Let's take our time," what came out was a sexy, soft request.

57

"Avinash, I need you. I . . . I need you."

Avinash pulled back more to look into her dark, vibrant, green eyes, as though he needed some reassurance that she was ready for him. With that, he hit the OPEN button and the elevator doors released them directly into his sumptuous flat. Avinash escorted her inside, as Ari stepped clumsily into his den, half-dressed with her breasts still prominently exposed. Avinash took off his jacket, and reached for her hand. He smiled as he led her to his sunken living room, an area plush with soft pillows, rugs, and Indian art and sculptures, and stopped in front of a large mirror. He stood behind her, as Ari got a glimpse of her disheveled appearance, her hair a wild mess. Her lingerie enhanced her femininity, and Avinash let his hands travel down to the center of her universe.

Ari gasped and stepped away. *This is really going to happen,* she thought. Ari wanted him, but now she was fearful of making a mistake. She watched in the mirror as Avinash walked toward her, a hungry look of longing on his face. In that split second, she knew she needed him, no matter what.

Avinash froze as she turned around and laid a trembling hand on his chest. "I-I need to know if you're ready for this. Do you have . . . ?" she asked in a shy whisper. It was not the most romantic thing to say, but she hadn't been with anyone since Santos, and she certainly wasn't taking any chances.

"Don't move," he said as he hurried from the room. Less than a minute later he was at her side, unclothed and sheathed. Ari was shocked at his bravado, yet it aroused her.

Avinash leaned in close, his eyes smiling, and she reached for his neck, kissing him softly as he moved her backward onto the large pillows scattered about on the floor. She settled herself and pulled him down to her.

He slipped his tongue between her lips, and Ari moaned in delight, excitement washing over her. After pleasuring Ari with long, all-consuming kisses, he slowly removed each piece of intimate clothing as if she were a delicate piece of porcelain. Finally, Ari lay before him in nothing more than the bracelet that Devyani, her childhood nurse, had given her. Avinash examined every inch of her with his eyes, touching her softly with the tips of his fingers as he trailed them across her body.

"You're beautiful, Ari," he whispered as he lowered himself on top of her. His touch sent electrical currents through her body, and she was a mass of tension and excitement. Avinash took his time, kissing and suckling her, starting with her fingers, wrists, arms, and across her shoulders and neck. His mouth moved to her breasts, and he left tender kisses there, sucking on her hardened nipples as his hand dipped between her thighs. Ari shuddered, lifting her hips and pulsing against him, as if to beckon his entrance into her with the movements.

They drank each other's passion like it was the last drop of water in the desert—an imaginary oasis where two parched souls became one and the eternal thirst had been quenched. Avinash seemed in no hurry to finish, choosing instead to pleasure Ari and enjoy her. They spent the evening together in his flat, playing, touching, and fondling as they moved from the living area to the cavernous master bedroom, finally ending up in the huge Roman tub. Few words had been spoken, with only the occasional moan or whisper to excite passion in the other. While Ari lay against him in the tub, Avinash reached around her, using the sponge to caress and wash her breasts, his hands gentle as he sprinkled sweet, delicate kisses down her neck. Ari could not believe that after hours of lovemaking, she still wanted more of him. She took his hand and eased it down, across her stomach and beyond, moaning as he slipped two fingers inside her. He increased the pressure, and when Ari moaned again, he muffled the sound, his lips covering hers as he breathed in her sexual release.

Avinash kissed her again and stepped out of the tub. He dried off quickly and left her for a moment. When he returned, he had a plush white robe, a bottle of champagne, and two ornate flutes. Avinash helped Ari out of the tub, and his eyes stayed on her for a moment. He slipped the robe around her shoulders, playfully grabbing her bottom and then tying a knot at her waist as he brought her closer to him. They laughed, happy to be in each other's company. The rest of the evening was beautiful, magical. No remorse or troubles—just passion and desire. As the evening fell into the night, Ari and Avinash finally rested in his king-size bed, holding on to each other as if to life itself. Ari slept well that night, better than she had in days, and Positano and the house on Viale Pasitea were but distant memories.

The next morning, as the sun crept through the wooden blinds, Ari awoke, naked and alone in Avinash's bed. She opened her eyes, panicked for a split second until she remembered where she was. She swiped the hair off her face and sat up, smiling at the memories of the previous night and everything that had happened. She still couldn't believe it was real. She slipped from the bed and headed for the bathroom to tidy up before going in search of Avinash. A few minutes later, refreshed and with no clue as to where she'd left her clothes, Ari spied one of Avinash's shirts draped across a brocade chaise lounge in the corner of the bedroom. She slipped it on and made her way downstairs. She could hear someone in the kitchen and realized she was starving.

She found Avinash preparing eggs, and he had set out placemats with orange juice and an assortment of fruit and breads. Ari tiptoed in and Avinash looked at her, smiling with his eyes as he always did. She stopped, laughing as if she'd been caught red-handed.

"Good morning, darling. How do you feel today?" he said as he smiled from ear to ear and scanned her up and down. "Breakfast?"

Embarrassed to be wearing his expensive designer dress shirt, still doused in his cologne, Ari tugged at the tail and crossed her arms over her chest. "Sure! I haven't eaten anything in twenty-four hours, and I think I worked off the calories last night."

Avinash walked out from behind the large center island. "Bring that lovely body over here." He pulled her nervous hands away from the bottom of the shirt and kissed her for what seemed to be an eternity. Then he took her by the hand and sat her at the table before placing a heaping portion of eggs on her plate. "Enjoy, love. I have a couple conference calls this morning, but once I'm done we can do something this afternoon, anything you'd like. Okay?"

She nodded, nibbling on the inside of her cheek instead of her breakfast and fumbling for the right thing to say.

"Avinash, what will happen to the house? In all the turmoil yesterday—"

"Ari, I have to apologize for my actions yesterday. I'm very sorry. I crossed the line with my interrogation about Santos. I was too blunt with you, and I treated you unfairly." When Ari opened her mouth to reply, Avinash put a finger gently to her lips. "Let me finish. About the house . . . we can move forward. It will take some time, considering this development with your ex-husband, but we will be able to close. I suspect it will be a slow process in Italy, but if you really want to do this, Sam suggested we change the original deed to one in your name to make matters move faster. Can you get Santos to agree?"

Ari didn't answer.

"My question is," he said as he placed his hand on hers, "do you want to move forward now? You asked me Sunday what I thought about your plans. That was before we spent the night together, and now that we have, I have a dilemma. I could be the better man and let you move to Italy as a simple business transaction. No questions asked. Or I could be the man I think you want me to be and tell you it's not the right time, that we should give us a chance. Think about it, Ari. You can still have your home—fix it up as a hobby; put it back on the market as a rental with Sam's help—and we can spend summers there, just you and me. Only you can answer that question, but I want you to know how much last night meant to me. I truly would like for you to consider staying here with me."

Ari smiled at him and nodded. She needed to do some serious thinking. She had a decision to make—one that would be even harder than the one she'd made to leave everything behind and start a new life in Italy.

"Just give me a little time," she said.

"Take as much time as you need." He kissed her goodbye and headed out the door.

***

At World Bank, Anjali set up the room for the conference call. She took a moment to call Avinash to remind him of the meeting and to see if he had heard from Ari. He didn't answer, and Anjali had no time to leave a lengthy message. Ten minutes later, Avinash returned her call from the car.

"What's up, Anjali? I see I missed a call from you."

"Good morning, sir. Just wanted to remind you about the conference call at ten this morning. Are you on your way?" Avinash confirmed he knew about the call and would be there shortly. "I see. Very well then. Anything on Ari, sir? I'm awfully concerned. Should we call the police?"

"*Nahim*, Anjali. It's not necessary, dear. Ari is fine; she was with me last night. I'll be at the office in a couple of minutes, okay?"

Anjali was not satisfied with his answer. What did he mean about last night? Was Ari with him just part of the night or the whole night? Perhaps he meant the whole night and into the morning? She scurried about in the office and couldn't concentrate, not even for a moment.

***

Ari finished her breakfast, enjoying the leisurely morning but unable to settle her mind. Suddenly, she remembered that Kash had called the day before and hurried to her bag to retrieve her phone. She was curious as she played the voicemail he'd left her.

"Ari, this is Kash. I just wanted to apologize for the other day. I was truly not myself, and I need to see you again. I can still taste our kiss, and you have been on my mind a lot. Please call me. Thanks, love."

Ari couldn't think of calling Kash now. Perhaps tomorrow. Today she had too many things to do, decisions she had to make. Avinash was now an important part of all those decisions. She closed her eyes for a moment, and she could see her home at 87 Viale Pasitea. It was finally fixed the way she wanted, with the bougainvillea's hanging over the indoor terrace that overlooked the blue Mediterranean. But now she could see herself with a man—a man she was starting to truly care for—and the idea of being alone forever in a beautiful home, in a far-off place, seemed daunting to say the least.

One of the first things Ari needed to do was call Anjali and Sam. She knew they would be worried and would have many questions about her disappearance. She knew Anjali would be busy setting up the conference call, so she tried Sam first. He answered immediately.

"Ari, is that you?"

"Yes, Sam, it's me. I'm fine. I'm so sorry about yesterday. I hope you can forgive me . . . after everything you've done for me. I owe you such a big apology."

"Nonsense, Ari. As long as you're all right. There's no need to apologize. Will you be coming to the bank today? I have several options for moving forward—that is, if you still want to do so."

"That's just it, Sam. I'm a little confused right now, and I need some time to think. I would certainly like to change the deed on the home to my name somewhere down the road. Can we put it off for, say, a week or two?"

Sam agreed and asked if she had discussed it with Avinash. "He was quite worried yesterday after you left his office."

"He knows that I'm in agreement about putting it off, but we haven't discussed my decision just yet. Can it just be between you and me for now?"

"Yes, of course, Ari. I understand. Whatever you decide, we are here to support you."

Ari thanked Sam and thought about how much his friendship meant to her. After the death of her parents and grandparents, she really had no family support to speak of. Santos's family cared deeply for Ari, but they were living in Lisbon and had their own family issues to deal with. Her friends in the States were few, but those who had been there for the good and the bad were thrilled she had made the decision to move to Italy, even if it meant she would be moving far away. They had all planned to visit her the following year when she was settled in and have the biggest "Happy New Beginnings" party they could muster up. She smiled as she thought of it. At one point, before she met Santos and even during their marriage, they traveled so much together that she had christened them the "What a Life" club! Interesting choice of words, she thought. What a life, indeed! Here in London, removed from everyone she knew, her life was taking an interesting turn. Ari decided to embrace the change with a positive attitude. She'd wait

patiently for Avinash to call, but first she had to call Anjali
and explain what happened.

***

Once the conference call ended, Anjali sat with Avinash and
questioned him about Ariadne. He smiled and assured her
everything was fine.

"We will be seeing each other this afternoon. I was
thinking of taking her to Bath, having a nice dinner, and . . .
well, who knows what."

"Well . . . I certainly 'know what!' You shagged her last
night!" Anjali said with a mixture of disbelief and curiosity.
"I can't believe it! You're too much, Avinash. She hasn't
even been here forty-eight hours and already you've been
intimate? What happened to dating, courting, and getting
to know each other? My God, Avinash! So . . . how was it?
Was it hot? I need to know every detail."

Avinash laughed and enticed Anjali with just enough
information to drive her over the edge. She pinched his arm
and harassed him until Avinash finally gave in and spoke
discreetly about their night together.

"Anjali, it was great. I think I am starting to have real
feelings for Ari, honestly. You'll be happy to know that, for
the first time, I think I could have a life with someone. I'm
not sure where all of this will take us, but for now I'm a
happy man. And I must admit you were right about
Ariadne. She's a treasure."

Anjali fought back tears as she watched him pour out
his feelings. She hadn't seen this side of him in a long time,
and it was sweet watching him begin to see how life with
one person was truly possible. She hugged him and left his
office to dry her eyes.

Anjali was back at her desk when she received Ari's call, and the sound of her voice led Anjali to believe that she and Avinash were extremely happy with each other. Ari explained how things with the house had transpired, including information neither Avinash nor Sam had yet to share with her. She told Anjali that the home-buying process in Positano would be put on hold until she and Avinash could figure out where things were heading.

"We had a wonderful night, Anji. It was . . . how can I explain it?"

"It was hot, sweaty, sexy, and brilliant!" Anjali replied.

Ari laughed, but Anjali detected a hint of nervousness in her voice. "Yes, well, all those things . . . but what honestly made the moment so beautiful was how much we needed each other. You know what I mean, Anji?"

"Of course! I have been telling Avinash that for years, but I don't think he understood the true meaning of it until now. I'm so happy for you guys; I really am. I will need to start charging for this matchmaking business, you know?"

They chatted and laughed a while longer, as if they'd been friends for years rather than just a few days. They were still on the phone when Avinash strolled out of the office, his black T-shirt half-tucked into his jeans.

"I'm off, Anjali. See you . . . uh . . . when I see you. Friday, perhaps? We need to talk about preparations for my cousin's wedding."

"Sounds good," she said before turning her attention back to Ari.

"Oh my God, Anjali!" Ari said. "Just the sound of his voice makes me . . . . Anyway, we have to shop for the wedding. It's in two weeks!"

"Don't worry yourself, dear. I'll pick out some nice dresses with saris, and you'll look like a queen. This wedding will be special in so many ways."

Anjali was hoping that this time together could change Avinash the scoundrel into a one-woman man and, more importantly, that Ari could recognize the game before it was even played on her.

Chapter Four

I n Sorrento, the news that a problem had delayed the signing of the home sale documents reached Marcelo. The source at the courthouse—a woman he met with a bit of flirting—and his prayers to Santa Rita were paying off. Marcelo also knew the American had another shot at getting the house, and before she could attempt it, he wanted to find out more about her. Always the charmer, Marcelo decided to ask the generously proportioned courthouse worker out to lunch. She accepted, and he headed to the *barbiere* for a shave and haircut. Afterward, he doused himself with a little Acqua di Parma and stopped to purchase a nice linen shirt. *This just might work*, he thought as he strolled to the café—a quiet, quaint little place overlooking the Bay of Naples.

Constancia, the courthouse worker, arrived shortly after the waitstaff showed Marcelo to his table. He watched as she fussed with her hair and tugged at her clothing, her eyes darting from table to table in a frantic search for him. A heavyset woman in her late fifties with a body like a cantaloupe, void of shape and femininity, Constancia reminded Marcelo of a German prison frau during the war. *She could probably beat me to a pulp*, he thought as he stood to greet her.

"Are you sure it's okay to talk here?" Constancia asked, her eyes still scanning the area for possible eavesdroppers.

Marcelo did his best to reassure her. "Surely a beautiful, enticing woman such as you can have lunch in public with a man. No one here will think twice about it." She finally made eye contact with him but said nothing. "Are you unable to enjoy the company of a man who finds you beautiful and a pleasure to be around?" He swallowed hard, hoping the heavy dose of compliments would do the trick. Indeed it did. The woman batted her eyes and leaned forward to touch his hand.

"Well, of course I can," she replied. "Having lunch with you is such a treat for me."

Marcelo smiled. *"Perfetto, signora."*

Marcelo let her do the talking. This is easier than I expected, he thought, playing the part of the captivated listener with ease. Two hours and a couple of proseccos later, Marcelo managed to convince Constancia that the house at 87 Viale Pasitea was his, and the American had stolen it without remorse or guilt. A hardworking, lonely man like him, without a love in his life and no place to rest his tired soul at night, should not be treated in such a fashion—especially by those imperialistic Americans!

"How dare she!" Constancia said, indignant and now on a mission to save Marcelo's house, promising him a complete file and information on the American as she invited Marcelo to her home just outside Sorrento in Priora.

Marcelo agreed and hurried to jot down her information before she changed her mind.

He left the café feeling more alive than ever. Revenge provided just the adrenaline he needed to take back what was once his.

When Marcelo arrived in Priora that evening, Constancia welcomed him into her home and invited him into the dining room. As she scurried back and forth from the kitchen, he wandered about the room, hoping somehow to work up an appetite for whatever she had brewing. A curio cabinet caught his eye, and when he approached it he was amazed to see a massive collection of sewing thimbles of every shape, size, material, and country of origin imaginable.

How can someone be so attached to a thimble? he thought as he took one last look through the pristine glass curio doors before taking a seat at the table.

Constancia came in with the last steaming dish. The dining table held enough food to feed an army. *With any luck, she will eat it all in one sitting, and I can polish off the wine,* he thought as Constancia lit the candles placed in tall candelabras and sat across from him. She smiled often—a little too often, Marcelo realized as he examined her worn and stained teeth, making him less hungry than before. He finally managed to down some greasy sardines and aubergine that was in season but could eat no more.

After dinner, they moved from the dining table to the outside patio, from which hung thirty to forty colorful birdcages. Before Constancia could shriek out a warning, Marcelo slammed his forehead into one and cut himself. He settled himself in the nearest patio chair and cleaned off the blood with a handkerchief he had in his back trouser pocket, not wanting any blood to drip onto his new linen shirt. Constancia fussed over him as she sat him down, leaning into his face as she tried to dab arnica paste on his forehead. Marcelo, all but smothered by her pendulous, sweaty breasts, scooted out of her reach and got to his feet.

"Thank you, my dear. I'll be quite fine. Now, do you have the file you mentioned earlier?" Marcelo breathed a sigh of relief when she waddled inside to fetch it. "The torture one must endure," he mumbled. "I've got to get out of here."

When Constancia returned with the file, Marcelo decided to make his move. He kissed her on both cheeks and explained his need for a hasty departure.

"I'm exhausted and my head is pounding," he said, praying the sorrowful look on his face matched the fake whine in his voice. "Surely it must have been all the wine and delicious food, *amore*."

Constancia's mouth opened, closed, and opened again without uttering a sound—her words frozen from the kisses, perhaps—but it reminded Marcelo of a desperate fish out of water. He grabbed the file and strode toward the door with the woman in tow.

"When will I see you again?" Constancia asked when she finally found her voice.

"Soon. Very soon." Marcelo placed a hand on her shoulder, determined to keep her at a safe distance.

"I think," Constancia said in what Marcelo surmised must be her most romantic voice, "we have a connection. A love connection. Don't you agree, Marcelo?"

"*Si, amore, sicuramente.*"

He dashed out into the chilly evening and down the streets of Priora, looking for a taxi. Marcelo opened the file on the ride over to Sorrento which gave him a good twenty minutes to skim over some of the details. There were photographs inside, and two in particular caught his eye. The first was of the home, dated four years ago; the other was of three people, but his eyes were drawn to the tall, striking woman in the center of the photograph, flanked by an older gentleman holding a file of some sort and yet another gentleman, his arm draped casually around the woman's shoulders. *Could this be her?*

Marcelo examined the photograph again and stuffed the rest of the material back into the file. For a moment, time stopped, and he couldn't help but stare at the beautiful woman, wondering why she wanted the house—his house. His anger tripled as he stared at her. *Of course she would have to be gorgeous,* he thought as he struggled to concentrate.

The woman had such a kind smile and angelic eyes. Her hair was blowing across her face on the always-windy Viale Pasitea he remembered. What would be a terrible flaw in a regular photograph, at least for most women, made this woman seem like a goddess. Marcelo slammed the file on the seat and uttered a string of colorful Italian indecencies.

The next morning, in a dusty café near the marina, having slept not a wink thinking about the American, Marcelo examined the documents in more detail. He realized the sizeable deposit the couple gave the owner several years back was probably the reason the home was not sold sooner. No matter what document he was reading, he kept referring back to the photograph. *Just as well that she's beautiful; it will be easier for me to destroy her dream. If she were some lifeless waif, I would need a different plan.* Marcelo knew he had a short window of time and decided to visit Lorraine in Positano once again.

***

At World Bank in London, Anjali was just getting ready for lunch when someone she hadn't seen in years strolled into the office. "Hello, Anjali," the suave, handsome, Indian man said. "Remember me?"

Anjali's mouth dropped open. *What that hell is he doing here? And in Avinash's office, of all places!* "It's been a long time, but the years have been good to you. You're no longer that skinny, pestering boy. What in the name of God brought you here, Akash?" she said, getting a better look as she stared him up and down with suspicion.

"Anjali, please call me Kash. We've known each other for too many years to be so formal with each other. You never had a problem with me, and . . . well, Avinash and I—"

"Yes, you and Avinash had your issues, big issues that never got resolved. You know Avinash never wanted to see you again, so what are you doing here? Akash, I'm not going to ask you again. Tell me, or I will call Security."

"No, don't do that! I'm not here for Avinash. I wanted to ask you something important."

"What are you looking for, Akash? This is all highly suspicious. You're lucky Avinash is out of town for a couple of days, or he would have you thrown out on your arse!"

"So, he's away then. Surely he is with someone?" Anjali raised her eyebrow at him, letting him know full well she would not give him that information. "All right, all right. To the point, Anjali. Don't lose your temper. Is he with Ariadne Cordero?"

Anjali tried to hide her astonishment, but her mind raced. *How does he know Ari?* It didn't seem remotely possible that the two might be friends, and Ari had never once mentioned Akash to her. Well, I haven't known her long, so maybe . . . .

"Oh, you know Ms. Cordero? What a coincidence," Anjali said, determined to sound nonchalant.

"We met on the flight over from Los Angeles. I really like her, Anjali, and I haven't heard from her in a couple of days. She doesn't answer my calls or return my voicemails. I've left messages at her hotel, but it seems Ari has disappeared. And since you said Avinash was away for a few days . . . well, that would explain a lot of things."

Anjali walked over to Akash and stared into his dark, deep eyes. "Akash, you know how much Avinash means to me. I owe him my life. I would never betray him, and now that I've met Ari, I would not betray that girl either. She's a good person, someone who deserves a shot at happiness. Leave her alone. Do not return here, and do not pursue her. She has made up her mind. If she's not returning your calls, she's trying to tell you something. Respect her and leave now, Akash. I am warning you for the last time."

Akash smiled. "You know, Anjali, I really like you. You're honest and loyal. Unfortunately, I'm not." He grinned at her again before heading for the door. "We'll be in touch."

"No, we won't!" she yelled at him as he walked away.

Anjali returned to her desk and plopped into the chair, frustrated and confused. *Why is Akash so interested in Ari?*

Especially if they'd just met once. Does he want to destroy any chance Avinash has at happiness after all these years?

One thing was certain: if Avinash thought for even one second that Ari had anything to do with Akash, he would not be the slightest bit forgiving.

***

That evening, after a full day of touring Canterbury and Bath, Avinash and Ari checked into a quaint boutique resort just outside of town.

"Are you tired, darling?" he asked, unlocking the door to their room.

"Just a little, but this place is so beautiful! I may never want to leave." She smiled as she kissed him lightly on the cheek. He returned the kiss to her lips and shut the door behind them.

While Ari unpacked the clothes she'd picked up from her hotel and placed in a day bag, Avinash opened the wooden shutters, revealing a panoramic view of the peaceful hills before them. The setting sun provided the perfect backdrop, casting a brilliant orange hue across the landscape, and he asked Ari to come see it for herself.

She stood in front of him, comfortably nestled against his chest, and Avinash wrapped his arms around her like a blanket as the sun went down for the evening.

"Vhat do you like, ma'am?" he whispered in his most exaggerated Hindi-English accent. "Vhy do you love being here with me, ma'am? Vhat's your favorite color, ma'am? Vhat do you want to eat, ma'am?"

All Ari could do was laugh and enjoy his humor.

"Nothing? Ma'am has no answer?"

She tipped her head back and smiled. "You're too much, you crazy Indian!"

"Really?" he said. "I'm the crazy one, and you're the mute one? Fine pair we turned out to be." He was going to start another round of rapid-fire questions, but Ari pulled his head down for a kiss. He moaned as he turned her around to face him. "Hmmm. I like that answer much more."

They stood there, wrapped in each other's arms as the sun slipped below the horizon. Avinash caught on to the Lionel Richie song playing in the background and started to slow dance with Ari. They shared an animated laugh, as they always did when they were together. Avinash took off his leather jacket and dove onto the bed, scattering plush pillows in every direction.

"*Idhar aao,*" he said sweetly as he patted the bed.

She joined him as he requested and rested her head on his chest. "I remember my grandmother saying that to me when I was a child. I also know how to say *Tū hai mera dila kā pyāra.*"

"Do you know what you just said?" Avinash whispered, feigning a look of wide-eyed astonishment. He ran his fingers over her lips and asked her to say it again.

"Have you never said you care for someone with all your heart?" Ari retorted.

Avinash smiled, certain she'd made an error in the Hindi translation. "Well, darling, I care for a lot of people, but you just said, 'I am the love of your heart.'"

Ari kissed him, and then she sat up and thought for a moment. "Actually I do have many people that I love with all my heart, though in different ways." Ari explained how she loved her grandparents, who took her to so many places, showing her a love of art, people, and different cultures. She loved her parents, and though they were distant from her, they showed her the meaning of true character.

Avinash listened intently as Ari listed other people and things she loved. Then she got up from the bed and asked Avinash to open the wine they'd bought in the city of Bath. As he uncorked it, she decided it was time to tell him about Santos. "I loved him very much, Avinash. I won't ever deny that to you or anyone. Santos was my soul mate, my partner, the love of my life—until he left me. He meant everything to me. Santos was the balance to my life, the positive to my negative, the good side to my bad side, the calm in my torment. It may sound corny, but he completed me in so many ways. Santos helped me become a woman who could feel true love, enjoy it, and return it without fear."

"Tell me how you met," Avinash said when she paused to gather her thoughts.

"We met while I was working at a marketing firm in Los Angeles. It was a one-year contract, and I was twenty-six years old and newly divorced from my first husband, Joseph. My marriage to Joseph was a nightmare. He was emotionally abusive, and it was a horrible mistake to marry him, but I felt sorry for him, thinking I could fix him somehow. But like so many things we try to fix in our lives, it was impossible. I realized too late into the marriage that you can't fix someone who doesn't want to be fixed. You can only mend your soul once the damage is done and move on. Before I met Santos, I spent a couple of years alone trying to find out who I was and what I wanted in life."

"Were there others before Santos?" Avinash asked.

"Yes, but no one of any consequence."

"Then tell me more about how you met Santos," Avinash said, pushing Ari to get everything off her chest.

"I was in Los Angeles, like I said before, and one of the agency's biggest clients threw a launch party for a new tequila brand at Chateau Marmont. Have you been there?" Avinash nodded but didn't speak. "Well, it was a swanky party. The Who's Who of Beverly Hills and Hollywood were there. I had been to those sorts of things in Los Angeles and a couple when I lived in Spain, but the vibe was special that night. It sort of felt the same the night we met in London. The evening couldn't have been more amazing. It was enchanting and inspiring for a new career woman like me. Anyway, Santos was invited by the launching company since he was investing in the tequila brand, Vida Blue."

"Catchy brand name for tequila," Avinash said, noting the good business sense of that name. When translated, *vida* meant life, and blue was the color of the agave plant used to make the tequila.

Ari was thrilled that he caught on so quickly but continued her rendition of the story. "He was just standing there, admiring all the beautiful people, as I was, and suddenly we scanned each other from a distance. Our eyes met and we smiled at each other, almost as if we knew what the other was thinking. I looked away, and moments later he appeared at my side. He was sweet, almost angelic in nature, and complimented my agency on the launching. Santos told me he was born in Portugal but mainly grew up in the US and in Mexico. I figured that was the reason I couldn't put a finger on his accent. I had to work at the event and tried to excuse myself, but he gave me his business card and asked me for my telephone number. Santos had a way of making you feel secure. There was no evil intention in his eyes. Normally, I would never give a stranger my number, but we had many things in common in Los Angeles and Spain and so . . . we left it there, agreeing to see each other again and have a coffee or cocktails somewhere. I must admit, I spent the rest of the evening thinking about him, and I hoped he would call me. When I returned home, my roommate told me a mysterious man with a sexy accent had called me. I knew it was Santos, but I waited a couple of days before returning the call."

Avinash hung on every word, not taking his eyes off Ari for even a moment. He wanted every detail, needed to see her reaction as she spoke of Santos, gauge any residual feelings she might have toward this man who, though he'd never met him, was indeed his rival. He smiled when she laughed at old memories and held her when she spoke of sadness. If Avinash could learn everything about Santos from Ari, all of the information about her and what she wanted in a relationship would be known to him. This, after all, was the most important strategy for winning Ari over and making her forget Santos—and, most importantly, forget about moving to Italy once and for all.

***

The hours went by and Ari realized she had been talking about Santos for too long. It was way past eight in the evening, and she quickly stopped her story and asked Avinash if they could take a break for dinner somewhere. He agreed and they headed into the quaint town for a quick bite. The evening had cooled down, and despite her white, long-sleeved pullover, jeans, scarf, and ankle boots, Ari shivered at the night's chill and leaned into Avinash for warmth. They walked into town, arms wrapped around each other, and finally reached a little bistro that seemed to beckon to them from the street. They found a table near the fireplace, and Avinash ordered the meal with his usual confidence and knowledge.

Ari didn't care that he knew exactly what she wanted that evening. In fact, she appreciated the idea that someone—a man other than Santos—really understood her.

Avinash warmed her hands with his, rubbing them together, and Ari giggled as other patrons stared at his antics. He leaned closer, put his lips to her ear, and began to sing the soft, haunting melody of an old Indian folk song.

"That's beautiful, Avinash. What does it mean?" Ari asked when he finished. Avinash looked at her hands and translated as best he could.

"On meeting you, it feels like I should keep admiring you. On meeting you it feels like I should keep liking you. The mystic hills are enchanting and my heart is desiring you . . . again and again."

He gazed into Ari's eyes and continued. "In spite of the number of times I see you, it never seems to be enough. I cannot see anything other than you." Avinash suddenly seemed far away, as if lost in a pleasant memory.

"That's beautiful, Avinash," Ari said. She kissed his hands, still wrapped tight around hers. She thought of asking him if that song reminded him of someone he had loved and lost, but she knew better than to ask a womanizer for details. In the past, such particulars would have haunted her, but Ari had grown up quite a bit and knew what questions to ask and when. She opted to change the topic and asked Avinash about the upcoming wedding and how it would be celebrated. It seemed to snap him out of his reverie, and he quickly smiled with his eyes, agreeing to fill her in on the upcoming nuptials. Ari mentioned what she remembered most of the American-Indian wedding she'd attended and boasted about the beautiful songs, the ceremonies, and the tradition.

"This will be a traditional Indian-Punjabi wedding. My nephew is quite modern, but his mother is traditional, so some of the traditional customs we observe will be used," Avinash explained. "My nephew was born in London and rarely makes trips back to see the family. I'm sure they will observe customs like the *mehndi*, since the women seem to enjoy the henna hand painting so much, the *vivah-homah* or sacred fire ceremony, and the traditional groom's arrival. The bride is also Punjabi, so you will see some of those customs woven into the wedding as well. It should be beautiful. I'm sure you will enjoy it. I-I mean, we will enjoy it together." Ari stared at him, surprised that Avinash, for once in his life, now seemed unsure of himself.

***

In the days leading up to the wedding, Avinash and Ari spent every waking moment together. Though Avinash loved his work, he could think of nothing more than coming home to be with Ari, who had left the hotel and was living at his flat, her one-month stay in London having turned into three. The nights of partying with a variety of women were over. The calls and messages from his list of girlfriends, all hoping for a hookup, were erased, and he did not long for the emptiness of those times any longer. Now the evenings were filled with Avinash's closest circle of friends, including Anjali and Sam, who told stories about India while Ari filled them in on her interesting life in America and Spain.

***

Try as she might, Anjali had not managed to find the right time to tell Ari that Kash had been looking for her or that he had appeared at the bank. During an evening when Avinash, Sam, and some friends from his gym were watching a gut-wrenching Indian cricket league match, Anjali pulled Ari into the kitchen.

She got to the point quickly. "Ari, how do you know Akash Ramkissoon?"

"What?" Ari said. "Kash? I don't understand."

"Well, the fact that you just called him Kash tells me you know him better than I thought. Let me tell you, dear, that I am not asking you this question because I wish to pry into your private life. I am asking you because your relationship with Avinash is in jeopardy, and you need to tell me."

Anjali watched as disbelief clouded Ari's face. She was certain a million questions must be running through her friend's head.

"Okay, okay. It's nothing, really," Ari said, speaking slowly as if measuring her words. "We met at the airport in Los Angeles, in the VIP lounge, and he just came up to me and said hello. We struck up a nice conversation, and he managed to arrange that we sit together on the flight. All we did was talk. He was incredibly sweet, and I felt comfortable with him. I told him about the house in Positano, that I would be meeting some people at World Bank in London,

83

but I did not tell him about Santos or my reasons for buying the house. Later, after we arrived in London, he called me."

"On the way to our dinner the first night, in the car, you received a call. Was that Akash?" Anjali asked.

"Yes. He invited me to breakfast the next morning. I agreed. It was before I met Avinash. Honestly, Anji, after that night I didn't even want to go to breakfast with him. Avinash and I had a connection, and all I could do was think of him and . . . well, you know the rest. Kash and I met up that Sunday around two in the afternoon, and we had a nice time. Suddenly he excused himself. I do remember Kash seemed different after that, but then you called me and invited me to your home, and I didn't really think about it again."

Anjali waited patiently as Ari told her the rest of the story, including Kash having words with a woman at the café and his hasty, nervous retreat afterward.

"It was strange. I wondered who she was, but I didn't ask and I couldn't read him. When we got to the car, he . . . well . . . he—"

"He what, Ari? Come on!"

"Kash kissed me. It was all very innocent, as if he needed to be needed at that moment. I didn't think anything more of it. Really, Anjali. It meant nothing."

"I believe you, Ari. Then what?"

"He took me home. End of story."

"That's it?" Anjali asked. "You mean to tell me there is nothing more than that?"

"Yes! He's been leaving me messages, but I haven't answered them. Kash means nothing to me. He's just a stranger I met on the plane but nothing more. Avinash means everything to me, Anjali. I even feel guilty that I haven't thought of Santos in so long. Positano seems so far away now. What can I say? I think I love Avinash."

Ari had tears in her eyes as she confessed her feelings, and Anjali felt the need to hug her and tell her it was going to be fine, though she knew in her gut that this innocent meeting between Ari and Akash would somehow come back to bite her in the worst way.

Suddenly, Avinash entered the kitchen and stopped short. "Is everything all right, Anjali?" Ari turned around at the sound of his voice, tears still lingering on her face as Avinash approached her. "*Kyāhu'ā*, what's happening, darling?"

"Oh, it's nothing. She just got a little emotional—woman things," Anjali said, quickly saving the odd moment.

Avinash cradled Ari's face in his hands and examined her eyes, trying to read her. Ari stared back at him, and Anjali could feel the emotion flowing between them. Ari played it strong, smiling and giving Avinash a peck on the cheek.

"It's okay, darling. Just girl talk. Don't worry."

"Are you sure?" he said as he looked to Anjali for an answer.

She reassured him again, and the evening ended on a quiet note, though Anjali knew Ari must be filled with unanswered questions about Kash and Avinash.

Anjali waited until the next morning, two days before Avinash's cousin's wedding, and invited Ari out for lunch and some shopping. They spent the afternoon in Southhall, a lively, diverse community in the West London borough of

Ealing, an area oftentimes referred to as Little India. There, Ari found colorful saris and street food stalls selling samosas and Indian sweets alongside bright fabrics hanging in shop fronts. Bhangra music filled the air, and the streets bustled with activity from the thriving local community.

Anjali hoped Ari would stay in London for Diwali, the Festival of Lights. She explained to Ari that the festival was celebrated in late October or early November, and it was one of the biggest festivals of the year. "You can't miss it, Ari, honestly."

"We'll see. I would love to be here," Ari said. "Maybe things between Avinash and me will continue to grow and I can make the festival."

After some sweets with tea, Anjali took Ari to the *Sri Guru Singh Sabha Gurdwara* on Havelock Road, one of the largest Sikh temples outside of India. The stunning building, finished in marble and granite with a gilded dome and stained glass windows, was peaceful and welcoming. Prayer and chanting could be heard as they entered, and Anjali asked Ari to take off her shoes and cover her head with a scarf that was hanging from her purse. They made their way to the foyer just outside the prayer room, and Anjali found space for them to sit next to each other on the floor.

"I know you have lots of questions, Ari," she whispered, leaning close to her friend so as not to be overheard. "Now is as good a time as any to fill in the blanks. Akash Ramkissoon was the only nephew of Mr. Harvash Dutta, the wealthy banker who took Avinash in as a son and later left him much of his wealth and his powerful position at World Bank. Akash was the only son of Mr. Dutta's sister and was brought up selfish and spoiled. Squandering most of his youth in gambling and drinking, his mother sent Akash to London to become a man and study for a career in finance. She had hoped that eventually Akash could take over the family banking business, but Akash had other ideas. Once in London, he was uncontrollable, and his uncle found it impossible to tutor him.

"It was during this time that Avinash was a promising director at the bank, where his diligence earned Mr. Dutta's trust and admiration. After an incident at a pub that landed Akash in a London prison for destroying public property in a drunken brawl, Mr. Dutta commissioned Avinash, who was a couple of years older than Akash, to be his tutor and help him out of his wasteful life. Avinash declined at first, thinking it was a huge undertaking; after all, if he failed, then Avinash would be blamed and Mr. Dutta's trust in him would be lost. Nonetheless, Avinash accepted after Mr. Dutta, too old and tired to do the job himself, insisted. Avinash paid the fine, got Akash out of prison, and brought him into his own home, spending some difficult weeks trying to detoxify Akash and put him on a healthier path, until he finally came around and started to act responsibly.

"I forgot to mention that Avinash was dating one of the daughters of the bank's largest investor. The investor had one of the wealthiest pharmaceutical companies in the UK and his homeland, India, and his daughter Suniel was a beauty. One evening, Avinash asked Suniel to help find a suitable girl to date Akash. The girl she chose was a friend of mine, Pritam, and she immediately hit it off with Akash. Unfortunately, he was more interested in Suniel—not because he loved her, but her money was much more attractive. He planned to win over Suniel's love with his charm and the help of Avinash's busy bank schedule. Soon she found Akash too dashing to refuse. Pritam confessed to me that there was something odd between Suniel and Akash. I met him several times and also thought he was irresistible and a true devil. Once Akash won over Suniel, the two schemed to get Avinash fired so Akash could assume his position at the bank, using her wealthy father's influence to coerce Mr. Dutta into agreeing to the plot.

"Akash would finally have the prestige and the money to marry one of the wealthiest girls in London without much effort. Soon thereafter, there was a joint meeting of the heads of the bank. At this meeting, the pharmaceutical giant asked the committee and Mr. Dutta to remove Avinash from his position and to put his future son-in-law in his place. Mr. Dutta was shocked to learn that it was Akash, his own nephew, conspiring against him and his longtime employee. Obviously, Mr. Dutta refused at first, but the committee threatened to withdraw their money and support from the bank. Before Mr. Dutta could answer the committee, he called in Avinash, and, as you can imagine, his world came tumbling down in a matter of minutes. He learned of Suniel's betrayal, how his friend Akash had conspired against him, and that he was about to lose his job at the bank."

"I can't believe what you're telling me!" Ari said when Anjali finally stopped to catch her breath. "Kash did all of that?"

"Yes, but there's more, Ari. Mr. Dutta tried to buy more time, asking the committee to give him twenty-four hours to return with an answer. However, what happened next made the day's events seem like child's play. Mr. Dutta received an urgent call in his office during the meeting with the committee—Akash and Suniel were involved in an accident, and both were in the hospital. The other driver was killed, and there was no word on the status of Akash or Suniel. Mr. Dutta and Avinash rushed to the hospital, telling Suniel's father the news as they all ran out of the meeting. Once at the hospital, they learned that Akash was unconscious but alive. Suniel's fate, however, was different; the poor girl died on impact."

"Oh my God!" Ari said as she covered her mouth with her hands. "Poor Avinash! What did he do?"

"As you can imagine, Suniel's father was destroyed and later withdrew his proposal from Mr. Dutta. As for Avinash . . . well, his life was changed forever. I truly believe this is the very reason why he has never committed to any other woman until you came along."

"Then what happened?" Ari asked.

"When Akash finally awoke, he learned from Avinash that he had killed his girlfriend and that his scheming plans were also destroyed. With the consent of Mr. Dutta, Avinash had Akash deported back to India and made the drunken brawl incident and a manslaughter charge due to the accident stick to his record. Avinash vowed that if he ever saw him again, he would not be forgiving and would make him pay for everything he had lost. Suniel's father accused Akash of killing his daughter, and Akash was indicted. Even in India, Akash could not escape the charges against him. The courts sided with Suniel's influential father, citing that he had killed another Indian citizen even if it was in a foreign country. Akash was convicted and served five years of a seven-year sentence before being released.

"We heard he moved to Australia and somehow later made it to the US. I believe he returned to England for revenge. It's where he was headed the day you met him in Los Angeles. Another thing, Ari. His interest in you may not be so pure. He has a wife and a child in Mumbai."

The prayer session ended and the mass of people exited quietly from the room. Ari and Anjali gathered their belongings and followed behind the group and out of the temple.

***

It was early evening when Ari returned home from her outing with Anjali. She'd spent the ride home trying to sort out everything Anjali had told her, but she simply couldn't believe it was true. Why hadn't Avinash mentioned any of it to her? She had so many questions and a lot of thinking to do.

Ari was surprised to find Avinash already there waiting for her. "Where have you been, darling?" he said, his eyes smiling at her.

With the story of Kash and Suniel still swirling in her head, Ari dropped all her shopping bags and rushed to him, hopping into his arms and wrapping her legs around him in a tender embrace.

"Kyāhu'ā, Ari," he said, laughing as she showered him with kisses. "What's going on?"

"Do you know how much I love you?" she whispered in his ear, as she had to Santos every night before going to bed. It just slipped out, but she meant every word. She kissed his ear and nibbled at his neck. Ari found his lips and surrendered her mouth to him. It startled her how easily he could make her toes curl. They kissed, it seemed, until all reason left them, and Ari could swear they were floating.

Suddenly, he seemed to have crashed back to earth. Avinash put Ari down and looked at her in amazement. "You love me?" he said, his eyes piercing hers. "How much do you love me?"

She smiled and ran her finger over his lips. "I love you from here to the stars and back."

Avinash wrapped his arms around Ari and pulled her close. "What would I do without you, Ari? I love you, darling."

CHAPTER FIVE

For the nuptials, Avinash looked dapper in a crisp, white *kurta*, teamed with fitted pants and a black waistcoat. Ari wore a two-toned fuschia and black Chantilly lace sari with a lace wrap that had beautiful intricate gold-threaded stitching on the bottom. The small of her back was showing, and her hair was curled and tied back with gold-colored clips placed an inch apart and cascading down through her hair. Avinash had a surprise for her before they left for the wedding. It was a beautiful necklace, kundan-set with table-cut 'polki' diamonds, rubies, emeralds, and pearls, strung on multiple rows of seed pearls and joined by an adjustable silk cord. It was a work of art on her neck and hung just above her cleavage. Avinash then applied the traditional *bindi* on Ari's forehead, completing her look for the wedding.

"Won't people think we're married if I wear the red dot?" Ari asked.

"For now," Avinash explained, "it's meant as jewelry for your beautiful head, and it also stands for the third eye."

Ari too had a surprise she had bought Avinash—a necklace with a coin that had the heads of Hindu Gods Brahma, Vishnu, and Shiva, and a beautiful silk handkerchief that was just a darker shade of fuchsia to match her dress. It was a perfect contrast to his white *kurta*. Avinash looked amazing.

***

On the ride to the wedding, Avinash went over some of the names of the cousins and family members for Ari to remember. Heading up the long driveway of the beautiful mansion about forty minutes outside of London, Ari caught a glimpse of the numerous guests, some in modern-day evening wear and others in the most colorful Indian attire Ari had ever seen. Ari's eyes caught Anjali first, there with Sam as her date. She looked beautiful in her golden-yellow attire with her hands decorated in henna as was the custom. Sam, a dead ringer for American actor and namesake Sam Elliott, was dashing in his black tuxedo, opting for the more traditional look. Ari noticed all the young girls swarming around Avinash, calling him "cousin" as he playfully pulled at their ponytails, squeezed their cheeks, and carried the smallest ones on his back. Seeing him so happy with his family and friends made Ari think of her own family and how much she missed being around those she loved.

***

The rooms in the home were colorfully decorated with garlands of flowers that hung from the ceilings and staircases. The numerous rugs leading to the altar were impressive, and the smell of incense and the sound of soft music playing in the background mesmerized her. It seemed to Ari that she was dropped into a dream as she floated through the house, marveling at the guests and taking it all in like a schoolgirl. From a distance she could see Avinash proudly greeting all the wedding party and being such a loving host. His second cousin, the groom, was a twenty-four-year-old law student who was so handsome he almost had the features of a God. The turban worn at Punjabi weddings matched the groom's beige-and-gold-colored *kurta*, and he had lovely jasmine and orchid garlands hanging from his neck like leis. His bride, a twenty-year-old Bengali and university accounting freshman, was also breathtakingly beautiful in her red and gold wedding outfit and *Mangalasutra* (Thread of Goodwill), a necklace worn as a symbol of their marriage. Both bride and groom wore impressive, elaborate jewelry on their bodies and hands. The bride gushed from the altar, occasionally smiling at her parents who were seated among the guests.

***

While Ari sat watching, Anjali called over one of the girls who skillfully painted her hands with beautiful henna colors. Anjali and the henna artist explained the different ceremonies during the course of the wedding.

There was the *Jaimala* or the Exchange of Garlands. Here the couple exchanges garlands as a gesture of acceptance of one another and pledge to respect each other as partners. For the *Madhupak*, the bride's father offers the groom yogurt and honey as an expression of welcome and respect. The *Kanyadan* is a sort of giving away of the bride, where the father of the bride places her hand in the groom's hand, requesting him to accept her as an equal partner. The concept behind *Kanyadan* is that the bride is a form of the goddess Lamxi, and the groom is Lord Narayana. The parents are facilitating their union. During the *Havan*, Lighting of the Sacred Fire, the couple invokes Agni, the god of fire, to witness their commitment to each other. Crushed sandalwood, herbs, sugar, rice, and oil are offered to the ceremonial fire. This aroma fills the room and is so enticing that you are transported to another world, another time, and, frankly, another universe.

Avinash assisted during the *Bandhan*, where a knot is tied with scarves placed around the bride and groom. They are tied together, symbolizing their eternal bond. This signifies their pledge before God to love each other and remain faithful. The *Saptapardi* is a series of steps that the bride and groom walk together to signify the beginning of their journey through life together. Each step represents a marital vow:

> *First step*: To respect and honor each other
> *Second step*: To share each other's joy and sorrow
> *Third step*: To trust and be loyal to each other
> *Fourth step*: To cultivate appreciation for knowledge, values, sacrifice, and service
> *Fifth step*: To reconfirm their vow of purity, love, family duties, and spiritual growth
> *Sixth step*: To follow principles of Dharma (righteousness)
> *Seventh step:* To nurture an eternal bond of friendship and love

During the *Sindhoor* (Red Powder), the groom applies a small dot of vermilion, a powdered red lead, to the bride's forehead and welcomes her as his partner for life. It is applied for the first time to a woman during the marriage ceremony when the bridegroom himself adorns her with it. Avinash looked at Ari during this moment and smiled from a distance.

There was food everywhere, in all corners of the house; there was not one soul without sufficient food and drink. The waiters in white suits served some dishes cocktail-style, while other elaborately designed tables held dishes beyond the imagination. Ari and Anjali had their fill of pastries and samosas, and they both dove into a comfortable, intricate, and probably dreadfully expensive Indian rug with plush pillows facing a fireplace, where other guests warmed themselves during the cool night. Avinash walked around like a proud father, and though he didn't spend much time with Ari, he checked on her from time to time to make sure she was comfortable.

She didn't mind his absence; it was a beautiful thing to watch him welcome and thank every single guest, making sure everyone had enough to eat and being so loving with his family. It didn't really bother her either that Avinash had not formally introduced her to his family members. They were only together a couple of months, and in a semitraditional Indian family she knew he had to be careful. The fact that she was there with him as his guest and wore the *bindi* was a symbol of their relationship. Besides, every time he helped a grandmother or elderly guest into a seat or brought them a drink, she fell helplessly in love with him.

***

The music switched from Bollywood tunes to pop, waltzes, tangos, and romantic ballads during the course of the evening. A beautiful, full moon rose high in the sky, coupled with a mist that seemed to envelope the crowd like a big blanket of love. A song was playing while Ari studied Avinash from a distance. He was speaking to a group of elderly men and looked so handsome and dashing that she could not keep her eyes off of him. Every once in a while he would look at her and smile, acknowledging her presence, not caring if guests noticed. Midway through the song, she caught onto a tune she had heard before but couldn't remember where.

"You could be the keeper," the lyrics repeated over and over. Avinash was a keeper indeed. As the song played softly, she so wanted to dance with him, hold him and feel his breath on her neck.

She wandered up to the second floor of the house toward the terrace. The view was stunning. At this hour of the night, all you could see were the twinkling lights of the small towns scattered in the valley below. The mist was intoxicating, as was the scent of what her grandmother used to call *Galan de Noche*. Known in English as Hero of the Night or Gallant Gentlemen of the Night, the flower only bloomed at night, its aroma a mixture of sweet jasmine and sandalwood. Ari looked around for her hero, Avinash, who had suddenly disappeared into the evening mist. While she scanned the guests, the song continued to play. "You could be the keeper," she kept hearing as she hummed the melody. Suddenly he stood before her, leaning against one of the large columns which was wrapped in garlands of flowers. He had brought her a drink, and though Ari was already narcotized from the evening, Avinash was like a drug, a very good drug that she could not get enough of.

"Look," he said, "it's Vida Blue." Ari smiled wondering if this offer to drink Santos's famous tequila was a joke or the universe was sending her a karmic message. With the tumbler of Vida Blue in her hand, Ari stepped closer to see his big, smiling eyes, and he trailed his fingers along her cheeks, caressing her chin and neck. Ari wanted to kiss him but the song was fading. She hoped that neither the song nor the evening would end, so she could remember this night forever.

Suddenly, Avinash took the drink from her hand and, without removing his wanting eyes from hers, slowly drank the tequila and licked his lips. Ari did not know what to make of this, but he then grabbed her wrist and pulled her off the terrace. Ari followed closely behind Avinash as he made his way through the mingling guests, past the gardens and beautiful fountains, deep into the dark night's mist. *Where is he taking me?* Ari wondered. *Did I break some traditional Indian wedding rule by standing on the terrace?*

Ari was soon out of breath. The sari she was wearing didn't allow her to run exceptionally fast, and she was doing everything in her power to keep up with Avinash who was still tugging at her wrist like he was on a lifesaving mission. They finally reached a small cottage, and Avinash let her go to pry open the old door.

"What is this place?" Ari asked, gasping for air. Avinash didn't answer, but he managed to open the rotting door and inside they went. Avinash closed the door behind them and looked for a lantern that he remembered was near. The light from the moon that evening peeked through a window allowing Avinash to find an oil lamp, and light the wick. He turned to her out of breath, panting, and finally spoke.

"This place belonged to my uncle. He was an artist. It was a place for him to paint and meditate. It was one of my favorite places to visit when I was in college."

"Oh," Ari said. "For a moment there, I thought I did something wrong."

Avinash had that look in his eyes—that I-want-you-right-now look—and he was awfully good at getting his way.

With that, he walked over to Ari and kissed her like he hadn't seen her in years. He was moist from sweat, and his kisses tasted like the whiskey he had been drinking all night mixed with the sweet *paan* dessert given at the end of Indian weddings. Ari was shocked and felt excited. She'd spent most of the evening wondering if he would ever acknowledge her. She grabbed his lapel and pulled him down to her lips as he pushed her slowly into another room. They were both breathing heavily, and the cottage was musty and hot. He picked her up, and they collapsed into a bed that was barely off the ground, making a frightening sound when they landed. Avinash unwrapped Ari's sari and removed her undergarments like a child opening presents on Christmas Day. *A professional at undressing*, she thought. *Obviously he's done this before.* It was cold, and her nipples were aroused. *Or is it how he touches me?* The room was dark, but Ari could still see her beautifully decorated *mendhi* hands. She wanted to touch his manhood but was afraid someone would walk in. Avinash continued taking off his clothes.

Despite the shadowy darkness, Ari could see that he was excited and she welcomed him, reaching up to touch his chest. She softly kissed his torso, running her tongue down the center of his core, into his belly button, and working her way down. When Ari saw that he was nearly overcome by the pleasure, she hesitated, thinking for a moment that if she deprived him just a little, the torment would unhinge him. He'd ignored her all night, after all, and Ari wanted to be in control. Avinash was quivering from desire, so Ari did the only thing she could do. She caressed him, stroking his beautiful manhood, which excited her even more.

Avinash moaned and asked her to continue. The excessive amount of cocktails, however, did not deter Avinash. His thrust into her practically lifted her off the bed, and she gasped as her heart accelerated. Avinash tried to hold back, even though her exquisite tightness almost made him want to explode. Ari was flushed and wet with pleasure. The old bed creaked and groaned and her back arched as Avinash reached her golden spot. Ari dug her fingers into his back as they came together in an almost sexual rapture, collapsing into each other's embrace. The old, musty cottage was the only witness to their love.

Avinash laughed with Ari as she told him the shack was really quite disgusting and smelled horribly. "I wanted to be with you all night, Ari. I'm sorry I appeared distant."

Suddenly Avinash felt the desire to tell Ari something. While she lay against the musty bed sheets where they had made love only moments ago, both of them naked and vulnerable, Avinash said the words she wanted to hear.

"Ari, I love you. I love you so much. Don't leave me, darling. Stay with me forever."

CHAPTER SIX

I n the spring of 1975, Sorrento was alive and full of people from every corner of Europe and abroad. The streets vibrated with the footsteps of those looking to shop, eat, or lay a wager on something even though it was seemingly prohibited in those days. The *stradas* were decorated with the flowers of the season, and expensive automobiles, with their shiny hoods and pristine tire spokes, adorned the sidewalks. The chauffeurs, dressed in their best attire, waited next to these beautiful pieces of steel as their owners either ate or gambled in underground casinos while their wives shopped.

A villa, situated high on the cliff overlooking the ocean, a perfect view of Capri at a distance, was the place to see and be seen by everyone. The castle-shaped architecture, with its broad columns and domed ceiling, hovered over the city like a beacon of prosperity and success.

Everyone called it the Castellammare. If you were extremely righteous or religious, it might very well be a pit of everything sacrilegious and worldly, a pit of sin and damnation. No matter how you saw it, the truth was, it was a place that everyone wanted to visit at some point in their lives, and today was no different for a young, beautiful, hopeful model from Porcari named Sofia.

For Marcelo, however, it was an exceptionally stressful day. Just recently being appointed manager of the casino tables by Marco Batalli, Castellammare's owner, Marcelo was doing his best to live up to expectations. To make an impression, Marcelo was dressed like a mannequin, not a thing out of place except for the drop of sweat running down his brow.

Batalli was yelling orders at him like a short-order cook. Under normal circumstances, Marcelo would have told old Batalli to take a hike, but he owed him the respect; after all, casino manager was quite a position for a scoundrel like him. The lobby and ballrooms of the villa were full of guests, and the bars were overflowing with drinks. Not one patron was without a cocktail, cigarette, or a casino chip in hand. It's truly a special day. Batalli pulled Marcelo aside, putting his short, fat fingers around his pristine white tuxedo collar, and asked him to entertain the ladies at the roulette table. "Get them to bet everything," he ordered him.

Marcelo took off, straightening his collar as if to get the feel of Batalli's grubby hands off his neck, and strolled over to their table in his usual swagger. The women saw him coming at a distance and marveled at his walk and self-assurance.

From the corner of his eye, Marcelo caught a glimpse of a beautiful blonde standing alone at the bar, and he stopped dead in his tracks. He couldn't help but notice that she was the most beautiful woman he had ever seen—*a mermaid, a princess, surely a mirage*—dressed in a long, yellow gown. The girl had placed him in a complete trance. Marcelo caught a passing waiter and asked that he take a walk with him. He had hatched a plan.

At the roulette table, the ladies from Amsterdam were melting at the Italian stallion and flirted aggressively. Unable to understand a word they were saying, Marcelo smiled and flirted back and asked the accompanying waiter to open a tab for the ladies. Without missing a beat, Marcelo kissed the cheek of the woman closest to him and excused himself. The ladies pouted in unison as the handsome Italian left them.

"Buona fortuna a tutti." Marcelo yelled as he sprinted back to find the blonde beauty.

***

Marcelo's five-foot-eight frame didn't allow him to walk any other way than proud. He walked as if he had bags of heavy coins in his shoes, a sway that showed the world a hero was entering. As a child he was told he wouldn't amount to much; as an adult he was determined to prove otherwise. Meeting the blonde beauty at the bar, Marcelo asked if she was waiting for someone and if he could assist her with anything. The beautiful girl smiled shyly and said she wasn't sure who she was looking for. Marcelo took her hand and lightly kissed it.

"I should present myself then. My name is Marcelo Donati. I am the manager of the casino. Perhaps I can help you find the person you're looking for."

The beauty felt comfortable with him and explained that she was a model from Rome looking to find someone to represent her. "I was told this was the place where important people gathered. Do you know if there is such a person here who can represent me?"

Her tone was desperate and full of desire. All Marcelo wanted to do was to dive into those blue eyes and rescue her. Before he could even think of what he was truly saying, Marcelo blurted out that he could help her find such a person.

"Wait here and I will introduce you. Do not move. Excuse me, but what is your name?" The beauty stood from the bar stool and shook his hand with her long delicate fingers,

"My name is Lucia. Lucia Ferretti."

As luck would have it, Marcelo didn't need to supervise much at the casino tables; the bets breezed along all evening, and the house pulled in a record amount of winnings. He spent much of the evening introducing Lucia to several photographers and magazine editors who made assurances that they would introduce her to the right people for modeling jobs. .

A chance meeting between Lucia and Marcelo set her career in motion. Within months she had become one of the most sought-after models in Italy. The two lovers were suddenly living a life that anyone would envy and had everything to go with it: youth, beauty, money, fame, and love. They were inseparable and had more money than they ever imagined. What they did not have was a place to call home and a family. Together Marcelo and Lucia owned the Amalfi Coast, and Sorrento had surrendered to their charm and beauty. There was no venue that did not know about the Amalfi Coast lovers. They were in fashion, and it was fashionable to have them as your guests. The rich invited them to their parties, whether they knew them or not. Just having them on the guest list guaranteed every paparazzo in the region and a front-page cover story in magazines and via news media outlets.

A casual stroll down any street was nearly impossible for Marcelo. Women swooned and men either envied him or wanted to be him. The couple had no privacy, and it was during these tumultuous times that Marcelo decided to build a fortress to ensure the seclusion they longed for. He bought a dilapidated bungalow in Positano on 87 Viale Pasitea for next to nothing, with the purpose of converting it into a home they could enjoy and live in forever. Marcelo remodeled and rebuilt the home for Lucia, and they moved in on her twenty-fifth birthday. In 1976, life was just beginning for Marcelo and Lucia. Their love seemed indestructible—or so they thought.

***

In life, the one thing you can count on is the fact that when you really want something to happen quickly, it usually doesn't. Marcelo was quite aware of this annoying truth. After spending months with Lorraine, trying to find out more about the house purchase, Ms. Cordero, and the whole story behind the delay, Marcelo was at his wits' end. Lorraine, too, was frustrated that Marcelo's plan wasn't moving forward, and though she enjoyed his home-cooked meals, she was tired of his conspiring. She longed for her privacy and, to make matters worse, had gained several unwanted kilos in the process.

In town, the gossip mill was set ablaze when several women recognized Marcelo with Lorraine. The rumor quickly spread that not only was the infamous Marcelo in town, but he was planning on rebuilding the house he designed for poor Lucia Ferreti into his love nest with Lorraine.

"What a bunch of bloody nonsense!" Lorraine huffed when Marcelo let her in on the torrid gossip about town.

"I'll be sure to straighten them out today at our meeting for the Festival Musica d'Estate."

The International Chamber Music Festival was one of the largest music gatherings in the Campania region. This year it was in August, and Lorraine was one of the main organizers on the Amalfi Coast.

"It's best to ignore it," Marcelo said, shaking his head as if remembering a similar time in his own life. "If you show interest, you will throw petro oil to the fire, but if you are indifferent, it will go away in time."

Like everything in life that has no explanation, Marcelo had no answer for this new dilemma. He put down his coffee and walked out of Lorraine's house, going who knows where.

Whatever it was, Lorraine could not be bothered with Marcelo's obsessions. The house and the new owner who had been keeping him up at night and giving him the most horrendous moods were not on her radar now. The music festival needed her attention, and the committee was meeting that afternoon.

A list of musical acts—those confirmed and yet to confirm—had been sitting on her coffee table, and she was unable to get to it. She missed her husband in times like these. He was such a good organizer, had promotion and public relations in his blood. This would have been a piece of cake for him, but now she had to rely on a couple of snooty, wealthy women from Ravello and Amalfi and the mistress of one of the music festival's board of directors. The purpose for having these musical festivals was to bring romance, elegance, and culture to the city. She remembered how, years ago, such festivals were the best place to meet a new love, but now it was all about the funds for the festival and what municipality was getting the credit for bringing in the best musical act. *What a shame,* Lorraine lamented. *No romance, no culture. It's all gone.*

***

There was certainly no romance in Marcelo's life as he sat at an outdoor cafe on the beach in Positano, watching the ferries to Capri and Sorrento come and go. He wondered if it would rain that day and why Positano still meant so much to him. Marcelo had no one there who truly needed him; everything he cared for had gone long ago, including most of his fortune.

"I'm crazy to be here . . . to want this life and this house back. What was I thinking?" he mumbled in contempt.

At that moment, he searched his coat pocket for a cigarette and felt something else; it was the snapshot of the American woman. He stared at her, wondering why he couldn't get her off his mind. Marcelo reasoned that maybe something about her reminded him of Lucia.

Gazing down the beach toward Amalfi, Marcelo remembered the day he asked Lucia to marry him. They had just left a dinner party hosted by a prestigious modeling magazine and were tired and worn from all the picture-taking and elbow-rubbing with famous guests. Marcelo had ordered a bottle of champagne from a nearby restaurant, and they sat on the beach to drink it. He loved that Lucia could go from being a beautiful model to a simple girl who just sat on the sand at a moment's notice. When he offered the champagne to her, Lucia refused to drink, saying she wasn't feeling up to it. Marcelo knew that she'd been trying to get clean from the sleeping pills she'd been taking in the past; the mixture of alcohol and narcotics had taken a toll on her health. Marcelo had threatened to take her to a hospital for detoxification if she continued on her destructive path, but Lucia had finally taken his threat to heart and stopped cold turkey. He certainly was not going to force her to drink if she didn't want to. Marcelo had told Lucia how much he loved her and that he couldn't live without her. Perhaps it had been the wrong time, but he'd asked her to marry him without thinking.

Lucia had placed her face against her knees and cried. *Certainly a dubious reaction,* Marcelo thought. "What is wrong, Lucia?" he'd said. "Don't you love me? We've been together for three years. We have shared everything. Why this reaction?"

Lucia had cried even more. Then she'd gotten up from the sand and ran from him toward the center of town, leaving Marcelo no other recourse than to follow after her, calling out her name and pleading for her to stop. At the top of the town, on Viale Pasitea, Marcelo had caught up with her, now angry and at his wits' end. He shook her, as if this would make her come to her senses. Nearby paparazzo had taken pictures of the scene, and Marcelo had to take Lucia into a nearby restaurant, dragging her to the back and asking the waitstaff to hold the press from coming in. Lucia would not explain what she was feeling, saying only that she wanted to go home and forget the whole day. Marcelo, tired and disappointed, had given in to her request. Her dismissal of him had been a blow to his ego, so he'd spent the rest of the evening with Lorraine and some of her friends after dropping Lucia off at the home they shared in Sorrento. Marcelo had told no one of the incident; after all, he wanted to forget it, and so he drank—more than he should have. Later that evening, he'd left Lorraine's and spent the night elsewhere. Drunk, tired, and frustrated, he'd had sex with several women in the hallway of an apartment building.

***

Lucia and Marcelo separated for two months after that incident. Marcelo's pride was hurt, and Lucia just wanted her space. As he continued to work on the home on Viale Pasitea, it became his obsession, something to help him cope with the disappointment of their relationship.

The women in town had heard of their breakup and came in droves to console him. Marcelo accepted their contributions of kindness. During this time, Marco Batalli was forced to sell Castellammare. The economy and loss of jobs in Italy made for the lack of clientele, and thus the sale of the villa was imminent.

Marcelo worked day and night on the home. His passion for its completion made him drink and smoke more than he wanted. When he lacked money for supplies, he gambled away what he could—jewelry, cars, property— until he was almost destitute. For the next weeks, Marcelo gambled heavily, his wins and losses as predictable as a weather forecast. He spent hours betting on horses, soccer matches, or whatever any group of avid gamblers was betting on. Winning or losing was inconsequential to him.

Finishing the home, however, was taking a back seat, and Lucia was not there to help him out of the destructive slump he was in as she had been in the past.

One rainy evening, he returned to the home and found Lucia waiting inside. She was wet and cold, but he didn't care; he treated her with no compassion. Lucia explained that she had been in Porcari with her family for the last two months, thinking about what to do with her life. She was not happy. While she was there, she'd met a prominent lawyer, and he was willing to help her out of the craziness her life had become. Though she was not in love with him, he promised to give her a real life and a real home. The more Marcelo listened, the more enraged he became.

"I have spent the last year building this house for you with my money. I have worked like a dog to build a home and the life you wanted. You never loved me. You used me, and then when you tired of me I was tossed away like an old newspaper."

Marcelo came at her and Lucia went running up the steps, but he was too quick for her. He dragged her through the house and showed her everything he had built for her, in her image, as if she were a goddess, as she wept and tried to release herself from him. At the top of the steps looking down into the foyer, he turned to her and said, "This entire house is made out of love."

Lucia looked at him with sorrow and whispered, "This house was made to hold what you believe to be love. There is no love here, only emptiness. You have gambled at everything in life—this house and even my love for you. I will not let you gamble my life away too." Lucia headed down the stairs, and Marcelo tried to stop her.

"Let me go!" Lucia warned. "I'm pregnant and I don't know if I want you to be this child's father. I will always love you, Marcelo, but not like this."

Lucia released herself from his grasp, and as he tried to stop her from leaving, she slipped on the recently polished ceramic steps and tumbled down the stairs. Marcelo hurried after her but could not stop her fall. At the bottom of the beautiful staircase that he had built for his love lay his Lucia, lifeless on the floor, her blue eyes gazing up at him.

***

Marcelo was arrested and served twelve days in jail. He was later released when the coroner's department found that her death had been accidental. There were no markings of abuse or violence. The child she was carrying, a three-month-old male fetus, was also pronounced dead. Marcelo Donati had suffered enough. In one blow he had lost his girlfriend, his son, and his house.

All the creditors and loan sharks in Sorrento came to collect, and Marcelo had to leave the Amalfi Coast for Tuscany to look for work and another life. Lorraine helped him relocate and find work as a house builder in the region. His life in Italy's north province was empty and meaningless; at times he would take odd jobs in Switzerland just to get away.

Marcelo never got to see Lucia's body or her burial place, and he never had a chance to say goodbye to her. It was too tragic to recall when he was awake, so the memories came while he slept, usually in the form of nightmares.

For Marcelo, days, months, and years came and went with no special meaning for him. He was alive but there was no life or burning desire in him, as he disassociated himself from his life on the Amalfi Coast and all his friends. Marcelo became a mere shadow of the man he once was. The only good that came of the tragedy was his sober lifestyle and cleaning up his gambling debt by working various odd jobs. One thing was true: though Marcelo never had a problem seducing a woman, there was only one woman he thought of day and night. It burned and tore him apart. Lucia's death removed layers of his soul until he could no longer feel.

Now, thirty years later, destiny had placed him in the town where the tragedy had taken place. Marcelo's desire to reclaim the house somehow brought him an energy he had not felt in a long time. This woman, Ariadne Cordero, was his target, and getting her out of the house was his mission. He would do anything to make it happen, and if seducing her and making her fall madly in love with him was part of the plan, he was sure he could do it. Every good plan has a strategy and an outcome. His was simple. It was important for Marcelo to clean up, look a little younger and desirable for the lovely American beauty he was about to destroy.

CHAPTER SEVEN

I t had been more than six months since Ari worked professionally, except for some editing side jobs and several press releases she did for Sam at the bank, she was getting a bit antsy. The new life with Avinash was wonderful; after all, he showered her with love, gifts, attention, and, more importantly, his time. He had cut back significantly on his work hours and was home every night before the start of the evening news. Ari was happy to cook and plan meals or outings, but she missed the creativity of her work, and she wanted to discuss with Avinash the possibility of finding a part time or consultant job that would allow her to feel more useful.

Avinash arrived that night especially tired, and Ari had prepared one of his favorite dishes, *fideuà* with squid ink and calamari. The sauce's aroma—a delightful mix of garlic, onions, red peppers, saffron, and white wine—permeated the flat as he walked in, tossed his coat on the chair, and headed straight to the kitchen. Ari had just showered and was wearing a white cotton summer dress that showed off her perky assets.

"Hello, darling," he said, smiling and hugging Ari from behind. "Mmmm . . . that smells great, and so do you! Is that all for me?" He buried his face in her hair and nibbled on her neck.

"No," Ari said. "You have to pay the cook first." Avinash then turned her around and paid, indeed, with a long sensual kiss as Ari fell hopelessly into his embrace.

During dinner, Ari looked for the right moment to bring up the job. Avinash was a modern Indian man with many traditional and nontraditional points of view, but when it came to women and equality he was all for it. He was, however, the type of man who wanted his partner to run big decisions by him, and he did the same in turn. It was a level playing field in his mind—no surprises, no mis-understandings. But Avinash was not one for drama. Just a small taste of it, and he bolted like the roadrunner.

Ari was a bit more free-spirited with her decisions, and at times she had to remember to keep Avinash in the loop. She did not want her decisions to make him insecure, so she kept him informed. On this evening, it would seem that Ari and Avinash had big news to share with each other. It was just a matter of who was willing to speak up first. When Avinash finally brought up a business trip to Dubai, Ari perked up.

"Dubai? That's great! When are you going? Can wives and girlfriends attend too? I always wanted to go to Dubai. How exciting."

Avinash just smiled. He loved how Ari was always willing to go at a moment's notice, but he had to burst her bubble.

"Darling, I leave this Monday for five days and, unfortunately, it's a business meeting. No wives or girlfriends will be attending. I'm so sorry, Ari. I would love to take you to Dubai someday. We can—"

Before he continued to give her more reasons, Ari jumped in. It was a good time to segue into the job proposition.

"That's really disappointing," she said as she looked down at her half-finished plate. "Oh well, what's a girl to do all alone in London?"

"Listen, Ari, I know it's not fair. I'm the one who really doesn't want to go. We've been together for the last three months, and I enjoy being with you all the time. Trust me, this was planned last year before I met you. I will make it up to you when I return," he said as he caressed her arm.

Ari wanted to let it sting a little more and came up with a good comeback. "I understand. Maybe . . ." she said, as if a light bulb has just turned on in her head, "Anjali and I can take a girls' trip somewhere. Isn't that a good idea?" She smiled like the cat that just ate the canary and relished Avinash's discomfort as he tried to maintain his composure

"Well . . . uh," Avinash muttered, unable to find the words.

"I don't want to be alone while you're away," Ari said. "If I had a steady job here, well, I certainly wouldn't leave." *The perfect red ball in the side pocket!*

Avinash was not one to make rash decisions but he was always fair, and Ari knew he would take the idea into consideration and do what all men want to do with their women when there is a problem at hand—come up with a solution.

"All right, darling," he said, getting up to move into the living area. "Let me think about your proposition."

Which one? Ari thought, *the trip or the job?* In any case, Ari was smart enough not to pry or act needy to get a response. After all, she didn't need his approval to do anything, but she did respect and value his opinion. She also knew all too well that when it came to men, letting things simmer always rendered the best results.

The next morning, Ari had just come back from her jog in the park, and Avinash was having a seemingly contemplative breakfast.

"Good morning, love," he mumbled as she entered the kitchen.

Ari replied in her most cheerful voice. "Beautiful morning! Everything is so alive in this city. Did you sleep well?"

Responding in a monotone voice, Avinash answered, "Not too well. I had a lot of things on my mind."

Ari noticed he was not in the mood for chatting, so she grabbed a cup of coffee, kissed him on the cheek, and headed toward the shower.

"Have a nice day, love!" she said from a distance as Avinash wrestled with his thoughts.

***

Avinash arrived at the office with a scowl on his face, and Anjali could tell he was moping. She greeted him with a cheerful "good morning," but Avinash didn't even acknowledge her. Anjali knew something was brewing.

"Good morning, boss! Thank you, I had a wonderful evening, and I'm just happy to be here working with my cheery boss." Anjali waited for the look Avinash usually gave her when he was not in the mood for antics. Two seconds later, she got it.

"There it is! You're brooding, Avinash. What's up?"

"Anjali, you always know the exact moment to bother me when I don't want to be bothered. What do you want to know? Must I tell you everything that is troubling me?"

"Well, actually, yes. Because I have to work with you, and I certainly don't want you to be all up in my face, so spit it out! Well?" Anjali pushed on.

Avinash gave in. "I just don't know what to do with a woman for the first time in my life. Ari is . . . she's . . . ." Avinash stopped and thought for a moment before continuing. "She's special to me."

Anjali understood that he was at a relationship crossroads and, more importantly, that he probably never had these feelings for anyone else, except maybe Suniel. She knew not to push but to let him think and give him support, so she quietly left his office and dialed Ari.

That evening Ari and Anjali met up for drinks at a bar near the bank. It was on Smithfield Street, a swanky spot housed in a large Georgian townhouse with multilevel bars and a fabulous restaurant. Ari was excited to inform Anjali of her plans for the two of them to take a girls' trip.

Over drinks Anjali told Ari that Avinash was worried, and that his being worried was a good thing. Ari wasn't surprised.

"I know he's apprehensive about our trip, Anjali. Usually it would be the woman who was in this predicament. I got use to this with Santos. He was away a lot during our marriage, but I trusted him and he trusted me. With Avinash, I think maybe he's used to extremely needy, high-maintenance women—two things I'm not. If he can go to Dubai for a week on business—and by the way, we both know it will not be business the entire time he's there—then it's only fair that I should be able to take a trip somewhere. If I were working, we wouldn't be having this conversation, and he would have no reason to worry, right?"

Anjali assured her she was in agreement. "Avinash is now in a totally different world with you. All I'm saying is that you need to be a bit careful with him. Don't impose the trip; work it in, you know?"

"In other words, you want me to use Vaseline to make it less painful," Ari quipped.

Anjali cringed. "Well, yes. That's sort of nasty, but yes. Sweeten up the proposition of the trip by being a little . . . how should I say . . . lost and in need of him—and more loving than normal. Even if you're more than capable of opening a jar of honey, ask him to do it for you. You need his help to finish a recipe. The remote control doesn't seem to work when you use it. Let him zip up your dress, and ask him for advice on everything, understand me? Indian men are a special breed. Avinash is extraordinarily modern in comparison to other Indian men but give him time and a loving nudge."

Ari agreed. "Now can I propose our trip? I think we should go to Positano."

"What?" Anjali didn't even want to hear the rest. "If Avinash finds out you want to go to Positano, he will surely think you still have plans to move away, Ari. Are you crazy? This will certainly drive him over the edge. Don't you dare, girl!" Anjali was not so sure Ari had the bug of moving to Positano out of her system.

"Look, Anj," Ari reasoned, "we can spend two or three days in Madrid or Barcelona. Then we can take a flight to Naples and drive down along the Amalfi Coast. It will be fun and relaxing. Besides, you told me that you've always wanted to go to Spain with a native. Well, here's your chance. Who knows, you might meet the man of your dreams on this trip."

Ari was persuasive, and Anjali was a bit more accepting of the idea, as long as she told Avinash that Positano was not on the itinerary.

Ari agreed. "Fine. No mention of Positano, and tonight and for the next couple of days I will be the most seductive and lost little lamb Avinash has ever met."

"Dear God, help us all," Anjali said as she cupped her hands in prayer mode. Ari couldn't help but laugh while she sipped her martini.

***

An hour later, the two women left the restaurant. It was a beautiful London evening, and Ari wanted to walk home. She flagged down a taxi for Anjali but did not get in with her.

"What are you doing? The flat is not anywhere near here," Anjali said while stopping the taxi driver from moving the vehicle.

"I know. I just wanted to walk to the flat. It's a beautiful night, and it will give me time to think about our itinerary."

Anjali shrugged and cautioned her to be careful.

Ari started walking home, but somewhere along the way she made a wrong turn and crossed the street onto the main thoroughfare to White Chapel, a working-class neighborhood that is known to be dangerous if the wrong person happens to wander through. She continued in that direction, completely lost, and stood at the edge of the road near Aldgate. It was a ghost town at that hour of the night, but she knew many buses made their routes through there during the night and decided to wait for one instead of calling Avinash. Suddenly and without warning, two men on a motorbike sped toward Ari, nearly hitting her. Her move to avoid them caused a misstep onto some wooden produce crates that were left on the curb overnight. The thugs laughed and yelled obscenities at her as they drove off into the evening fog. Ari felt a sharp jab of pain on her side that was coupled with the sting of landing on her back. The pain was getting worse, so she reached into her purse to ring Avinash while she struggled to get up. Just then, she heard the men coming back on their motorbike, heading straight toward her as she slid into a dark alley away from plain sight. The thugs circled several times, and Ari trembled in the cold night air. She could feel a wet substance on her shirt.

Avinash, who had been listening the whole time on his cell phone, called out to her as she struggled, but the call was suddenly disconnected.

Ari was so dizzy that she needed to sit on the ground to get her wits together. In the cold, dark alley, between garbage bins and rotting waste, Ari rang Avinash again, and he quickly answered.

"Ari, can you hear me, love?" Avinash yelled.

"Avinash, I'm hurt. Please, I need you to come get me. I don't know where I am. I must have made a wrong turn. I don't know . . . I think I'm bleeding, and I'm really scared. Somebody is trying to hurt me."

Avinash asked her to get somewhere safe and tell him what street she was on. Ari gave him an approximate location. It was important for her to get within view of the route he would take, but she was afraid the thugs would see her, so she hid behind some crates within eyeshot of the passing vehicles. Within minutes, she saw Avinash approaching in his black Porsche Carrera, an unlikely vehicle in this neighborhood. Ari stepped into view, and he flashed his high beams at her. The car was barely in park when he opened the door and ran to her.

"What happened, Ari?"

He quickly noticed that she was completely covered in blood. Avinash helped her into the car and drove her to St. George's—not the nearest hospital, but he had friends who were physicians there and knew she would be in good hands.

Once they arrived, the emergency staff took Ari from Avinash's arms as he stood there powerless, his shirt drenched in Ari's blood. Ari was rushed away where he could not see her. On route to the hospital, Avinash had called Dr. Kiran Patel, a dear friend and his own physician, to explain the incident. Dr. Patel assured him he would personally take a look at Ms. Cordero, but he would need to report it to the police.

***

It seemed like an endless nightmare as Avinash waited impatiently to hear some news on Ari's status. Suddenly, he heard Ari's phone ring in her bag and decided to look for it. The caller ID said *AKASH R*. Avinash thought it was a joke.

Could this be the same Akash? And if so, why is he in her contacts list? Deep in thought, Avinash did not hear the nurse approach.

"Mr. Batra, please follow me. Ms. Cordero is now responding and able to see you." He was stunned. Between the call and Ari's accident he was not listening to the nurse's instructions.

"Mr. Batra? Please come this way," the nurse insisted.

Once inside the room, he saw her pale, lifeless body on the stretcher and momentarily forgot about the call. "Ari," he whispered into her ear. She slowly opened her eyes, mouthed his name, and fell back into a deep trance.

A few minutes later, Doctor Patel entered the room and filled Avinash in on her status. "Avinash, it seems she was attacked by some men on a motorbike. She tried to move out of their way as they drove into her, but she seems to have landed on some wooden boxes. A piece entered her side and caused the excessive blood loss. I see you have some of it on your shirt. You may want to clean up, Avinash. We are in a sterile environment here. In any case, she also has severe lacerations to her back from the fall. Miss Cordero will be fine with a bit of rest and antibiotics. Nothing to worry about other than to watch her for a while due to the blood loss. Some ice on her back and rest, and she'll be brand-new."

The doctor shook Avinash's hand and walked out. Avinash dialed Anjali, asking her to bring him a clean shirt since she had an extra set of keys to his flat. Within the hour, Anjali arrived with his clothes and asked Avinash about Ari's status.

"You can go in and see her. She's sleeping but she'll be fine."

He took the clothes from Anjali's hands and headed toward the men's washroom. They spent the night with Ari, Avinash staring out the window into the cold London night. He could tell Anjali was beside herself with guilt. She kept asking Avinash to forgive her for allowing Ari to walk home unaccompanied.

Anjali walked over to Avinash and asked, "Are you okay?"

"No, I'm not okay," he said sharply and reached for Ari's bag, pulling out her cell phone and pressing the recent calls list. "Why is he calling her, Anjali? How do they know each other? You know, don't you? Tell me!" His voiced echoed in the room.

"Shhh, Avinash, you'll wake her. All of this has an explanation. Come outside with me. Let her rest."

Avinash rushed out of the room with Ari's phone in his hand and sat outside, waiting for Anjali's story. "You'll be glad to know that Ari has not seen Akash since she arrived here months ago. She met him on the flight over from Los Angeles, and he has been after her ever since. Ari is not interested in him, and aside from one breakfast they shared the day after you met her, she has not seen him or taken his calls. Akash came to my office when you were away with Ari on holiday, and he deduced that you two are together. Frankly, I didn't deny it."

Avinash clenched his jaw, and his eyes were now red with anger.

"Please, Avinash, let me tell you what happened," Anjali cautioned him. "Akash came looking for Ari, and he told me she had not taken any of his calls or returned messages. What you need to worry about is not if Ari is interested in Akash; you need to worry that he will relentlessly pursue her now that he knows you two are a couple. I'm sure if you were to check her cell phone, you will find all his incoming calls and no outgoing calls.

"You need to protect Ari from Akash. You need to protect yourself from him, or I fear this will have a very unseemly ending. You have worked too hard to get where you are now. Do not let Akash take over your life or harm Ari, because I fear he will harm her to get back at you."

Avinash was not worried that Akash could hurt him, but he believed Anjali and thought that perhaps the attempt to harm Ari tonight could very well have come from Akash. He definitely was that unscrupulous. Avinash thanked Anjali for the talk and asked her to go home. He would stay with Ari the rest of the night, and in the morning she could relieve him.

"One more thing, Anjali," Avinash said as she opened the door to leave. "I will forgive you this time, but if you ever fail to tell me that Akash Ramkissoon is anywhere in the vicinity of the bank or Ari, I will not be forgiving a second time. Understand me, Anjali?"

She looked down in shame. "Yes, Avinash. I'm sorry."

Avinash hugged Anjali and sent her on her way. For the rest of the night, Avinash watched over Ari. She struggled with pain but occasionally opened her eyes, murmuring his name while squeezing his hand. He was convinced that he had to protect her. Ari would not have Suniel's ending, even if it meant that she had to go away for a while.

***

After a couple of days in the hospital, Ari wanted to go home. Anjali and Avinash shared their time with her, and she was grateful for their support. She had spoken to the police several times, but nothing could be done; Ari had not seen the faces of her attackers.

On Thursday Ari was given the green light she so desperately wanted; after all, Avinash was leaving on Friday, and she wanted to see him off. While she was getting her things ready, Avinash came in with some flowers and a proposition.

"Ari, I was thinking about our conversation before this all happened, and I want you to go on your trip. It will be good for you to take some time after such a difficult week. It will make me feel better that you are entertained and traveling rather than being at home waiting for me."

Ari could only kiss him sweetly and wonder how God had blessed her with such a great man. As they kissed, the nurse walked in with a wheelchair, and Ari was finally discharged.

Once they arrived at Avinash's flat, Ari had a delayed reaction from the accident. An overwhelming fear came over her—the same panic she'd felt when Santos would travel for months at a time, always fearing something would happen to him. Though Vida Blue Tequila had been a financial blessing for her and Santos, somehow his frequent trips without her put her in a panic, the same panic she was feeling now. Ari would have constant dreams of Santos getting kidnapped or fighting off some thief, or worse, dying in some horrible accident. Without even thinking, she hugged Avinash, trembling.

"I don't know what I was thinking," she explained as Avinash held her. "I thought I could just walk about town like I've lived here all my life. It was so scary, and I'm so sorry, Avinash. I need you so much. Please don't go to Dubai."

***

She looked up at him with those vibrant green eyes, and he could not resist her. Avinash kissed her and moved his body so close to her that he could feel her heart pound against his chest. Avinash felt a bolt of electricity take over his body and surrendered to her as he took her inside his flat, still clinging to her lips as if to life itself. The flat was dark, other than the lights of the city below them glowing against the terrace door, but Avinash managed to find his way around and softly lowered Ari onto the large T-shaped leather couch where he had entertained all his past girlfriends. They were all a distant blur now. Avinash only wanted Ari. It momentarily occurred to him that if he hadn't met Ari at the restaurant that night, she just might be with Akash right now, and this realization sent an even stronger need to protect her than he had ever felt before.

Avinash pulled down at her strapless blouse, lowering it just enough for him to kiss her shoulders. He knew he would be away from her for a while, and he wanted to take his time, enjoy every part of her body, show Ari how he needed her. He moved his fingertips down her body, feeling every inch as if it were for the last time.

"Please wait here for a moment," Avinash said, hurrying out of the room to gather up some oils. When he returned, he undressed her slowly, one piece of clothing at a time. Then he took off his shirt, leaving only his trousers, and began pouring the oils into his hands and rubbing them to bring heat to his palms. Avinash kept his eyes on Ari's face, now flushed and glowing with excitement. Avinash began with her shoulders and worked his way down, softly rubbing and kneading her breasts and nipples. He was careful not to touch her wound and the five small stitches that were now almost invisible.

The oil smelled of lemongrass with a hint of jasmine and patchouli. It warmed her breasts as he worked them slowly, softly pinching her nipples and blowing on them gently. When he moved down toward her stomach and pelvis, Ari reached for his fly, her breath coming in short, heated bursts. Avinash could tell she was aroused and eager for him, but he made her wait. He ran his hands down the inside of her thighs and worked the oil down to her feet, massaging and kissing every single toe. Ari moaned and ran her hands up and down his back, grabbing desperately at his hair every time he touched a sensitive area.

Suddenly, Ari sat up, her body glistening with oil and her eyes blazing. She took Avinash by the hand and led him to the couch. He didn't resist as she unzipped his pants and slowly tugged them off. He watched as Ari's lips parted to pleasure him. Avinash was tormented with desire, jealousy, and a feeling of protection. Normally Ari's friction was what he longed for, but tonight was different. He wanted to please her. It was all about Ari.

As she hovered over him, he slid down past her breasts and drove his tongue inside her. Ari moaned the way he liked it. It was music to his ears. He could feel her legs quivering, and when he looked up to see what he had done, Ari was just as he wanted her to be—her hair a tumbled mess, her face red from desire, and a satisfied smile on her face.

Avinash took a long look at her, and she opened her eyes to meet his. He smiled with his eyes, the way she liked it. That night, the two oily, sweaty lovers lay next to each other, falling asleep in each other's embrace. Ari, exhausted, slept soundly, holding tightly to Avinash. He, however, slept with one eye open. It would remain like this, he feared, until Akash was out of his life and away from Ari forever.

In the morning Avinash and Ari showered, and as Ari lathered him up, he stood quietly, gazing at her. Later, while drying Ari with the towel, Avinash finally spoke.

"I love you, Ari. I love you very, very much. I hate going to Dubai without you. Will you miss me, darling?"

"You still don't know how much I love you?" she said, smiling at him. "I will call you every day, I promise." She hugged him, and he returned the embrace with a kiss of acceptance, sealing the sweet moment.

***

Ari was surprised that she hadn't needed to use *Operation I Need A Prince Right Away*. The incident with the motorcycle had done the trick, but she had hoped it wouldn't have been so painful. Even so, she decided to use up a couple more needy points, and Avinash was thrilled to oblige until it was time for him to head to the airport on his way to Dubai.

In the car, Ari told him that they would be heading to Spain, explaining that Anjali had this secret desire to hook up with a Spanish lover, and she was hoping Ari could hunt one down for her. Avinash laughed and warned Ari that Anjali was difficult with men.

"Your mission will not be easy, but I am happy that you're helping her, Ari. Anjali certainly deserves a good man to love her."

They embraced each other in front of the Emirates gate at Heathrow. Ari gave Avinash a silk, gold-colored veil she had doused with her favorite perfume. She placed it inside his black Hugo Boss hoodie as she whispered, "This is for you to think of me, love."

He smiled with his eyes, as only Avinash could do, and kissed her again before he turned and headed toward the gate. He patted his hoodie as if to say, "Your heart belongs to me," raised his hand, and waved goodbye.

With Avinash finally off to Dubai, Ari hurried home to pack for her trip to Barcelona that night.

***

While waiting for his flight in the Emirates lounge, Avinash phoned Sam and explained that the security team was to have a full watch on Ari in Spain, twenty-four hours a day. He told Sam that he was sure Akash Ramkissoon had planned the attack on Ari, and he wanted proof.

"I knew Ari and Anjali were planning a trip, but how will the team follow her on the journey without her knowledge?" Sam asked.

"I don't know, Sam, but make it happen. Her full protection is extremely important to me. No mistakes. Understand, man?"

"Yes, yes, don't worry. I will personally handle the investigation and will get the surveillance team together," Sam assured him.

"Good. Let me know if you need my input while I'm in Dubai. If that bastard gets anywhere near her, I want immediate extraction of Akash from her location."

Avinash left London with some hesitation, but he knew Ari's trip away from London would take Akash off her scent, at least for now.

CHAPTER EIGHT

When Ari arrived back at Avinash's flat to pack for her trip, she found a shipping notice from the Los Angeles port. During her whirlwind trip to London, meeting Avinash and putting the move to Positano on hold, she forgot her belongings had arrived at the port in Naples, Italy, and now this trip was needed to track down her things and ship them to . . . God knows where!

Her plan was to stay in Barcelona for three nights and then head to Positano for four nights, perhaps meeting up with her longtime buddy, Lorraine. Ari was not worried that she hadn't seen Lorraine in years. Locating her would not be a problem; after all, everyone in Positano knew Lorraine. All she'd have to do is ask around.

When she finished booking the hotel in Barcelona and their flights, Ari phoned several properties in Positano where she knew Lorraine had worked for years as their wedding planner. It was six in the evening, and she hoped Lorraine would be found working in one of them. She called the Poseidon hotel, and when the clerk at the reception desk answered, Ari spoke in Italian, requesting to speak with

Signora Lorraine Newly. The receptionist explained Lorraine was not in, but if the call had to do with booking an event at their property, she could supply her with a mobile number. Ari agreed and took down the digits.

***

In the meantime, Lorraine and Marcelo were dining with some of her friends at Chez Black, a beachfront restaurant right in Positano's best section. Lorraine picked up a call, not recognizing the number.

"*Mi scusi un momento*," she said as she hastily got up from her table. "*Si*, this is Lorraine. Who is this?"

When she returned to the table a couple of minutes later, Lorraine was pensive and concerned. Marcelo asked what had happened and she looked at him.

"Oh, Marcelo . . . we must talk right away."

The dinner ended abruptly, and Lorraine took Marcelo for a walk on the beach.

"Marcelo," she said in a voice only a loving mother could use with her unruly child—though this child was sixty-two years old. "The woman you want to meet, the owner of your home? I know her. She just phoned me."

Marcelo jumped, his grey eyes nearly bulging out of his head. "*Che cosa*? What?"

"Marcelo, this girl, this woman, is a friend of mine. I renewed her wedding vows some years ago here in Positano. It was during that time she and her husband, Santos, put a deposit on the house. She has dreamed of this house with her husband, and now he is no longer in the picture. You cannot go through with this plan of yours."

Marcelo walked away, huffing and puffing as he spewed Italian expletives.

"Marcelo!" Lorraine yelled after him. "Do you hear me? You cannot do this to Ari Cordero!"

She could not make him reason, but soon thereafter he returned with a proposition.

"Introduce me to her as the best builder on the Amalfi Coast. That's it. If I work in the house, I will feel better and forget the crazy plan. Okay, Lorraine?" Marcelo begged.

Lorraine agreed. "Ms. Cordero will be here in four days and you will finally get to meet her."

***

During the days just before Avinash left for Dubai, Anjali became increasingly curious about Akash and what he had done since he left England years ago. If she meddled in Sam's business, that would surely send Avinash into a tailspin, so the digging started on her end. It would seem Akash had held several aliases and had a "wanted" status, according to the Interpol website, for money laundering, arms trafficking, and a list of other unmentionables. Indeed, he had been busy, but how could she tie this to the gut feeling she had about Akash wanting to do Ari harm—and if so, *why?*

She kept it all hush-hush, but the trip would be an excellent time to probe Ari on her life. Maybe, just maybe, there was something that would connect Ari to Akash, and she could help bring him out of hiding for the authorities to arrest him.

On the tarmac, ready to take off to Barcelona, Anjali encouraged Ari to talk about Santos. She framed the conversation as if there was a worry that Ari still had Santos in her heart and sheepishly pushed for more information.

"Tell me about him. What was he like?"

"Anji, are you some frustrated FBI agent?" Ari joked. Nonetheless, after several minutes of pleading, Ari caved in as Anjali begged her for more details.

"Tell me. It will make the flight shorter, and I will be less nervous about flying."

Ari took a deep breath as if to jar her mind, digging into its data bank to pull out the most beautiful, yet painful, history of love in her life. "I will now bore you by starting at the beginning," Ari said, giggling.

"Santos was the oldest child to Juan Echegui, a Spaniard from the Basque country of Spain, and Consuelo Murquia, who grew up in Madrid but was the daughter of immigrant Italian-Judaic parents who moved to Spain during the war to avoid extradition for their beliefs. The Echeguis had a family jewelry store and were financially stable during the war and fascist uprising all over Spain. On a business trip to Madrid, Juan met Consuelo, a dark-haired beauty who was waiting for a group of friends outside her parents' business on the Gran Via. They married soon after, and Juan's businesses later took him to Lisbon, where he arranged for a pregnant Consuelo to move with him. Once Santos was born, they had two other children—his middle brother, Jacobo, and the youngest of the three, Maria del Carmen."

Ari explained that he came from a wholesome, loving family, something she loved about him because her family was so broken up during many moments of her life.

"What did he look like?" Anjali asked, even more intrigued.

Ari smiled as she remembered him. "Santos was a handsome man. Not pretty like Brad Pitt but extremely masculine, about six feet tall, with a beautiful head of wavy salt-and-pepper hair and a distinctive Spaniard Roman nose. He had great fingers, long and slender with an incredibly soft touch. Like Avinash, he dressed impeccably, always in fashion though it looked like he didn't put much effort into it. He was naturally stylish. Santos loved to swim, so he had a swimmer's body, with long legs and torso. His upper lip was thin in comparison to his meaty bottom lip. For this reason he always had a mustache or a beard. Santos was adorable, Anji. He was so loving, never irritated or spiteful, and he made me a better person. I was always so angry. I wanted to blame everyone for my lonely childhood, and Santos taught me to forgive and move on. He wasn't the most detailed of men, not as detailed as Avinash is, but always loving, always touching and hugging. He was the essence of pure love. Anjali, I loved him so much."

Ari's eyes watered as she remembered, and she took a minute to collect herself before continuing. "We moved to Madrid together, and he helped me open my first public relations company. He was good with business ventures. We hardly ever separated, only during those business trips of his. Our relationship was uncomplicated, and it transitioned easily into love with no drama. We never fought. We agreed on almost everything except his long work hours and frequent trips. Our relationship was fun and sometimes goofy and playful. Soon after Madrid, I went back to Los Angeles and he spent some time in Lisbon. We realized we couldn't live apart from each other, and when he finally came back to Los Angeles, we went out to dinner at this romantic restaurant and I asked him to marry me."

"You did what?" Anjali said.

"I asked him to marry me," Ari responded with a smile.

"You did not, you tramp!" Anjali laughed with Ari.

"Yes, I did. I said, 'I love you. I don't want to live without you. Will you marry me, Santos Echegui?'" Ari said.

"And? What did he say? For God's sake, Ari!" Anjali was now on the edge of her seat.

Ari leaned close to Anjali's ear. "He said . . . yes!"

Anjali started clapping and jumping in her seat while Ari tried to quiet her. Ari explained that when they finally married a couple of months later, they honeymooned on the Amalfi Coast, and that is when they were the happiest. Santos didn't think about work or anything else but being with her.

"It was such a beautiful moment in my life. We awoke to amazing sunrises, made love all day, ate like crazy, and saw the most beautiful sunsets we had ever seen. The nights were filled with millions of stars, and I would wake up in the middle of the night, walk to the terrace, and want so desperately to pluck them from the sky." Ari explained how moving to Positano had become an obsession for Santos. All the friends they made in the small coastal village were like family, including Lorraine, the woman who renewed their wedding vows five years later and still remained a close friend. They had lost track of each other after Santos left; in fact, they hadn't spoken in a couple of years. She would certainly be surprised to learn that Ari was in the process of purchasing the home on Via Pasitea—a home that, according to Lorraine, had some infamous history attached to it.

"So it was during this time, I think Avinash told me, that Santos had a tequila company, right?" Anjali said, pushing for the end of the story. "And then his partners did what they did . . . but let's not talk about that. So Santos comes out of jail, and you're so happy and in love that you want to buy this dream home in Positano. I don't get it, my friend. Why did he just leave you?"

Ari smiled as she looked deep into Anjali's eyes. Suddenly, Anjali saw so much pain in hers that it was clear to her now.

"Santos didn't leave you willingly, did he?" Anjali placed her hands over her mouth in disbelief. "Santos is not among the living, is he, Ari? Why did you have us all believe he left you? Oh my God, I feel sick to my stomach."

Anjali quickly unbuckled her seat belt and headed toward the back of the plane. Inside the small lavoratory, she truly felt sick that she made Ari tell her the whole story. Sick that she was investigating her life. *What kind of friend does that? What was I thinking? Poor Ari must be traumatized from losing Santos in such an unfair way. That's why the house was put on hold. That's why she needs to fulfill their promise. That's why she has to return to Positano. It's a promise she has to keep. It has nothing to do with wanting him to return to her life. For God's sake, he can't be dead.* Anjali nearly hyperventilated in the small bathroom.

When she returned to her seat, Ari appeared calm and hugged Anjali to assure her it was okay.

"I never said anything, Anjali, because, honestly, until this very moment I couldn't even bring myself to believe he had passed away. After meeting Avinash, I felt guilty that I could have feelings for someone other than Santos. In my mind, he was the love of my life. How is it possible that I could fall so madly in love again?

"How can someone find the love of their life twice in one lifetime? I have struggled with these feelings for months, thinking if I kept quiet, maybe I could actually be that lucky. What can I do if Avinash makes me so incredibly happy? I never want this to end, yet I'm afraid that it will, that something will happen to Avinash, and I'm frightened to feel anything real."

"Does Avinash know about Santos? I mean, does he know he's . . . you know?" Anjali asked.

"No one knows but you and, of course, Santos's family," Ari explained.

"How did it happen?" Anjali asked.

"Santos was in Mexico, and there was a horrible storm. He died in a car accident trying to get back home to me. He had brought up the subject of the house in Positano again and wanted us to move quickly to be safe. It was the last time we spoke. He didn't suffer, but it was a horrible accident. I lost my Santos in one moment. All of our dreams, all our love, everything we planned together vanished."

Ari and Anjali spent the rest of the flight in comfortable silence. Talking about Santos seemed to have been therapeutic for Ari, and Anjali could finally take a break from her sleuthing—though there was so much more she was curious about now.

Once they arrived at the hotel in Barcelona, Ari pulled out a vase from her carry-on bag. Anjali stared at the vase, wondering where it came from.

"This is the vase my nurse, Devyani, gave me. Remember the story I told you about getting sick as a child in India?" Ari said. Anjali remembered fondly.

"Well, I decided that Santos should live here until I could bring him to Positano. I plan to drop his ashes overboard on a boat ride to Capri. He loved that trip so much, and he told me that is where he wanted his ashes to be scattered."

Anjali hugged Ari and assured her it would happen.

***

While Avinash was in Dubai, his security team reported that Akash Ramkissoon had returned to the UK in March aboard a flight from Los Angeles using the assumed name of John Ronit. Interpol was interested in hearing how Ronit showed up unannounced at World Bank and wanted to speak with Avinash and Ms. Cordero. It seemed Avinash had plenty to worry about. He was responsible for putting Akash in jail and making sure he didn't inherit any of Mr. Dutta's vast dynasties, and now news of his whereabouts was vague. Akash had managed to keep his identity quiet and moved discreetly under the radar. They were unable to tie him to the hit on Ari, though Sam was still waiting to view the film from the traffic cameras. The security team in Barcelona reported to Sam that the two women had arrived and were staying at Hotel Arts, near the marina. All seemed to be quiet, though they were checking the guest list at that hotel for a possible match with John Ronit.

Ari phoned Avinash, wanting to hear his voice, and once they spoke she felt at ease. Anjali also reported to Avinash that things were okay, but when Ari stepped out of the room for a moment, Anjali asked Avinash to be extra attentive to her when he returned from Dubai. She told him she had found out some things about Santos and would tell him later, but it was an extremely difficult time for Ari, and he needed to be more caring than normal. Avinash agreed, his curiosity piqued.

"Be careful. Anjali. Do not let Ari out of your sights," Avinash strictly cautioned her.

***

The evening in Barcelona with Ari was filled with music, food, and great people-watching. They headed to one of the many famous restaurants of El Bulli's brother, Albert Adria. Anjali loved to hear Ari speak in perfect Castilian, ordering food left and right like a native. She sometimes switched to Catalan, the native language in Barcelona, and Anjali was amazed at how she zoomed through the menu in both languages. Ari was a real foodie and followed the latest food and wine trends all over Spain, Italy, and Portugal. Anjali realized that Ari's vast knowledge of food was a key to Avinash's attraction to her—among other beautiful qualities that Ari held.

Once they dined, they headed to the Palau de la Musica for a concert and later settled into a long walk through La Ramblas, Barcelona's most picturesque pedestrian street. Ari showed her everything Barcelona had to offer—the good, the bad, and the magnificent. She was in her element, and obviously felt quite at home in Spain. Anjali noticed she missed Avinash more than she admitted, buying him trinkets and clothing that he would love.

The last day in Barcelona, Ari took Anjali to Sitges, a colorful seaside village about forty-five minutes from Barcelona. They spent the day on the beach, eating seafood and drinking white wine sangria. Ari made sure Anjali got the attention of the men on the beach by going topless, and Anjali was horrified! Even so, the topless Ari managed to lure a couple of handsome Spanish lads over to their camp on the beach, and Anjali was in heaven.

That night, one of the men, a nice lad from Toledo, accompanied the ladies to dinner in town and later exchanged numbers with Anjali. On their way back to Barcelona, the driver Ari had hired explained that two gentlemen dressed in dark clothing had been following them but had suddenly disappeared. The driver was worried that the ladies had a jealous boyfriend or husband and warned them to behave.

Ari straightened him out right away and told him to mind his own business. "Just drive. That is your only job. Do we understand each other?" she snapped. The driver obeyed and drove them to their hotel without another word.

***

The next morning, they would have to be ready for their flight to Naples, and the drive from Sorrento to Positano would be beautiful but quite scary for any novice motorist. Ari needed sufficient rest to take on such a trip—one she hadn't taken in quite some time, a trip that would lead her back to the most pleasant time in her life. Ari was sure she was on the right path, on the road that would take her back to Positano. She called Avinash when they arrived in Naples at 10:20 in the morning. It was two hours earlier in Dubai. Avinash quickly answered, and while they waited for their luggage to come through the belt, Ari recounted the last three days in Barcelona in short bullet points. She wanted to hear how he was doing in Dubai.

"That sounds like fun, Ari. We have to take that trip together someday, just you and I," Avinash said. "Dubai is good . . . a lot of meetings, but last night we had dinner in the desert under the stars, and it was quite beautiful. I miss you terribly, darling. Just four more days and we'll be together again." He spoke sweetly, lowering his voice as he often did when he wanted to melt her.

"Yes, love! I can't wait. Listen, we're off. Please call me tomorrow morning, okay? Te quiero, amor."

"I love you too, Ari. Safe travels."

While they wrestled their luggage into the tiny trunk of the Mercedes-Benz A-Class rental car, Anjali entered the address of their two-bedroom apartment overlooking the ocean in Positano and right off the main road, Viale Pasitea, into the portable GPS.

"We won't need that, Anj. I know exactly where it is, and besides, we're stopping for lunch in Sorrento."

Ari explained to Anjali that she had received word that her furniture and belongings had arrived at the port of Naples, and she had to claim them while she was there.

"What are you going to do? Leave your stuff here or ship it to London?" Anjali asked.

"Not really sure, Anjali. I need to figure out what to do with the house in Positano first. If Sam is right, the situation stopping the closing has been fixed, and all I need to do is sign the paperwork in Sorrento. I'm hoping this might become a summer home for Avinash and me."

Ari sped onto the highway in the direction of the Strada Statale Amalfitana.

***

It was the last day of the music festival in Positano. The major acts would be performing that evening, and Lorraine had made sure to secure the best seats for her guests. Marcelo knew she had been trying to keep him at bay most of the time, but he managed to find out Ms. Cordero and her friend would arrive today and would be staying in a flat near town. That was all he needed to hear. Marcelo headed to a nearby barbershop to clean up. A trim here and there and he was looking a bit more presentable.

After all, getting the contract to remodel the home was not going to be easy. He had a lot of competition in town, but he knew he could sway the American to choose him. In any case, who would know better how to restore a house than the person who rebuilt it? The idea was to see Ms. Cordero at the closing ceremony party. He wasn't interested in all these new and flashy bands that were yelling and screaming nonsense and daring to call it music; he wanted to meet Ms. Cordero one-on-one and have her full attention. Marcelo was prepared and more excited about this than he had been about anything in a long time. *This is my night,* he thought.

***

The drive from Naples to Positano was mainly on the Corso Italia SS145. It was a broad highway with jaw-dropping land and sea vistas. After arriving in Sorrento, Ari invited Anjali to lunch at Terrazza Bosquet, a lovely restaurant in one the city's most luxurious hotels, the Grand Hotel Excelsior Vittoria. They dined on the beautiful terrace overlooking the ocean. Ari made sure she didn't drink any alcohol, because the one-hour ride ahead was treacherous. She opted for juice and later a strong caffè to cut the edge off those late nights in Barcelona.

Anjali was stuffed. She wasn't use to eating this much food and discreetly unbuttoned her trousers letting out a sigh of relief. "If there is such a thing as being food-drunk, this must be it," she said pointing to her stomach. "Must we take this long drive now? I'm starting to feel a bit nauseous.' Anjali pleaded. "Sorry Anjali, there is no time to waste." Ari assured her she didn't want to take that road at night and off they went. By the time they arrived in Positano, Anjali developed a horrible headache. Luckily her malaise hit her after the twists and turns on the drive there, or maybe it was the very reason she was sick. As Anjali waited in the car for Ari to checked in to the flat they rented, Ari brought in their luggage and situated Anjali in one of the bedrooms, bringing her plenty of water with two aspirins.

"Sleep, Anji. We still have plenty of time before the concert tonight." Anjali moaned as she covered her head with the white down comforter.

***

Ari really wanted to take a walk in town. The weather was perfect: sunny, blue skies, about sixty degrees Fahrenheit with a warm breeze sweeping into town from the Mediterranean. It was all she needed. She had some loose ends to tie up regarding her belongings at the port of Naples and started to make some phone calls.

With all the excitement, she hadn't remembered to talk to Avinash about the house. Then she realized he didn't even know she was in Positano in the first place. *It's best to keep this under my hat until I return to London. We'll talk about it then*, she thought.

The main centre of Positano was a virtual hornet's nest of vendors and trucks unloading everything from food to chairs and supplies. Corporate promotional banners were strung up everywhere, with the concert's logo and their sponsors, while the guests waited for the final setup before taking their places on the bleachers and chairs arranged arena-style. Many roads from the main highway were blocked, with access allowed only for trucks and approved personnel who were part of the preparation for the concert. It was a good thing Ari and Anjali arrived when they did, or else poor Anjali wouldn't have been able to rest at all.

From the terrace window of their flat, with Viale Pasitea humming below it, Ari could see the beautiful ocean that called to her so often. It was so clear that day that she could just make out the Li Galli islands from a distance. The warm breeze hit her face and she closed her eyes, breathing in and out slowly to take it all in.

***

Across the street, Marcelo Donati had gotten his first look at her and liked what he saw. Leaning against a tree and smoking a cigarette, Marcelo took Ms. Cordero in. She had taken off her jacket and was in a tight tank top and jeans, her reddish-brown hair with streaks of gold blowing in the wind. She looked like the same goddess in the photograph. Marcelo did not move his eyes away from her, nor was he afraid of being noticed. He continued to watch her, studying her from afar until the faint sound of a ringing phone broke the spell. He watched as Ari pulled her phone from her pocket before hurrying inside to take the call.

***

In London, Sam received some disturbing reports from the London police. The two motorbike thugs had been found a couple of kilometers east of the city and had been arrested. The police camera had captured their motorbike tag and traced the license plate of the bike to a repair shop just east of that location. The extensive questioning by police had led one of them, a Sudanese national who was already in the country illegally, to talk about the evening. During his confession with an interpreter, the Sudanese man explained that they were contracted by a man with a British accent but they never saw him. They were to simply pick up the woman and bring her to a designated location. No harm was to be done to her, and they did not know the reason for the job. The payment was 5000£. Their plan was spoiled when the woman fell on their approach and they had to return to find her. She managed to escape, and they were unable to make the pick-up. Their mobiles were confiscated and call traces were being made, but they got no hits on any particular number. The news was shocking to Sam; in fact, Avinash had been correct in his assumption. Ms. Cordero's life was in danger, and he had to inform Avinash immediately. It was obvious that Ari would be safer if she could stay out of London, and Sam knew that Avinash would not be pleased to hear this news. Sam also knew this report would change the lives of a couple who were in love, and if this proved to be the work of Akash Ramkissoon, neither of the men would give up until one of them was destroyed.

***

Ari was happy to hear she could come to Sorrento and sign the paperwork on the house whenever she wanted. This prompted her to think about ways to tell Avinash and make it a proposition that he could not refuse. She tiptoed into Anjali's room with a cold glass of juice and found her awake and looking much better.

"I brought you some juice, Anji. How do you feel?"

She rubbed her head. "Oh, I guess I'm okay, but I still have the headache."

"Do you think you'll be able to make it tonight? I need you with me, girl." Besides needing a wing-woman, Ari wanted Anjali to enjoy the town and the festivities.

"I think so. I just need some fresh air. Does this place have a terrace with a breeze or something?"

Ari smiled. "Sure, come with me. The sun is perfect."

Ari led Anjali to the terrace and positioned her under an old, potted lemon tree that provided great shade. Anjali stared wide-eyed as she took in the beauty of the town, the sea, and mountains around her, all in such perfect harmony.

"It's beautiful, Ari, simply breathtaking. You go do your thing. I'll just lie here and be a diva. Don't worry about me. I'm a tough Desi chick. I'll be ready in no time," she said as she covered her eyes with her large sunglasses.

***

Marcelo continued to walk the streets with the vision of the beautiful *donna* in his head. He wanted to meet her immediately and could feel the adrenaline boost up and down his body. Marcelo had never felt this invigorated before. He would make sure Ms. Cordero felt comfortable in his presence, making her laugh and trust him. *This shouldn't be too difficult for me*, he thought. Once she confided in him, using some elaborate scheme to entice the woman to sign over the house would be easy. First, he had to get up-close and personal, get inside her head and heart. Only this way could he win her over and gain her trust. The plan was perfect, but first he had to meet her and seize the moment.

***

Lorraine was busy with last-minute preparations. The committee was helping, but she was the heart and soul of the concert, knowing every intricate detail. The phones never stopped ringing at Chez Black, a restaurant set up as the Grand Central Station for the concert. It was a virtual madhouse and she was drowning. Lorraine called the one person she knew had done something similar to this before and could be her right arm. She called Ariadne Cordero.

***

Ari and Anjali arrived on the *spiaggia* ready to get to work. Ari knew that organization and control of the itinerary for the concert was the key. Within a matter of minutes, Ari set up a station for all vendors to check in and gave them their security bracelets, allowing them to enter the venue without question. Anjali worked the coordination of the acts and had them situated in a trailer that served as a green room before their performances. Lorraine took care of the rest, and things were moving smoothly. The concert would open within two hours.

Ari spoke with the police and asked them to position themselves at all entrances of the concert. Designated music festival committee members would be taking tickets and tearing them in half to keep control of the masses and prevent overcrowding. At a certain time, the entrances would be blocked off and no further entry would be allowed. The stage was positioned near an area known to the city as "the cave," and the stands were supported by wooden floors to prevent sinking in the beach sand. The concert needed to take place before the tide came in, and once it was over, the stage would be quickly dismantled before the ocean waves swallowed it. There was a short window of time, and this had never been done before, a first in Positano, and hopefully with an ending that would be long remembered.

***

The first act took the stage after the mayor of Positano welcomed all the guests and the crowd sang "The Chant of the Italians," the Italian national anthem. The first act was a pop group from Naples, and their music got the crowd pumping. Ari and Anjali were manning some of the information booths and set up a first aid tent with staff from the hospital in Sorrento for injuries or drunken fights. Marcelo watched Ari from the terrace pool at the Covo dei Saraceni, a hotel that hovered over the marina and beach with a perfect view of the crowd but too far to see the acts on the stage. He wasn't interested in any of the acts. He wanted to see Ari in action, and she was a virtual worker bee that didn't stop for a moment. Marcelo noticed some of the men gawking at her. *This could potentially turn dangerous,* he thought. *An opportunity for me to assist the American.* Marcelo made a dash toward the beach. He had his ticket, so the entry patrol let him by without question.

Once there, he noticed a young man who'd had one too many beers approach Ari, grab her by the arm, and attempt to dance with her. Ari was trying to refuse, but the young man was strong-arming her. Marcelo approached without fear, having boxed in his youth. He knew exactly how to momentarily disable the young punk without harm.

"Let her go," Marcelo said, stepping behind Ari. "She obviously was working the event and didn't want to dance."

Ari pried herself loose from his grasp and hurried behind Marcelo. The young man ignored the warning and called Marcelo and old goat that needed to go take his nap. Marcelo took the insult and stopped him from moving forward, his chest puffed out like a male sea lion protecting his cubs. In his drunken state, the young man called Ari a whore and yelled that he would have his way with her. That was enough. Marcelo struck the man in the neck with a chop and then finished him off with a blow to the nose. He fell in slow motion and hit the sand face-first. After the police came and took the man into custody, Marcelo took Ari by the hand and led her to the first aid tent, sitting her down and motioning for the nurse to check her over. Her arm was visibly bruised but nothing serious.

"Are you okay?" Marcelo asked, kneeling in front of her.

"*Si, grazie.*"

"*Parli Italiano, signorina?*" Marcelo asked.

Ari answered in perfect Italian that she understood the language better than she could speak it.

"I'm working on my Italian, signor."

Marcelo excused himself for not making an introduction sooner. "Signor Marcelo Donati, at your destruction."

Ari corrected him with a smile. "You mean at my disposal, Mr. Donati?"

"Yes, yes. Sorry. My English is like your Italian. Not so good," Marcelo replied.

The nurse applied an ice pack to Ari's arm which was now turning purple.

"I'm okay," she assured Marcelo, who was fussing over her. "Lately I just happen to be in the wrong place at the wrong time."

As Ari got to her feet, Anjali came flying into the first aid tent.

"There you are! Dear God, what happened?"

Ari explained the incident and Anjali thanked Marcelo for protecting her.

"It was my pleasure," Marcelo said. "I don't believe we've met."

"I'm Anjali," she said with a smile, her eyes scanning him from head to toe. "Will you be attending the closing ceremony dinner tonight? There's one more seat next to me, Mr. Donati."

Ari coughed and told Anjali that perhaps Mr. Donati had other plans.

"Oh, no," Marcelo quickly replied. "I'm free tonight. I will join you. *Mille grazie.*"

Ari excused herself, letting Marcelo know she had to get back to work. "Thank you again, Mr. Donati. I guess we will see you tonight at the dinner then."

Marcelo simply nodded and walked away lighting a cigarette.

***

"Anjali, you're so forward with men!" Ari said as the two of them headed back to work. "You can't do that here in Italy! Do you know what subtle means?"

Anjali just smiled. "Do you know what hot, sexy, Italian man means? Let me have some fun. I might get lucky tonight!"

Ari could only laugh, and they quickly got back to work. A few minutes later, Lorraine stopped by to check on them.

"So you've met Marcelo, have you?" Lorraine asked. "I was wondering where you'd wandered off to. But then I saw Marcelo drop that drunk guy down the beach, and I knew something was up."

"Do you know him?" Ari asked. "Well, of course you do. You know everyone. Anjali is quite smitten with him. She's invited him to the closing dinner tonight. I hope that won't be a problem, Lorraine."

"Oh no," she answered. "Marcelo has a way of popping up everywhere."

Ari wasn't sure what that meant, but beween the loud music and the sting of her bruised arm, all she wanted to do was find a quiet place to sit. Anjali had wandered over to a nearby vendor's tent and seemed to be having a rather serious conversation on her cell phone. Ari could tell she was arguing with whoever was on the line and hoped there was no bad news from Avinash. She hurried in Anjali's direction and got close enough to hear the end of the conversation.

"It's okay. Yes, yes, I will take care of her, but I don't understand your decision. You need to think about this more," Anjali said, pleading into the receiver.

Ari hadn't see Anjali this distraught in a long time and approached her as she finished the call. "Is everything okay, Anjali? Is Avinash okay? Please tell me."

"Oh, he's fine. It's Sam and work. They're changing the computer system at the bank, and he wants me to take another week of vacation with you. What do you think?"

Ari was surprised. They had return flights in three days, and she knew Avinash would be waiting for her.

"We can't, Anjali," Ari replied. "You know Avinash will be back from Dubai, and I'm missing him so much. How could we possibly stay another week? He wouldn't hear of it."

"Okay, okay. It was just a thought. I don't even think Avinash will be able to work with all the system changes. Who knows, he might decide it's okay for you to stay longer. I certainly would love to get to know Mr. Donati better."

Ari didn't want to listen to Anjali's nonsense. "We'll talk about it later," Ari huffed as she turned and walked out of the tent. The music was deafening, and Ari covered her ears as she pushed through the crowd. She got a cold chill up her spine like something was truly wrong, but she tried not to think about it as she continued helping Lorraine with the festival's last details. The show was almost over, and the tear-down of the event would be quickly underway.

***

That evening when Avinash returned to his room at the luxurious Burj al Arab resort in Dubai, he found a report from Sam waiting in his email inbox. He read it and put in an immediate call to Sam, who answered promptly on the first ring.

"Yes, Avinash. Did you read the report I sent to you?" Sam asked.

"This is worse than I thought. Ari was in real danger of a kidnapping. Have you told anyone where she is?"

"No," Sam responded. "I told the police she left London on holiday and could not be reached, whereabouts unknown. Knowing how you felt and since we had discussed this subject previously, I took the liberty of calling Anjali, encouraging her to stay longer in Spain and not return until we could tie Akash and his accomplices to this kidnapping. God knows what else he's planning. I'm afraid I won't be able to hold off Interpol. An Agent Valverde keeps calling, asking questions and wanting to meet with Ari."

"Good job, man. Let's keep in touch, and please update me on any news," Avinash said as he closed his mobile phone.

Avinash was now distraught with fear for Ari. His first instinct was to get on a plane and run to her, but that would just lead Akash straight to Ari, and he couldn't afford to take that chance. With Interpol in the picture, at least he knew the hunt for Akash was international, and they had been on his tail for quite some time.

***

That evening, at the finale of the music festival, Lorraine instructed Ari to go back to her flat and change for the dinner being held at The Terrazze restaurant on the Via Grotte dell'Incanto, not too far from her flat. Because it was on a steep, sloped road, Ari would definitely need her vehicle to get there.

When Anjali and Ari arrived at the flat, they began drinking, and Anjali poured Ari more than she should have. Ari was parched and drank without thinking. She showered and dressed in a black cocktail dress with one shoulder and arm exposed, black pumps, and a teardrop diamond necklace that Santos had bought for her in Milan while they were dating. Anjali wore a simple black pantsuit with a colorful scarf and diamond earrings. They were both feeling no pain when they arrived at the dinner. Ari could barely parallel park the small Mercedes but finally managed, and they headed inside.

The view from the outdoor terrace was spectacular. All you could see were the twinkling lights of the town and the ocean below, and the breeze was exceptionally welcoming that night. They were escorted to their table and found an interesting mix of women who Lorraine had invited.

Lorraine introduced Ari and Anjali to Marcelle from Luxemburg, the owner of a women's fashion shop in town, and Claudia, a tall and Amazonian-looking woman who hailed from Brazil and would make tongues wag as she walked—her breasts were a good double-D, and she shamefully wore a push-up bra to expose them even more. The introductions continued with Paulette, a petite French woman who owned several French pastry shops along the Amalfi Coast, and Angela, another British expatriate who had moved in the 80s after a long romance with an Italian jeweler. She now enjoyed the finer things in life after he left her much of his fortune when he suddenly died ten years before. The other three women were Italian: Carmen from Sorrento, the owner of several restaurants on the coast, including one in Capri; Guiletta from Palermo, a robust woman who had a history of being the cougar in the group and was proud of it; and finally Daniela, a petite, mousey brunette from Genoa whose husband was the president of the music committee for the festival. Daniela was a retired nurse and was a lot of fun to talk to. Anjali and Ari rounded out the table of ten exceptionally interesting women who would be doing a lot of gossiping and drinking and entertaining the rest of the music festival guests who were dining that evening.

"Has Avinash called?" Ari whispered to Anjali.

"No, Ari," she answered as she poured more prosecco into her flute.

The evening was filled with lively tales of men and could-have-been relationships. When the conversation turned to Ari, Paulette asked her why she was in town.

"It's a long story," Ari said as she poured herself more prosecco. She gave the women few details, other than to say that she and a former love had once planned to live in Positano, and she was in town to fulfill that dream. "In fact, I bought a house in the process, just up the road at 87 Via Pasitea.

"What?" Guiletta quickly responded. "Don't you know that house has a *maledetto*? You certainly won't find any romance in that place."

"It's cursed?"

Claudia chimed in mockingly. "And it's *Viale* Pasitea, darling." Ari smiled but ignored her correction.

"Perhaps it's time you hear the truth about that house," Lorraine said. She described a young, Italian man who made a life for himself in Sorrento and later Positano. The story of the underground gambling ring, the women, money, fast cars—it all seemed fascinating to Ari who had skipped over the first and second entrees and had been performing on alcohol fumes for the last two and half hours.

Lorraine described how the young Italian met the girl of his dreams, Lucia. That he built a house for her with details that would befit a queen. Then fame and fortune hit them, and everything went downhill in the relationship.

"Your house, Ari, is a small version of the Taj Majal in Positano, an homage to a woman loved so much by one man that all he could do was worship her with a structure built in her image."

Ari, her words slurred, fell in love with the story and begged Lorraine to continue. Those who knew the tale or had witnessed it soon joined in.

Lorraine finished by telling of Lucia's tragic death. "In your house, Ari. 87 Viale Pasitea." By this time, Ari and Anjali were weeping, though perhaps as much from inebriation as from the sad story itself.

Then Guiletta, who could hold her liquor, nodded toward the bar. "Oh my God! There he is!" she whispered to the group. "That's the man who built your house. That's the poor dog who never got to finish that house."

Ari turned around to take a look. "That guy?" she said. "He doesn't look romantic or even capable of building such a house for a woman. That can't be him."

"In fact, it is, Ari," Lorainne replied. "That is Marcelo Donati, the gambler, Amalfi Coast playboy, and lover that you see before you. If anyone can fix your house, it's that bloke."

***

Ari, still reeling from the story and an overload of prosecco, managed to get out of her seat, determined to meet her patriot in arms, someone who understood true pain, love, and suffering, and had survived it.

Anjali kept telling the women that she had invited the poor bastard to the dinner and had no idea of his life, as Ari struggled toward him in her high-heeled pumps, bumping into tables and waiters along the way. All Marcelo could do was watch in delight as the American made a complete fool of herself.

Ari was as drunk as a sailor, and when she was just a few inches from him, she fell over some steps and right into Marcelo's arms. He held her against him as she looked up at him, only to see his chin, nostrils, and grey eyes staring down at her.

"Mr. Dooooonati?" she mumbled.

"Yes, Ms. Cordero. Can you stand or shall I just hold you up all night?" he said.

"No, it's okay. I can stand. Am I not standing now?" Ari asked in disbelief.

He muttered something sarcastic, but Ari wasn't listening. All at once, she saw Santos in Marcelo's eyes and Avinash in his smile and could not resist the temptation to lean in and kiss him—a lip-lock that lasted longer than she would have wanted if she were sober. Marcelo pulled her close, holding her and caressing her back in the process.

Ari, lost in the moment, heard the women hooting and laughing in the distance.

Suddenly, Angela yelled, "Get that bastard!"

Within minutes, the dinner party became a Roman circus, but the guests seemed to be enjoying the show. Marcelo continued to kiss Ari, and when he pulled away for a moment to catch his breath, she fainted in his arms. It was all too much for her—the drinks, the stories, Santos and Avinash on her mind, and now this Marcelo character. She hung lifeless in his arms until he picked her up and swung her over his shoulder like a sack of potatoes.

***

"Take her to my flat, Marcelo," Lorraine said. "And be good to her. No funny business." Marcelo marched off with Ari like a pirate carrying a loot of gold and placed her gently in his truck. He arrived at Lorraine's flat and carried her up the steps. For one moment he wanted his way with her—she was so beautiful—but he quickly took his mind off that and placed her on the bed he had been using for the past months. Marcelo then took off her shoes and went to the bathroom for some towels and cold water. As he patted her forehead and neck, Ari began to mumble, calling out for Avinash . . . whoever that was.

She awoke moments later, and Marcelo had already prepared a pot of strong coffee. Ari tried to get up from the bed but could not, and Marcelo signaled to her that she should not move.

"No, no, *signora*. Here, drink this," he said as he held the cup of coffee to her mouth and removed the towel from her forehead."

"Where am I?" she asked.

"This is Lorraine's house. She told me to take you here. She will come soon. Now drink."

After a few minutes, Ari came out of her alcohol stupor. "Why are you helping me?"

He didn't think he was helping her; rather, he was helping himself. But he gave her the answer he assumed she wanted to hear. "You are a woman with much love to give, and you have lost your love. I understand you."

159

Ari seemed satisfied with that answer. She handed him the cup and fell back to sleep on his bed. He heard her mobile ring and took the phone out of her bag. The caller ID read, Avinash. Marcelo smiled and placed the phone back in her bag.

***

Avinash had been calling Ari and Anjali all evening long, and neither had answered. He was worried, restless and unable to sleep. Not being able to locate them was killing him. At 2:00 a.m. he rang Ari again.

"Hello? Who in damnation is calling at this hour?"

Avinash paused as he tried to place the voice. *It's not Ari or Anjali, so who――*

"Hello?"

"This is Avinash Batra. I'm trying to reach Ms. Ariadne Cordero."

"Mr. Batra, it's two in the morning and she's asleep."

"I know and I'm very sorry. I have been trying to reach her since last evening, and she has not responded. Is everything okay?"

"She's fine, Mr. Batra. She told me all about you. This is Lorraine Newly, her friend from Positano. She's a bit under the weather and is resting. I'll have her call you tomorrow as soon as she wakes up. Don't worry and good night."

Avinash didn't know if Lorraine had met Ari and Anjali in Spain or if they were actually in Positano. Why didn't she tell him? At least he knew she was fine and would get the full story tomorrow. Avinash did not sleep well that night, and his fear for Ari's life became his obsession.

***

By one in the afternoon, most of the guests in Lorraine's flat had started to show some signs of life, while Lorraine prepared a late breakfast of scones, mixed fruit, and strong tea. Marcelo had left early after sleeping miserably on the undersized sofa in Lorraine's living room. He'd check on Ari before he left and found her sleeping like an angel. Anjali woke and managed to get to the bathroom, cringing at the sight of herself in the large antique mirror. Ari, in the meantime, was still asleep and lifeless when Lorraine went to check on her.

"Ari, wake up, love," Lorraine said as she gave Ari's arm a gentle shake. "It's almost two in the afternoon. Your boyfriend called last night wondering where you were."

"He called?" Ari whispered, forcing her eyes open at the mention of Avinash.

"Yes. It was two in the morning, and I picked up your phone because it wouldn't stop ringing."

Ari, her brain still foggy, sat up and tried to process the situation. "Does he know where I am?"

"Well, I should hope so, dear," Lorraine quipped. "The poor man was beside himself."

Ari struggled out of bed and met Anjali passing in the hall. "Do I look as bad as you?" Ari asked.

"Yes, you drunken slut, but you still manage to look beautiful. I hate you," Anjali said as they headed for the kitchen.

"Did you hear Avinash called last night?" Ari asked.

"Yes, Lorraine told me. I think he may already know where we are. You're going to need to break it to him."

***

After a few bites of a scone and nearly a gallon of water, Ari called Avinash. He picked up on the first ring.

"Ari? Are you okay? Hello?"

The worried tone in his voice made her stomach churn.

"Yes, love. I'm fine, baby. Just had a little too much to drink last night. I need to tell you something," she whispered.

"You're in Positano, aren't you?" Avinash said.

"Yes, love. Let me explain," Ari said apologetically.

"You don't have to, Ari. I think it's a good idea. As a matter of fact, I think you should stay and finish what you went there to do. You wanted a job? Well, remodeling your house will definitely give you something to do. It all came together for you, love. Congratulations."

Taken aback by his response, Ari paused for a moment, unsure as to his true intent. *And why doesn't he want me to return to London?* she wondered. "So you're okay with the house purchase? I'm doing this for us now, you know. We talked about a summer home for us, and since I'm here—"

"Absolutely, darling. Makes perfect sense. Stay a couple weeks more and get it all organized the way you want. We'll see each other soon. I'll call you tomorrow. I love you."

With that, Avinash ended the call, leaving Ari to stare at her phone in disbelief. *This is not a good sign. If he truly loves me, he would want to be with me. Something has changed, and I bet Anjali knows what it is.*

As Ari and Anjali prepared to leave, Ari apologized to Lorraine for whatever happened the night before, though she couldn't remember much of it.

"Don't worry, darling," Lorraine said with a chuckle. "It's exactly what this town needed, a little scandalous incident to keep the fires burning."

They said their goodbyes, and Ari and Anjali headed out in search of a taxi to take them back to the restaurant where they'd left the car. They passed their flat on the way and noticed a silver Mercedes parked on the curb in front.

"Is that our car, Anjali?" Ari asked. "It is! How in the world did it get here?" Ari dug through her purse, but no keys were there.

Then she noticed a handwritten note taped to the door: *Sig. Cordero, I drive your car to the albergo. No safe in street. Feel best, Marcelo.* Ari stared at Anjali who had a smile from ear to ear.

"If Avinash finds out this guy has the hots for you, you're doomed, darling."

Once they got settled in the flat, Ari asked Anjali what she meant when she called her a drunken slut at Lorraine's house.

"You don't remember?" Anjali asked. "Not a thing?"

"I only remember that Marcelo brought me to Lorraine's house, and he made me some coffee. That's all." Ari wanted to hear the rest.

"Well, the ladies at the table started talking about a story of a playboy who built a house for his lady. It had a tragic ending and supposedly, I say this because I didn't personally see it, you got up from the table and planted dear Marcelo with a wet one that he thoroughly enjoyed. I also hear he felt you up quite a bit, including your perky Spaniard buttocks." Anjali laughed at the look of horror on Ari's face.

"I did that? That's so unlike me," Ari said.

"Well, you did. Then he picked you up like Prince Charming, threw you over his back, and took you to Lorraine's."

Anjali waited for a response from Ari, but what she heard next was totally unexpected. "I spoke with Avinash," Ari said stoically, "and he wants me to stay and finish what I came to do. I think it's a good idea. Perhaps he's having second thoughts about our relationship, and the time apart will let us know if we were meant to be together or not. It all happened so fast. I was vulnerable and feeling guilty about loving him, and he was charming and seductive. Everything happens for a reason."

The call from Avinash had been like throwing a bucket of ice water on her, and his strange response made her wake up from the dream.

"There is no such thing as finding the love of your life twice in one lifetime, Anjali. This is where I belong."

Anjali said nothing but listened intently, which was exactly what Ari needed from her. She let Ari ramble to get it out of her system.

"I never got to say goodbye to Santos. The last time we spoke, all he talked about was Vida Blue and Positano. I think life is pointing me in the direction I need to go. Strangely enough, all I feel right now is loss. It's all I've ever had."

***

The next day, Ari could barely drag herself out of bed. During the trip over from London, she had picked this day to take the ferry to Capri for Santos's fond farewell, but she didn't have the strength for any of it. It was too heavy an assignment, and she needed to be free from all of the pain.

But never one to stay in an emotional slump for long, she told Anjali they would go to Sorrento, sign the papers to the house, wire the money to the bank in Naples, and then finish off the celebration in Capri. They could take the last ferry back to Positano at six in the evening and be home for an early dinner.

Anjali agreed and hurried off to make a few phone calls while Ari gathered picnic items and documents she needed for the purchase of the home. As she packed the car, Marcelo stopped by to make sure she'd received the keys.

"I did, Marcelo. Thank you so much . . . for everything. And please accept my apology if I embarrassed you in front of everyone. It was certainly not my intention. I'm afraid I had a bit too much prosecco."

Marcelo wouldn't hear of it. "It was my pleasure to assist you, signora." Then he offered his services to fix the home on Viale Pasitea. There was no able-bodied soul on the Amalfi Coast who knew that house better than he. He handed Ari a preliminary quote on materials at cost and showed his services reduced in price.

Ari didn't know what to think. *Why would he want to be involved with a house that held so much pain for him?* She took his hand and thanked him again for his kindness the night before. "I will have an answer for you by tomorrow, *va bene?*"

***

Anjali punched Avinash's number into her phone and watched from the terrace as Ari and Marcelo chatted on the street. "I don't know what you told her, but she is a changed woman, Avinash. Do you know why we're here? Do you think it's all about the house and Santos and their dream of living here?"

Avinash's tone was icy as he explained that he was only trying to protect Ari from Akash. "I can't give you much detail, Anjali, but this is serious."

"We're here to bury Santos. He has been dead for four years! He died in a car accident in Mexico. I think there is something more to Akash being in London, but Santos didn't leave Ari the way she led us to believe. He made her promise if he died, she would take his ashes and throw them overboard on a ferry ride to Capri. He made her promise that she would buy this house and live in it, be safe and find the love of her life again. Basically, move on. Why did he need for Ari to be safe, Avinash? Safe from what? Who? Ari only understands what she promised Santos, nothing more. You need to tell her the truth. Ari is destroyed, and yet she's given you so much love, so much to live for, so much for you to believe in. Ari hid all of this pain away and gave you 100 percent, and I know she's taken Suniel's place in your heart. If you do this to her, if by trying to protect her you decide it's best to leave her here in Positano alone, you will finish her off, Avinash. She is not Suniel. If she's in danger, she needs your help but more than anything, Ari needs your love. There will be no more of the caring and loving Ari you found a couple of months ago. Do you hear me, brother?"

Anjali stressed her concerns to Avinash, but there was no response. For the first time in his life, the famous London businessman, the ever eloquent and dashing playboy, Avinash Batra, was silenced.

CHAPTER NINE

A vinash marched into World Bank the next morning, his usual swagger, brilliant smile, and cheerful greeting replaced by a cold, intense scowl. He went straight to his office, closed the door, and called into Sam's office on the intercom.

"I need you in my office straight away, Sam," he said, banging the receiver down so hard that the picture of Ari on his desk went crashing to the floor.

"Why didn't you tell me Santos Echegui was dead?" Avinash asked before Sam could close the office door behind him. Sam did not respond. "Here I am, the president of World Bank, and I am not privy to important information on my clients? You were supposed to do a background check on this man. What the hell did you give me in this file?" Avinash slammed the file on the desk in front of Sam. "Speak, man!"

"The information was there all along. You were only interested in knowing the reason for the indictment, the trial, and subsequent imprisonment of Mr. Echegui. You were only concerned with getting Mr. Echegui out of the way so you could pursue Ms. Cordero. Had I told you she was a widow from the beginning, would she have been interesting to you? Anjali and I knew you needed someone like her, but I took the initiative to show Ari to you in a different light. Otherwise, you would have had no need to fight for her or pursue her the way you have these past few months. She would have been easy prey in your hands . . . too easy. But with Santos abandoning her, the wounded Ari would need to be protected; she would need the support of a strong man like Avinash Batra. Did you become her hero, Avinash?"

Avinash swiveled his chair around, his back to Sam, and stared out the window at the view of the city below him. He had nothing to say—he knew Sam was right. Avinash asked to be alone, and Sam obliged him without further comment. When the door clicked to a close, Avinash turned back to his desk, opened the Echegui file, and read it with a fine-tooth comb.

Santos had left Ari a large fortune; she had no need to be with him for money. Then it dawned on him that this may be the initial reason, aside from her beauty and charm, that Akash pursued her. Perhaps she informed him of her dealings with World Bank and Akash put two and two together. Then everything fell into his lap and he was going to use Ari as his bait. *But there has to be more*, he thought. *How did he find Ari? Did he know Santos somehow? That's impossible. He died a couple of years ago. Why is he after Ari now?* Avinash checked his mobile for calls, but there were none from Ari. Her absence hit him hard, and he decided to visit the local pub alone, to let it all sink in.

***

Anjali sobbed as she stuffed her carry-on with magazines and finished packing on Saturday morning. Soon, the cab would arrive to take her to Naples for her evening flight back to London.

Ari wrapped her arms around her friend. "What's wrong, Anji? Please don't cry. I'm a Spaniard; I won't be able to stop crying once I start. And we don't need a reason to cry."

"You're not even upset, Ari. I can't believe how strong you are. Avinash hasn't called you, and I'm leaving you here alone. Aren't you scared at all?"

Ari smiled. "Not really. I realize this is where I need to be. I will complete Santos's wishes and move on with my life here. I love this place, and I will be fine. Don't think I won't miss you, Anjali, because I will. You can always come and visit me. But I do want you to promise me something."

"What?" Anjali asked.

"Take care of Avinash. I love him so much. He needs your support. Promise me, Anj."

Anjali's tears began anew as she clung to Ari. "I promise," she said. "And you need to promise me something, Ari. I want you to attend Diwali in October. You won't have to see Avinash. Thousands of people attend, and the odds of us bumping into him would be slim. Please? It's six months away. Promise you'll come to London and celebrate the festival with me."

Ari knew she didn't want to see Avinash just now, but the festival was too good to pass up. "I'll be there. I promise, Anjali."

***

When Anjali arrived in London that evening, she found Sam waiting for her. She hurried over and smothered him in a bear hug, a display of public affection she knew Sam would abhor.

"What's up, you crazy old goat?" Anjali joked as Sam took her bags.

"Not much," he said. "But I will warn you, Avinash has hit rock bottom these last few days." Anjali shook her head, knowing full well where he would be hanging out to drown his sorrow.

On the ride home, Anjali filled Sam in on the details of Ari's life, her conversation with Avinash, and how he coldly told her to stay in Positano and make her life there.

"Is there any news on Akash?" she asked.

"No, nothing new, but we're keeping track of him, and when he sticks his head out of the hole we'll be waiting," Sam assured her.

"I just don't want to see those two have another Indian showdown, Sam. It will not be pretty.'" Anjali sighed and settled back in the plush leather seat to enjoy the ride.

***

Avinash went back to his bachelor life—long hours at the bank and frequent stops at the latest hangouts to meet women. In his attempt to forget Ari, which he could not, Avinash drank a little more and returned to being the womanizing player he once was. Ari's things—her perfume and the love notes he'd written her—were still at his flat. Her clothes still hung in the closet, including the beautiful dress she'd worn to his cousin's wedding. It seemed like a lifetime ago. The ring he'd purchased for her in Dubai, meant to be a symbol of his commitment to her, remained there, abandoned and forgotten.

One evening, Avinash came home from the bar, poured himself a drink, and opened his laptop to check his email. As he browsed, he came across the pictures he'd taken of Ari during their visit to Bath and Canterbury. "I'm sure she has a new lover now," he grumbled as he clicked through the online photo album. Probably some hot Italian guy who can't keep his hands off her. The thought of it sent him into a rage, and he strode to the bedroom, intent on packing her things to have them shipped to Positano.

As he tossed her belongings into a suitcase, he came across the veil she'd given him before he left for Dubai — the one drenched in her favorite perfume. As he held it to his nose, breathing in the familiar scent of her, he picked up his cell phone and punched in her number. It was a bad idea, but he wasn't thinking. It had been three weeks since they last spoke, and Avinash was hungry for the sound of her voice. And then Ari answered.

"Hello? Avinash?"

He was breathing heavily into the receiver, but he could not speak.

"Avinash, are you there?"

Overwhelmed by the sound of her voice, he opened his mouth to reply, but his words were powered by whiskey and rage and loneliness rather than love. "Who are you with, Ari?"

"I'm alone, Avinash, the way you wanted me to be. Remember? You made that choice. What do you want?" Ari asked. Her tone, firm and controlled, only angered Avinash more.

"You fucked Akash, didn't you? That's why he's after you. That's why he wants you so badly. Who are you fucking now? Who, Ari? Tell me!" Avinash yelled, his words slurred.

"You're drunk, Avinash. I won't talk to you when you're like this. I'm hanging up now. If you want to talk when you're sober, I'll take your call then."

As Ari ended the call, Avinash threw his tumbler of whiskey against the wall and cursed at himself for having made the call in the first place.

***

Marcelo finished his dinner and, with no other plans for the evening, decided to stop by to show Ari the samples of blue tile he'd found for the kitchen backsplash. He was delighted that she'd decided to allow him to do the remodeling, and the cucina had become the biggest part of the project, since Ari decided to move it from the front of the house to the back with its full panoramic view of the Mediterranean.

Ari was visibly upset when she opened the door, but it did nothing to dampen the emotion Marcelo felt as he looked at her. It was late, but Ari looked stunning in a long, grey cotton sundress with thin straps and a plunging neckline which did little to hide her ample cleavage.

"What is it?" Ari said, huffing and puffing at him as he stuttered and fumbled his way into the living room. The back of her dress was more lowcut than the front, dipping all the way to the small of her back. Marcelo noted that she wore no bra.

"I thought perhaps you'd like to see these tile samples," he said as he laid them on a nearby table. Marcelo rattled on about how beautiful the kitchen was going to be, but he could tell Ari was distracted.

"How much longer until I can stay in the house?" she asked.

Marcelo said the house would be going through a process to remove the mold in some of the rooms, and it would be best if she stayed away completely to avoid being sickened by the dust. "Aside from that, the roof needs to be redone. You would be uncomfortable there at night."

"It's just as well," she said. "I think I may have to visit someone in London to set the record straight."

After a few more minutes of one-sided conversation, Marcelo announced his departure. As he drove away, he received a call from Lorraine, who needed to speak with him as soon as he was back in town. When Marcelo pressed her for details, Lorraine said little, other than to indicate that it had something to do with Ari.

Curious and a bit alarmed, Marcelo put the pedal to the floorboard and hurried home.

***

That night, Ari wrestled with her sleep, tossing and turning until it was useless. It was then she made the decision to face Avinash in London.

They had not seen each other since he left for Dubai, and over the phone it was impossible for Ari to detect what was truly happening in his life. If he no longer loved her and truly wanted her out of his life, then Mr. Avinash Batra would have to tell her face-to-face.

***

The next morning, Ari called Marcelo from the airport. She'd been terribly dismissive of him the night before and wanted to make amends. When he didn't answer, she left a voicemail.

"Marcelo, buona sera, sono Ari. I'm at the airport on the way to London. I should return in a day or two. I'm sorry I was such bad company when you came by last night. I do love the tile you picked out for the backsplash. You have control of the house and the workers, and I trust you with my home. Please be careful with the mold and don't get sick, okay? Ciao."

Ari arrived at Heathrow at one forty-five in the afternoon and asked the taxi driver to take her straight to World Bank, no stops. She had not told anyone she was coming, not even Anjali or Sam. Ari wasn't sure what her approach would be or how she would react at the sight of Avinash, much less how he would react upon seeing her at the bank. All she knew was that she needed to see his eyes— they would speak the truth—and nothing would stop her.

When Ari walked into the reception area, Anjali dropped the stack of files she was holding. "Ari! What are you doing here?"

"That's funny," Ari said. "Everybody seems to be asking me that question today. Before, I was able to come in and out of this bank unnoticed, and now everyone wants to know why I'm here. Well, it's none of your business." With that, Ari opened the doors to Avinash's office and stepped inside.

Avinash was seated at the head of a massive mahogany conference table, surrounded by what Ari assumed were clients. She didn't care. Avinash got to his feet, a look of shock on his face, and asked the gentlemen to excuse him for a moment.

"Are you going to ask me why I'm here too?" Ari asked as the men scurried from the office and closed the door behind them.

"Ari, did you come here alone?" he asked as he returned to his desk and sat down, shuffling papers to avoid looking at her.

"Yes, I'm alone. I came to talk to you. I want to hear from you why you wanted to leave me." Her voice cracked and tears began flowing down her cheeks. "I need to look you in the face when you tell me you don't love me."

As Ari walked toward him, Avinash reached for his phone, punching at the buttons without looking in her direction. She stood between his legs and grabbed him by the shirt collar.

"Look at me and tell me you don't love me." When he looked away, Ari grabbed his face in both hands, but Avinash still managed to avert his eyes. Ari repeated the question over and over, but Avinash did not answer.

Suddenly, Ari heard the pounding of footsteps, and Sam rushed through the door with two security guards in tow. They made it halfway across the office before Avinash motioned for them to leave. Ari turned to Avinash in disbelief.

"You called Security on me? What have I done to you?" Ari was rapidly coming apart. She thought she could be strong, walk in and out and take the news in whatever shape it came, good or bad. But she never expected this cold detachment or that he'd have her escorted from the premises. As Ari stared into the eyes of the man she loved, she suddenly realized that he was a stranger. She knew nothing about him.

Before Avinash could say a word, she blurted out, "You know everything about me. I have told you everything, yet all I know about you is your name, your age, and that you were born in Mumbai. Aside from that, I have willingly given my life to a complete stranger. Who are you, Avinash Batra?"

Suddenly, a feeling of fear came over her and Ari stepped away from his desk, slowly backing toward the door as if he were a dangerous animal. Avinash tried to explain, but Ari wouldn't hear it. She ran toward the door, but Avinash was faster, one palm securing the door in place, the other hand on her arm as she reached for the doorknob.

"Stop, Ari. You don't understand anything. Damn it! I'm trying to protect you. It's not safe here."

Ari pried herself from his grasp. "Yes, I know it's not safe around you. You're a coward. It's your image you're trying to protect, not me!"

Avinash locked the door and pinned her arms to her sides. Ari struggled to break free of his grasp, but he was much too strong for her. He tried to reason with her, but she wouldn't hear it.

"Let me go! You know nothing about love. You don't know how to fight for someone you care about. You're a fake."

Avinash let her go, but she didn't run. Ari stood there crying, searching his eyes for the truth. Then Avinash took a step toward her and kissed her with savage desperation, as though the only thing keeping him alive was the passion and love he felt for her.

"Ari, I love you. I love you," he whispered. "I swear I would die for you."

Avinash took Ari by the hand and led her to the white couch, the one where she had received the bad news about her loan months before. He ravaged her with kisses, and she did not stop him. He kissed away every tear on her face and held her like a child. Ari knew he wanted to take her right then and there, but she was in no hurry to give in. He no longer seemed concerned about his business or his image or what his clients might think or say about the sudden disruption of their meeting. He was a determined, hungry man.

When Avinash started to undress her, Ari got to her feet. Still angry and defensive, she taunted him, undressing herself slowly, one piece of clothing at a time, watching as he eyed her slim, toned body. Ari stood naked in front of him, and he reached for her but she backed away. When Avinash approached her, she moved behind his desk and sat in his chair, her long legs and feet on the polished mahogany desktop.

"Ari, what are you doing?" he asked.

She said nothing, only smiled. She was in control. As Avinash stood next to her, he swung the chair around, and Ari placed both of her feet on his chest.

"Stop this. You're making me crazy," he whispered, holding tight to her ankles. Ari continued to smile and Avinash surrendered to her, kissing her feet and inner thighs as he made his way up her body. Suddenly, Ari shot up from the chair and pressed Avinash back onto the desk. She climbed atop him, took his rigid manhood in her hand, and pushed him inside her. Avinash made no attempt to stop her, grabbing her butt in both hands and lifting his hips to drive himself deeper. Ari was in charge and Avinash seemed to be enjoying every minute.

Ari had her way with him in his prestigious office, on his high-dollar mahogany desk, and it was heavenly. Being with him was all that mattered to Ari. What she knew or didn't know about him was inconsequential—this was the man she loved.

When they finished, Ari got down from the desk and Avinash stood up, his beautiful, naked body drenched in sweat. She made no effort to avert her eyes from him. He kissed her and disappeared into the washroom, returning a minute later with a warm washcloth and a dry towel. Ari watched as he delicately cleaned and dried every inch of her body. Then he gathered up her clothes, lovingly caressed her chin, kissed her on the lips, and asked her to dress.

When both of them were presentable, Avinash strode over to his desk, picked up the phone, and asked Anjali to send in the Security team.

***

Avinash turned his back to Ari as the team entered his office.

"Take Ms. Cordero to Heathrow, and do not let her out of your sight. Make sure she is on the next flight to Naples—and no mistakes this time."

Ari watched, wide-eyed, as Sam approached her. *How could I have been so stupid?* she thought as he took her by the arm. In shocked silence she allowed him to lead her from the office like a lamb heading to slaughter, willingly and without question. She did not turn to take a last look at Avinash. She never saw the tears rolling down his face.

They passed Anjali, who tried to offer words of comfort to no avail. Ari was too stunned to offer up a show of resistance.

They reached the elevator, and Ari stepped inside. As she turned around, she caught a final glimpse of Avinash, standing in the outer office doorway with a pained look on his face. She held his gaze until the elevator door slid shut between them.

On the way to Heathrow, Ari said nothing to Sam or the security team. There were no tears. When they arrived, Sam made the flight arrangements and escorted her to the TSA screening area. She offered no objections.

"I know you don't believe it, but Avinash loves you," Sam said, kissing Ari on the cheek. "And he is doing this for you."

Ari walked away from Sam without a goodbye. Every inch of her body longed to be back in Positano, in her house and with the people who cared for her.

Ari made it through the security screening without issue. As she exited TSA, a group of men dressed in black and looking like they meant business approached her.

"Ms. Ariadne Cordero?" a tall, serious-looking man said as they formed a barricade around her. Ari looked at them with a glazed expression, still uncertain what was going on. "I'm Victor St. John, Interpol. Will you accompany us, please?"

The men took her to a stuffy room with no windows. It was like a scene from a Jason Bourne movie. There were four men in the room. Two were from Scotland Yard, and one man was an agent from Italy, Mr. Gianni Baromeo, who she recognized, having seen him in Positano recently.

The Interpol agent, Detective St. John, informed Ari that she was there because she was being warned and needed protection from a wanted killer they had been tracking for quite some time. *Protection.* A word she had heard plenty of times in the past weeks but still had no meaning for her.

Ari finally spoke. "Who or what, may I ask, are you protecting me from?"

The agent offered Ari a seat at the table. "What does the name John Ronit mean to you?" he asked once she was settled.

Ari looked up, her green eyes intense and cold. "That name means nothing to me."

For the next twenty minutes, St. John fired questions at her, and Ari was not able to answer. His voice became a decibel louder, and Ari shrank into the chair. She was relieved when the agent from Italy suggested they take a break. When he returned to the room a few minutes later, he handed her a cup of coffee and a photograph.

"Tell me, Miss Cordero, do you know this man?" he asked.

To her surprise, it was a photo of Kash. *All of this is about Akash? This is what Avinash is trying to protect me from?* Ari looked up at Agent Baromeo.

"This man is Akash Ramkissoon. At least that is the name he used when I met him in Los Angeles at the airport."

She did not stop talking until she had spewed everything she knew up to present moment, even showing the agent the missed calls and messages on her mobile phone.

"Check them all," she said to Agent Baromeo. "Everything he has contacted me about in the last months is all there. I have not talked to him, nor have I seen him since the day after I arrived in London."

But there was much more to come. She learned Ronit—Kash, as she knew him—had led a seemingly busy life of crime that included dealing illegal arms and drugs around the world.

***

The questioning lasted hours as Interpol, Scotland Yard, and other unknown security personnel pulled out files, pictures, and other paraphernalia on Ari's life. They suspected her because she moved around frequently; they suspected her because she'd been married to Santos. And Ari, who was growing tired of the cross-fire interrogation, could not give them the information they needed. What came out next was a piece of information Ari could never have suspected. Agent St. John reached into a file and pulled out a report filed by someone Ari knew all too well. It was a detailed description of Akash's underworld dealings.

The report further alluded to a partnership with two other men who Ari knew were associated with Santos and the Vida Blue tequila business. As she read, her hands trembled and she couldn't concentrate. The words jumbled, and it was too much to take in.

"What is this?" she asked, astounded.

St. John took the report from her hand and let Ari know that Santos Echequi had found out about John Ronit, as Akash was known to him, and his underworld by accident and did the right thing—he reported Akash to Interpol. Mr.

Echegui, unbeknownst to Ari, became an agent for Interpol to help bring in Ronit. Santos Echequi had been on a mission when he died in a car accident.

"Ms. Cordero, it was no accident. Your husband was murdered. The crime team found the tracks of another vehicle nearby. It was raining heavily on that day. The mud tracks leading to the accident showed someone tampered with the car's brakes to make it look like an accident. Mr. Echequi had reported to us that he'd found evidence and was on his way to meet us with it. No evidence was found in the wreckage."

Ari was horrified and stood up, visibly shaken by the news.

"Why wasn't I informed of this when it happened? Why have I been led to believe that he had an accident when my husband was murdered by a maniac on the loose while he was trying to help you?"

Agent Baromeo tried to calm her, but there was little he could do. "Please sit down, Ms. Cordero. While I realize this news is distressing, we really need your help."

"Help? My husband died helping you find this character. Why should I help you?"

"Listen, Ms. Cordero, there is no other choice but for you to help us. This man is a danger to you, and you will be next if you don't assist us."

Ari returned to her chair, a cloud of despair settling over her. "Okay. What do you need from me?"

Baromeo's line of questioning shifted to Avinash and what she knew of him. Ari simply said they had been together a short time and, as far as his business dealings, he was highly successful and honorable. St. John asked about their personal relationship and why she was now living in Positano while Batra still resided in London.

"Could you have, by accident, helped Ronit in some way and this caused a problem between you?"

"If Mr. Batra and I have decided to part ways, it's because it was the best for both of us. It certainly has nothing to do with Akash. I'm sure all of that information is in your neat, concise file."

Agent Baromeo sat on the table next to her as the agencies and their representatives argued among themselves in the back of the room.

"Ms. Cordero, do you want to go home?" he whispered.

Ari nodded.

"Then follow my lead."

"Gentlemen," Baromeo said as if they were in a courtroom and he was the lead attorney. "I don't think Ms. Cordero should remain here for further questioning. I think the best plan of action is that we continue our surveillance in Positano, station one of our men undercover in her home, and wait for Ronit to make contact."

As the men went back and forth, Ari stood up and the room was silenced. She'd clearly had enough.

"Gentlemen, I'm not going to have you disturb my life any further. If you want to observe me you may, but at a distance. I moved to Positano to bury my husband and have peace. You will not disturb me unless you have a warrant for my arrest. Thanks to you, I have missed my flight and now have to spend another night in London where, according to you, my life is in danger. If I need someone in Positano to watch over me then it will be with someone I trust."

Baromeo asked if that someone might be Mr. Donati. "He's no first-class citizen. For years Donati couldn't even set foot in Naples. He is the man you trust?"

Ari walked over to Baromeo and stared him down. "Yes, for now he is the only man I can trust. Mr. Donati has lived in Sorrento for many years. If someone wanted to finish him off, they would have had plenty of opportunities. He's paid for his mistakes, Agent Baromeo. Now, if you don't mind, I'm tired and I need a place to stay tonight. Any suggestions?"

Agent Baromeo offered to take Ari to a hotel nearby and escort her back to Heathrow the next morning. She agreed, but before they could leave, St. John had one more question.

"Why did you come back today, Ms. Cordero? In and out of Heathrow so fast? What did you and Batra talk about?"

Everyone in the room waited for her response. Ari looked away and swallowed hard.

"My house. We talked about my house."

"A simple phone call would not suffice?" St. John asked.

Ari knew she was caught but just went with the first thing she could think of.

"I needed Mr.Echegui off my home deed to proceed. It had to be done in person."

Ari left with Baromeo but not before Detective St. John warned her again that Ronit was a dangerous man. "He has killed many times before, Ms. Cordero. Your husband was one of his victims; trust me when I say he won't think twice about dispatching you."

***

184

As Baromeo drove, Ari stared at him with a smirk. Agent Gianni Baromeo was an extremely good-looking forty-two-year-old Italian from Rome with brown, wavy hair and light blue eyes. He was fit and walked like an emperor, despite his five-foot-seven frame. Interpol did not allow him much time for anything other than work, and his past relationships had been minor flings here and there.

He caught her eye and asked Ari what she was smiling about. "I know how to drive, you know," he said with a chuckle.

"It's not that," Ari said. "I just remembered where I saw you in Positano. You were one of the waiters at the after-party dinner for the music festival. That was a good cover. You must have heard all of us talking about men and other juicy topics. I remember you keeping my glass full of prosecco that evening. It must have been a very interesting night for you, Agent Baromeo."

He finally smiled, and Ari noticed he had the most amazing dimples.

"As I remember it, Ms. Cordero, Mr. Donati had a much better night than I did."

Ari felt her cheeks redden as she remembered Anjali telling her about the drunken kiss she'd given Marcelo that evening. Too embarrassed to reply, she stared out the window. They rode the rest of the way in silence.

***

Too much had happened for Ari to take it all in. In a matter of weeks, she had learned her husband had been murdered, presumably by Akash—John whatever his name was. Her belongings were in crates somewhere in Naples, and she was a resident, albeit a renting resident, of Positano. And to add insult to injury, she and Avinash were over. Learning that Santos had been working with Interpol when he was killed brought shivers to her spine.

Now she was faced with the grim reality that there was an actual plot by Kash to have her kidnapped or killed. This only proved that she was now a guinea pig for Interpol and Scotland Yard and live bait for the illusive Ronit.

After a sleepless night, Ari had a quick breakfast and was ready when Agent Baromeo picked her up the next morning. Much to her surprise, he was flying back to Italy with her on Scotland Yard's orders. On the flight, Agent Baromeo explained that he would be nearby, keeping watch along with Donati.

"He's not experienced in these things, Ms. Cordero. You will need someone of my background, not only to watch over you at home but to make sure things are safe for you in town. Perhaps you can ask Mr. Donati to hire me as one of the workers. That way, you get a bodyguard and another helping hand for your house repairs."

Ari agreed, on the condition that Mr. Donati was made aware of his presence and the danger she was in.

"That's fair enough," Baromeo said.

They settled in for the flight and before long, Ari was fast asleep.

They arrived late that evening at her flat just up the road from 87 Viale Pasitea. Ari showed Gianni to the upstairs bedroom that Anjali had occupied when she first arrived in Positano. It had a terrace from which Baromeo could easily see anyone coming down from the main strada into town. Ari was physically and mentally exhausted, but spiritually weary more than anything else. She attempted to call

Marcelo, but he didn't answer. She carried her bags to her room and considered taking a bath, but before she could run the water, the doorbell rang.

Before she could reach the door, Agent Baromeo was down the stairs with his hand at his hip, his weapon at the ready.

"Put that away," she said. "It's only Marcelo. He usually comes over at this time of day to update me about the house."

Ari let Marcelo in and immediately jumped to introductions.

"Let me introduce you to Mr. Gianni Baromeo. He's from Rome, and he will be staying in town. He's looking for a job. Perhaps you might consider him to help with the house?" Ari asked.

"Ciao, Mr. Donati. Nice to meet you," Baromeo said.

Ari watched as Marcelo's eyes flared. This wasn't going to go well, but she didn't have the strength to intervene.

***

Marcelo did not believe the man standing before him was looking for a job. His Salvador Ferragamo boots said otherwise. Aside from that, he may have ended up in Rome but his accent was clearly from the north of Italy, perhaps Bologna or thereabouts. Marcelo asked Ari to join him outside.

"What is going on, Ari? Who is this man you've brought back with you?"

Marcelo listened as Ari struggled to explain what was going on. "I'm so tired, Marcelo. And now they say my life is in danger. Scotland Yard has sent Agent Baromeo to protect me while they attempt to catch Akash."

Marcelo nodded, trying his best to understand the situation. He asked a few questions, and Ari did her best to fill in the gaps.

"Marcelo, I can't talk anymore," she said, motioning to her throat.

"What is wrong?" Marcelo asked. "Can I get you a drink?"

Then he watched as Ari simply broke down, as if a tidal wave had just sideswiped her and lifted her off her feet. Marcelo held her as she cried, not quite understanding why she was so distraught. At that moment he made a decision to get rid of the agent as soon as possible. He placed Ari in the terrace garden and it was starting to get cold that night; he quickly turned on the gas fireplace just next to her.

"Stay here," Marcelo said, leading Ari to a chair in the terrace garden and turning on the gas fireplace nearby. I come back."

***

Ari curled up on the big chair and continued her descent into a world of darkness. Everything had hit her at once. Perhaps she had repressed Santos's death and the dream of living in Positano for too long, but the news of his murder was more than she could accept at the moment. Ari couldn't remember how long she'd slept outside, but when Marcelo finally returned, she was unable to respond to his questions. He lifted her in his arms and carried her to the bedroom.

***

For the next two days, Ari slept and only drank water when Marcelo made her. She succumbed to a world of depression that consumed her. The ever-happy, optimistic Ariadne

Cordero had fallen into a precipice and was unable to climb out. On the third day Marcelo, still unable to communicate with her, brought down all her belongings from Naples as Lorraine watched over her.

The work continued at 87 Viale Pasitea. The mold was removed from the home and the walls were treated, but only the main bedroom on the second floor could be occupied without a risk to Ari's health. Marcelo arrived at the flat with a doctor who was a friend from the city of Ravello, and he examined her.

Ari seemed almost in a state of shell shock and needed intense medical attention at a specialized hospital. The doctor informed Marcelo that the best one was in Rome. There was a worry that everyone in town knew Ari, and news of her hospitalization would become gossip. Lorraine asked the doctor to prescribe the needed medication. They would make arrangements between herself, Marcelo, and Daniela, the wife of a Music Festival Committee member, to take turns caring for Ari. Lorraine explained to the doctor that Ari would come out of her depression only if surrounded by people who truly loved her, certainly not in a cold, strange psychiatric hospital. The doctor agreed and prescribed the needed medication. He administered an IV that needed to be changed every ten hours since Ari was not eating willingly.

After the doctor left, Marcelo and Lorraine sat on the terrace, dreadfully unsure about Ari's mental state.

"Do you think it would be a good idea to call Avinash?" Lorraine asked.

Marcelo lit a cigarette and took a few deep drags before replying. "I feel that would be pointless. Perhaps it would be best to call Anjali. It would be good if she was informed."

They talked awhile longer and set a plan in motion for the next weeks. Daniela would administer the IV in the mornings and give Ari her medication, while "Boom Boom" Claudia stayed with her. Marcelo would arrive for lunch around two in the afternoon and stay until it was time for him to head back to 87 Viale Pasitea to supervise the construction. Lorraine would be with Ari until Marcelo returned in the evening to stay with her until the next morning.

Ari still wouldn't speak or acknowledge anyone's presence. Her days were spent either in bed or sitting in a chair on the terrace getting some much-needed sun while she stared at the ocean. The team tried to make her life as easy as possible. Perhaps Ari noticed their tender care, but no one knew for certain. Marcelo was patient and sweet with Ari, even feeding her as if she was a feeble bird, placing morsels of food in her mouth which she nibbled and chewed endlessly. At some point, he decided to treat her as he would if she were in a perfect mental state. He told Ari stories about the war in Italy—big, elaborate tales of his youth. Then Marcelo read her books and love poems in Italian, hoping she'd find his deep, raspy voice soothing.

Several weeks later, Ari began to improve, smiling as Marcelo and Lorraine recounted a story from the crazy seventies. Marcelo was finally able to make Ari eat, so the IV was removed and Daniela was no longer needed in the mornings.

Finally, arrangements were made to move Ari into her home. The repairs were not making much progress because of Marcelo's absence, but it was at least livable. Marcelo knew that placing Ari in that house would help with her recovery.

The physician was called back to reevaluate Ari. He reported that she had gained a few kilos since he last examined her, and she was much more responsive than before. Ari was definitely on the mend.

***

Life continued on Viale Pasitea. Agent Baromeo had received feedback from his superiors that Ronit originally had placed a hit not only on Ari but also Avinash the night of the supposed kidnapping. The two motorbike hit men who botched the assignment were found dead and floating in the Thames. All the underground chatter pointed to an Indian man who had arrived in London just months before. The kidnapping had turned to a murder plot, and now Ari and Avinash were at the center of the investigation.

Agent Baromeo explained to St. John that Ari was in no condition to take care of herself, as she had fallen into a deep depression that had her bedbound for weeks. At this point, Baromeo asked that the focus should be on Avinash Batra. He would continue to monitor Ms. Cordero and report back when she was feeling better.

***

One late rainy evening, as Marcelo read to her, Ari asked him if he believed in love. Marcelo hadn't heard Ari utter more than one word for the last three months and was amazed at the clarity of her question.

"Why do you ask me? I am no expert," Marcelo said. "Does anybody really know the answer to that question?"

Ari looked at him, eyes dull and her face pale and sullen as one tear trickled from her eye. She pointed at a book and Marcelo reached for it, placing it in her hands. The book, a translated version of *Rumi, Fountain of Fire* by Nader Khalili managed to touch Ari and her feelings, she explained. "Humans are born with unlimited freedom and infinite bliss if they choose to have it. In order to reach it, we must surrender to love. I gave love and need it to survive. Do you believe in love, Marcelo?"

Ari looked up from the book to see Marcelo in tears. He knew how much she had suffered, but now Marcelo was feeling guilty for even entertaining the thought of destroying her.

This brought a new realization to him about his past with Lucia and what he was willing to do to Ari for love. He remained quiet.

"I still believe in love, Marcelo. Love saved me from death itself, from wanting to die every day. Because of love, I live."

***

After three months in the gallows of depression, the sun slowly started to shine in Ari's vibrant green eyes. The cure? A group of people who cared for her, but especially Marcelo who was now more concerned with Ari's recuperation than he was on snatching the house from her.

During the time Marcelo cared for Ari, he realized he probably would have cared for Lucia the same way if she would have survived the fall that took her life. Ari's well-being and delicate life were in his hands, and all he could do was nurture her with love, kindness, and understanding. Strangely, Marcelo still hoped that Ari would return to him and that the closeness that had developed in the silence of her illness would grow into a friendship built on trust. Her illness gave him someone to talk to, though in her semi-catatonic state he often wondered what Ari could hear or understand.

Most people judged Marcelo without knowing the truth behind Lucia's death. At least Ari listened intently and at times nodded in agreement, symbolizing to Marcelo that she understood somehow. Ari became his salvation, a cleansing of his soul and an honest attempt at redeeming himself from the abyss his life had been in during the last years. They were together in some strange life story, precisely at the moment they needed each other. Finishing the house for Ari would be good for her, he thought, and he set out to make a masterpiece of the home on 87 Viale Pasitea. This time, however, not for Lucia or himself but for someone who truly needed a home to love and protect her . . . his dear Ari.

***

One early morning, Ari awoke and walked to the outside terrace in nothing more than her long nightgown. She stood there shivering and gazed out into the ocean. It called to her, and she asked God to take her; the pain was more than she could bear. Ari headed toward the water, slipping back into that dark place, the one that did not allow her to cry, void of feelings except for profound emptiness, back to a life that was meaningless. All of a sudden, she felt a strong force envelope her and forcefully grab her from behind. The energy pulled so hard that it made Ari lose her balance and fall to the cold, wet ground. When she turned there was no one there. The terrace door that she had closed behind her now stood wide open in the distance. *What was that? Who was here?* Ari, cold and scared, got to her feet and ran toward the house. She searched the place from room to room, peering into every nook and cranny, but there was no one in the house, not a soul. Sobbing, she prayed to God to forgive her for even thinking of ending her life.

When Marcelo arrived later that morning from a trip to Naples, he saw Ari curled up on the sofa, her eyes closed and her hands folded in prayer.

"Ari? Are you okay?" he asked.

Ari looked up at Marcelo and smiled. Her eyes were clear, and the darkness that hung over her for so long seemed to have dissipated. She walked straight and strong over to Marcelo and hugged him with all her might. Marcelo held her, trying to understand if something scared her or she was just relieved that he had returned.

Pulling away from Ari, he looked closely into her eyes for answers. "I hope you are feeling better today," he said.

Ari took him by the hand and led him to the kitchen, opening the cabinet where all her daily medications were stored. She took each bottle, one by one, throwing them into the trash bin as Marcelo watched in stunned silence.

"Ask me again if I want to live, Marcelo."

Marcelo looked down. He didn't realize that in all these months of care, Ari actually heard him ask her that very same question during those times when she was seemingly in an unconscious state from the heavy dose of medication. Marcelo played along with her request.

"Tell me, do you want to live, Ariadne?"

Ari smiled and said, "Someone told me today that I must live, that the road does not end for me now."

"Who told you this, Ari?"

She stood in front of him, stronger than she had been in many months. "Santos, told me this. Do you believe me?"

Marcelo walked over to the panoramic window that was still without its glass panes. It was covered with dark-blue plastic wrap that popped and crackled in the wind. He leaned against the half-sanded wooden cabinets and took out a cigarette, placed it in his mouth, but did not light it. Then he looked at Ari and answered.

"Yes, I believe you."

CHAPTER TEN

The summers in London can be pleasant, but this particular year it was miserable, and most people who could afford it headed to the beach or somewhere in the mountains. The only people crazy enough to be in London this time of year were tourists who didn't know better or Londoners who could not afford to travel.

Anjali decided to escape the heat by visiting Ari in Positano. Lorraine had explained her devastating plight over the spring months, how Ari suffered and was still too weak physically and emotionally to leave the house. Lorraine let Anjali know that if not for Marcelo, Ari would have given up long ago. She also mentioned her hope that Avinash would hear about Ari's difficulties and would learn how invaluable Marcelo had been in her recovery. It seemed to Anjali that Lorraine was eager to make Avinash squirm.

During this time, Anjali had grown distant from Avinash, watching him slowly self-destruct. He had taken up smoking, something he had kicked in his youth, and was now a shadow of his former self. Still, he played the part of the composed businessman in most of the meetings he attended. Avinash was thinner and had lost most of his body mass. He ate poorly and drank too much. Anjali did not tell him about Ari's illness. She did not want to give him the satisfaction of knowing that he had destroyed her, just as she had predicted. Neither did she tell him that her digging deeper into Santos's tequila business showed signs of some shady partners.

Anjali was almost sure that Vida Blue Tequila was a good cover for something. Just what that something was, she didn't know, and it was keeping Anjali up at night. *Who were these guys, and why did they disappear when Santos was convicted if they were clean?* There was more there than what the press was sharing. Sure, there was a successful tequila business, but something lurked in the shadows. If Santos somehow found out and was getting ready to expose them, perhaps his death was a consequence of these findings.

Scotland Yard and Interpol were now daily fixtures at World Bank, but Anjali did her sleuthing on the side, unbeknownst to the official investigative agencies. Finally weary of it all, she asked permission to visit Ari in Positano. After all, having a chance to visit her was more important than any demons Avinash was fighting.

***

The case against John Ronit started growing tentacles. The more the investigation probed into his life, the more it became clear that his capture was of utmost importance. Ronit managed to skirt around every trap they placed for him. He was always ahead of the game and for now, there was no evidence that Avinash or Ari were in any danger.

Nonetheless, Avinash played the London scene with a low profile and had little if anything to do with life outside of business. Sam decided he wanted to accompany Anjali, but he was afraid to leave Avinash alone, and so it was decided that it was best for Sam to stay and for Anjali to visit Ari. She was going to convince Ari to come back for Diwali in October, hoping that by then Akash would be in prison where he belonged and Avinash and she could work things out. Anjali had created a rapport with Agents Baromeo and St. John, who were investigating a new lead on suspicious funds that had been transferred from a bank in Prague to one in London—he was hoping John Ronit would be the recipient by tracking the money trail using the resources at World Bank.

As Avinash sat preparing for a speech at an organization meeting for one of his children's charities, he happened to skim over information on one of the largest donors, an Indian woman who was photographed at a similar event in Mumbai and looked extremely familiar. Avinash called Sam to the office and he came at once. He gave Sam the photograph and asked him to look closely at the woman in the photo.

"Yes, she looks familiar but her name is not."

"Exactly what I thought," Avinash responded.

He called Anjali into the office and asked the same question. Anjali remembered her too, but again, just as with Avinash and Sam, could not remember how she knew her.

"She's one of the charity's largest supporters, yet she has never been outside of India and is now coming to this meeting? Why now?" Avinash asked.

Before they could dig any deeper into the mystery woman's identity, Anjali switched gears and went straight for the jugular. "I'd help you figure this all out, but I'm going to visit Ari in Positano for a week. Her home is coming along nicely, and it's time for my holiday. It's been way too long. Oh . . . and I'm leaving this Friday," she added as she turned and left his office.

"Anjali, wait." Avinash called her back in. "How's Ari?"

"I'm going to find out, Avinash. We haven't spoken in three months," Anjali replied unsympathetically as she hurried out.

Avinash looked at Sam and sighed. "She hates me since the incident with Ari in my office. I can't say that I blame her. I was cruel." He swung his chair around to look at the beautiful view of London and the Thames below.

"I can't stop thinking about her, Sam. I just can't get her out of my mind."

"I understand. Do you want me to find out about the woman, Ms. Singh?" Sam asked, quickly changing the subject.

Avinash turned his chair back around to face Sam. "Yes, I need to know who she is. That's all, Sam. Thank you."

***

Ari was still weak and was now also anemic. Though her weight was back to normal, the aftermath of weeks without solid food, exercise, and regular activity had taken a toll on her. Doctors said it was a slow progression to get healthy again, but her iron and hemoglobin levels were alarmingly low. She needed to get back to normal activity and begin slowly eating healthier.

It was exceptionally hot in Positano, and this too was not helping her to recuperate, forcing her to remain locked inside her room and unable to take in the cool breeze off the Mediterranean that she loved so much. It was customary that on Thursday's the Dolce Vita Club, as Lorraine dubbed them, came over to play Scopa, an Italian card game. The game was unfamiliar to Ari, but she enjoyed watching Lorraine, Claudia, Angela, Daniela, and Paulette gang up on Marcelo and curse each other in multiple languages. When she was feeling a little more energetic, she made them paninis but she never ate them.

Most of the time, Ari would just lie in her reading room, snuggled in a large, round chaise lounger under bougainvilleas that cascaded from a trellis in the ceiling. It was Ari's favorite room. As she slept, her mobile rang. She tried to check the numbers but the glare from the sun bouncing off the ceramic tile of the terrace did not allow a clear view. Ari answered.

"*Si?*" There was silence. "*Si?* Hello?" Then she heard his voice.

"Ari, have you missed me? I certainly miss you, love. Enjoying Positano? Do you think you will be safe there?"

Ari took the phone off her ear in a panic and dropped it. She tried to get up from the chaise but got tangled and fell to the floor. Marcelo came running and asked what happened. She looked up at him in a panic and said, "Akash!"

As she fainted in his arms, the other women came running.

"Who is Akash?" Marcelo desperately asked the women. None of them knew except for Lorraine, who had the same horrified look on her face.

"It's John Ronit," she said.

Agent Baromeo arrived within minutes and tried to speak to Ari, who was locked in her room with Lorraine.

"This could not have come at a worse time. *Il cazo!*" Marcelo said angrily.

Agent Baromeo understood the complexity of Ari's health but also had a job to do. Catching John Ronit was the only thing he was concerned with at the time.

"We need for him to call again. We need to trace that call, Marcelo."

"How much does she have to take, Gianni?" Marcelo asked.

In the bedroom, Ari alternated between nervously staring out her window and pacing in a panic as Lorraine tried to calm her down.

"It was him. It was him! He found me! What if he's already hurt Avinash and now he's after me? I have to know if Avinash is okay. I have to call him."

Lorraine finally calmed her down enough to pry the phone from her hand and give her a high dose of medication.

"It's okay, Ari dear. Let's just give the phone to Gianni so he can trace it if he calls again. I promise Baromeo won't leave the house."

Lorraine led Ari to the bed and helped her get settled beneath her favorite blanket. In minutes, Ari was fast asleep.

***

Victor St. John was meeting with Avinash about Ronit's money transfers when Agent Baromeo called to report the incident in Positano.

"Thank you for the update, Baromeo. I want you to stay put. Don't move from Ms. Cordero's until further notice." Before he could return the phone to his pocket, Avinash fired questions at him.

"He's at Ari's? Why? What's going on?"

St. John filled Avinash in without going into great detail, explaining that Ari had received an unexpected call from Ronit and that it had upset her, especially given the delicate condition of her health.

"Her health? What do you mean? Is she ill?" Avinash asked, concern on his face and in his voice.

"I'm sorry, sir. I thought you knew. Ms. Cordero had a nervous breakdown some months ago and has been under a doctor's care while she recuperates at home."

Avinash pushed the agent for more information, but he either didn't know anything else or was hesitant to share it.

A flood of thoughts filled his head as St. John tried to continue but Avinash was not listening. He rushed out of the office looking for Anjali, but she had already left for the day. Completely distraught and anxious beyond belief, blaming himself for her illness, Avinash stayed in the office, drinking and remembering his days with Ari.

His first impulse was to call her, but now her calls were being traced. Avinash decided to email Ari, but as he sat to write, no words came forth. The eloquent and versed man was not able to express his love or his pain. The frustration made him call Sam, who had not yet left the office, and they spoke openly. Sam reported to Avinash the turn of events that Ari had taken after they last saw each other. He also told Avinash that the original owner of the house had been taking care of her along with Ari's friend Lorraine.

"These people have brought her back," Sam said, "and she is improving but slowly. Thank God she made friends in Positano. She's not alone, but I imagine she—like you—needs strength and positive reinforcement. You're not in the best state of mind, Avinash. That's why you should not attempt to call or write to her. You need to shake whatever it is you're going through and, for God's sake, get your shit back together!"

He picked up the half-empty bottle of whiskey and shoved it in Avinash's face.

"And this cannot continue," Sam admonished. "The only person who can save Ari is you. Not Interpol or Scotland Yard or anyone else. Only you can protect her, and you must do it to right the wrongs that Akash committed years ago. You are the only one Ari needs right now, old chap, but in the state you're in, I'm afraid you won't be able to help anyone, including yourself."

Sam had never spoken to Avinash in this tone, but he quietly took his counsel and accepted the error he had made in his attempts to protect Ari. He realized what he had done was called abandonment, especially when she needed him most. He felt a sense of failure on his part and knew he could not continue on this path of destruction.

Avinash called in his personal trainer and a physician to help him back to his healthy self. He apologized to Anjali for his treatment of Ari and for failing to listen to her. It was the worst thing he had ever done to the two women he cared most about, and he was truly ashamed. Anjali cried with Avinash as he explained himself. She couldn't help but forgive her friend, her boss and mentor. Though she wanted to help him get back on his feet, she needed to see Ari first. Avinash agreed that it was a good idea and instructed St. John himself to take her to Positano.

***

Agent Baromeo moved into the study of the home at 87 Viale Pasitea and made his base there. His setup of elaborate tracking devices and computers required poor Marcelo to amp up the electrical wattage just to keep the rest of the transformers in the house from popping.

"Who is going to pay for this additional electrical cost?" he asked, joining Ari in the kitchen. "It is not part of my proposal."

Ari, now unable to finish the dinner she'd been preparing because of the electrical issues, was just happy that Baromeo was moving in. Having him there gave her a sense of security, not only for herself but for Marcelo and the ladies who visited the house almost daily.

"Sorry, Marcelo. Dinner is ruined. Maybe we should eat out today?"

It was the first time in months that Ari had asked to leave the house and Marcelo was thrilled.

"Yes, yes! Grand idea! I know just the place, a quiet trattoria in Priano, Salerno, near the beach. *Meraviglioso!*"

Ari smiled as she watched Marcelo make the preparations that now needed to include Baromeo, someone Marcelo was not too thrilled with at the present time. As Marcelo was getting ready to call the rest of the group, Baromeo asked him to do it on a secure line or not call at all.

"We can't take any chances now," he admonished. Marcelo agreed and made the call from a secure line.

That evening in Praiano, the group spent a memorable night eating, drinking, and enjoying some young, hip foreign musicians who had shown up unannounced but who completed the perfect dining experience. Ari still did not eat much, but she tried a spoonful of each of the dishes that Marcelo and Agent Baromeo ordered. Claudia, the Brazilian bombshell, danced with Marcelo as the others watched him try to teach her to tango. Ari said it looked more like they were "tangled," and the others laughed with her. Her humor was slowly returning, and Lorraine was pleased that she could enjoy herself without panicking.

Marcelo ushered Ari onto the dance floor, and she playfully refused before finally joining him in a slow dance as the sun set over the ocean. Ari embraced Marcelo and whispered in his ear.

"*Grazie*, Marcelo. *Si è salvato la mia vita*. What would I do without you, my friend?"

Ari lightly kissed him on both cheeks, and the two friends danced to "Parlami d'amore Mariu," one of Ari's favorite Italian songs.

"Even after everything you go through, you are still so beautiful," Marcelo told her.

"The most beautiful things come from wreckage." Ari knew Marcelo would not understand what she said, so she entertained him with a twirl and laughed.

The group and the rest of the diners watched them dance. Soon, they all joined in, the ladies taking turns with

Baromeo and Marcelo. At the dinner table, Marcelo pulled out a small pouch from his pocket and placed it in Ari's hands. Inside was a dainty necklace made of gold with a sun on one side and an inscription on the other.

Marcelo leaned in and whispered, "Wear this when you need to feel stronger."

The end of the magical day was a symbol that they were both out of the darkness that had enveloped them, for Marcelo more so than Ari. In a couple of months, he was almost the man he'd once been, thanks to her.

***

In London, as Avinash was taking a run in the gym of his flat, Sam arrived with some news on Ms. Mahima Singh and had previously called St. John to fill him in. It would seem that the Ronit crime network was now taking on better form. According to sources in India, Ms. Singh was not the woman's real name. She had changed it years before when her son disgraced the family name and she disowned him, preventing him from acquiring the family empire. The gossip indicated she allegedly had not seen or spoken to him in years. Avinash finally spoke as he stared at her photo.

"This is Akash's mother. I saw her once when she came to his deportation hearing, but of course back then her name was Reeva. Her brother was my mentor, Mr. Harvash Dutta."

St. John was on the story like it was the last drop of water in the desert. He understood that Ms. Singh was probably here with the ruse of attending the charity event, but hopefully she wanted to reach out to her son, Ronit. Together in Avinash's office, they hatched a plan to set up a meeting between Avinash and Ms. Singh. The sting included a complete backup unit ready to pounce on Ronit if he showed up. Avinash did not see the danger in the sting or to his life. He simply agreed and went along with the plan.

The surveillance team agreed that the only way Avinash would get a meeting with Mrs. Singh would be for him to go undercover. Sam would set up the meeting with her charity board, claiming a prominent, wealthy businessman wanted to make a sizeable donation before the charity event and would only deliver it personally to Ms. Singh.

Later that day and after several hours of planning at Avinash's flat, he headed toward the kitchen for a drink of water and Sam later followed.

"Anything wrong, boss?" Sam asked.

Avinash, pensive and without quite knowing what his gut was telling him, said, "This is all too perfect. Why would Reeva come to London knowing that World Bank is a sponsor and that I would show up representing it? Moreover, why take the risk that I may recognize her? Don't you think this is all wrapped up in a sweet little package and placed at my feet?"

Sam had to agree, but getting a meeting between the two would help the investigative agencies get closer to Ronit. What other alternative did Avinash have?

"Are you going to tell St. John what you think?" Sam asked.

"No, it doesn't matter to them one way or the other. I'm the bait, and this trap is needed. You can be sure I won't attend that meeting with just a wire. I will be prepared."

Avinash would not flinch if Ronit showed up, and this time he would not fail to put him away forever, even if it meant going back to jail or heading underground.

***

The plan was set in motion. Sam would make the appointment with Ms. Singh, and Avinash would attend in representation of a bogus organization. They took all the necessary precautions and incorporated a business, renting a storefront for the offices and staffing it with personnel to appear legitimate. The corporation, called Anguila Group, would handle stocks and high-end investments. At the head of the organization, Avinash used the moniker Robert Scorpio, a name he took from a soap opera, *General Hospital*, an American show he was now ashamed to say he watched for years when he was learning to speak English in Mumbai.

It took several days for the charity committee of Ms. Singh's group to confirm the appointment, but the call came in to Anguila Group and Mr. Scorpio's assistant confirmed it. It would be on Friday, the day before the charity event, at three in the afternoon. The team would be assembled just outside in unmarked vehicles and on nearby rooftops. A sniper was called in just in case Ronit showed and attempted to escape. The plan was to take Ronit alive. The mousetrap was set.

***

As Ari continued to improve, she felt like it was time to venture further out of the Amalfi region. Marcelo had talked about the Larix or Larch, a wood in northern Italy that had been brought in by Eastern Europeans many years ago. This would be the most appropriate wood for the repair of the roof.

In Italy, Marcelo explained, it grows at high altitudes around mountaintops. Its timber can withstand sudden climatic changes, from icy winds to high temperatures on sunny summer afternoon. It is excellent for use in the building of exposed structures such as bridges or roofs. The best place to find it was near the Fusine lakes near the Italian Alps on the border with Slovenia. The route north would be by train to just outside Venice and then a hired car using Cortina d'Ampezzo as the base. Marcelo had a friend with a small villa that he could use to scout out the best sellers of the wood. Ari was eager to go with Marcelo, but aside from Avinash and Santos, she had not taken a trip with any other man.

There was also the issue of Santos's last wishes; he wanted his ashes spread in the Mediterranean on a clear summer day. Ari was feeling much stronger now, and she thought Santos had spent too many years bottled up in that beautiful vase. On a clear Sunday morning she called Marcelo up to her bedroom to explain. Ari had already told Marcelo that Santos had passed away, but she had not told him that Interpol had alluded that he might have been murdered by someone in Akash's entourage, if not by Akash himself. Marcelo was aghast at the news. Ari also explained that Santos's ashes were in a vase, and it was time to give him a proper send-off. After she finished, she asked Marcelo for his help getting the solemn job done. He had, after all, been her rock all these months.

Marcelo walked over to the open double doors of Ari's bedroom. Looking out into the expanse of the beautiful sea he turned to her. "I wish I could be next to Lucia when I die. She's buried in Tuscany, a town called Porcari near Lucca."

Ari was deeply touched. "You can have your wish, Marcelo. I will take you there if you die before me. I promise. But for right now, you're here with me, and you're very much alive. I need you to help me with Santos. Please say you will." Ari knew Marcelo could not refuse her. They hugged each other to seal the promise they had made, and Marcelo set out to find a boat that would accommodate them.

At about two in the afternoon, Ari had enough with Agent Baromeo and his delusion that her plan was dangerous without his presence. Marcelo was ready. The vessel and the skipper had been hired to take them out that same day.

"Listen, Gianni," Ari reasoned. "I have to do this alone. You can watch me from any rooftop in this town. Or rent a dingy and follow us around if you want to. Frankly, I don't care. But you are not coming with Marcelo and me, *capito?*"

"I will be on a boat nearby, and I will not interrupt your plans. But if I see anything suspicious . . . ." Before Ari could thank him, Baromeo stormed out of the room.

"*Lui è matto!*" Marcelo said, his pronouncement of Gianni's questionable mental state punctuated by a flurry of gestures.

Ari went to her room to change clothes and returned soon after in a black wrap dress and flats, the vase cradled in her arms. She was wearing the beautiful necklace Avinash had given her for his cousin's wedding, and her hair was tied back in an elegant bun, her face free of makeup. Marcelo watched her coming down the staircase like a wounded angel. Her appearance was beautiful, even though she was dreadfully sad. Together they walked to the marina for the trip just outside Positano's bay.

***

Ari had practiced the beautiful words she wanted to say to Santos and found a befitting poem by American poet Amelia Burr. The boat left the shores of Positano on a beautiful clear day, the sun shining brightly and specks of light bouncing off the waves. The captain moored the 60-foot fishing vessel a couple of kilometers off the shoreline in the direction of Capri, and the moment came for Ari.

She talked about Santos into the wind as if he were present, the love she felt for him pouring out like a cascade of endless water. The tears flowed as she recalled their marriage and honeymoon in Positano, and the city—the only true witness to their love—stood ever-present, again in attendance for this momentous occasion in her life. She turned to Marcelo and handed him the vase with tender care. Then she read the poet's words—words befitting of her beloved Santos:

Because I have loved life, I shall have no sorrow to die.

Ari wept as she finished the poem. Marcelo gave her a moment and stood at a distance just behind her marveling at the beautiful woman before him. *Could I had fallen in love with her? Taken her away from all this pain if only she would see me differently, if only she could forget Avinash and I could forget Lucia?*

Ari spent time staring off into the ocean below and looking up at the beautiful city in front of her. Marcelo, like a faithful guardian angel, waited patiently. She turned and motioned for him to come to her. Ari gently took the vase

211

from his grasp and opened the seal shaped like an elephant to uncover the remains inside. She said a prayer in Spanish and Marcelo followed in Italian. Ari let Santos go, peacefully weeping and yet strong in her resolve to complete his wish. When the last of his ashes poured out, she threw the vase into the water and looked at Marcelo, eyes clear and strong. She took a deep breath as if to say to herself the *task is complete*.

"It is done, my friend. Let's go home," she said.

Agent Baromeo, who had been watching from a nearby boat, arrived first to the shore. He hurried to Marcelo's truck and was waiting when they arrived. Ari was still heavy with emotion as Marcelo helped her up to her seat. She sat in silence, her eyes focused on the sea as the vehicle pulled away from the marina.

***

Marcelo opened the large doors leading to the terrace. The sun was almost setting, and a cool breeze filled the room. Baromeo had settled in his room to check on updates for Ronit. Ari walked straight through the half-opened double doors, touching the bougainvilleas that were hanging above, and Marcelo watched as she floated by in a trance. He poured her a glass of prosecco and one for himself as he headed out to the terrace, where Ari stood staring off into the ocean beyond the cliffs. The seagulls flew majestically above, making their beautiful calls. The evening cooled and the sky was glowing with orange and yellow hues.

"*Auguri, Signora*. It was a good day for your Santos and for you. In Italy we celebrate these . . . how do you say . . . *trionfo*."

"Yes," Ari said, "triumph."

"I think you should take this trip with me to Ampezzo. It will do you good to see the rest of this country."

Ari smiled and placed her nose close to the rim of the glass, allowing the bubbles to tickle her.

"I need time to feel like myself again. You know, sometimes feeling right after feeling bad for so long is the hardest thing to get used to."

Ari looked out again into the blue ocean, wondering when her life would feel right again. She closed her eyes and breathed deeply, as if the air were hope itself.

"Let's go tomorrow, Marcelo."

Marcelo smiled and clinked his flute with hers. "Yes. *Domani, Signora.* Tomorrow is perfect."

***

Avinash dressed down for the meeting with Ms. Singh; he wanted to appear totally different from his normal *GQ* magazine-prototype. This time he wore jeans and a polo shirt topped off by a sports jacket and baseball cap. He was accompanied by Sam, who would play the role of CFO. Agent St. John fitted Avinash with a wire and gave him last-minute instructions.

The London agencies and local police were in place, providing surveillance of the charity offices where Ms. Singh would meet with Robert Scorpio aka Avinash. The support team outside was ready to take action if John Ronit arrived. Avinash was not nervous, and St. John warned him to keep his anger at a minimum and let Ms. Singh do all the talking.

"Be in control of the conversation but do not run it. You're a sharp guy. Get this woman to open up to you and steer her in the direction we want. Your mission is to get

Ronit out from hiding. If she is who you think she is, a mother will do anything to defend her child, even if she has washed her hands of him. Got it?"

St. John continued to brief Avinash. Avinash nodded, asked a few questions for clarification, and then he and Sam headed into the building that housed The Singh Children's Foundation. St. John followed at a discreet distance. When Sam and Avinash entered the elevator, Agent St. John performed a sound check.

"Can you hear me?"

"Yes," Avinash answered. "Now keep quiet and let me take control." He pulled his jacket aside to check that his small-caliber pistol was still secure in his shoulder holster.

"Aren't you nervous?" Sam said.

Avinash smiled. "No, Sam. She's been expecting me long before this meeting was set."

"What do you mean she's expecting you?" he heard St. John mutter in his earpiece.

Avinash ignored him and walked into the office. He greeted the receptionist and placed the briefcase on top of the prominent reception desk before them.

"We have an appointment with Ms. Singh," Avinash said. "My name is Robert Scorpio, and this is my financial officer, John Abbott."

"Yes, Mr. Scorpio, the committee has been waiting for you. Please come with me."

The receptionist ushered them down a long hallway toward a massive set of double doors. When she opened them, Avinash whispered, "We're finally here."

The backup team listened intently but made no move. Once inside, Avinash and Sam saw no committee members, only Ms. Singh seated at the end of the long conference room table. When he was close enough, Avinash extended his hand to greet her. She ignored the gesture without making eye contact and motioned for them to sit.

"Let us not continue this charade," Ms. Singh said as Avinash and Sam settled at the table. "You have gone to great extent to cover your identity. However, you know it would be impossible for a mother to forget the man who ruined her child's life." She paused for a moment, but when Avinash said nothing she continued.

"Having said this, I am also acutely aware that he has put himself in a position that can bring harm to you and to him. You are here, Mr. Scorpio, only because I fear he will be hurt or killed if I don't help you stop him. I know my son has committed grave mistakes. At first I attributed these bad judgements to his spoiled youth. Next to you, he felt inferior and wanted to prove himself. His mistakes, however, have tarnished our family name, and I could not help him any longer. It is my understanding that he has made an attempt to harm you."

Avinash could hold his silence no more.

"He has made attempts to harm my girlfriend and tried to abduct her. These are not the mistakes of a foolish, inexperienced boy. These are crimes punishable by law, and I will not allow him to harm my loved ones again, Reeva."

Visibly shaken, her face drained of color, she got to her feet and approached him.

"How can I help you stop him?" she asked.

Avinash stood and placed his hands on her shoulders. "I am here because of your brother. He made me the man you see before you, but I have worked extremely hard to honor his trust in me. You must believe me when I tell you that I don't want any harm to come to Akash. I simply want to stop him from hurting anyone else. Where is he, Reeva?"

She slumped into her chair, as if she was carrying a large load and needed to rest.

"I don't know," she said with a heavy sigh. "He sends me messages somehow, but I have no idea where he is. Akash needs money. That's why I thought this donation would be a good idea. I told him you would donate these funds, and I would give the money to him. That way he would see this as revenge and agree to it. Do you understand? If you want to find him, I must give him this money."

Avinash paused for a moment as St. John chirped into the earpiece.

"How will you get this money to him?" Avinash asked as he placed the briefcase on the table in front of her.

"I must go this afternoon at five o'clock sharp to a boat slip near the pier, number 47, and wait for him. This will be the first time I have seen my son in years. Please do not hurt him," she pleaded.

Avinash could not promise anything, but he let her know he would be near and she would be safe while authorities stood close by. "The task will be to catch him alive. He has information that Interpol wants. They will not harm him."

***

As the meeting came to a close, several units set out in the direction of the drop-off point. Avinash asked Sam to stay close to Ms. Singh to secure the money drop. Then he left the building and rode with the local authorities to the pier.

He could feel his heart pounding; his adrenaline was so high that he could have run to the boat pier himself.

Once there, they radioed the Thames River police to the site and asked them to moor off at a distance while the sharpshooters took their positions in buildings and on rooftops across the Thames. With their long-range scopes, they could shoot a fly on Ms. Singh's head if need be. The London police, Interpol, and Scotland Yard would station themselves near alleys and in abandoned buildings. They had not put a wire on Ms. Singh for fear that Ronit would somehow think his mother was there to give him up to authorities. She'd been instructed to stand at the end of the pier so that Ronit or his intermediary could arrive by boat and get close enough to reach out for the briefcase without stopping.

At seventeen hours sharp, a blue high-powered boat slowed down and coasted to the pier. Ms. Singh appeared nervous but stood her ground as the boat came closer. The subject appeared to be wearing a ski mask, and when the boat was close enough he reached for Ms. Singh. As she stepped closer to hand him the briefcase, a shot rang out. In a matter of seconds, Ms. Singh and the briefcase toppled into the boat and it sped away from the pier.

Seconds later, Avinash heard the rumble of powerboats as the river police followed in close pursuit and the ground units scrambled to locate the source of the shot that felled Ms. Singh. Still wearing his wire, Avinash depended on St. John to fill him in as the chase ensued, though he would have preferred to witness it all firsthand.

"We've got them in sight," St. John said, his words echoing in Avinash's ear. "Now there's a red cigarette boat approaching them."

Avinash listened as the agent explained that the masked subject had tossed the briefcase into the red speedboat before thundering off in the opposite direction with Ms. Singh still onboard. Now they were chasing two high-powered vehicles, one with the money and the other carrying Ronit and his mother.

"Forget about the money," Avinash heard St. John instruct the team. "Stop Ronit and his mother."

Moments later, with guns drawn, they had the blue boat surrounded. Ronit was instructed to turn off the engines and put his hands up. He obeyed without a word, and the team climbed aboard the speedboat. Two men pinned Ronit against the side of the boat and pulled off his mask as another kneeled next to Ms. Singh.

What Avinash hear next rattled him to the core. "Negative, gentlemen. We do not have Ronit. I repeat, we do not have Ronit. We're on our way back. Have an ambulance at the ready when we arrive."

The mousetrap had been sprung, but neither the mouse nor the cheese were anywhere to be found.

CHAPTER ELEVEN

M arcelo entertained Ari with rapid-fire jokes. He was an excellent storyteller, and it was the best method for keeping Ari awake while she drove on the Autostrada A1 from Naples to Rome. Besides, it was a welcome distraction from the queasy feeling in her stomach, which was unusual for her, as she was used to driving on all types of roads and terrains. She attributed it to the months she had been bedridden and laughed as Marcelo continued to entertain her with jokes and stories.

That evening they stayed in Riano, a small town just outside Rome. The *albergo* had a large living area, two private rooms, and a full bath. Ari was still feeling nauseous and eating was out of the question.

"I will bring you some soup. You rest up, *va bene?*"

"*Si, grazie,*" Ari said as she removed her shoes and stretched out on the bed.

***

The town of Riano had some serious flooding issues years ago but was now recovering slowly, and the people were out and about the next morning. Ari awoke feeling a little better, not having eaten a thing the night before, and decided to venture out with Marcelo for some coffee before the long trip ahead of them.

"Marcelo, why haven't you found anyone since Lucia?" she asked as they sat in the little café down the street. "You're such a nice guy. You're funny, intelligent, and handsome. Why are you alone?" Marcelo chuckled as Ari smiled, unaware of the irony in her question. "Seriously, you could find a nice woman to keep you company."

"Signora, this subject can only be discussed with a couple bottles of vino. I cannot say I have been truly alone for these past years; I have had women here and there. *Niente especiale, capito?*" He stopped to light a cigarette. 'Tell me, signora, would you be interested in someone like me?"

Ari thought about if for a minute. "Well, you remind me in many ways of Santos, the way you take care of me and fuss over me. You're kindhearted and you don't have an evil bone in your body. But you know who I love, don't you?"

Marcelo felt the sting of guilt in her words and changed the subject.

They sped toward Tuscany with a quick stop in Siena for some spices that Ari wanted. On the way, Ari talked about Santos and how good he'd been to her.

"He always encouraged me to go for my dreams. If it wasn't for him, I probably would have never owned a business. He was exceptionally good with numbers and always guided me. Every morning we would tell each other, "I love you." Every night we would say the same thing before we went to bed. We didn't say it as an automatic response; we truly meant it. Before every meal together, our way of giving thanks was to kiss. We could never keep our hands off each other. Avinash is slightly different in that aspect. I guess because of his culture. He's incredibly sweet, loving, and devoted when we are together and is such a romantic, extremely detailed.

Marcelo laughed. "So what's wrong with him?"

Ari smiled. "Nothing really. I just mean he's different about expressing love and affection in public. Not characteristically Latin in that respect, but he was certainly trying to be until . . . ." Ari changed the subject back to Santos. "It's strange, but when I'm alone, I feel him closer to me than any other time. I just wondered if you ever felt that way about Lucia."

Ari suddenly realized she'd been going on and on and Marcelo hadn't said a word. "I'm so sorry, Marcelo. Forgive me. I didn't mean to talk so much about—"

He stopped her. "*Cara mia,* when you speak of someone you love, it is never a waste for the one who is listening," Marcelo said sweetly. "Okay?"

Ari agreed.

***

The roads were dusty, as it had not rained in months. Siena appeared empty when they arrived midafternoon; most people did not venture out in the heat. They parked and took a walk along the city's narrow streets, and Ari began to feel sick again. Marcelo took her to a nearby café and bought her a Fernet, a digestif made from a number of herbs and spices which varied according to the brand but usually included myrrh, rhubarb, chamomile, cardamom, aloe, and especially saffron. This version also had mint.

"This is horrible, Marcelo. What is in this stuff?"

"Just drink it. You will feel better." Marcelo kept pouring more in her glass.

"It tastes like Listerine," Ari complained.

After a while, she did start to feel better and they continued looking for her spices. She remembered an old store she and Santos had visited on their honeymoon. There, the herbs were kept in wooden drawers labeled in Italian and English. They would weigh each item individually and let you taste them. She and Marcelo searched up and down and could not find the place. Finally, someone told them they had moved the location to a farmhouse just outside of Siena near Poggibosi.

"We shall search for it on our way out of town," Marcelo said. "But first I must look at the granite for your kitchen countertops." He found Ari a seat at a sidewalk café nearby, in the shade of a huge old tree. "If I find something suitable, I will come for you."

Between the heat and the queasy feeling that was returning, Ari nodded off briefly until she was awakened by an older Italian woman who asked her to get out from the heat and follow her to her store. She had a kind smile and a worn look to her face, perhaps from years of being in the sun. Ari followed her inside, and the kind woman found her a chair and placed her feet in a basin full of cool water.

"Grazie, signora," Ari said.

The woman, who spoke no English, told Ari that she should not be in the sun in her condition. The woman tried to explain in Italian and with hand gestures that Ari would soon experience motherhood and the death of someone she loved in the coming months.

Hoping she'd misunderstood but certain she had not, Ari became flustered. *"No, signora. Non darò alla luce.* I am not going to give birth."

Within moments she heard Marcelo calling out for her in the street and she yelled out to him. Marcelo rushed in, thinking she had fallen sick only to find Ari with her feet soaking in a basin of water, explaining to a strange woman that she was not headed into motherhood. The old woman, mistaking Marcelo for Ari's husband, congratulated him.

"What the hell is she saying about a baby and someone *morto?"* he asked.

"Nothing!" Ari removed her feet from the basin and grabbed her shoes. "Let's go!" she said as she rushed barefooted from the store.

Marcelo, still puzzled, thanked the woman and followed in Ari's footsteps. "Does she think you're pregnant, Ari?" he asked as he hurried to catch up with her.

"No! She's crazy. I am not pregnant. Let's go, please."

***

Marcelo drove them out of Siena, and they went in the direction of Poggibonsi for her spices. Marcelo was famished and hoped by then Ari would be willing to eat something.

After the spice farm, they stopped in Poggibonsi to eat. By now neither was in the best of moods, and Marcelo ordered up everything on the menu of the quaint trattoria without even asking Ari if she wanted something in particular.

"Sorry," Marcelo said as he put down his Peroni beer. "I'm very hungry right now. How do you feel?"

"I'm fine, Marcelo, thank you." Ari stared out the window, watching people come and go on the street.

"Are we going to talk like this all the way to Cortina d'Ampezzo, as if we are sending a telegram? 'I am fine. Stop. And you? Stop. Go to hell. Stop.'" Marcelo tapped his fingers on the wooden table as if communicating by Morse code. All Ari could do was laugh as she put her forehead on his shoulder and kissed his cheek.

"You can always make me laugh," she said, smiling.

"*Bene, signora,*" he said. "*Alora mangia.*" He put a platter in front of her, heaped high with fresh buratta cheese and warm bread doused in olive oil.

Ari nibbled at the cheese, trying to clear her mind. This may be some old woman's crazy intuition, but she remembered how difficult it had been to get pregnant with Santos. He'd wanted children so badly, but doctors said that a football injury to the groin in his youth may have been the cause. They'd even thought about surrogacy after they moved to Positano, but fate changed everything before they could do so. Now Ari was almost thirty-nine, and this was a dangerous stage in her life for pregnancy. What weighed most heavily on her mind was the part about someone dying. She feared for all the people she loved and hoped that this prediction would just pass. Ari was not particularly superstitious, but Santos had been, and though she would try to convince him otherwise, some of that fear of the unknown grew in her now.

Marcelo tore his day-old, crusty bread over the soup. While Ari played with her meal, Marcelo charted the day on a map. He told her he wanted to take a turn south and head to Porcari to visit someone. He said it was important, but before he could explain further, a call came into his mobile and he excused himself to take it outside. Ari wondered why he needed privacy every time he received a call, but decided he was just swearing at the workers at the home in Positano and didn't want her to hear it. Ari sat alone in the restaurant and thought about tomorrow. It would be the first day of August—Avinash's birthday.

***

The cancellation of the Children's Gala due to the disappearance of its founder, Ms. Singh, had hit news and media outlets like a wildfire. The caption of the *London Times* read: "Interpol and Scotland Yard Suspect Thwarts Capture." The foundation wanted answers, and they were pointing fingers at Avinash Batra, President of World Bank, as the last person known to see Ms. Singh the day of the failed event. The phones were ringing off the hook at the bank, and Avinash could do nothing more than to have Anjali screen the calls and inform people that he was preparing a press conference. What he'd actually say was as yet unknown.

By now the agents in Positano had advised Agent Baromeo that Ariadne Cordero and her friend Marcelo Donati had skipped town in his absence—yet another setback. Baromeo had been told by Marcelo that he would be traveling, but he never said Ms. Cordero would be accompanying him. She was to stay in Positano with Baromeo's backup, Agent Raoul Valverdi. The news was upsetting, and Baromeo sent a team to search for their whereabouts immediately, especially now that Ronit was on the loose.

Avinash sat in his office with the newspapers that held the latest gossip and updates on Ms. Singh, who had disappeared from the hospital where she was being cared for. He wondered what he would tell the press and if Akash's mother was still alive.

"So, boss, I guess there will be no birthday celebration tomorrow, right?" Anjali said as she walked into the office.

Avinash looked up at her, his eyes bloodshot and his beard unshaven, and swept the newspapers off the desk. "Do you know what worries me more than any of this news?"

Anjali nodded. "Ari?"

"Ari," he replied. "We set this elaborate trap to capture Akash, and now Ari is in more danger than ever before. To make matters worse, no one in Italy seems to know where the hell she is."

Anjali tried to reassure Avinash that Agent Baromeo had heard from Agent Valverdi that she may be in Tuscany. "It seems he's been in contact with Marcelo and knows exactly where they are. You don't have to worry. Ari is protected." Anjali walked around the desk and put her hand on his shoulder. "It's your birthday tomorrow, and I know Ari; she will not forget. Wherever she is, I know she will call you just to wish you a great day. You'll see, Avinash."

Avinash smiled at the thought of hearing Ari's voice, even if it was over the phone. He truly hoped she would call. Hearing her voice was exactly what he needed.

***

The next morning, Ari awoke with Avinash on her mind. It was his birthday and she missed him. She had been having recurring dreams of him—some beautiful images of them together and others quite frightening. She wondered if a quick call was a good idea, just to wish him a happy birthday. Would he even talk to her?

Marcelo had left early to run an errand and would return in a couple hours to head out to Cortina d'Ampezzo. They needed to order the wood beams for the roof before the rains came, and the factory promised to deliver sooner rather than later. Ari was feeling vulnerable; she couldn't bring herself to do a pregnancy test just to clear her fear of the old Tuscan woman's prediction. All she knew was that she had fears and raging hormones, neither one allowing her to think straight.

Ari stared at her cell phone, her heart pounding. She was alone, lonely, missing Avinash who would be returning from the gym at about this time. She took a deep breath, picked up the phone, and pressed his number in her Favorites list. Avinash answered on the first ring.

"Hello, Ari? Can you hear me?"

She froze. The sound of his voice made every inch of her body vibrate.

"Hi, Avinash. I . . . I wanted to wish you a happy birthday. I hope you're having a lovely day." Ari paused for a second to gather her thoughts before continuing. "I heard the news about Ms. Singh. Are you all right?"

"Ari, thank you for thinking of me. I miss you so much. Things are not great here. What can I say? It's quite a mess. Getting to Akash has proven to be very difficult."

Ari heard his desperation and wanted to reassure him, but Agent Baromeo had warned her that no call should be longer than thirty seconds. "I'm fine, Avinash. I need to go now. Be safe."

She heard Avinash whisper, "I love you" in Hindi and ended the call without replying.

Ari was strong, and after the call she felt that things would get better soon. She had a powerful need to shield herself from anything negative that would come her way. The pharmacy bag holding the pregnancy test was still sitting on her night stand. At that moment, she made a decision. *I need to know*, she thought, smiling. *It's time.*

When Marcelo returned, he was visibly upset.

"What's the matter?" Ari asked as he poured himself a glass of red wine and slumped into a chair at the kitchen table. "It's ten thirty in the morning. Why are you drinking? Tell me, *fammi sapere.*"

Marcelo responded, his voice cracking. "I went to see her. Lucia. I went to see her . . . how do you say it? *Tomba.*"

"You went to see Lucia's grave? Why didn't you take me with you?" she said as Marcelo took another good gulp of wine.

Marcelo walked away from Ari, knowing he should have. "No lo so. I wanted to be alone with her. I can't explain what I feel." Marcelo's eyes filled with tears.

Ari grabbed his hand and led him to the sofa. All she could do was hold him tight; she knew exactly how he felt. Losing Santos was still fresh in her mind even now, four years later.

"Lucia is not angry with you, Marcelo," Ari said as they held each other." It was an accident. She's simply resting, waiting for you."

They remained on that sofa in Porcari for a long time, until he could weep no more and Ari felt he was stronger. Ari packed the car and they headed to Cortina d'Ampezzo with a stop in Padua. Marcelo met with Agent Valverdi just outside town and got the go-ahead for them to continue, with Agent Baromeo's blessing. If they kept moving, finding them would prove more difficult for Ronit than if they stayed in one place for too long.

***

Avinash reached the office, happier than he had been in days. When Anjali caught sight of him she knew that he had spoken with Ari.

"So, birthday boy, did you get a phone call?"

Avinash smiled with his eyes and headed toward his office where his Media Relations staff was waiting with ideas for the press conference. Avinash was in a good mood. All he could do was think about Ari and the sound of her voice on the phone. He found himself distracted by the white sofa where he'd watched Ari undress and the desk where they had made love the last time he saw her. The memories gave him a high he hadn't felt in a long time.

Avinash gave the media team some ideas for the press conference, and they were instructed to make their revisions. He asked them to set it up for four in the afternoon in the main vestibule of World Bank.

"Sam, we need extra security today, so make sure we have enough to cover the event," Avinash instructed. The team and Sam were dispatched, and the pressure was on to get all the media outlets to the bank to hear from Avinash Batra himself.

In the meantime, the World Bank offices were buzzing with curious staff and media entering and exiting the building trying to find the best vantage point for coverage of the conference. Avinash Batra was never late, and the vestibule of World Bank was a hornet's nest of gossip. Anjali and Sam stood next to the podium as Avinash entered the lobby with two security officers and took his position. Impeccably dressed in a black suit, red tie, and crisp white shirt, he was ready. Avinash's brow creased as he positioned the microphone closer to his lips and cleared his throat.

"Welcome all. Thank you for coming. During the past weeks there has been much speculation and misguided talk about the association of World Bank with businesswoman and charity organizer, Ms. Maheema Singh from the Singh Children's Charity. Her unfortunate disappearance has left this community looking for answers. We at World Bank are deeply saddened by the turn of events that unfolded just a week ago, and we stand ready to assist local and international authorities in the search for Ms. Singh. More importantly, we are eager to bring to justice the person responsible for these events. I have personally been a victim of this individual and wish to reveal his name to you and the reasons that have led me before all of you today. The person responsible for the kidnapping of Ms. Singh and for the death of my fiancée, Suniel, over a decade ago and most recently the attempted kidnapping of my current girlfriend, Ariadne Cordero, is none other than the son of Ms. Singh, Mr. Akash Ramkissoon, who has been going by the assumed name of John Ronit."

The spectators gasped and talked among themselves as Avinash tried to continue.

"Please, please, let me finish. Mr. Ronit entered this country illegally several months ago and has been trying to seek revenge with repeated attacks on me and my loved ones since he arrived. Mr. Ronit is also the nephew of the late, Mr. Dutta, my mentor and previous owner of World Bank. Under an assumed name, Mr Ronit's mother reached out to me in an attempt to bring him in safely. In a cowardly act, Mr. Ronit kidnapped his own mother and escaped the capture of local and international authorities. We have no information on her whereabouts." He paused, took a sip of water, and continued.

"Therefore, I would like to announce a bounty for the capture of Mr. Akash Ramkissoon, aka John Ronit, in the amount of 300,000 pounds. Any information on his whereabouts or his capture will be rewarded. We at World Bank, our employees and shareholders, my family and friends stand ready to fight to bring Mr. Ronit to justice. Thank you."

With that, Avinash stepped away from the microphone. Sam thanked everyone for attending and told the astounded audience that there would be no questions or further comments made by World Bank or its employees. The noise in the lobby was deafening and boisterous as media members made calls and TV cameramen crashed into each other in an attempt to exit the bank and be the first to place a live feed directly to the studio from the trucks waiting outside.

Avinash felt like Gary Cooper in *High Noon*, his gun still blazing from taking the wounding shot. It was a gamble that he took, and he wanted everyone, including Ronit, to know that he meant business. Avinash closed the bank for the rest of the afternoon and let everyone go home early.

***

In Cortina d'Ampezzo, the wood beams were purchased and arrangements made to have them shipped to Positano immediately. Soon Ari would literally have a good roof over her head with no worries from the rainy season or winter. They left the car near Venice and took the train to Naples. They rode in silence, Marcelo battling an awful cold he'd managed to pick up somewhere along the way and Ari trying to find the right time to share her news with him. Finally, she could wait no longer.

"I need to tell you something," she said.

"What?" Marcelo said, closing his eyes and reclining in the seat to rest comfortably

"I'm not pregnant. It was probably something I ate. The old woman was mistaken," Ari said as she smiled at him.

Marcelo opened one eye. "That is good, no?"

Ari nodded, trying her best to hide the twinge of disappointment she felt deep in her heart.

The taxi left them at the front door of 87 Viale Pasitea, and Marcelo was in a much worse state by the time they arrived. Ari quickly made him get into bed while she searched the house for something to bring down the fever, but she could not find anything strong enough. She turned on the TV in Marcelo's room—he enjoyed listening to the BBC channel to perfect his English—and there he was, Avinash during the press conference. Ari froze. Marcelo sat up in bed, and they listened intently as the news made reference to his press conference and then replayed it in its entirety.

Ari was stunned that he would openly speak about a past he had hidden for so long and that he would call out Akash on everything he had done. She felt a sense of despair as she watched Avinash try to defend his honor and the empire he had built at World Bank, a bank full of people he cared about which was now being threatened by a ghost from his past.

Suddenly, Marcelo was overcome by a fit of violent coughing. "*Lui ha le palle,*" he managed to say.

Ari gave him a stern look. She knew that translated to *the guy has balls . . .* or something like it.

"I will go to the pharmacy for something, *tornerò presto,*" she said as Marcelo continued to cough uncontrollably. She rushed out of the house and down the street to the nearest pharmacy.

Ari was in a daze. She felt a need to be with Avinash now, and it reminded her of Santos. Especially during his trial, the way the press had hounded him. *It must be a terrible time for Avinash,* she thought. When she arrived at the pharmacy, Boom Boom Claudia was just turning the corner in her direction.

"*Cara mia, preziosa.* You've returned from your trip," she said as she smothered Ari in hugs and kisses.

"We just got back today and Marcelo is very sick." Ari quickly pulled Claudia into the pharmacy. "Can you help me get something for a fever and a chest cold?"

"Yes, sure." Claudia quickly spoke with the pharmacist, and he went behind the counter to prepare the order. "If you want a good doctor to come to the home, I have a friend, you know. He lives in Praiano and can come to the house. He owes me."

"That would be wonderful, Claudia. Thank you. Would you like to come back to the house with me?"

The pharmacist returned with the medications and instructions. As they headed back up the hill to the house, Claudia stopped Ari for a moment. "Is something else wrong?" she asked.

Ari couldn't hold it any longer. "Yes, it's Avinash. I saw him on the news today. Things in London are really horrible, and he had to tell the media what was happening. I don't know what to do. I don't know if I should do anything at all." Ari looked at Claudia for words of wisdom, but she just gave Ari a sad smile.

***

When they arrived, Ari and Claudia headed toward the kitchen which was now almost finished. She didn't even notice the beautiful cabinets and the white granite countertops. They had opened a panoramic window that stretched from the bar across to the other end of the wall, and the cobalt blue on the cabinets matched the Mediterranean Sea and sky just beyond the terrace.

Claudia marveled at the stunning view as Ari mixed the powdery substance from the pharmacy in a glass of water. "Oh my, Ari! *Bellisimo.*"

"Stay here and enjoy yourself, Claudia. I will return once Marcelo drinks this." Within minutes Ari returned and found that Claudia had already poured herself and Ari a glass of Tuscan red wine. They headed outside to the terrace, and Claudia prompted Ari to speak about what she was feeling.

"It's a strange mixture of feelings, Claudia. I feel powerless, the same way I felt when Santos was in trouble. It almost seems like I'm reliving those horrible days all over again, unable to help. Is life trying to tell me something?"

Claudia listened as she poured herself another glass of wine. "Fate is something you cannot control, *cara mia*. You are in Positano for Santos, but you really want to be in London with Avinash. Now this house and even poor Marcelo are keeping you here. Don't try to push life to bend to your wishes. Let it take you on the journey you were meant to take. If you are destined to be with Avinash, life or fate will pull you in that direction and nothing will stop it. The present is the only thing you need to worry about, Ari."

Claudia's words made sense, but they did not calm the anxious feeling in her stomach. Ari smiled and gazed out into the ocean as the sun began to set, the end of another day. Life in Positano was just beginning for her, and she had to be brave to face what may lie ahead.

Chapter Twelve

One week after her arrival in Positano, Ari awoke to a cavalcade of workers who came to unload the wood for the roof that had arrived earlier than expected from the suppliers in the north of Italy. She was sure Marcelo would not be able to rest properly with all the noise. Marcelo quickly awoke, feeling a little better and ready to command his workers, but Ari forbade it under penalty of institutionalization. She hired another contractor in town to take over the roofing project and gave Marcelo the ultimatum to rest up or abandon the project altogether.

In the chaos of the morning, Ari had missed a call. It appeared to be a US number from somewhere in New York. Ari held her breath as she connected to her voicemail, hoping nothing had happened to Santos's family, most of whom lived there, including his nieces and nephews. As she listened to the message, she placed some coffee beans in the French press and waited for the coffee to brew. Her intuition was right; Diego, the oldest nephew of Santos, was getting married. But he was thanking her for agreeing to come to his wedding—a wedding she knew nothing about. It seems he had sent an invitation to Ari's address in England and, according to the date he mentioned, the wedding was just two weeks away. The caller's voice was warm, insisting that his favorite aunt be present as the godmother of the wedding, and he expected that she and her guest would stay with him.

A million questions flooded Ari's mind. *What was he talking about? Where? When?* Ari had grown close to Diego when he came to do his internship at a prestigious law firm in Los Angeles. Ari and Santos had opened their home to him, and they were a family of three. The death of his uncle had hit him incredibly hard, as it had the rest of the family, but Diego had remained in communication with Ari and she loved him for it. The mystery was tugging at her. *Who had RSVP'd for this wedding, and why hadn't Avinash forwarded the invitation to Positano?* Whatever the reason, Ari had to think of a way to get back to the US. How could she leave with Marcelo so sick? What about Akash? Would she have a problem traveling with him still on the loose?

Before she could figure out what to do, she received a call from Claudia asking about Marcelo. She advised Ari that the doctor couldn't come the day before because he had been in an accident but would send another doctor in his place.

"Good God, is he okay?" Ari asked in disbelief.

"Yes, *cara mia*, he's fine. Just a bit out of sorts and with no vehicle. But you needn't worry. The doctor he is sending is also a friend and will see Marcelo today."

"Thank you, Claudia. Will you be over tonight to watch movies with us?"

"You just try and keep me away, dear," Claudia said.

Ari had turned one of the dining rooms into a makeshift theatre room with a large screen and comfortable loungers. She usually had all her friends over for Friday movie night, with each guest bringing something to eat. Afterward they'd stay late into the night to discuss the plot on the terrace.

During the afternoon, when the workers left for lunch or went home to rest, the doctor arrived to check on Marcelo. Ari rushed him into the bedroom where Marcelo lay still under the covers trying to sleep after a restless morning. Ari hated to wake him up but insisted that the doctor check him over. With that, she left the room and let the kind, overweight man who looked more like a fisherman than a physician examine the grumpy patient. While she waited, Ari phoned Anjali.

"Hey, bambina. What's up?" Anjali said. "It's so good to hear your voice."

"I'm doing well, my friend. But Marcelo is sick."

"Oh no! What's wrong with Musi?" It was a nickname Anjali had for Marcelo, one he despised as it referred to Mussolini, but she didn't think Colgate, the nickname he'd given Anjali in reference to her pearly white teeth, was any better.

"He has a terrible cold. A doctor is with him as we speak. How are things after the press conference? I saw a piece of it here. Avinash did really well."

Anjali explained that the situation with Ms. Singh had calmed down a bit but she was still missing, along with Akash. There were even suspicions that she was in on the bait and switch the whole time but no one knew for sure.

"Avinash is doing much better. He misses you and wants to see you. He even mentioned that we should visit you in Positano. Can you imagine? Mr. Work-all-the-Time wants to take a sabbatical?"

The thought of Avinash coming to Positano sounded magical, but she first had to find out about the wedding invitation from Santos's nephew. And more importantly, she needed to know who had responded on her behalf, promising she would attend with a guest.

"Anjali, has Avinash said anything to you about a wedding invitation that arrived for me? Did he say he responded in my behalf or speak to you about it?"

Anjali said she knew nothing about the mysterious wedding invitation. When Ari explained the strange circumstances of the call from her nephew, the only assurance Anjali could offer was that Avinash still had her things, including her correspondence. There was a possibility that Interpol could have confiscated the correspondence for security measures, but she was not aware of the wedding invitation.

Ari's head spun with scenarios. *Could this be the work of Akash? Did Avinash RSVP to the wedding for me?* With that, Ari had to close the call, explaining that the doctor examining Marcelo had just appeared in the living room and needed to speak with her.

***

"Will he be okay, Doctor?" Ari asked with a lump in her throat.

"I'm not sure. I need to examine him further and take some tests," the doctor said, speaking in perfect English. "He has been a heavy smoker, and these things can get complicated. Could be pneumonia or something else. I need him to visit the hospital in Sorrento for a more thorough examination."

Ari promised to bring him to Sorrento in the next day or two. She thanked the kind doctor and offered to pay him but he refused. *Perhaps Claudia took care of the fees without letting me know.* Whatever the case may have been, it was imperative that she get Marcelo to the hospital for some tests, and she knew she would need a brigade of troops to maneuver the ever-stubborn Marcelo to even consider the possibility of going to Sorrento, of all places, to get examined. *Tonight is the perfect night,* she thought. The troops would all be gathered at her home, and she would plot her strategy with them. The movie they planned to watch that evening was *Vincere*, the story of a woman's relationship with Mussolini. *Perfect!*

That evening, with the food and wine flowing and Marcelo sleeping peacefully inside, Ari finally began to relax. The woman had gathered on the terrace for dinner, each having brought a dish from their native province or country. The favorite by far was Ari's orecchiette pasta with grilled in-season vegetables.

The ladies discussed Ari's trip to New York. All were in agreement that she should attend, but Ari was still worried about the situation with Akash and leaving Marcelo when he needed her the most. Lorraine volunteered to take care of him, but Ari felt a sense of commitment to Marcelo. After all, he had been there for her while she was ill and brought her back to life.

Claudia and Paulette didn't want to hear more sour news. They started dancing on the terrace, and the ladies laughed as they tried to tango across the floor. Ari, still unsure about what to do, moved her chair closer to Lorraine.

"In Tuscany a woman I met predicted that I would have a child and that someone close to me would die," Ari whispered as the other women continued to entertain themselves. "I have been trying to erase the thought from my mind, but I can't."

Lorraine smiled and assured Ari that predictions are like the weather—completely unpredictable. "I think you need to be with your family, Ari. This trip will give you strength. You haven't seen them since Santos died, and they must feel that you still have that connection with him. I think Marcelo will understand."

Ari took a sip of her wine and smiled at Lorraine. She had a lot to think about, and the wedding was drawing closer.

***

Ari and Agent Baromeo accompanied Marcelo to the Ospedali Riuniti Penisola Sorrentina. While they waited for him, Ari informed Baromeo that she needed to travel to New York for a wedding. Baromeo voiced his concern and told her this was not the time to travel.

"When is it ever going to be the time for me to travel? I need my life back. I feel like Akash is in control of my every move."

Baromeo nodded. "Yes, he is in control of you and Avinash now, that I can assure you. Unless you want to travel with one of the agents, you cannot leave Italy alone, Ari."

She knew the conditions would be rigorous, and she felt a sense of frustration but at least she would make the wedding. "What about Marcelo?" she asked.

"Marcelo is in no condition to travel or protect you." Baromeo, unshaven, his blue eyes more intense than ever, was stern and would not hear of it.

"Then why don't you accompany me to New York, hotshot? By the way, do you mind?" she said as she pointed at the exposed weapon neatly tucked into a holster at his hip. "It's making me nervous." Baromeo grinned and repositioned his jacket to cover it. Ari shook her head and smiled back at him. "You're terrible, you know."

"*Si*, I know. And you're beautiful." Ari looked away and blushed.

"By the way, you know Anjali has been doing her own investigation on the side. I didn't think it was good for her to snoop, but she's actually quite good at it." Baromeo laughed.

"Oh? I was unaware. Is this perhaps to help Avinash remember things about Akash that may help the case?" Ari reasoned.

Baromeo went silent. He pulled a small jute bag loosely wrapped in twine out of his pocket and placed it in her hands. Ari looked astonished.

"How did you find this? Who gave this to you?"

"Is it important Ari?" Baromeo asked. "I wonder because you took great lengths to keep it hidden, but a wooden jewelry box can easily be broken into."

Ari was now breathing heavy and ready to lash out at Baromeo, but this could be important. *If it leads to Akash or Santos's killer, I'm going to cooperate.*

"It was given to me along with Santos's things when they found his body. I don't know what the dirt inside the bag means. I thought maybe it was some new blue agave plant that Santos was interested in harvesting, but honestly, I don't know why he had it. I just kept it. In case."

"In case what, Ari?"

She stood up and walked away from Baromeo, tears flooding her eyes. "In case it was a message to me somehow. Something Santos was trying to tell me. I don't know, Gianni! You're the investigator! You tell me why he called me twice the day he died and didn't leave me any reason to doubt him."

Baromeo stood up and approached Ari. "Santos called you twice, Ari? You told police he called you only one time. Was it one time or two times? What did he say to you?"

"He said he'd be home later than he thought. Then he said . . ."

"Ari, please. What did he say?"

Ari looked up at him, gasping. "He said, 'green valley.'"

"What?"

"You heard me. He said two words: green valley. I don't know what it means, but that's what he said."

"Green valley . . . green valley," Baromeo muttered as he stared at her. Then he pulled out his mobile phone, punched in a couple of numbers, and hurried out of the hospital.

Ari remained in the corridor, the small jute bag in her hands.

***

It would take at least a week for Marcelo's test results to come in, and he was crankier now than he'd ever been. He decided to take Ari and Baromeo to a restaurant he enjoyed off the Via Correale, near the Piazza Angelina Lauro.

"Is it safe for you to walk about in Sorrento?" Baromeo joked.

"Well, aren't you here for protection? So then protect, ragazzo."

Marcelo was not having any of what Baromeo was dishing out today. He had been poked and prodded all morning long. "Follow me," he said as he walked out of the hospital onto the busy maze of streets just ahead.

As they followed, Ari wondered how it might have been for Marcelo when he was lord of the underground gambling ring in Sorrento. She envisioned an Alain Delon look-alike in a white Italian suit making his way up the streets with a peacock strut that wooed women and made men envy him. He still had the swagger, and though he was older, she could see that he was in his element. She enjoyed how he took them about town, showing them everything that had some meaning to him. Marcelo no longer looked ashen or sick. This trip was like an infusion of life, a concoction of memories from a past that now gave him a different objective in life.

They dined at O Parrucchiano, a historical restaurant of Sorrento that is said to have invented the cannelloni but back then it was called *strascinati*. Marcelo explained that the restaurant was founded in 1868 by Antonino Ercolano, a seminarian who mastered the art of cooking in the kitchen of the local archbishop's palace. Later he transformed two rooms on the main road into a tiny *trattoria* and named it La Favorita. The place was soon frequented by his friends, and because of his past vocation of priesthood, Antonino gained the nickname of "O Parrucchiano," which meant parish priest in the Neapolitan dialect. In the forties, Antonino left the *trattoria* to his young nephew, Giuseppe Manniello, a boy who lost his father at the tender age of seven and had been raised by his uncle. Giuseppe, to whom his uncle had taught all his secrets about cooking, improved the tiny *trattoria* and passed his secrets on to his sons who now owned the famous restaurant.

Ari finished off her profiterole and sat back with a sigh. They'd been dining for three hours, and she wondered how the three of them would get back to Positano after ingesting such a feast. When Baromeo took his leave to the washroom, Ari brought up the trip to New York. Marcelo listened intently and was alarmingly quiet, only looking at Ari when she described her relationship with Diego and how much she missed him. Marcelo smiled as she recounted her life with him. When she finished, he spoke.

"I think you should go to this wedding, but I will go with you. I won't know the test results until next week. By that time we would have enjoyed our time in New York and returned," he explained. "I will not let you go alone, even if you are accompanied by Baromeo."

Ari smiled and kissed him lightly on the cheek. "Very well then," she whispered in his ear. "We will go together, you and me."

Baromeo returned to the table just as the waiter arrived with the check. Ari was relieved when Marcelo graciously picked up the tab.

***

The day to travel abroad came for Ari, Marcelo, and Agent Baromeo who had received clearance from Interpol and

Homeland Security to travel to New York. Ari felt nervous as she waited at the gate, fidgeting endlessly and unable to relax. Marcelo wanted to reassure her but thought best to let her wrestle her demons alone, at least for the time being.

Though Diego had invited her to stay with him, Ari had made arrangements to stay at the Waldorf Astoria on Park Avenue, the same location as the ceremony and reception, since she was traveling with Marcelo and Baromeo. She spoke with Diego a week before and asked if she could include one more to the guest list without explaining her ordeal of the past months and the groom lovingly agreed.

Upon arrival, they only had time to change at the hotel before heading out to the rehearsal dinner at Budakkan on West 37th Street. Ari wasn't surprised at the choice. She had thrilled Diego with her stories of the East and of her time in India, and he had been fascinated by the tales.

The wedding ceremony and reception would be held the next evening at six o'clock sharp, and she would have a small role as the godmother for Diego. Ari quickly showered and dressed in a simple white pantsuit with a champagne-colored lace top and matching pumps, accented with an ornate and colorful Indian necklace she had bought in London. Her hair was now longer, wavy and draped down to her mid-back. She looked stunning.

When she caught up with Marcelo, impeccable in a simple black suit, he could not help but stare at her approach. Ari glowed with happiness.

"Salute," he said as he offered her one of the flutes of Champagne he had ordered. When Ari took her first sip, she saw Marcelo look past her. He tightened up and clenched his jaw. Ari's curiosity made her turn in the direction of his gaze. Suddenly, she became weak in the knees. Standing there in a dark blue suit, his white shirt open just enough to show the hint of a familiar necklace, was Avinash. Ari could not speak as he crossed the room and kissed her lightly on the cheek. Just behind him she saw Agent St. John and two other men. He too was well-accompanied.

"Avinash, what are you doing here?" She suddenly realized that he had responded to the wedding invitation knowing she would attend. The jazz music playing in the bar seemed to swirl around her—or was it his presence that had her in a trance and barely able to breathe?

"You look beautiful, Ari, breathtakingly beautiful. I'm so happy to see you." With that, he leaned over Ari and shook Marcelo's hand firmly. "Thank you for accompanying Ari. I will take over from here."

Avinash ordered an open tab for Marcelo and offered his arm to Ari, ushering her away from the bar. Ari was torn. Poor Marcelo was here to attend the wedding with her, not to be left at a hotel bar alone.

"Have a good evening, Ari," Marcelo said as he gingerly pushed her toward Avinash.

Ari looked back at him over her shoulder. "I'm sorry," she mouthed to him.

He raised his glass to her in a gesture of good luck. "*Lui ha le palle,*" he muttered.

*** *

With St. John and the other agents following behind them, Avinash escorted Ari to an awaiting SUV. As they pulled away from the curb, Avinash raised the privacy window, separating the two of them from the others.

"How did you—?" Ari tried to ask, but Avinash could not hold it any longer. He leaned into her and kissed her softly, wrapping his hand around the back of her neck to bring her closer. She could feel his passion in the way he kissed her, and she responded as she always did. They kissed, it seemed, all the way to the restaurant, and Ari was now yearning for him so much that she could barely think of meeting the family.

When the vehicle parked in front of the restaurant, Avinash pulled away from her and spoke. "I wonder what goes through your mind when someone mentions my name to you. Can I tell you what goes through mine? Do you really want to go in there now?" he said.

"I have to, Avinash. They're waiting for me."

"Can they wait a little longer for you? It's still early, dear." Avinash pressed the button to lower the window and signaled the driver to take them somewhere else.

"No, no. We're here. Let's go in. Please, Avinash."

He could never say no to her and they exited the vehicle. Avinash opened the door on her side and gave her his hand. Ari exited and walked toward the entrance with Avinash and two agents following closely behind. When they reached the hostess, Avinash took over, as always, and requested that they be taken to the Echegui/Dominec dinner party.

Ari studied Avinash as he spoke with the woman. He was in much better shape; his arms were fuller, and he seemed more muscular than before. He took her hand and they followed the hostess to the back of the restaurant and up the stairs to the second level. Budakkan had its history in Manhattan; it was the place where the famous dined.

In the quaint room with gold and turquoise décor, Ari made eye contact with Santos's younger sister, Maria del Carmen, and the groom's future mother-in-law. Maria made her way through the guests and hugged Ari.

"My precious sister, how long has it been?" Maria said. Tears flowed as the two looked at each other in amazement. "How is it possible that you can be more beautiful now than before?"

Avinash smiled and Ari introduced him to Maria. "This is Avinash Batra, my . . . ." She paused, and Avinash hurried to her aid.

"Her boyfriend, with all due respects to your dear brother, Santos."

Maria kissed Avinash on the cheek and raised her eyebrows at Ari in acceptance. Then Diego appeared with his fiancée, adding to the hugging fest.

"Thank you, thank you," he said as he hugged his beloved aunt. "Tia, this is my beautiful bride, Madeline. This is my favorite aunt, Ariadne."

The beautiful dark-haired beauty hugged Ari. "I've heard so much about you and Santos. I'm so happy to finally meet you." Ari could tell from her accent that she was either from Argentina or Uruguay.

The introductions came and went that evening and Avinash was patient, doing his best to make out most of the conversations either in Portuguese, Spanish, or a mixture of both. After a beautiful evening of dining and recounted stories, Diego stood up to make a toast. His demeanor was so much like Santos's that Ari became emotional hearing him speak; even the tone of his voice was identical. Ari was grateful when Avinash reached out in support and gently took her hand in his.

"When we think of true love, we sometimes think of fictitious characters in books, plays, and movies," Diego said. "We wish in our lifetime that we could find a love so deep that it transcends time and distance and even death. A love so committed that imagining ourselves away from the one we love can cause pain. We need this love like the air we breathe, like a drink of fresh water. It nourishes us and sustains us. When I think of true love, I have to look at my Aunt Ariadne, so beautiful and strong. I think of my Uncle Santos who I loved so deeply and who showed me that when you find your true love, no matter what, you should never let any circumstance in life take you away from them. I know my uncle is here in spirit, telling me to make Madeline my wife and never let her go. This evening is for my new bride-to-be, for my Uncle Santos, and my Aunt Ariadne. The love you possessed is my shining example that love never ends. Thank you all for coming. Gracias, Tia. I love you."

Tears rolled down Ari's face and she smiled knowing Santos was present. And she was sure he approved of Avinash; she felt it. As the guests gathered to leave the dinner, Avinash spoke with Jacobo, Santos's brother, and Ari caught up with the other family members. She let them know that she was now living in Positano, in the house Santos wanted for her. Ari recounted how she gave Santos the bon voyage he wanted. She cried as she told the story and the family held her, expressing amazement that she managed to be strong enough to go through with his wishes.

As they said their goodbyes, Avinash gathered up Ari's clutch and the gift from Diego and Madeline. They made their way out to the SUV, which St. John already had running and ready to go.

"Thank you for being so understanding, Avinash," Ari said as they settled into the rear seat. "I know it must all be quite confusing for you, meeting Santos's family tonight."

Avinash smiled with his eyes, and Ari smiled back at those wonderful, deep pools of his. "I expected it, Ari. I hope it wasn't uncomfortable for you that I was there. I wanted to be a part of this, of everything you do. I never want to leave you again, darling."

"Where are we going?" she asked when she noticed they were heading in the opposite direction from the Astoria. Avinash smiled again, like a fox.

"It's a surprise."

***

Ari had no idea where she was. They had travelled only a short distance, but she had her eyes on Avinash and lost track of where they were. The SUV finally pulled to the curb, and Avinash helped Ari from the car. They were in front of a loft building of some kind with an art gallery below in what looked to be the Meatpacking District. They took the steps up and past the center gardens of the gallery and entered a mysterious room.

"I hope this isn't like your uncle's cabin," she said, laughing.

"Oh no," he said. "I wouldn't do that to you again."

The apartment was quaint and unlike Avinash's style, but it had an amazing view of the Hudson. "This is not your place, is it?" she asked sheepishly. Avinash smiled as he pulled a bottle of wine out of the bar.

"No, this belongs to one of my cousins. Her family set her up to study art in New York, and she interns in the gallery below us. The art gallery belongs to her boyfriend. She was not at the wedding in London but she knows about you."

"Oh? How does she know about me?"

He turned to her and smiled with his eyes. "Ari, I held a press conference in London and sort of let the world know that you're my girlfriend," he said.

"Ah, yes," she said. "How could I forget?"

Ari stood in the center of the room, not quite knowing what to do. Avinash followed but sat comfortably on the sofa. He opened his arms to her and, like a little girl, Ari curled up into them. She could feel his warmth. Avinash made no effort to take things further, content at that moment with her mere proximity. Ari felt safe. She felt cared for, and it was just what she needed.

"I know you have doubts about me, Ari. I realized it on the ride to the restaurant when I asked the driver to take us somewhere else and you didn't want to go. I must say I was surprised. What do you want to do?"

She spoke softly into his chest. "I want to talk about us."

Avinash got up and sat on the coffee table facing her. "Very well then. Let's talk. You first. Tell me what's on your mind."

Ari breathed in heavily, searching for the right words. It served to clear the months of pain that enveloped.

"You hurt me deeply. In London, the last time we saw each other . . . that was horrible. It took a long time to recover from your dismissal of me. Despite all of that, I'm stronger now."

Avinash listened intently without interruption. Ari explained her spiral into depression, all of it, even the parts she cringed to discover about herself. Avinash got an earful about Marcelo, what he had done for her. She mentioned all her friends in Positano, naming and describing each one in vivid detail. Ari explained that at times she felt alone, banished from everything she knew, but during those times, as crazy as it sounded, she felt Santos's presence the most, and it usually came accompanied by dreams of her nurse, Devyani.

"Do you see what I have done for you, Avinash Batra?" she said when she was finished. "I have told you everything about myself from the time we last saw each other until now. My question to you is this: what do I truly know about you? Why do you continue to keep me in the dark about your life? Why do I have to learn about your life from a televised press conference? If you can answer these questions, perhaps I could trust you again. Until you do, I'm afraid you're just another stranger to me—a stranger I love deeply, but a stranger nonetheless."

Avinash puckered his lips and proudly lifted his chin. "I believe that you think you don't know me. May I ask what I can tell you that you don't already know about me? Is my past so important that it will not permit you to move forward? Where I was born, what I did in Mumbai, who is my father, my mother? Will that make you trust me or love me more or less than you do today? How much information is enough for you to begin to trust me again? Ari, I feel I need to apologize for hurting you, from the bottom of my heart. I did all of it to protect you. Tonight, Diego's words helped me see that I was wrong for leaving you, and I am truly sorry. I want to move forward now. Can we forget about the past, Ari? What can I do from this moment on to show you that you can trust me? Tell me what you want from me and I will deliver it."

Ari thought about it as she gazed into his eyes, and she realized that she did not want to enter into a long discussion about their breakup or his past. His demographic profile was unimportant. Where he came from and where he lived before she knew him was not why she loved him. Her love for him was so strong that nothing he could say would change her mind about how she felt. Ari knew life had broken her just as badly as it had broken him. But for some crazy reason, when they were together all the broken pieces became whole. *Only together can we mend.*

Ari moved in closer and kissed him. He put his arms around her waist and smiled. "I love you so much, Ari," he whispered. She brushed her lips against his and could feel his hot breath on her face. He smelled divine, the way he always did. Ari noticed he did not attempt any more than what she wanted from him, and he kept his hands on her waist, restraining his desires and trying to regain her trust. She ran her fingers through his dark hair, flecked now with strands of gray. Ari trailed her long fingers down his jawline, over his lips and down his neck.

Avinash began to breathe heavier and she liked it. She continued to touch him, running her hands down his chest and planting tender kisses from his neck to his ear. Still he did not move. She knew he was enjoying it and wanting her to do more . . . much more. Ari pushed Avinash back into the cushions and climbed into his lap, facing him. She unbuttoned his shirt down to his waist, pulled his shirttail from his trousers, and repeated the same steps, running her fingers lightly over his skin, from his waist to his neck, around his ear lobes and into his hair.

"I need you. I need your body pressed against mine, your warmth, your smell, the taste of your kiss, your hands wrapped around me," Ari said taunting him.

Avinash was now panting but kept his eyes fixed on her. Ari moved her body closer, pressing her torso and chest against his. He closed his eyes and whispered in her ear a Hindi phrase she knew well. And though she'd heard the words before, each time felt like the first. "On meeting you it feels like I should keep admiring you. On meeting you it feels like I should keep liking you. The mystic hills are enchanting and my heart is desiring you."

Ari brushed her lips lightly over his and Avinash lost control. He grabbed her hands and closed his eyes, as if one more touch from her would shove him over the edge. Ari was full of longing. She had oceans of want, and Avinash was the tide coming in. His perfect stubble was a bit rough against the inside of her thighs, his licking and kisses only augmenting the fire that was ahead. Avinash went straight for the danger, for the thing that drew him to her. *How do you rush something that you want to last forever?*

Avinash pleased her more. He didn't want her to lose the look of desperation. That look when a woman knows you're close and she doesn't want you to lose the intensity. She pulled him toward her mouth and she tasted him with passion and desire as he hung over her, wet in arousal. Ari and Avinash consumed each other that evening in that loft.

Exhausted and lying side by side until morning, Ari never once let go of the arms wrapped around her.

The next morning while Avinash lay in bed sleeping, Ari sneaked into the living room. The tiny gift box from Diego and Madeline was still on the coffee table. Inside was an antique charm with a beautiful gold filigree border. On the back was an engraved inscription that read, "If love does not make you happy, it was never love." This was something Santos's mother said all the time, and Ari remembered her love and devotion. She held the tiny charm in her hands and kissed it in the woman's memory. It was the perfect gift and it came at the right time.

Ari recalled that almost all of her moments with Avinash had been happy ones. He had been a shower of happiness in her life, a life that was empty because of Santos's departure. Ari started to see Avinash differently— not as a passing love affair but the love of a lifetime. This lifetime, the one she was living now, the one that fate had put in front of her. Ari had to grab hold of it or risk losing it forever.

***

Marcelo arrived at the Waldorf midday after touring the city on his own. Strong coffee and a shower were at the top of his list before the wedding. As he headed down the long corridor, Agent Baromeo approached, looking concerned.

"Have you seen Avinash or Ari?" the agent asked.

"No. Why?"

"I need to inform him of something important," Baromeo said as he hurried off.

Within minutes, Ari arrived at the hotel with Avinash and the security team. Agent Baromeo asked St. John to meet him immediately in one of the small conference rooms adjacent to the ballroom where the wedding would be held. The news? Several bank accounts they'd been tracking for possibly laundering funds, believed to belong to John Ronit, had now been mysteriously changed to another account holder.

"Who's the lucky devil?" asked St. John.

"The twelve million dollars in funds located in Belize, Andorra, Switzerland, and Bruges are now in Avinash Batra's name," Baromeo said.

"Is this a joke?" St. John said.

"It's clear that Ronit or his accomplices want to implicate Batra in a money-laundering scheme to destroy his reputation and remove him as a majority shareholder at World Bank. When this news hits the media outlets it will be devastating, and to make matters worse, we don't know how to stop it."

Unbeknownst to Ari and Avinash, the news would be a media shower of epic proportions within a matter of hours in London

***

Ari left Avinash for a moment and went to check on Marcelo. She nervously knocked on his door and watched as Marcelo appeared half dressed, his bow tie hanging to one side as if he had tried to tie it but gave up.

"Ciao, can I help?" Ari asked as he stepped aside to let her in.

"Happy, *carisima*?" Marcelo smirked as he tugged at his bow tie.

Ari smiled and went to assist him. When she did, she felt he was warm and touched his forehead. "Fever, Marcelo?" she asked.

"No, no, I took a hot bath. I am fine. *Perfetto*."

Ari fussed with his tie again and helped him slip into his jacket before leaving his room. "See you downstairs," she said.

Ari wore a black corsette top and a pink-champagne-colored, flowing skirt with a slit up to her midthigh. One side of her hair was swept up in perfect waves complementing her face exquisitely. The new charm from Diego and Madeline hung daintily from her neck.

"You make me very happy," Avinash said. He wore a black, Prada dress suit, white shirt, and black tie. As always, without much effort, he managed to look like a king, wearing his secure demeanor with effortless style. Together they truly looked beautiful as they walked out of the elevator onto the mezzanine level of the hotel where the ceremony would be held. One of the bridesmaids clipped a beautiful dark-purple calla lily on Ari's wrist and one on Avinash's lapel. Marcelo, who was already waiting, had been bestowed with a similar boutonniere.

In the back of the room, members of the security team were stationed in every corner, trying to appear more like hotel staff than Interpol, though their $8000 ear pieces gave them away.

At the altar, Diego stood with his best man, his uncle Jacobo, and they waited nervously for the bride to make her entrance. The intimate group of about forty guests rose as the beautiful bride arrived with her father to the melodic strains of Debussy's "Clair de Lune." When Madeline finally reached Diego, she kissed her father and took Diego's hand. The resemblance between Diego and Santos was so amazing that Ari felt she was reliving her own wedding. It took every ounce of strength inside of her not to weep like a child.

Ari then took her place alongside Diego for the ceremony of the mantilla, a beautiful Spanish tradition where the godmothers or other special guests tie one end of a Spanish mantilla to the bride and the groom as a symbol of togetherness. Ari stood proud next to Diego, and he held her hand as the officiant read the words that Madeline and Diego had written.

***

Later, as Ari and Avinash danced during the reception, a young boy no more than ten years of age approached Marcelo with an envelope that was securely taped shut. Once the envelope was in Marcelo's hands, the boy sprinted out of the ballroom. Agent Baromeo caught the exchange. Marcelo told him there must have been some mistake. The envelope had the initials AB on the front. He did not know the boy, nor did he know anyone in New York.

Baromeo rushed out of the room with the mysterious package and the security team followed. Ari saw the powerful exchange between the agents and Baromeo from the dance floor and asked Avinash to follow her.

"What happened?" she asked Marcelo.

"It is nothing," Marcelo said. "I was given an envelope by mistake, and Baromeo is making an issue of it."

"An envelope? What was in it?" Avinash asked.

"I don't know. They took it," Marcelo grumbled.

Avinash firmly put his hands on Ari's shoulders and told her to stay with Marcelo. "I'll be back in a minute." He rushed through the wedding party and out of the venue as Ari and Marcelo waited.

Avinash, St. John, and the security team quickly met up with the Manhattan Crimes Unit. Within minutes the van took off with Baromeo, St John, and Avinash inside. They parked several blocks away in a secluded alley, and the crime unit team asked the men to exit the vehicle in case the contents of the envelope were hazardous.

As Avinash paced the sidewalk, his cell phone rang. He pulled it from his pocket and looked at the screen but didn't recognize the number.

"Put it on speaker and answer it," St. John said.

Avinash did as he was told, and what he heard chilled him to the bone.

"Your whole life will come crashing to an end, just as my life did . . . because of you. Checkmate, my old friend." John Ronit ended the call before Avinash could respond.

"Shit!" Baromeo yelled.

"Ari! She's alone! I have to get back to her," Avinash said.

Just then, the doors of the van swung open, and a member of the Crimes Unit informed Avinash and the others that they'd gotten a positive hit on the contents of the envelope. Anthrax. There's no doubt this was an attempt on Avinash's life.

***

Ari answered her phone on the first ring.

"Avinash, where are you?"

"Ari, listen to me carefully. Go quickly with Marcelo and the agents to your room, pack your bags, and wait for me. I am on my way. Do it now, darling. Do you hear me?" Avinash insisted.

"Yes, yes. Okay. I will do it now."

Ari was beside herself as she stuffed her phone back into her clutch.

"Bad news?" Marcelo asked.

"Yes." Her eyes filled with tears. "We have to leave now. Please come with me, Marcelo."

In an instant, two of the agents arrived with instructions to escort Ms. Cordero and Mr. Donati to their rooms. The orders were to get them to the basement level quickly and securely. They would be leaving New York through La Guardia tonight. As the agent rushed her from the ballroom, Ari asked for a brief moment to say goodbye to Diego and Madeline. She ran to them.

"I have to go, my dears. I love you. I love you both. Please visit me in Positano."

And with that, she was gone.

***

Avinash arrived and went up to his room, grabbing only what he needed before rushing to Ari's side. Ari saw him exit the elevator on her floor and yelled out to him.

"Are you all right?"

Before he could respond, Marcelo joined them, and Baromeo and Agent Valverde ushered them into the empty service elevator and pressed the button to the basement floor. Ari clung to Avinash, who did his best to keep her calm.

Marcelo leaned against the elevator wall, his face ashen. As they exited the elevator, Ari turned to Baromeo and whispered, "Help Marcelo, please. He is not well."

Two black SUVs pulled up behind the hotel near the loading dock. They slid into the back seat of one of the vehicles as St. John climbed in front. He picked up his phone and called one of the lead agents at closest to the Airport to ask for a security sweep that included a search and apprehension of John Ronit in case he was trying to leave the city.

"The threat is real. Avinash almost headed back to London in a casket!" St. John said to the agent on the line.

Ari let out a shriek and covered her mouth in shock. "What? You were almost killed today?"

Avinash tried to quiet her as St. John continued his round of calls, but Ari was beside herself in fear. She held Avinash tightly as he comforted her.

As they were ushered through the gate and into the ticketing area, Avinash told St. John that Ari was coming with him to London. Marcelo overheard and said he would be returning to Positano. It was too much excitement for him. Ari, confused by all the commotion, said nothing. It didn't matter where she went as long as she and Avinash went together.

St. John briefed Avinash, explaining that the British media had gotten ahold of the fraudulent bank account news and advising they go somewhere other than London in order to avoid the press. Avinash did not want to go anywhere but back to London and refused. It was settled. Ari would go back to London with Avinash, and Agent

Valverde and Marcelo would head back to Positano with Agent Baromeo.

To avoid suspicion, Avinash and Ari quickly changed clothes in a TSA office near the gate. Ari peeled off her beautiful gown and quickly jumped into jeans, a white pullover, and a long-sleeved sweater but was unable to change her shoes. Avinash gave her a baseball cap and switched his trousers for jeans. It would have to do; it was all they had time for. They headed toward the ticket agent who was already rushing them into the jet.

***

On the flight back, the only thing St. John could do was hope that the media would not be waiting to ambush them when they arrived at Heathrow. First thing Avinash would have to do is hire the best barrister in London to defend himself from the alleged accusation of laundering money for trafficking arms. It would be easy to prove the accounts did not belong to Batra. Agent Valverde had been closely watching the same accounts for quite some time and knew that the original account holder was Ronit.

Nonetheless, the worst part of this would be hearing the higher-ups slam the Interpol team for letting a ten-year-old chap hand a lethal envelope to Donati in the middle of a wedding reception. St. John could just hear the hacks making fun of them. They'd never let him live this one down.

As he watched Avinash trying to calm Ari and reassure her that all would be well, the hardened Interpol agent only hoped their love could withstand the mountain of trouble that lay ahead of them.

Chapter Thirteen

The flight was long and Ari awoke to find Avinash speaking with St. John a couple of rows in front of her. Ari wondered why Akash always swooped in and managed to ruin any happiness Avinash and she shared. She also worried about Marcelo and his medical test results. They would be in soon, and she knew he would not make the appointment without her.

Ari closed her eyes and tried to calm herself, not allowing the anxious feeling to take over and run her thoughts. She replaced the bad thoughts with those of the beautiful wedding and her night with Avinash. When she opened her eyes, she found Avinash sitting next to her. She had no idea how long he'd been there.

"How's my Ari? Sleep well, love?" Avinash said, smiling as he ran his finger under her chin.

Love. How wonderful those words sounded coming from his lips.

"Yes. I guess I'm okay and you?"

"I'm ready," he said as the sky team announced their final descent into Heathrow. Avinash smiled as he squeezed her hand. "We need to be ready."

***

At Heathrow there was no media waiting. . After clearing customs, he was taken by the agents into a room where Scotland Yard and other Interpol personnel were waiting to meet with him. The investigation would be done quietly. Indictments were not in the immediate future unless they couldn't prove Avinash was not the original account holder.

While Avinash met with investigators, Agent Valverde escorted Ari to Anjali's home. During the drive, Ari phoned Marcelo but there was no answer. She left him a message to phone her once he reached Positano. She was hoping the news from the hospital in Sorrento would help ease her fears about his health. Perhaps recruiting Lorraine and Claudia, the strongest in character of the Dolce Vita Club, would get him to the appointment.

When they arrived at the house, Anjali welcomed Ari with open arms and had already prepared some tea. As they spoke, Ari updated her on everything that had happened in New York at her nephew's wedding and the events that brought her back to London.

"Avinash called me to fill me in about the money-laundering charges," Anjali said. "The media will mangle the truth to sensationalize this against Avinash; it's going to be horrendous for the bank, but especially for Avinash. We have to be strong for him. He's going to need our support now more than ever."

Ari smiled and embraced her. "I know," she said. "Our love has gone through so many tests. This is just another one."

***

Before long, fall was upon them. Ari loved that time of year, with its cooler mornings and nights. September proved to be a series of media interviews, with the press chasing Avinash and hounding him for answers. He tried to impress Ari with his air of strength and fortitude, but she was his rock at home and in public, standing beside him at all the press conferences and interviews. Ari was soon the focus of the local press, who speculated about the beautiful, mysterious woman who was always by the World Bank leader's side.

At night, Avinash would come home early to cook for her. Ari's appetite was voracious, and she noticed that it seemed to help him decompress from the negative energy of the day. Her nerves always got the best of her. At times, the monsters of depression wanted to drag her back into the cave of darkness, but Ari bravely fought them off. Whether these recurring feelings were stress or anxiety, the truth was that Ari had never looked better, and Avinash spent as little time away from her as possible. She was his refuge.

***

During a moment of alone time while Avinash was at a meeting, Ari's mobile rang. It was Claudia and she sounded extremely upset. Lorraine was also on the line.

"What's wrong?" Ari asked. "Is it Marcelo?"

"Ari, dear, it's bad news. Are you sitting?" Lorraine said.

"Yes. Tell me, Lorraine."

Lorraine's voice cracked. "Marcelo has lung cancer. He needs to begin chemo in the next weeks. They are hoping the cancer hasn't spread."

Ari dropped the phone and sobbed. *How could he be this sick?* She picked it up again and Lorraine tried to comfort her.

"We will take care of him now, Ari. You need to stay with Avinash. This is what Marcelo wants. He will be in Rome for one week, a rest, and then another series of chemo sessions. They want to blast the hell out of those cancer cells. This will leave him weak, and once he returns he will stay with me. The workers at your home have been dismissed, and when Marcelo is feeling better, perhaps you can let him stay in his room. You know how much he loves that house."

Ari agreed and promised to be back in Positano for his return home. The news was devastating. This was worse than anything Akash could do to her.

***

Ari had promised to join Avinash and Anjali for dinner at Sam's house that evening. She was determined to be there, despite the terrible news about Marcelo. Ari could not go back to that dark place in her soul that gnawed at her from time to time. This stretch of the road in life needed a strong and able-bodied driver with a strength she did not possess. Avinash and Marcelo needed her more than ever. Ari needed to lead them out of the maze and stay the course.

As they sat down at the dinner table, Ari felt sick and nauseous. She picked at her food, moving it around on the plate without truly eating anything.

"Ari, are you okay, dear?" Anjali said. "You're looking a bit pale, and you've hardly taken a bite. Avinash says your appetite has been great lately."

Ari shrugged. "My stomach is unsettled for some reason. Maybe if I lie down for a minute it will pass." Avinash jumped to his feet and escorted her to the nearest bedroom.

"What is it, love?" he asked as he helped her to the bed and covered her with a nearby blanket. "You're ice-cold and certainly not yourself tonight."

"I'm fine, really. Just let me rest for a minute. I'm probably a little worn out from cleaning out the closets today. Please go finish your meal."

Avinash kissed her forehead and rejoined the others. Ari was asleep before the door closed behind him.

***

The next morning, Ari poured coffee into a mug, but suddenly the smell was overwhelming and she couldn't drink it. She made herself a cup of mint tea instead and made Avinash a protein shake that he liked after returning from the gym. He kissed her on the lips and headed to the shower. When he returned, he was dressed for business and looking dashing as always.

"Ari, I've been worried about you lately. Perhaps you'd feel better if you had something to keep you busy here in London. What about working at World Bank in the media department? You're more than prepared for the job, and you can keep me abreast of the news that's happening, while it's happening. I'm afraid I don't often hear what is going on until it's too late to react."

Ari was surprised by the suggestion, but she knew Avinash was right. When she thought of Marcelo and the need to return to Italy in a few weeks, she hesitated—but just for a moment. *I'll work that all out when the time comes,* she thought.

"I would love to work at the bank. When do I start?"

Avinash smiled. "That's the Ari I know. You can start today."

***

Ari spoke with Marcelo daily, even getting the nurses to do face-to-face calls with him so she could see his progress. She was happy that his spirits were up and that he had taken this test with strength. Ari told Marcelo about her job, and he listened intently, asking questions about every detail. The daily chats with Marcelo were moments Ari used to disconnect from work and talk to a friend, and they proved to be a source of strength for her. If Marcelo could withstand the cancer treatments with determination despite the pain he was obviously in, she could be just as strong and help him and Avinash through this rough time in their lives. Ari recalled that she always felt the happiest when she was helping someone else. It must be what Devyani had taught her when she was a little girl, and it remained with her to that day.

Ari's media relations position at World Bank proved to be quite a challenge, but she managed to juggle it and public relations simultaneously. With respect and a firm hand, Ari ran a tight ship, and her staff loved her for it. It was the first time in many years that anyone had truly taken the time to understand the ins and outs of the department or had taken an interest in each staff member, using each of their skills to the fullest potential. She had also become the lead charity organizer and had Avinash involved in many corporate events that not only placed World Bank but Avinash himself in a favorable light with the London press.

Ari and her team managed crisis control with expertise, and the daily news about Avinash and the laundered funds for arms trafficking had fallen back to the last segment of the talk shows, no longer front-page news. During that time, Interpol and local authorities managed to prove that Avinash Batra never owned those accounts and the smoke screen that John Ronit created was now just that—smoke. The indictment was dropped and the case was closed, at least for now. They continued to monitor Ronit's movements, and he continued to prove himself to be elusive, always one step ahead.

During a meeting that Ari organized for the children's charity art event for orphaned children in Darfur, she was having a particularly hard time with one of their largest fundraising corporations. Samboor Traders had been a constant charity sponsor for World Bank for years but for some reason or other was resisting the funding for the charity this time around. Ari and her staff were making no progress in securing a meeting with the head of the company, Ms. Jeanette Samboor. Ms. Samboor, the daughter of a Saudi oil tycoon and a British socialite, was one of the richest women in the United Kingdom and also a beautiful, single cougar in her fifties who usually got what she wanted or, according to the gossip about town, she paid for it. Ari's assistant, Gaby, had heard through the grapevine that she had pursued Avinash relentlessly after the death of Suniel, but he was never interested in her romantically. She also learned that Ms. Samboor once held one of the largest corporate accounts in World Bank history, but there had been some tension between her and Avinash and he'd decided she should bank elsewhere, though they remained friends.

Ari found this new information and her suspicions were tied up in a neat little package that needed some unraveling. She knew Anjali would be out on errands that afternoon, and Avinash would have just returned from his workout at the gym. Ari entered the office and found Avinash in the washroom finishing up his grooming ritual.

"Hi there," she said to Avinash as he walked out of the washroom.

Avinash jumped and then smiled at the sight of her. "Ari, darling, you startled me. Did you need me?"

Ari rarely entered his office unannounced. She did not believe that her romantic ties with him had anything to do with normal business protocol, and she kept a formal business relationship with him at all times, especially in front of staff.

"Well, yes, actually, I need some information that will help me with the charity event for Darfur. Do you have a few minutes?"

Avinash took her by the arm. "Of course! Would you like some tea first?" Ari nodded and he poured her a cup. "What do you need to know?"

Ari took a seat on the sofa. "Do you know any logical reason why Ms. Jeanette Samboor would not return my calls with regard to the charity event participation? I find her silence quite unusual, considering she has been part of this event for many years. Now, for some reason, she wants nothing to do with us. I have checked, by the way, and she's in town. We keep leaving her messages, emails, and yet . . . nothing. Not a word. Think you can help?"

Avinash squirmed in his chair and looked down at his desk, trying to find something to do other than look at her. Ari knew that her hunch was spot-on and pushed further. "Avinash? Any suggestions?"

He cleared his throat. "I don't really know what would keep her from the event, Ari. Perhaps your approach has been different this year? Have you changed your funding request for sponsorships, or maybe we didn't give them the prime spot they had last year?"

Ari had to bite the inside of her cheeks so that the tea cup didn't leave her hand and land on his head. *How can he think this is my doing? Does he think I'm some amateur corporate event organizer?* Ari spoke with calmness but clenched her jaw.

"Avinash, all of the other corporations, some larger than Samboor, have responded with no problem." *How dare he doubt me!* Ari kept her cool and took another deep, cleansing breath. "My approach has been the same with Samboor as it has with all the other corporations that have agreed to participate. I have not downsized their level of participation; in fact, I have even offered Ms. Samboor exclusivity."

Avinash remained silent and wrestled with his papers. Ari knew that it was in his protective nature to give Ari the cleaned-up, Disney version of those dark pieces of his past. Though it troubled her that he was still unable or unwilling to completely open up to her, be it because of his personality or his culture, at least he told her some of it. This time however, the bits and pieces she needed to know about Jeanette Samboor were left in the dungeon, and Ari began to worry. She took the last sip of her tea, stood up, and headed toward the door.

"Ari, please don't leave angry."

Ari turned around at the door and smiled. "Do I look angry to you?"

Avinash came around from his desk and approached her. "You look disappointed," he said.

Ari opened the door and marched toward the elevator. "Congratulations. That's the first truthful thing you've said since I entered your office, Avinash." With that, Ari stepped into the elevator, and the doors slid to a close.

***

"I am so frustrated, Anjali," Ari said that evening as the two of them slipped into a booth at a local pub. "Avinash is giving me the runaround about Ms. Samboor. I guess he's never going to trust me completely."

As they ordered their drinks, Ari's phone rang incessantly. She didn't need to look at the caller ID to know it was Avinash. He'd be home by now and was accustomed to finding Ari there each evening to greet him.

"That was Avinash, wasn't it?" Anjali said as Ari tossed her phone back into her purse. "Tell him where you are. He will worry, especially knowing that Akash may be somewhere close. He loves you, Ari."

Ari had heard enough. "Loves me? He can't even bring himself to tell me the most mundane things about his life."

Anjali smiled as she sipped her martini. "Trust me, *laraki*, Jeanette Samboor has never been an important part of his life. Well, maybe in a business sense, but that's it. So she pursued him like a she-devil. Who cares? She has pursued half of the rich and famous men in this town. Everybody knows that. Ari, listen to me. They had a falling out about business, and he's ashamed that he fell for her plan—which, by the way, was really a trap she elegantly put together with her rich father to snare Avinash into marriage. When he learned what she was really scheming, he pulled out of the deal. The bank lost a lot of money, but Avinash preferred to take the loss rather than marry that harlot."

Ari was even angrier than before. "You mean to tell me that he doesn't want to talk about Jeanette Samboor because he's ashamed that he made a bad business decision?"

Anjali laughed at Ari's naïveté. "Haven't you figured out Indian men yet? They are hardwired to keep honor in everything they do, especially family and business. When you break a business deal, you are someone who cannot keep your word. Avinash is a modern Indian man, but you can't part with these things that are in your DNA. It was an extremely disgraceful part of his business career, but he managed to live through it, and with his personality and good sense, he remained business associates with Samboor. I'm sure Ms. Samboor knows you're his girlfriend, and she will probably make your life a living hell before she gives you her money, dear. Her battle against you has been declared."

Ari couldn't believe the nonsense she was hearing, but she knew it was all too real for Avinash. She decided to finish her drink and head home sooner rather than later. Anjali saw one of the agents at the door of the pub. "Look. There's your ride. Go home, be safe, and go easy on Avinash."

***

When Ari arrived home, she found Avinash at the table scanning the paper. He paid no attention to her as she walked in and hung her coat in the closet. She was extremely tired and didn't want to discuss Samboor, their messy business past, the charity event, or anything else that night.

Ari headed straight to the bedroom and undressed to shower without uttering a word to Avinash. As she let the hot water wash over her body, she felt a sense of peace that took away all the stresses of the day. When she finished, she opened the shower door to find Avinash standing in his pajama pants and T-shirt, a towel in his hands.

She stepped into his arms, and he dried her body slowly, with a soft touch. Then Avinash dropped the towel and felt her warm, damp body with his fingertips. Suddenly, Avinash picked Ari up and carried her to their bed, placing her gently on the plush down covers and pinning her there so he could have his way with her. He kissed her breasts and ran his tongue to her navel and then downward, but Ari refused to open her legs for him. Ari was not budging until she knew the only body he wanted was hers.

***

Avinash had pleasure on his mind, and his lips said it in a thousand ways. He was hungry for Ari and distraught that she had not made more of a move on him. He needed her to touch him; it turned him on. Instead, Ari rolled onto her side, her back to him. Avinash was distracted at her dismissal. She'd never been so distant in bed before. As he considered his next move, Ari arched her back, sliding her bum up toward him. No more cues were needed. His lovemaking was desperate and deliberately needy.

Avinash reached across her hip and used two fingers to caress her right where she liked it the most. Before long she was wet and moaning as she responded to his touch. When Ari threw her head back to reveal the curve of her perfect neck, Avinash knew she was his, and he didn't care how Ari would interpret it. She had such a strong hold over him that he could not live without her for one moment, and he needed her to know that no one mattered more than she.

Afterward, Avinash held Ari as she slept. He brushed a strand of hair from her cheek and watched the steady rise and fall of her breasts. He had never felt this strongly for any woman in his life. Before Ari, he'd been able to take his mind off the sexual pull a woman had on him by replacing those thoughts with something else—usually work or some challenging sporting event. He was an expert at placing women on perpetual hold whenever he wanted and for as long as he wanted. Sometimes he was cruel, but he always managed to win them back with his suave style. As he lay next to Ari, he knew there was nothing that could ever replace her or his feelings for her. She was always on his mind, whether it was during a business meeting or during a game of cricket or polo. For the most part, everything he did was for her or because of her . . . never in spite of her. She was forever in his heart.

***

Ari awoke to a full breakfast that Avinash had prepared for her before heading to the office. There were fresh flowers in a crystal vase on the table and a beautiful envelope on the placemat. Ari was intrigued by the note. She sat down, still in her robe with her hair pulled back, her face just washed, fresh and beautiful, and opened the envelope to read it.

My Ari:

I want to tell you so many things, and yet the only way I know how to tell you is when I make love to you.

I am sorry for keeping things from you. I want to protect you from everything that can harm you. In doing so, I feel that I leave out pieces of my life that you believe may be important. Please know I do not do this deliberately, I do it because I love you.

You are the most important person in my life. You are the most important part of my life. There is no one or anything more important than you. All I want is to love you, to delight you, and to be with you. For this reason, I will personally call Ms. Samboor and ask her to come to the office for a meeting. I will introduce her to you and ask her to participate in the charity. Furthermore, I will ask her to help us as our exclusive sponsor for the charity event for the children of Darfur.

This is difficult for me. I am sure Anjali has filled you in on our business dealings with Samboor. It is the past and you are the present, the now, my future and my forever. For this reason, I will put aside my reservations and help you.

I love you, Ari. You are my life; I cannot be in this world without you. I am yours, and I surrender to your love and to your wishes.

I love you, Avinash

Ari had never read such a simple, yet heart-grabbing, love letter in her life. She did not cry but merely let the love enter her soul and surround her being. The words cradled her and moved her so deeply that she could do no more than to read them over and over again.

If Santos was the most romantic man she had ever met, then Avinash was truly the most inspirational one and, more importantly, the most honest man who had ever crossed her path.

***

Later in the week, the meeting finally took place with Ms. Samboor, Avinash, and Ari. It went smoothly as Avinash explained his desire to have Samboor Traders as the exclusive contributor for the Darfur charity event. Ms. Samboor was a beautiful woman with light skin and Moorish features, not tall but toned and fit. Avinash explained the event in full detail, giving Ari credit for creating a new level of participation and deciding to offer it first to Samboor Traders. Ms. Samboor agreed to the terms of participation, and the rough patch between her and Ari was smoothed out.

***

The charity gala was held at The Mondrian, situated in the vibrant South Bank area on London's Cultural Mile. Ari and the gala committee members had chosen the forties as the theme, with a Casablanca ambiance that included a black-and-white backdrop of an old Hollywood set. No detail was left out, including several Phantom Rolls Royces that were situated at the entrance of the hotel. Gorgeous models dressed in the era's most glamorous gowns beckoned guests to enter the gala.

Ari dressed in a tight black evening gown that covered the front but exposed her beautiful back. The dress hugged her frame down to mid-thigh and then fanned out around her knees in layers of cascading chiffon.

Her hair was pinned up and combed in sleek waves, which complemented her long neck and the strand of dainty pearls that looped around it and dangled down her back. Avinash wore a white dinner jacket, a white shirt, and a black bow tie with black trousers and charol shoes. He greased his hair back and had stubble on his face. Together, they looked like they had stepped out of a Metro-Goldwyn-Mayer movie.

The gala was a success and as it was winding down for the evening, Jeanette approached Avinash, who was seated at the bar enjoying a cigar and admiring Ari's tireless spirit from a distance. Jeanette smiled at Avinash as she leaned against the bar and gazed at Ari with him.

"She's a beautiful soul, Mr. Batra. You did well this time."

Avinash smiled, knowing her words were the truth. In celebration he ordered two flutes of Vintage 2003 Dom Perignon. As they clinked their glasses, Jeanette revealed a hair-raising truth to Avinash that he did not see coming.

"I was approached by John Ronit some months ago," she said. "He was interested in getting my help, wanted me to invest in a project he had. Of course I refused, but I wanted you to know."

Avinash took the cigar out of his mouth and swung the barstool around to face her. "What did he want, exactly?" he said, his tone stern.

"Ronit wanted me to arrange a meeting between him and Ari at an unknown location, and if I refused, he threatened to expose one of my associates who was quietly let go from Samboor Traders some years ago for embezzling. It would have been a media shower of negative press for me, but after hearing your press conference and learning of the kidnapping of his mother and the whole mess with Interpol, I knew that the end result would be worse for me if I got involved with this man. I knew Ari would be hurt, maybe even killed, so in exchange I offered him a sizeable amount of money for his silence. I told him Ari was not in the country and that I was dealing directly with you on the charity. I'm sorry I didn't tell you before, Avinash. I thought it was best not to say anything. This is why I tried to stay away from you and Ari. Giving you the money for the charity was not the problem."

Avinash felt a chill up his spine. He realized that, despite all these months of happiness with Ari, the threat of Akash was still extremely real. Avinash kissed Jeanette's hand, thanked her for her loyalty to him, and then stood up to face her.

"Stay away from John Ronit," he said, warning her as a friend would. "He will be back for more money, and when he returns I suggest you call this man." Avinash handed her a business card with Agent Victor St. John's contact information.

With that, he took the last sip of his 2003 Dom Perignon, placed the flute firmly on the bar, and strutted toward Ari, unbuttoning his tuxedo and loosening his bow tie as he walked. She watched his approach and fell into step with him as he reached her.

"What's happening, Avinash?" she said.

"Let's go," he said. "This party is over." He took Ari by the hand, smiled with his eyes to calm her, and led her out of the venue.

***

The next day, Anjali and Avinash were preparing for the Diwali festival in London. Though Avinash was apprehensive about Ari being in such a large crowd with Ronit still on the loose and Jeanette's terrifying confession, Anjali convinced him that the odds that he would dare come out in public with so much police and security on a day like Diwali was not his style. In the meantime, Ari was still trying to convince Avinash that they needed to visit Marcelo in Positano now that his chemo sessions had ended and he'd returned home. Avinash kept avoiding the issue, telling her that work and her staff needed her now more than ever.

What Ari didn't know is that Avinash had a talk with Sam and Anjali about their future as a couple, and he was entertaining a more serious arrangement between the two of them.

Anjali had argued with Avinash. "You make it sound like a business transaction that you have to close. Have you even thought about calling it what it truly is? It's a proposal of marriage."

Avinash laughed. "You don't think I can go through with a marriage proposal to Ari? I bought the ring on my trip to Dubai. The thought of marrying Ari has been on my mind many times."

Anjali shook her head. "I can't believe my playboy mentor and friend is seriously entertaining thoughts of marriage."

"Well, I think it's a splendid idea. The Diwali festival is full of hope and joy. It would be perfect timing," Sam added.

***

That night, Avinash arrived home with an arrangement of calla lilies and orchids. Ari was sitting in the dining room in a white sweater that wrapped around her waist and a white cotton skirt. She was fuller than before, and her long hair was shiny as it hung in waves past her shoulders. She was going over media clippings and trying to put them in some semblance of order. The dining table was stacked high with papers, and her black-rimmed reading glasses made her look lovely.

"Flowers? How thoughtful. What's the occasion?" Ari asked, smiling from ear to ear.

Avinash leaned in for a long and sexy kiss. Ari breathed heavily as she touched his face with desire.

"I love you, Ariadne Cordero. I was thinking of you on my way home and made a stop for these flowers." Ari smiled and took off her glasses,

"You're so incredibly sweet, handsome, sexy, adorable, and charming," Ari said with a giggle.

"That's all you can think of? Isn't there more?" Avinash asked.

After dinner and a conversation about visiting Positano in the next weeks, Avinash slowly led Ari to the bedroom where he kissed every inch of her body. Ari removed only her top and left her hair in a loose bun. She then undressed Avinash and placed his dress tie over her head, letting it hang seductively between her breasts. With mischief in her eyes, Ari pulled Avinash toward her and then sat him on the edge of their large bed.

She sat on his lap and he slid one hand beneath her skirt as his mouth enveloped hers. Ari relaxed, allowing her legs to fall open and his fingers to find her silkiness in slow circles.

"Don't make me scream just yet," she whispered in his ear.

But nothing would satisfy Avinash more than seeing her lose all control. Then, Ari's back arched and she tightened around his fingers. Avinash was an extremely generous and expert lover, and Ari was just as good at receiving pleasure as she was at giving it. Together, the two lovers were invincible when they were in each other's embrace.

***

After several weeks with Lorraine, Marcelo moved back to 87 Viale Pasitea with renewed energy. This added vigor impelled him to finalize the renovations at the home and give it the touches it needed for completion. Upon entering the home, there was light and harmony. The ocean was center stage, with a jaw-dropping view to the blue waters of the Mediterranean from almost every room. The Cuban floor tiles glowed after the industrial marble polisher brought in from Naples was finished with them.

Marcelo built a shrine-like prayer alcove under the staircase. It would serve as a meditation room and provide a protective shield from tremors or possible earthquakes. The kitchen was large and spacious, and the cabinets were strategically placed so Ari could have a view of the ocean any time she wanted. The old terrace with those cascading bougainvilleas, where Ari spent much of her time recovering from her illness, was now a reading and entertaining room.

The sun terrace that once had no protection from the sun or privacy from the neighbors living in the houses above had a built-in remote-control canopy that was set to close with the morning's light and opened automatically at sunset to showcase the spectacular shower of stars on a clear night. A massive gas fire pit was also installed. Ari bought a sectional sofa and three loungers in Capri, setting them around the fire pit to create a cozy area perfect for visiting with friends or a bit of romance.

Marcelo continued to create his masterpiece with the home as the canvas and Ari as his inspiration. Upstairs, her bedroom was a brilliant white with touches of warm chocolate colors and its own gas fireplace. The original windows were torn down and double Plexiglass doors installed to showcase a view of the marina and the coastline beyond it up to Amalfi. Marcelo knew Ari was always looking for inspiration in everything, and he knew words were important to her, so he brought in a skilled artist to write in flowing script on the wall above her headboard. The words read: "Two sleepy people by dawns early light too much in love to say good-night."

The bedroom furniture Ari had chosen came from Morocco and had Arabic influences. Ornate mirrors were propped against the wall and on top of the dresser, never hung on the walls. The dim lighting was supplied by all types of lamps from India, and additional Moroccan lamps and lanterns were powered electrically or manually by lighting a wick the old-fashioned way. Some were strung over the bed and others rested on the floor alongside oversized white pillows and Indian rugs. Marcelo had done his best to make sure the home was exactly as Ari had envisioned it. All that remained was her final approval. Only then would he feel his job was complete.

It had been a long day. Marcelo, exhausted and alone, sat on the third step of the staircase—the same staircase where Lucia had taken the fall that ended her life—sipping a glass of Campari, a bitter cordial that he had mixed with tonic water to kill the stomach pain he was feeling lately. As he sat in silence, he wondered what his life would have been like if he'd lived in this beautiful home with a family of his own. After a moment recalling his memories, he realized one fact he could not hide any longer—87 Viale Pasitea had never been his home. It had been the escape valve for his passion for gambling, and Lucia had been his way of righting all the wrongs in his life. After a while, there'd been no life between them, and her resentment had grown to the point of wanting to leave for good. The home witnessed all this negative energy and still withstood the test of time, until Ari and Santos saw it and wanted to make it a home of their own. The home was not cursed after all; it was simply waiting for someone to fill it with love and hope and life. Finally, Marcelo understood. The home belonged to Ari. Love would find a home within its walls once again, but only if Ari was inside it with the man she loved.

***

This year, Diwali came to London a little later than usual, and a cold snap was in the air. The Festival of Lights is timed to coincide with the new moon, the darkest night of the month, in October or November, so the actual date varies from year to year. The practice of stringing bright lights and giving sweets or gifts appealed to Ari, who was a big fan of local festivals and celebrations from any country. She fondly remembered the festival of Saint Jordi in Barcelona and joining Santos and his family for the Festa de São João do Porto to pay tribute to Saint John the Baptist in a party that mixes sacred and profane traditions.

Diwali represents the victory of good over evil and light over darkness. The word *Diwali* or *Deepavali* literally means "a row of lamps." Enthusiastically celebrated around the world, Diwali marks new beginnings and a renewal of commitment to family values. It represents joy, love, reflection, resolution, forgiveness, light, and knowledge.

As Ari was getting ready to head out with Avinash, who would be home after his morning run, a cold chill crept up her spine, similar to the one she felt when she was attacked by the two men on motorbikes. Ever since her illness, Ari was much more perceptive and unexplainably sensitive to foreseeing the future. The feeling was strong this morning, and Ari felt a need to protect herself from whatever evil was out there. She fell to her knees and prayed, asking God to take this feeling away. Ari begged God for help, for guidance, and as she clasped her hands in prayer, she asked for forgiveness if she ever was pretentious in the way she handled life. Rarely did Ari feel the need to pray in this manner, but the feeling was powerful. As she cried for help, she heard a voice tell her to "get up and be strong." As she did so, she heard the front door open, and she quickly wiped the tears from her eyes. Avinash found Ari washing her face in the bathroom basin.

"I'll take a quick shower and we'll be on our way," he said. "Anjali is already there with Baromeo. It seems that security will be tight today, but you need not worry. I'm with you, and we are being accompanied by an agent." His gaze caught hers in the mirror and he cocked an eyebrow. "Are you all right, love?"

Ari dried her face and smiled as big as she could. "Of course! Hurry or we'll be late," she said as she hurried from the bathroom without another word.

CHAPTER FOURTEEN

Trying to park in London was a mission on any given day, but trying to find an open space during Diwali was next to impossible. Ari and Avinash decided to take the tube to Trafalgar Square with several task force agents. The ride over was crowded, and the agent asked for backup when they arrived at the station. This time, St. John had taken every precaution, and a special task force had been set up in and around Trafalgar Square.

They arrived and two more agents joined them as they were escorted from the busy station and onto the street above them. They met up with Anjali, Agent Baromeo, four special forces agents, and Sam. The sea of people was overwhelming. Though the majority were Indians, every other culture in London was represented. A group of children sang on stage as Avinash explained the festival to Ari and how it is typically celebrated in Mumbai. Ari tried to listen but it was difficult to hear in the noisy throng, and Avinash signaled the group to move to a less-crowded area of the square.

Ari was immersed in the music, and she paused to listen to the children who were singing and dancing. Anjali, Avinash, and the agents went on ahead without noticing she was no longer with them. Ari felt a strange force, an all-encompassing, negative energy in the midst of the joy and love that surrounded her. The feeling penetrated her soul and something told her not to look in the direction it was coming from; there was danger if she did. Ari felt the hate and saw it in the eyes of John Ronit as he walked in her direction.

Everything in her body told her to run, but she was frozen with fear. She wanted to yell for Avinash but could not. Suddenly an elderly woman bumped into her and woke her from the trance. Ari shoved her way through the crowd and into an abandoned building nearby. She spied the rusty remains of an ice cream stand and instinctively ducked behind it. Ari watched from her hiding place as Avinash searched for her, frantically yelling out her name into the crowd. She wept as quietly as she could, holding her hand to her mouth to quiet the sobbing as she saw Avinash desperately searching for her in panic. Ari hid deeper in the old ice cream vendor stand and whispered, "Please God, help me. Please don't abandon me now."

She waited a few more minutes and then stepped out from the safety of her hiding place. As she did so, she was grabbed from behind. A massive hand was slapped over her mouth, and a covering of some sort was lowered over her head. Her abductor tucked her under one arm and began to drag her. She couldn't see her attacker, but she sensed it was Ronit, and she struggled unsuccessfully to release herself from his grasp.

The path they were taking twisted and turned until her attacker stopped in his tracks and shoved her to the floor. She hit her head but managed to right herself. Ari yanked the hood from her head and found herself in complete darkness. She couldn't see anything and was too scared to yell or call for help. Ari could hear someone shuffling closer to her and tried desperately to crawl away from them.

A click echoed around her, and the room was suddenly bathed in light. She squinted, blinking hard to adjust her vision. And then she saw him. Akash Ramkissoon stood before her wearing a smirk that implied he had trapped his prize. He held his cigarette lighter high as he kneeled before her and ran his dirty fingers down her leg. Ari kicked him with all her might and dragged herself away from him, but he came at her with force and lifted her by the arm, throwing her against a wall and crushing Ari with his own body. Again, the room was engulfed in darkness.

"Let me go, Kash! Let me go," she pleaded, trying to free herself from his grasp as he whispered something to her in Hindi over and over again.

Akash grabbed her face and kissed her as Ari struggled to break free.

"Stop!" she yelled, spitting at him as he pulled his lips from hers. Suddenly, a warmth enveloped her, and a peace she could not explain settled over her. A powerful strength filled her. Ari was ready to die if she had to, but first she needed to tell her attacker something.

"I just realized why I came to London, Akash. All of this makes sense to me now—the chance meeting with you, then Avinash, and later learning that you were trying to hurt me. I couldn't understand any of it before, but now I see it."

Ronit moved in closer. "What do you understand now?" he said, his voice angry in the darkness. Ari scrambled to her feet, and Ronit flicked on the lighter to see her.

"I'm glad Santos found out about you and told the authorities. You might have killed him, but you will never be in peace. You have been hiding like a rat ever since his death. I clearly understand what brought me to London first. It was Santos who pushed things—life, destiny, whatever you want to call it—so I could meet Avinash and he could protect me from you. Santos was the one who nearly put you away forever, and Avinash will do it now, once and for all."

With a horrific, chilling laugh, Ronit spewed the worst of his venom. "Ari, you're so fucking innocent. You know you've wanted me from the moment we met. That wasn't a chance meeting. I've been after you for some time. All I was trying to do was take your beloved Santos's place and steal the millions he made from the tequila. I'm not hiding, love. I'm preparing to bury someone, that protector of yours, the one Santos, in his so-called spirit life, is telling you to run to. The only problem is, both of the men who are trying to protect you will soon be dead. In fact, one already is. You will finally be mine! And if that doesn't work out, I'll find a way to dispose of you too.

"So there you have it. The cycle will repeat itself again. Isn't it funny, Ariadne, how life has a way of doing a 360 on you? Here I am again, with you, and I have the power to choke the life from you. Can you imagine the guilt Avinash will feel when he sees your lifeless body?"

Ari held her breath as he ranted. Suddenly, he stopped, cocking his head to listen as the sound of footsteps and muffled voices echoed from somewhere in the building. The crackle of radio chatter in the distance gave Ari hope that the police were coming to rescue her.

Akash opened the door, and Ari caught sight of a shadowy figure lurking just beyond it.

"How close are they?" Akash whispered to whoever waited in the hallway. "Dammit! You were supposed to watch the car. You're useless, Green Valley!"

The figure disappeared without uttering a sound. Green Valley? Ari dare not say how she knew those words, but she was angry. The pieces were starting to fall into place.

"Now about that something you have...I want it right now. Where's the tiny bag with the dirt Ari?"

Ari could see he meant business. His presence in the tiny room was getting more and more aggressive. However, the irony of the question was too much for her. *He has gone to great lengths to capture me.* Ari decided to press further, she had nothing to lose.

"All of this is about a bag of dirt? Are you kidding me?" Ari laughed mockingly.

"Why don't you just tell me how you killed my husband, Kash? Before I die, I deserve to know."

***

Akash came at Ari with a vengeance. He was in no mood for games. He picked Ari up by the neck with one hand, pushing her up against the wall.

"You want to play games with me, Ari?" he said, his fingers pressing tighter on her neck.

Suddenly Ari could feel the warm comfort that always surrounded her when she was in trouble. As she drifted in and out of consciousness, the peaceful presence lifted her away. She could hear Akash screaming at her from a distance, but her mind played a dreamlike scene and Ari wanted to be taken there. She sensed the answers to her many questions waited just beyond.

Ari hovered over a desert. It was cloudy and windy, but she saw two men before her. One was in a car, and the other was standing nearby. They were talking, and one of them was very familiar. Ari could sense one of them was in trouble, he had something to hide. Then she heard his voice and knew- it was Santos! She listened as their voices floated around her, eager to know more.

"So, amigo, meeting up with the team?" the man asked

"Yes, sir," Santos seemed to answer obediently.

"What was in the warehouse?" The man was nervous and realized Santos was no fool.

"I'm heading there, you know. The Place. Where you should be. Is this normal protocol?" Santos asked. "All this protocol stuff is way out of my league."

"Don't worry about that. Let's take a look at what you have. Is it in the trunk? Get out of the car and open it."

Ari could see Santos move out of the car slowly. He opened the trunk and the man, Green Valley, as Santos referred to him, pried the box open. Closing it abruptly, he pulled out his gun and held it to Santos's head. Ari was consumed with fear, and it had nothing to do with the life being choked out of her by Akash. She needed to see more.

"Okay, buddy, take it easy. If you want this, take it. Take the car too. Just go and leave me here," Santos reasoned with the man who was nervously pacing and pointing a gun at him.

Suddenly, Ari was relieved when Green Valley asked Santos to leave with the box of ammunition and the money. She smiled as she watched Santos get back in the car and drive away.

Akash watched the smile cut across Ari's face. "What the hell do you find amusing about being choked to death?" he said as he dropped her to the floor.

Ari floated in and out of the scene she was being shown. "He's coming home," she said.

Akash became frustrated and yelled at her. "What? Who the hell are you talking about?"

Ari saw Green Valley in a car chasing behind Santos, the vehicles driving fast through the twists and turns of the canyon's wet road. He caught up with Santos a couple of miles ahead and rammed the back of his vehicle, sending the car on a tailspin on the wet road. It plunged down into a steep ravine.

The last thing she saw was her love gasping for air. Ari awoke holding her neck.

While she was getting her wits together, she saw Akash open the door slightly to check the position of the agents again, but no one was there.

Ari cleared her throat and finally spoke.

"You couldn't do it yourself, so you sent someone to do it for you. Santos had proof in the car, the proof you want so badly. But your guy couldn't find it in the wreckage, and so your thug cleaned the car for prints and left him there to die. You coward! I would rather die than give you that bag."

Ari delighted in the look of astonishment Akash had on his face. It was impossible for him to comprehend the power

Santos had on Ari and what he showed her about that horrific day.

Ari sat on the floor, fighting back the rage over Santos's death that threatened to overtake her.

Ari listened as the shouts grew louder. Whoever was coming was getting close. Akash opened the door again, and she could see him more clearly in the shadowy light from the doorway. She looked around, hoping to find something she could use as a weapon if she got the chance. She noticed a bottle on a shelf above her head and reached up for it, tucking it behind her back when Akash wasn't looking.

Ari was filled with rage. The threat to Avinash was more than she could bear. With her rescuers close at hand, she snapped. Ari threw the glass bottle at Akash, and it broke in his face. Whatever was in it ran down his neck and into his shirt, and he screamed as the liquid burned his face and eyes.

A strong voice told her, *Fight, Ari! Fight!* Ari obeyed. Functioning on pure adrenaline, she picked up the lighter that Akash had tossed aside, flicked it on, and threw it at him. The burst of flames engulfed his shirt, and she scurried away as he came at her. Ronit ran past her and stumbled into the hallway as Ari called out to the approaching men.

The first one she saw was St. John, with Agent Baromeo and the rest of the team close behind.

"That way! He went that way!" she yelled, pointing in the direction Ronit had fled.

St. John and the rest of the team followed in pursuit as Baromeo reached out to her.

"That's a nasty cut on your forehead," he said. "We need to get you out of here."

"I'm okay," she said, swiping at the blood that coated the left side of her face. "I think I set him on fire. I threw a bottle . . . there was something in it. He must be burned. You'll be able to find him. Go! Don't worry about me! Just go!"

***

On the street, St. John passed Avinash and Anjali who were desperately searching for Ari. They stopped St. John and asked him what happened.

"Ronit had Ari. She's been hurt. We're tracking him down. Go inside and help her. Go!" he yelled.

Avinash ran into the building, pushing his way through the multitude of parading bystanders. Anjali could not keep up with him and followed as best she could from a distance. When Avinash turned the corner of the long, dusty corridor, he spotted Ari slumped against a doorframe. He ran to her and she collapsed in his arms, her face and torso covered in blood.

"My darling, are you okay?" Avinash said as he knelt beside her.

"Avinash," she whispered, fighting to remain conscious. "I . . . Green Valley."

Avinash held her in his arms and rocked her as he cried, praying she wasn't seriously injured. He struggled to his feet with Ari in his arms as Baromeo returned.

"She torched the son of a bitch," the agent said. "We found pieces of his burnt clothing not far from here, but he's disappeared. We found his getaway car too, in a nearby alley. There were computers and mobile devices inside.

Ronit's whole network and databases have been confiscated. We also found Ms. Singh in the back seat, bound and gagged. She's dead, Avinash. Even if we don't find him today, we can shut him down. We have him! We have him, do you hear me?"

Avinash was bewildered. The news on Ronit was great, but Ari wasn't moving and he couldn't focus on anything but her. Blood still oozed from the gash on her forehead, and Avinash wiped it away from her eyes.

When Anjali finally reached them she was horrified. She knelt next to Avinash and gazed at Ari's pale, bloody face.

"Get an ambulance, Gianni! Dammit, call an ambulance!" she yelled. Baromeo assured her they were on the way.

As Anjali did her best to clean Ari's face, Avinash stopped her. "Ari said the words 'Green Valley' right before she fainted. You once told me those words meant something. What does it mean, Anjali? What does it mean?"

***

Ari was rushed to the hospital and was placed in the Intensive Care Unit. Avinash and Anjali did not leave the waiting room. The extreme loss of blood and the blow to the head left a concussion that healed slowly, but within two days Ari was awake and responsive. When she finally opened her eyes, Avinash was by her bedside.

"Am I dead?" she whispered as he caressed her cheek and gently kissed her hand.

"No, darling, you're very much alive." He kissed her on the lips.

"I've had a hard day, Avinash. Tell me something beautiful, please," Ari said, her eyes filled with tears.

Avinash smiled and said the most beautiful thing he could think of:

"Ariadne."

***

Anjali called the ladies in Positano, who informed Marcelo of Ari's abduction. He was given medical clearance to get on a flight to London, though Anjali did her best to talk him out of coming, knowing full well that he was in no condition to travel. Within a matter of hours, Marcelo arrived at the hospital in London with Lorraine and Claudia.

When Anjali saw the three of them coming down the hospital corridor, she ran to them. "It was all my fault," she said, tears streaming down her face as her friends embraced her. "I shouldn't have insisted she come to the festival knowing Akash was still out there."

All of them did their best to reassure and comfort her.

"Don't worry, Colgate. Ari is a strong woman," Marcelo said, patting her arm. "Now tell me, where is my girl?"

"She's in room 408. Avinash is with her. He doesn't know you have come," Anjali said.

"That's okay, *cara mia*. It's about time we met again, no?"

***

The agents had waited for Ari's health to improve before beginning the interrogation process, but her harrowing experience with Ronit was still fresh. Avinash sat beside her, holding her hand as she answered their questions. She recalled everything with acute detail and told them he was not alone. She recalled with great clarity that he had called out "Green Valley" to someone in the hallway.

298

"I'm convinced that this Green Valley is a person of great interest to the investigation," Baromeo said. "But we've been unable to put all the pieces together. We know he had something to do with your late husband's death, willingly or otherwise. And someone—Green Valley, perhaps—removed evidence from the car. And apparently he's here now and is somehow tied to Ronit. These details are irrefutable. The rest is still up in the air, including his true identity. But we're definitely on the right track, Ms. Cordero."

Ari shrugged. "I'm not a sleuth. I simply needed to know how my husband died." Ari broke into tears and the agents let her mourn. She didn't tell the agents what she saw in her mind that day. They would not believe her. It was hard even for her to believe it, but she knew it was Santos showing her the way. Ari decided to keep quiet.

Before Ari could regain her composure, the door to her room burst open and in strolled Marcelo.

"Marcelo!" Ari carefully stood up and hugged him so tight that he nearly lost his balance.

"*Ragazza*, strong and ready to fight," he said, laughing. "How are you, *carissima*?"

Ari quickly noticed Marcelo's ailing state but chose not to mention it. He seemed frail and looked to be about twenty pounds thinner. Marcelo turned and stretched out his hand to Avinash, who stared him down for a moment before shaking his hand.

"I'll be outside, Ari. You two seem to have a lot of catching up to do." Avinash cast an intimidating glance at Marcelo and hurried from the room

***

Lorraine and Claudia finally got a good look at the famous Avinash Batra as he stormed into the waiting room. With Avinash still within earshot, Claudia leaned over to Lorraine and said, "I'll take one of those with whipped cream and strawberries. Delicious!" Lorraine poked her and asked her to control herself. Anjali watched him, waiting for Avinash to explode, but he managed to calm himself down.

"What is he doing here, Anjali?" he asked.

"He's a good friend."

Avinash snapped, "Yes, I know that. Ari has already told me that he is a *good friend*. What is he doing here?"

Anjali sat down and motioned for him to join her.

"Look, Avinash, you already know the story. When you left Ari, he helped her. Marcelo has been with Ari in the good and bad times, but mostly the bad ones when you weren't there. You should be grateful that he was a faithful and loving companion for Ari. There's nothing between them. At least I don't think there is. Relax."

When he didn't respond, Anjali rolled her eyes at him and crossed the room to join the ladies.

Avinash felt like the outsider on this one. For the first time in his life, he felt like the second baseman in a woman's life, and he was not comfortable playing that position. Avinash decided to restrain his discomfort and wait patiently for Ari to recover. He walked over to Lorraine and Claudia and introduced himself.

"Pleased to meet you both and thank you for taking care of Ari in Positano."

Claudia was awestruck and positioned herself uncomfortably close to Avinash, nudging her voluminous breasts up against him. "*Cara mia*, you should have been taking care of Ari in Positano and not leave it to a sexy Italian man to do this job for you," she said.

Avinash clenched his jaw but managed to smile as he excused himself and left the waiting area.

***

Ari told Marcelo the wild story of Akash and how she narrowly escaped him.

"I had a feeling something bad was going to happen that day. I prayed for God to save me and help me. I know he answered me, Marcelo. A voice told me to get up and fight, similar to the one I heard on the terrace that day. Remember? Perhaps you don't believe in these things, but when I return to Positano, you and I will go to mass every Sunday."

Marcelo raised one eyebrow. "Maybe you don't have to go to church to pray."

Ari asked Marcelo for some water and took a few sips. "So, what do you think of Avinash?"

"Ahh. Avinash. Well . . . I don't know him at all . . . but he seems like an interesting gentleman. He loves you. I can see that, Ari. What are your plans with him?" Marcelo asked as Ari returned the glass of water to him.

"I know that I love him, Marcelo, but I need time. All of this trouble with Akash is wearing down our relationship." Ari looked away, pensive.

A sudden knock at the door startled them.

"Well, Ms. Cordero, I have your test results," the doctor said as he strolled into the room. After Marcelo excused himself and left to give them privacy, the doctor continued. "The results of the brain scan came back normal. You'll be pleased to know that you are cleared to leave the hospital tomorrow. Luckily, none of the trauma you received will affect the baby. I'm sure you were worried about that."

Ari stared at him, dumbfounded. "Baby? What baby are you talking about, Doctor?"

"Ms. Cordero, you're almost 13 weeks pregnant. You were aware of this, weren't you?"

Ari wasn't showing, and aside from missing her period the month before and having an unusually hearty appetite, she had no apparent signs that motherhood was in the picture.

"I-I . . . I see, Doctor. I had no idea," Ari said. "Thank you for all your attention. Please don't inform my friends outside of this news. I would like to be the one to tell them. I appreciate your discretion."

The doctor agreed and left Ari alone with her thoughts. She placed her hands on her belly and smiled. *Baby?*

***

Agent Baromeo and two other uniformed officers returned to keep watch outside Ari's room for the evening. Avinash, Marcelo, Claudia, Lorraine, and Anjali headed out for a light dinner, where they were joined by Sam. They made uncomfortable small talk in the quaint English bistro just a block away from the hospital. As Marcelo wrestled with the flavorless steak he had ordered, Avinash watched him intently. He realized Marcelo was probably a strong contender for Ari's attentions. Though he was sick, he was still handsome, interesting, and could hold a conversation. Worst of all, he was Ari's constant companion. *Yes, indeed,* Avinash thought, *he could easily lure Ari over to his side.* Avinash decided it was time to do something about that.

"I wanted to thank you for taking care of Ari all this time, but when she's feeling better that will no longer be necessary. Ari will be my wife soon, and I will take care of her from now on, Mr. Donati."

Avinash was brash and cocky, but Marcelo was no pushover. He cocked his jaw to one side and stared at Avinash, his grey eyes narrowed and more intense than they'd been a few minutes before.

"Ari will do what she wants when she is ready, and only Ari will decide who she wants to be with. It will be hard to pull her from her home in Positano. She has made a beautiful life there. *Buona suerte*, Mr. Batra. I wish you both much happiness," Marcelo said, his voice dripping with sarcasm. He raised his glass of red wine to everyone at the table. "*Salute a tutti.*" Then Marcelo excused himself, got up from the table, and headed toward the door.

The women all looked at each other. Marcelo had just punched Avinash's ego where it hurt the most.

Avinash did not know what to make of it all, but he wanted Ari back in his life and was ready to fight for her. The battle was not against the ghost of Santos anymore; it was now strategic warfare to win her heart back and have her stay in London—at any cost.

***

The next morning, Anjali and Ari had a long talk about the little bag of dirt. It was concerning to Anjali that Ari had not told the agents that Akash was after it.

"You realize he can come back for you, Ari. You still have what he wants. Something in that damn little bag has had him chasing after you for the last four years. Please let me tell Gianni about this. You must."

Anjali was firm but Ari was not conceding this. It was hers alone. Something deep inside told her to keep this to herself.

"Anjali, please try to understand. Our lives have been turned upside down since I arrived in London. Santos wanted me to have this. Why? I don't know. We still don't know why they want it or who this Green Valley person is. Please, just let this go."

When Anjali opened her mouth to protest, Ari silenced her with some other, more personal, news. Marcelo, Agent Baromeo and the ladies arrived a minute later and found Ari looking better and Anjali wide-eyed. Within minutes, Avinash came in and asked to be alone with Ari. They all excused themselves and headed toward the door except for Marcelo, who refused to leave unless Ari gave her approval.

"I'll be fine, Marcelo. Thank you," she said with a tender smile.

Once the door closed behind Marcelo, Avinash sat on the edge of the bed and placed her hands in his.

"Ari, I don't know how to start this conversation, but it's important. I have spent months thinking about us and all of this mess I have gotten you into. I'm sorry you had to go through all of this. Hopefully, Akash will be caught now, and we can put all of this behind us, forget it ever happened. All I know is that I love you. I want to be with you, and I don't want you to go back to Positano."

Ari moved away from the bed they were sitting on and stared out the window, looking for a way to be completely transparent with her feelings.

"I am stronger than I knew, Avinash. I survived a horrible illness thanks to the friends I made in Positano, incredibly good and caring friends, one of whom I'm sure is standing right outside the door. He is not my boyfriend, if that is what you're worried about. However, what he has been is a companion, a healer, a confidant, a support, and a loyal friend. Marcelo is sick. I'm sure you can see that. He needs me now and—"

"Ari, why is there always something or someone that needs you more than I do? First it was the house and Santos, and now it's Marcelo who needs you. When do I get my turn? Your life is here. There is nothing for you in Positano."

Ari's eyes, filled with tears of disbelief, turned a deep green.

"Wait just a minute, Mr. Batra. Am I not here for you now? Did I not change my plans, my life, for you, Avinash? I have always been here for you, despite my own needs, and have done so willingly, lovingly, for us. Can you say the same? Did you come to my aid when I needed you in Positano?"

Ari walked over to Avinash and stood face-to-face with him, more strength in her voice than she ever had before. "You should thank him," she said, pointing to the door. "That man saved my life. I love you, Avinash Batra, but I cannot stay with you when there is danger lurking in every corner. I have to protect myself, and I have to know you will do whatever it takes to be with me." She came closer and hugged him. "I'm leaving for Italy with Marcelo and the ladies later today. The rest I leave up to you. You asked me what is in Positano? Well, it's me. Ariadne Cordero will be in Positano, Avinash. If you want me, you know where to find me."

Ari walked out of the room and left him standing in a daze. No woman had ever denied him love or affection; after all, he was the powerful and charming Avinash Batra. What woman could turn him down? But Ari was different and she could, in fact, live without him—even if he could not survive without her.

***

Later that evening, the group waited at Heathrow to board their flight to Naples. Anjali was distraught that Ari could not work things out with Avinash, but Ari hadn't lost all hope.

"Perhaps something will bring us together again. Life has a way of returning the good or the bad you have done. Isn't that what the Hindu faith is based on? I know Avinash loves me. I think he has to figure out what the measure of real love is and what one is willing to do to keep it."

Anjali smiled. "You know him better than anyone else ever has, Ari. I'll keep hoping things will work out between the two of you. Safe travels. I'll visit soon, I promise."

"My birthday is in December. I expect you front and center at my party. The Dolce Vita Club can always use another member," Ari said, turning to pick up her bags.

Marcelo and the ladies hugged Anjali, and then she watched as Ari and the others disappeared into the crowd at Heathrow, joining Agent Baromeo who waited just ahead of them.

***

Ari followed the other travelers onto the crowded escalator. As she rose up and over the sea of people below her, she looked back, hoping for one more glimpse of Anjali. As Ari caught sight of her, her heart dropped into her stomach. Avinash stood with Anjali, raking his hand through his tousled hair as his eyes darted through the mass of bystanders. It stunned her momentarily but she managed to recover and waved her hand, smiling and hopeful. Avinash spotted her and smiled back, but the smile never reached his eyes. Even from a distance she could feel the sadness in his gaze.

When the escalator reached the top, Ari turned away and stepped off. When she looked back one last time, Anjali and Avinash were gone.

Chapter Fifteen

It was late when the flight touched down in Naples, and Ari was exhausted. They headed toward Positano, and the group decided to stay with Ari at her home that night. More than anything, they wanted to see her face when she finally saw the finishing touches on the home Marcelo had repaired to its current splendor.

Ari turned the lights on, dropped her bags, and gaped in amazement as she covered her mouth.

"Dear God! Marcelo, this is a masterpiece. Is this all mine?" she asked in disbelief. "You did all of this for me?"

"*Si, signora.* This is your home," he said, fighting back tears.

Ari hugged Marcelo so sweetly that she practically cradled him in her arms as she kissed his cheeks, clinging to him like a life raft. She was grateful that God or fate had put him in her life. "We should all pray, give thanks. I know it's late, but there are so many reasons to be grateful for everything we have."

Lorraine and Claudia opted for a less spiritual experience, heading quickly to the terrace and uncorking several bottles of wine.

"We'll be out here feeling grateful while you're praying, dear," Lorraine yelled from a distance.

Ari smirked, knowing her friends weren't particularly religious, and asked Marcelo to take her on a tour of the house instead.

Marcelo started with the kitchen; it was everything Ari ever wanted. The panoramic window was sure to offer a breathtaking view from sunrise to sunset. The center island with a grill and coal oven was a chef's dream.

He then led her upstairs to show her the other exquisite rooms, each with its own style and theme. The bathrooms were finished with the most beautiful granite rock she had ever seen. As she peered down into the living room from the top floor landing, Ari marveled at the shine of the Cuban tiles that had been restored to their original beauty.

"You can teach me to cha-cha on that tile," Ari joked.

Marcelo then led Ari into her bedroom and opened the electric blinds on the new sliding doors that offered a view of the city marina. Ari loved the writing on the wall. She sat on her bed and asked him to sit beside her.

"It's beautiful, Marcelo. I don't know what to say. Can you imagine? Ariadne Cordero does not know what to say?"

Marcelo laughed. "It must surely be the end of the world if you are quiet."

Ari laughed with him and put her arms around his shoulders. "I think there is something we must do first," she whispered.

Marcelo looked at her inquisitively. *"Cosa dobbiamo fare?"*

Ari smiled up at him. "We must babyproof the house."

"Cosa? What is this babyproof?" he asked.

Ari loved how Marcelo always got his feathers ruffled if she used a new word in English that he didn't understand. She dropped her arms from his shoulders and placed his hands on her belly.

"We must make the house ready for the bambino or bambina that is coming."

Marcelo jumped up from the bed, in such disbelief that he forgot to congratulate her.

"You have told Avinash?"

A hint of sadness crossed Ari's face. "Not yet, but I will. I just need to find the right time to tell him."

Marcelo grabbed Ari by the hand. "There is no time like the present to wish for a healthy baby." He took her down the staircase and around to the ornate door underneath it.

"What is this?" she asked.

"This is your church. You wanted to pray? Go! Pray now!" Marcelo opened the door, and Ari found herself inside a small prayer room with upholstered seats and beautiful altar pieces.

"Oh my God, this is amazing. It's truly magical in here," she whispered.

Marcelo pushed her inside. "Good. Pray now," he said as he closed the door behind her and went out to join the women.

***

Twenty minutes later, Ari joined the ladies on the terrace with a cup of hot chocolate. She was wrapped in a plush, long robe to shield her from the cool evening air.

"Where's Marcelo?" she asked as she settled on a lounger.

"Oh, Marcelo went to bed in a huff, saying something about you praying with a baby. I think he's lost it, the poor soul," Lorraine lamented.

Ari tried her best not to laugh. "Did you see the little chapel? I love it in there. It's so welcoming, and it feels sacred and spiritual. It's exactly what I needed tonight. By the way, ladies, I'm pregnant."

Ari expected the women to respond immediately, but there was a delayed reaction. Claudia was the first to scream and hug Ari, and Lorraine followed with a more subdued embrace.

"Does Avinash know?" Lorraine asked.

"No, I will tell him, just not now."

"When's the big day?" Claudia asked.

"In August, a year and a couple of months from the time I arrived in London. You know, as crazy and morbid as it sounds, when Akash had me pinned in that room he said that life had a way of doing a 360. I am at the same point I was almost four years ago with Santos. We wanted to make this place our home, have a child, raise him or her the best way we could, and then live out our days looking out into that beautiful ocean. Here I am, almost forty, and the last thing I expected was to fall in love again or have a child or to live in this house. Yet, it's so strange. I am here. He was right."

Ari warmed her face over the hot chocolate.

"It's fate, *cara mia*. We talked about this before. Fate and love have brought you here." Claudia smiled as she raised her glass and Lorraine followed. "The Dolce Vita Club will have one more member. Cheers! *Auguri!*"

Ari smiled and raised her cup. "Thank you," she said, gazing up into the dark starry night.

The ladies looked at her, but neither asked who she was talking to. Was it God? Santos? Only Ari knew.

***

During the weeks that followed, the hunt for John Ronit intensified, and Avinash decided that no more announcements would be made to the public. The bounty he had offered months before had no takers. The media attention had not helped, and with the death of Ms. Singh — accidental or otherwise — it seemed that any attempt to draw John Ronit out was futile. Interpol knew he had help but were no closer to identifying the person known as Green Valley or to figuring out what the payback might be for aiding him.

Avinash did not spend his time in the pub as he had before, but he was still living a lonely life, often wondering what he was doing in London. Anjali tried to support him the best she could, but it seemed she was spending more time with Agent Baromeo and the two were enjoying being in each other's company. Avinash didn't blame Ari for leaving, but this time he wanted to be the one to protect her. He felt powerless. He often had dreams of Ari screaming and crying out to him, and he would wake in a cold sweat. His ability to concentrate at work suffered, and the public relations team was blaming him for Ari's resignation.

***

Ari started taking long walks on the beach to physically prepare for the birth of her child. Marcelo would accompany her when he could or when he was feeling up to it, but it was Claudia who joined her most often on what they dubbed The Baby Patrol. On the walks, Claudia would encourage her to talk to Avinash about the baby, preferably sooner rather than later.

Due to her high-risk pregnancy, Lorraine and Claudia helped Ari find a wonderful obstetrician in Naples. The birth would take place in Rome, and Lorraine had already found a hotel literally a block away from the birthing hospital. Ari would transfer to Rome during her last month and prepare for the birth.

In the weeks that followed, Marcelo took a downward spiral and, worse, managed to get an infection that put added stress on his already weakened immune system. Ari visited him in Sorrento in the evenings and brought him homemade soups.

"When will you tell Avinash of this news?" Marcelo asked one day when she was visiting.

Ari gave him all forms of excuses, none of which Marcelo thought were of any value.

"I don't think you are being honest with him. You should tell him. He must know. I thought you were more honorable in your relationships." Marcelo jabbed at Ari with no mercy. Ari bit her tongue. She had never seen Marcelo so convinced of anything, and for him to be on Avinash's side was odd. Yet, he was relentless in his accusations. Finally, Ari had enough.

"How can you talk to me about being honest, when you have been plotting behind my back to take my house away from me? Do you think I don't know about your plans to get me to trust you so you could maneuver your way in and take over the house?" Ari said, shaking and in tears.

Marcelo pushed his food away and ripped off his hospital bib. "How do you know this, Ari? Did Lorraine tell you?"

"No, Lorraine would never betray you. I was approached at the bank by a woman named Constanza the day I went to sign for the closing. She told me you had asked her for my documents, and she thought you might want to take the house away from me. Perhaps you should have invited her to dinner or given her more of your time. It might have rendered you better results. Later, when we met at the music festival, you came to my rescue and you kept popping up everywhere unexpectedly. I figured Constanza was not too far off in her warning. Is that what you call being honest?"

Marcelo clenched his jaw and asked point-blank, "So why did you let me into your life if you knew?"

Ari put her hand over his. "I was planning to talk to you about it the day I returned from seeing Avinash in London, but that was the day I . . . well, you know . . . I became sick."

Ari felt a tinge of shame as she recalled that day. "You took care of me. You didn't leave my side, and I saw a different Marcelo. There was empathy in your eyes even though mine were empty and in pain. I was not gone completely; I could see how you struggled to bring me back from the darkness day after day. Marcelo, you became my rock, and it became clear to me that I could not remove you from my life. And now you cannot remove yourself from mine."

Ari paused to catch her breath, hoping Marcelo would say something, but he did not. "If it was meant to be, the house, in the end, will be yours. Destiny threw us together, and the house was the reason we were in each other's company. Who was I to remove you from a house that means so much to you?"

Marcelo could not hold back his tears. They streamed down his face as Ari spoke lovingly to him.

"Marcelo, I forgive you. Please forget all of this," she said.

"*Mi scusi*," he said, wiping his tears as he got up from the bed and headed outside.

Ari knew she had touched a sensitive spot, a part of him that lay dormant for along time. She gave him his time alone and read her baby books as she waited for him to return.

When Marcelo had not returned thirty minutes later, Ari became concerned. A few minutes later, she heard her name over the PA system, with a request to come to the nurses' station. The nurse at the desk made a phone call, and Ari was asked to wait. She waited patiently but was growing nervous, wondering if she had been too hard on Marcelo and maybe he had taken a turn for the worse. An older gentleman arrived a few minutes later and explained that he was the head of the Oncology Department at the hospital. He introduced himself as Doctore Marco Mauceri and asked Ari to follow him to his office.

Once inside, the physician explained that he had called her for this meeting, because Mr. Donati did not have any known relatives and he had important news.

"I am his family," Ari explained.

The physician, who had now switched to perfect English, explained to Ari that she needed to be strong. What he was about to say would not be pleasant.

"Please continue," Ari said, grabbing a tight hold on the chair arms.

"Ms. Cordero, I have bad news for you. Mr. Donati has not improved with the cancer treatments. His immune system is not responding to any medication we have given him in the last weeks, and now his heart is suffering. I do not know how long it will take, but Mr. Donati will not recover."

Ari tried to control herself for the sake of the baby, though everything inside of her struggled with this news. "But what do you mean when you say he will not recover? I don't understand. Can I take him home with me?"

The doctor offered a resolute smile. "It is best that you take him home. Let him spend his last days in a pleasant place, with your care, and let him go in peace. I will give you some morphine injections to apply only when the pain is very bad. The nurse will show you how to inject him."

Ari summoned up more strength and asked the question she dreaded to ask. "How long does Mr. Donati have?"

The doctor looked down at his papers before responding. "He has weeks, perhaps a month or two, Ms. Cordero. I am sorry."

Ari got up, willing herself to be strong. "Thank you, Doctor. I promise to take good care of him."

The doctor followed Ari to the door and put his hand on her shoulder. "Mr. Donati is a lucky man to have you in his life."

"No, Doctor Mauceri, I am the lucky one to have him in mine. Grazie."

When Marcelo returned to his room, Ari had packed his bags and was waiting for him. "What happened? Are they kicking me out?" he said.

"No. You're fine. And there is no reason to be here when you're fine. I think I would like to eat pizza for lunch. How about you?" Ari said, trying to appear famished when she was not.

Marcelo grabbed the bags from her grasp. "Well, I know where to go for pizza."

Ari knew he would say that. She followed him with eagerness in her step and sadness in her heart.

***

When they returned to the house, Ari told no one of the news, only that Marcelo needed more care. She could not risk any of the ladies crying or breaking down in front of him, and she had to prepare mentally for what was coming. She made arrangements through a lawyer in Porcari to build a mausoleum for two bodies and to transfer Lucia from her crypt into the new location. Since Lucia did not have any living relatives, at least none who would oppose, there were no issues with the mausoleum, but transferring the body from one resting place to another would prove more trying due to the bureaucracy in the courts. The lawyer was paid to make it happen quickly.

Ari made everything in the house more comfortable for Marcelo, buying him an adjustable bed and customizing the room for ease of movement. One evening while it rained incessantly, Ari watched over Marcelo who lay peacefully sleeping, and she wondered if Santos could have survived the car accident. *Would I be caring for him in this very home? Would I have had the strength to nurse him or, worse, perhaps even watch him wither away on a daily basis?*

Ari gazed at Marcelo, his beautiful body now withered and frail, and wondered if she could have fallen in love with him if she'd never met Avinash. Life was throwing all sorts of inquiries and tests at her, and Ari had to be strong to hold on. She remembered her father once told her that he loved palm trees because of their strength. They could withstand high winds, even hurricanes, bending and twisting, even losing their fronds. But despite the battering, the palm never breaks. It bends with the wind. Ari too had to bend and be strong for Marcelo, just as he had done for her months ago. Ari had to be the rock for Marcelo, and she was accepting of that truth.

***

During the nights, Ari often had to give Marcelo morphine to help him sleep. He frequently confessed to her that he wanted to get her out of the house. This subject tormented Marcelo nightly. Ari accepted his apology and forgave him over and over again, hoping this would help him leave this earth in peace. Once she did, Marcelo was able to sleep. Ari stayed with him, praying that he would be taken with dignity and that he would not suffer more than he could withstand.

The moment came when Ari had to tell someone about Marcelo. She'd always been good at writing. It expressed her feelings much easier than speaking ever could. She decided to send a long, handwritten letter to Anjali. Ari took her time, writing what she felt and how she took the news about Marcelo. The eloquent letter was a stunning piece of strength and resolve, and she knew that once Anjali received it, she would come to her.

Ari needed a friend, one she could count on. Within a week, Anjali arrived in Positano and entered the home at 87 Viale Pasitea. She asked Ari to let her see Marcelo alone and headed to his room. She quietly went upstairs and kissed Marcelo on the forehead. He opened his eyes.

"Colgate, you came home," he said, smiling at her.

Anjali held his hand and gave him water to drink through a straw.

Ari sat on the terrace under the bougainvilleas and wept. It was like the rains that had come several nights before. It washed away all the impurities, and Ari felt a sense of relief.

For the next days, Anjali and Ari took care of Marcelo in shifts, but he was not responding to the morphine. Anjali phoned Doctor Mauceri and pleaded for him to prescribe a higher dosage. The physician didn't think Marcelo's heart could take it, but Anjali argued that it was inhumane to watch him die in pain. The doctor agreed and the new dosage was delivered to the nearby pharmacy.

By now, all the ladies in town knew Marcelo's days were numbered, and they graciously helped with food and cleaning of the villa. With the help of Daniela, Ari bathed Marcelo on the bed daily, as he was always so scrupulous about his person; she wanted him to feel clean even if he could no longer take care of himself. Ari and Anjali watched over him vigilantly, lovingly, and prayed long and hard.

The days and night were sewn together. Time meant nothing. The waiting felt endless . . . or was it only minutes? The bond the three had in the home was clearly spiritual, out of body and undeniably tragic. Pain does that to you. Tragedy can rip you apart or bind you together forever.

***

In London, Avinash was meeting with Sam at the pub after work when he received a call from St. John letting him know that Akash was being treated by a holistic Chinese doctor who lived on Newport Street in London's Chinatown. The doctor's wife called police to say her husband was visiting an injured man at a farmhouse just outside of London and was worried that he would get into trouble. When the directions were given to Avinash, he realized it was the same address as that of his late uncle, the location where his cousin and his new bride were now living after their wedding. Fearing his family's life was in danger, Avinash dashed out of the pub, and Sam drove as fast as he could out of the city and toward the countryside.

When they arrived, local police and Interpol had barricaded the area and reported that a subject matching the description of John Ronit was inside. Police on horseback were patroling the grounds and helicopters flew over the home; it seemed like something big was going down, especially to the villagers that lived nearby. Avinash warned St. John that his family lived in the house and that he needed to find out if they were safe. As luck would have it, the couple had left on a trip to Amsterdam and had not returned, according to a report St. John received from the team. Avinash was relieved but wondered how they proposed to flush Ronit out. As they radioed one another, Ronit would fire rounds into the air to make sure no one moved in any closer.

The Chinese doctor explained to agents that Ronit was not following his medical instructions, and the infection had caused a sepsis that was taking a toll on him. Sam asked Avinash if he thought talking to him would help police maneuver around and catch him off guard. St. John would not have Avinash in the middle; in fact, he called to let him know about the latest update on Ronit, but he never expected Avinash to show up on the scene.

One thing was for sure—Ronit was weak, perhaps even dying. If they could get him to unload all his ammunition, they would have the signal to take him down. Unfortunately, there were no assurances that he didn't have a bigger set of guns or explosives inside.

***

Five hours had passed since they arrived at the scene, and Ronit was still holed up inside the house. Every time the agents spoke to him he seemed less eager to fight, but he was still unwilling to give up. Finally they received a call from Ronit asking if Avinash Batra was there. St. John was in a quandary. Should he let Avinash enter the home to appease Ronit and have a chance to take him down? It was risky but he wasn't sure he had any other strategies that would work, other than to let time run its course. With his weakened state, maybe they could wait it out.

Avinash asked to talk to Ronit, and one of the agents placed the call and switched on the speaker.

"What are you doing, Akash?" Avinash said when Ronit answered the phone. "You're surrounded. There is no way out. Give yourself up. You must stop this."

"You have my mother to thank for this, Avinash. She was not the saint you think she was. She hated her brother and she trained me to hate him as well. This was all her idea, but as she said, dear Avinash, I was always too weak to finish the job. She wasn't kidnapped. This was all her game to get money so we could leave you penniless and destroy your reputation. When we were younger I appreciated your help . . . at first. But eventually, the life you had . . . what you had become . . . the women and your money—I hated you for all of it."

Avinash let him talk as the agents circled the house. "I am a product of the hate my mother had toward uncle. I truly would have destroyed you. I still want to destroy you."

"Why did you come here, to my uncle's house?" Avinash asked.

Ronit was breathing heavier.

"You don't remember, do you? We came here with Suniel when your uncle was sick. You went to talk with your uncle and you left Suniel and me alone. We got to know each other very well, Avinash. That has always been your problem . . . leaving your women alone because you're too busy working. This was the place where Suniel and I got to know each other better. You're repeating the same mistake now, letting some Italian loser take care of your girlfriend." Ronit's laugh was maniacal and mocking.

"What about Ari?" Avinash asked. "Why would you want to hurt her?"

The mobile went silent and there was a long pause.

"She was my last hope. I would have left everything for her, but she has something I want more. I will get it eventually . . . but maybe not today."

St. John scribbled something on a piece of paper and handed it to Avinash.

"Will Green Valley be getting that something you want, Akash? Did Santos have something to do with Green Valley?" Avinash waited for a response.

St. John raised his hand and signaled to the agents to wait. Ronit began to fire at the walls, as if to summon them to come and get him. Suddenly, the agents burst into the home and more shots were fired. Ronit fell to his knees but continued shooting at the agents. Avinash yelled for the agents to stop, but they didn't listen. In an instant, the sharpshooter took Ronit down with a bullet to the head. Akash Ramkissoon, aka John Ronit, was declared dead at 6:22 p.m.

Avinash was held back from entering the home. He sat on the bumper of the police vehicle with his hands on his head in disbelief as Sam walked over to him.

"What is it, Avinash?"

He looked up at Sam in despair. "Akash was a puppet. If I'd known back then, I could have saved him from all of this."

"He made his choices, Avinash. In life we are free to choose, but we are not free from the consequences of the choices we make. Life is a series of decisions. Akash chose and lost." Sam continued to counsel Avinash like a brother. "It's over now. This horrible nightmare is over. You're no longer in danger and, more important, Ari will be safe.

Hopefully our lives will finally go back to normal. Now, old chap, let's get the hell out of here."

Sam drove Avinash back to London, and they stopped at a quaint pub. Avinash was disheveled and silent. At the table, he called Anjali to tell her about Akash, but she didn't answer. Avinash knew she was in Positano with Ari, and he felt a strong need to talk to her, to find out how Ari was doing. He couldn't get Akash's words out of his head no matter how hard he tried. Was he leaving Ari alone too long?

"Take me to the office, Sam," Avinash said, tossing back the last of his drink.

"Now? It's already nine in the evening," Sam reasoned.

"Now."

Avinash pushed back from the table and headed out the door. Sam paid the bill and followed behind him.

***

In his office at World Bank, Avinash sat thinking about all those moments when he could have helped Akash. Could he have been more of a teacher to him, shown more support, given him a position in the bank? He wrestled with his feelings of guilt, trying to reconcile all the memories to find an answer that made sense. Did Dutta's sister truly have so much hate for her brother that she was capable of fashioning her own son to destroy him? Avinash decided he would be the one to take care of Akash's wife and child by opening a sizeable trust fund for them in India. They would have no wants or needs, and their lives would not bear the mark of a murderous husband or father. Avinash would make sure of that.

Avinash was drained from the emotionally charged afternoon. As he gathered his thoughts, he saw a confidential file on his desk. Normally, Anjali placed these sorts of things in his drawer, but this was different. Avinash opened the file and found a note from Anjali.

This is the person you are in love with. Go to her.

He read the beautiful letter from Ari to Anjali, and it warmed his heart. There was goodness on this earth after all, and Ari was the personification of it. In one part of the letter Avinash read:

I knew that death was knocking at my door to take me away, and in those deep, dark moments of despair, I'm ashamed to say that I wanted to go. There was no inner voice, no survival instincts, no need to pray or hope - only darkness took over my soul. Slowly, gradually, a light pulled me back in, and it came in the form of a man who was lost and had given up too. This man nursed me back to life.

Marcelo fed me, combed my hair, read, talked, sang, and cried with me, accepted and held me. The man that once hated everything I stood for by owning his home was now the very man who cared for me because it was the right thing to do. How can I leave him now that he needs me the most? How can I abandon someone who means so much to me and whose love and care gave me the strength to love again?

There were also beautiful words about how Ari felt toward Avinash, how she fell in love with him from the moment they met. He was surprised to learn that her feelings for him made her memory of Santos appear distant and full of guilt. The more Avinash read, the more he wanted to run to Ari and hold her, be the man that she needed.

As he put the letter down, he also realized there was truly nothing more he could have done for Akash. He'd chosen his path in life and paid the price. For Avinash, however, life was handing him another opportunity, one he could not waste and one that had a short shelf life if he did not react quickly. React is exactly what Avinash Batra had to do. The powerful man of action took control and faced his mistakes. It was time to right all the wrongs, and he was not going to lose his chance.

That evening, Avinash phoned Anjali again to let her know that Akash was no longer a threat and that she and Ari were now safe. He also informed her that he had read the letter she left for him.

"Thank you, Anjali. I have much to do before I see Ari again. See you soon, my *didi*."

***

In Positano, the late nights for some reason gave Marcelo moments of lucidity where he spoke to Ari in clear sentences. But there were times when Ari had to give him a higher dose of morphine, and he seemed to speak in riddles.

Marcelo was fixated on a desire to be on a boat in the ocean, and there was a small boy who ran about while Marcelo took in the sun and fished. The boy was beautiful, blond and precocious, always running about, and Marcelo feared he would fall overboard and drown. He repeated the same thing, night after night.

Ari would ask who the boy was or where the boat was going, but there was never a clear answer no matter how she persisted. These repetitive dreams or hallucinations started to affect Ari's sleep—what little she could get. Anjali helped immensely, but Marcelo shared most of his inner

326

demons with Ari. Something tugged at her. It seemed that Marcelo was asking something more, but what?

On a day that he was more lucid, Ari asked him, "Marcelo, what does the ocean mean to you?"

He thought for a moment. "It is that one thing I would like to see for the rest of my life," he said.

Ari understood this to mean that he'd always loved the ocean, and being near it was his passion. Perhaps this idea of laying him to rest in the town of Porcari was not well thought out. After all, he never said that he wanted to be buried there; he said he wanted to be with Lucia. At that moment she realized perhaps the ocean was what he loved more than anything and that it represented Lucia. The little boy was the son he could have had with her, and he wanted to rescue him.

Maybe it wouldn't make much sense to anyone else, but it made perfect sense to her. The next day, Ari set out to find a place along the Amalfi Coast that had a perfect view of the ocean. Then she would arrange to transfer Lucia Ferretti's body to that location where they could be together forever.

***

On most evenings, and especially on the weekends, the ladies visited Marcelo. Afterward, they would sit outside on the ocean terrace near the warmth of the fire pit to speak about him. They talked about his crazy past on the Amalfi Coast, the rapid-fire joke sessions, always knowing the perfect spot to eat, the tango classes with Claudia and his ability to always have her breasts land on his face when he dipped her. They laughed and cried, recalling anecdotes and memories that only good friends can build through years of love and respect. It was no secret that the pain of watching their friend leave them slowly created a bond between them that was impossible to duplicate.

All of the beautiful homes Marcelo constructed with his expert style and attention to detail, many still scattered about on the Amalfi Coast, were a testimony to his skills and love of the region. The masterpiece, however, stood at 87 Viale Pasitea, and the women all knew they were a privileged bunch to have seen a dilapidated mess turned into an Italian villa of style and beauty. The home was already receiving numerous requests for feature stories from home and architectural magazines. But there was no story to tell at this time, only one harsh reality. The man who made it all happen was slowly leaving this earth, and Ari and her friends would do whatever it took to help him pass with dignity and grace. It was the only thing that truly mattered now.

***

Early one morning, Ari awoke Anjali and told her to take the small jute bag and to simply get rid of it.

"Remove it from my sight. Perhaps it brings bad things to me, and I have been keeping it like an amulet. Besides, it was the elephant vase that Devyani told me would bring me luck, not this." Ari was adamant.

As Anjali took the bag from her hand, they heard a faint sound coming from Marcelo's room and rushed to his side. Ari was unafraid and approached the bed, sitting beside him.

"*Sono qui, sono qui,*" she said. "I'm here, Marcelo." He squeezed her hand and smiled, his eyes watery and unfocused. Ari simply held his hands and kissed them. Marcelo was leaving her.

Anjali knelt at the foot of the bed and began praying in Hindi, wiping her tears with the hem of her sari. Ari remembered the words she'd told her grandmother when she was so ill— *Please don't leave me. Don't leave me alone.* All the memories of the people she loved, the losses in her life, flooded her heart and tore pieces from it.

Suddenly, Marcelo lifted her face from his chest and whispered in perfect English, "I will always be with you. I will always care for you. Be strong, my Ari. I am going with my family. *Ti adoro.*"

Marcelo took his last breath and left Ari early on that Sunday morning, when the sun was rising and its light flooded the room like a blessing. As Anjali raised herself from the floor and Ari stood up from the bed, one of those rays of light struck the mirror on the dresser and beamed over Marcelo, causing dust particles over his bed to rise up to the ceiling. It was beautiful and it calmed Ari as she watched the beam of light envelope her friend's beautiful face. Anjali came over to Ari and they embraced, watching over their friend in complete peace, knowing he left them and was now with Lucia.

The ocean waves were especially loud that day. All they could hear in the room was the roar of the waves as they crashed onto the shoreline. Ari walked slowly over to Marcelo and closed his eyes. She kissed him on the forehead and her tears washed over him. Anjali covered him and prayed as Ari backed away. Strangely, she didn't feel alone, and she was pleased that he passed so peacefully in the home he loved.

Ari was fortunate that during times of stress, God gave her a peaceful strength to move forward. This time would be no different; he would open another road for Ari to pass through. She went downstairs and phoned one of Marcelo's construction workers, telling him to send someone for the body. Within minutes, Lorraine came with the rest of the ladies and they prepared food and comforted Ari who was strong and with resolve but unreadable.

While they waited for the mortician to take Marcelo's body, she asked Anjali to leave her alone with him. Ari would clothe him for the last leg of his trip, and she wanted to do it alone.

***

The mausoleum that Ari found was abandoned by another family who could not afford to finish it. It was unfortunate, but it was a strange comparison to Marcelo's life years before, leaving behind his home because he was penniless. The mausoleum had been repaired by some of the builders assisting Marcelo on Ari's home. They finished it in two days.

The site was in the town of Vietri sul Mare on the Amalfi Coast, a small town on the cliffs with amazing views of the ocean. Just above the town, on the edge of a cliff and overlooking a view of the ocean that Marcelo would have loved, the two lovers would lie for all eternity. Lucia Feretti's remains were being shipped from a little cemetery in Porcari, *Valle Verde*. When she signed the shipping label, the name caught her eye, jolting a memory buried deep inside, but she didn't have time to think much about it. When Lucia's remains arrived in Sorrento they would be transferred to the Church of Santa Maria Assunta in the

Flavio Gioia square of Positano, where she would lie until Marcelo's remains arrived.

***

The mass was beautiful, and every corner of the church was filled with the people of Positano who either knew Marcelo or had heard of the Amalfi Coast legend. The two coffins stood next to each other as Father Nicodemo gave a solemn and tragic account of Marcelo's life. Ari sat in the front pew with Anjali and the rest of the ladies. There were ten of them in all, women who adored him, wept, and prayed for him.

At one point during the ceremony, Ari felt the need to approach Marcelo. The women looked at each other, and Father Nicodemo stopped his sermon to let Ari have her moment. Ari placed her hand over Marcelo's coffin, tears streaming down her cheeks. She reached behind her neck and unlatched a necklace she was wearing and placed it over the coffin. It was the necklace Marcelo had given to her when she recovered from her illness, the one made of gold with a sun on one side and the words *Cercare la luce*.

Marcelo had given her a message in her darkest moments. *Look for the light*. Ari leaned in closer and whispered, "I have found my light. Go in peace, my friend." She wept so sweetly over his coffin that it caused a profound silence in the church, a feeling of love that enveloped and comforted the audience.

"I ask you to stand and pay tribute to Marcelo and Lucia," Father Nicodemo said as the weeping subsided. The town held hands and prayed as Ari continued to mourn over the coffin of her friend.

Twelve men, including Agent Baromeo and members of Marcelo's crew from the home construction site, approached the coffins. Anjali hurried to the front and pulled Ari away.

"Come, dear, they need to take Marcelo and Lucia. Ari, please come with me."

Ari pulled herself away from the coffin and sobbed in Anjali's arms. The women comforted her and watched as the men, three on each side of the coffins, lifted the two lovers and carried them away.

There were two cars waiting above the city on the main road, the only road that led to their final resting place. The city folk followed behind in a procession with Ari, Anjali, and Lorraine in front of them until they reached the top of the city.

When the procession of vehicles finally arrived in Vietri sul Mare, the solitary mausoleum stood in front of them. They rested the caskets on two large blocks of granite while friends arrived to pray or say their final farewells. Ari had dried her tears and was feeling a sense of calm.

Whether it was the satisfaction of completing her friend's last wishes or the beauty and tranquility of the cliff where the mausoleum stood, she could not tell, but the truth was that it was a beautiful day. After an hour of praying and meditation, Baromeo told Ari and Anjali it was time and they agreed to finish what they came to do.

The men lifted the coffins and placed Lucia and Marcelo inside the beautiful stone mausoleum and closed the door. It made a solid noise as it closed, momentarily startling Ari. Aldo, one of the workers, took a plaque that Ari had asked an iron artisan in town to make and welded it to the top of the door of the mausoleum.

The inscription read:

Per un amore che non muore mai

Lucia Feretti e Marcelo Donati
Per Sempre
87, Viale Pasitea

It made sense to everyone. *For a love that never dies, Lucia and Marcelo, Forever,* in the home they loved.

CHAPTER SIXTEEN

W hen they returned home, Ari thanked the women who were with her that day and asked them to go to their homes and rest; she wanted to be alone. Anjali followed her inside and went to her room, giving Ari the space she needed. As she looked out at the ocean from her window, her fingers lingering on the small jute bag of dirt in her coat pocket—the bag Ari had given her to throw away. *Evidence or not, too many people have died over it*, she thought.

Anjali opened the doors and readied the overhand pitch. With all her might, she tossed the bag out over the terrace. As she did so, she heard a faint click as something hit the floor. Anjali looked down to find a tiny piece of metal at her feet.

"Do you have a story to tell me?" she said.

She scooped the piece of metal into a tissue and ran to call Baromeo.

***

Ari's thoughts took a momentary dark turn as she remembered the words of the old woman in Tuscany who told her there would be a death and a birth. She feared that she would return to the dark place, and it frightened her terribly. Ari reached into her dresser for the medication that would help, but she remembered she was pregnant; she had to be strong on her own.

The home seemed empty without Marcelo strutting about giving orders to the workers and without the constant noise from hammers and drilling that had annoyed her for so long. In the calmness of the evening, remembering all those things she and Marcelo talked about, she noticed more nuances and details that he left for her: an embossed figure of an elephant over the mantelpiece of her fireplace, almost identical to the one on the vase that held Santos remains for so long; a small altarpiece in the library room that was being used by Agent Baromeo had the image of the virgin of Montserrat, patroness of Catalonia, a region that was so dear to her.

Down the hallway of the long corridor upstairs, the ceiling had carvings of cala lilies, her favorite flower. Ari marveled at all the messages and details that Marcelo had left for her. It was like being on a treasure hunt.

Tired and drained from the day, Ari stayed in her room for the rest of the evening, no food or drink, just memories to nourish her soul—and prayer . . . lots of prayer.

***

Anjali was busy downstairs entertaining all the guests in Ari's absence, but between hosting and serving food alongside Agent Baromeo and the ladies, Anjali wondered how Ari was doing all alone upstairs. *Would this be another episode that would shake her to the core and leave her in a state of depression?*

"Did you find out anything about that piece of metal I gave you?" she whispered to Baromeo when they had a quick moment alone. "If Ari finds out, she'll kill me. She told me to just get rid of it."

"I sent it to the lab in London, Anjali. We won't know for a couple of days. Should we check on Ari?" Baromeo asked, trying to get her mind off the subject.

Without letting the other ladies know, Anjali and Baromeo snuck upstairs and found that Ari was not in her room. It was actually freezing without the warmth of the fireplace that Marcelo would fire up every night.

"Where could she be?" Baromeo asked.

"I don't know, but I'm worried about her. Let's start searching."

Baromeo agreed and they set off to find her, looking from room to room without success. Ari was gone. Anjali, beside herself in grief, hurried downstairs to ask the ladies for help.

The women set out to look for Ari. They sectioned off the town and worked in pairs, planning to regroup in front of the church in one hour to see if they'd made progress. If someone found her, they would call Baromeo and he would take care of the rest.

It was early February, and the windchill factor was high. Positano was a tourist area during the spring, summer, and fall months, but as soon as the warm climate left the region, it was a virtual ghost town. They searched all night and could not find her. At four in the morning, they abandoned the search and crashed at Lorraine's apartment to recover.

Anjali couldn't sleep. She prayed that the baby Ari was carrying would help her make the right decision.

"Everyone in town knows Ari," Baromeo said in an effort to comfort her. "If something terrible happened, we would know immediately. Ari is fine. Give her some credit; she is much stronger than you think."

***

The place to look for her was right under their noses the whole time. Ari was in the church—thinking, praying, recovering, asking for strength and, most of all, grateful to have had Marcelo in her life. Exhausted from the funeral and the long night, but feeling her spirits lifted a bit, she decided to return home. It was six in the morning when she arrived, and she was surprised to find the house empty. As she walked toward the terrace, she saw a figure near the window, but the early morning light cast shadows which did not allow her to clearly make out the person's face. Ari moved in closer and the figure turned toward her.

Could it be Green Valley? she wondered. *Is it Marcelo back to say something, or could it be Santos?* Ari was unafraid and stepped closer.

Finally, the shadowy form stood before her and smiled with its eyes. Ari did not hesitate for one moment and rushed to him, repeating his name and embracing him so tightly that he almost lost his balance. He laughed as he hugged her.

"My darling, *sundara rāni*. How I've missed you, Ari," he said sweetly in her ear as he held her with all his strength.

Ari kissed him as tears flowed down her face. "My God, Avinash, I can't believe you're here. I love you so much. You won't believe everything that has happened."

"What has happened, Ari? You're shaking," he said, holding her at arm's length.

Ari hugged him again. She didn't want to let go of him or spoil the moment between them.

"Please, darling, tell me what's wrong," he begged. "Where have you come from so early in the morning? The front door was open, and I didn't find Anjali or Marcelo home."

Ari could not hide her feelings any longer, not from Avinash. She looked down, trying to find the words, but the pain etched on her face told him something horrible had occurred. Avinash nudged her chin so he could see her eyes, and Ari said the words she never wanted to say.

"He's dead." She swallowed hard and continued. "Marcelo passed away. The funeral and burial was . . . I just came from there. I mean, it was yesterday, but I was at church now."

"No! I can't believe it," Avinash said. "Come with me, Ari. You're ice-cold."

He held her as they walked to the living room and settled her in front of the fireplace. He'd stacked some wood and little the kindling before she came home, but the room was still cold. Placing his wool jacket over her shoulders, Avinash sat beside her and rubbed her arms. "Tell me how it happened."

Ari told him the news of Marcelo's illness, the chemo, and his strength throughout the whole process. Avinash listened intently. He was always a good listener, keeping full attention and his eyes on her, feeling her pain or joy as she told any story. Ari knew she could tell him anything, and he would drop what he was doing to listen or give advice.

"I'm so sorry, Ari. He was a good man. I wanted to get the chance to thank him for being such a good friend to you, but I guess I came too late. I read your letter to Anjali. It touched me, and I want you to know I was a fool for ever doubting your love for me. I have left everything behind — my life, the bank; even the fear of Akash is gone. He was killed by police last week. The fool barricaded himself at my uncle's house in the country. Can you believe it? At first I blamed myself for his death. It was all so pointless."

Ari stroked his face and kissed him sweetly. "It's not your fault, Avinash," she whispered. "You tried so hard to help him, and he never understood the love of family or friends. Akash did so much to hurt our relationship, but all of that is over now. You're here with me."

As they kissed, the Dolce Vita Club made their return and found the lovers nestled in each other's arms. They were all eager to ask Ari where she'd been, but that could wait. Anjali was thrilled to see Avinash and wanted to say hello, but Lorraine quietly pulled her away to let the two lovebirds have their time together.

"This is the best medicine for Ari right now," she whispered to Anjali. "Let's go to Covo for breakfast."

***

Ari and Avinash spent the rest of the day together, catching up and talking. They both needed each other now after the turbulent months they'd had and the losses they'd experienced. They felt as if life had given them a second chance, and a whole new page had been left blank for their story to continue. Ari could not detach herself from Avinash for one moment as she explained all the details of the house and the wonderful things Marcelo had done to restore it.

With Ari, he discovered that the home had a soul that was undeniable. It had a charm and a pull that was unexplainable, and he felt like he finally belonged— in the home and in Positano itself. He never wanted to leave. For the first time, Avinash knew he had found a home, a life, a woman that he loved, and nothing else seemed to matter more than that. He didn't think of work, now that Sam was taking care of things. Avinash didn't care about the expensive home, fancy cars, or clothes; none of it was of any importance to him. His world was here, in Positano, in this beautiful home with the woman he loved, and he planned to enjoy every moment of it.

After a couple of days together, Ari decided it was time to host a gathering of their friends to celebrate, and Avinash was more than happy to help host. There were thirty invited guests, including all of the ladies and their significant others, Anjali and Baromeo, who were now an item, and some staff from their favorite restaurant in town. They would keep it low-key; after all, Marcelo had just passed away and Ari was still in mourning, as were many of their friends. The get-together would be a celebration of a new life, now that Avinash and Ari were together, and it was the perfect time to remember old friends and to celebrate new ones.

Ari and Avinash spent most of the morning devising a menu and cooking up everything from appetizers to first, second, third, and fourth plates and, with the insistence of Avinash, certain palate cleansers for his distinguished guests. Anjali rolled up her sleeves, cleaning the sardines that would be grilled with olive oil and garlic and peeling the tomatoes for the sauce with the pasta. The house hummed with guests, and though there were moments of sadness, there was also laughter, love, agape, appreciation, and a sense of joy just to be alive. Ari was starting to feel tired, and Anjali noticed her leaning back against the counter and taking a break.

"How's the little mommy? Feeling okay?" Anjali whispered.

Ari smiled. "Yes, the little one is taking a lot out of me, I guess."

Anjali looked over to make sure Avinash was not near and asked, "Will he find out tonight? Perfect occasion, *meree dost*." Ari smiled and patted her tiny bump.

Raising one eyebrow, Ari taunted her friend. "This may be the night. Stay tuned, dost," she giggled.

Ari and Avinash decided to place the appetizers in such a way that it would showcase the home. You would literally have to go into every room of the home to try all the delectable morsels of food and drinks they had prepared. Small chalkboards offered detailed explanations of each dish in both English and Italian, and the waitstaff prepared each guest their signature drink. The drink of the evening was appropriately named The M&L Cocktail, for Marcelo and Lucia.

From twelve in the afternoon until almost twelve in the morning, guests dined and drank, but mainly felt at home at 87 Viale Pasitea. They reminisced about many things, but there was no denying that the home held within its walls the love, hope, and happiness of the people that inhabited her.

***

Ari cleaned up the last of the dishes with Anjali and Lorraine, while Avinash, Gianni Baromeo and two locals smoked fine Cuban cigars on the terrace. Finally, Avinash came over to Ari and took her away from the domestic duties. After all, this was her home, a home she built against all odds, trials, and adversity. It was time she took a rest and enjoyed it like a queen, his *Rānī*. Avinash came up behind her and whispered something in her ear. Ari suppressed a loud laugh and followed him onto the covered terrace.

The evening temperatures dipped, so Avinash grabbed a thick, ornate throw and put it over her shoulders. He lay on the lounger and asked her to lie in front of him. Ari nestled between his legs and he wrapped his arms around her, kissing her neck and rubbing his hands over her arms to give her warmth.

"What you've done to this home and to see how the people of this town admire you is truly amazing, Ari. When we first met, I remember you said that you admired me and everything I had achieved and that I had raised the bar high. Those words stayed with me, but you have surpassed me in so many ways, darling. I am so proud of you. I am so honored to be the man you love and the man you wish to spend your life with. You have chosen me, and my heart feels so full of love. You know you're my queen, Ariadne Cordero."

Ari knew it was time. The new Avinash was opening up to her like never before and was ready to receive the news. She looked up at him, her eyes green and vibrant with love.

"Avinash, my heart belongs to you, my darling. It beats only for you, and so does the heart of the child I carry inside of me, your child, Avinash." Ari placed his hand on her belly and sweetly kissed him. When she pulled back to see those smiling eyes, they were full of tears.

"Ari, you're . . . you're—?"

"Yes, Avinash. I'm almost five months now. You're going to be a daddy."

Avinash sat up in disbelief, realizing that his life had made such a drastic and wonderful turn in such a short period of time, and it all started by just giving love a chance. He could not control his tears or his joy. He felt such a degree of thankfulness that he moved Ari aside, stood up, and walked over to the edge of the terrace overlooking the ocean without giving Ari a response to the news. He held on tightly to the banister, overwhelmed by his emotions.

The evening mist was coming in fast, but Ari gave him a moment. The idea of parenthood was new for Avinash, and it was a lot to absorb. With that, Avinash knelt to the floor and began to pray and chant. Ari could not understand what he was saying, but she heard in his humbled voice such honesty, his tone filled with thankfulness, forgiveness, piety, and honor.

She had never seen this side of Avinash, but she knew that although he gave the sense of being a modern Indian man, he held certain traditional beliefs that she hoped brought him closer to his culture, especially India's rich, spiritual one. As she waited, Ari heard a faint, calm whisper say, *Procura lo*—go to him, and it startled her. Enthralled by Avinash's reaction and obeying the voice, she walked over and knelt beside him, placing the throw over his shoulders to shield him from the cold. In prayer, the bracelet that Devyani had given her years before in India would be useful, and she placed it in his hands. Avinash whispered, "*Dōharānā*, please repeat," his face moist with emotion. Ari prayed with him, repeating his words as best she could.

Within moments, the haze that filled the skies that evening started to clear and the moon peeked through. Anjali arrived on the terrace, witnessing the moment, and she too dropped to the floor in prayer, feeling the blessings pour down and take over the home and everyone in it.

The remaining guests came over one by one to see what was happening, uncertain of what they were seeing. Lorraine explained that the couple had been through many trials, and they were giving thanks for everything they had. They were thanking God for the new chance to be together and for the new life that Ari had inside of her.

It was something everyone could understand, regardless of their beliefs. So, without exception, they all joined hands and listened to the soft hum as Avinash prayed in Hindi and Anjali and Ari repeated the beautiful words. It was a striking melody coupled with the crashing of the waves beyond the terrace.

It was a spiritual moment for the people there that evening, a cleansing for the home and everyone in it. Regardless of their religious beliefs, each person left there knowing something special had happened that night, something special lived at 87 Viale Pasitea.

***

That night Ari and Avinash couldn't sleep. They talked about their plans, where the baby would be born, where they would raise him or her, and even what name they would give the child. Ari was happy with the birthing team in Naples but realized it was too far and not very practical.

She was even thinking of renting an apartment in town to be closer to the hospital.

"Nonsense," Avinash retorted. "We first need to figure out what is best for you and the baby. Where we live after that . . . I'll leave that up to you."

Ari smiled in disbelief. She saw a changed man in Avinash.

"Stay here, darling. You need your rest," he said. "I'm going downstairs to be sure the staff cleaned up after the party last night."

Avinash made his way downstairs and found the house was spotless, except for the stacked wine bottles left out front for recycling. He prepared Ari some tea, yogurt, and fruit with toast and placed it all on a tray. Before heading upstairs he called Anjali in her room, wondering if she knew the name of Ari's doctor. He knew that Ari would have a risky pregnancy and wanted her to take all the precautions necessary. Anjali gave him the name of the doctor in Naples and the phone number, but also told him she was scheduled to go with Ari for an ultrasound this week and suggested perhaps he should accompanied her.

Before he left her room, Anjali asked, "What happened last night, Avinash? It was like the house was filled with a great spirit. Did you feel it?"

Avinash smiled. "Yes. I think it was God smiling down at us, perhaps smiling down at me for the first time in many years. It felt good, Anjali. I'm glad you were here with us."

After breakfast, Ari showered while Avinash walked through the home, marveling at the design and its prime location. For all the millions he'd paid for his flat in London, it did not compare with the breath of life this home gave you within its walls. For the first time, Avinash realized why it was so important for Santos that Ari move here and find a life that would bring her safety and happiness. If he were in his place, it would be his choice too.

Avinash stood on the terrace and scanned the ocean as far as his eyes could see. He knew that Ari had been put in his life for a reason. He analyzed his life and realized that perhaps with the loss of his mother and sister when he was a boy, he may have developed an unhealthy need to protect women and this created a pattern in his relationships. There was much more to loving someone than just shielding them from evil.

Avinash had to feel a sense of commitment and love, trust and forgiveness before he could move forward. He realized that this pattern of choosing young, inexperienced, helpless women may have developed as a mechanism to protect them from men like his father, who tried to forcibly take Anjali as his wife, or Akash, who convinced Suniel to act against him at the World Bank takeover and endangered Ari's life when he tried to destroy them.

More than ever, he wanted to share his life with Ari and their child—not because it was tradition or a sense of honor that was calling or because this is what people expected of him. Avinash wanted Ari and everything she represented. He wanted her friends, family, this town she loved so much, the house she turned into a home, her joys, her sorrows, the darkness, the light, and everything that came with her. Avinash understood why Ari loved Santos so much and why she could succumb to the darkness of depression, her life slipping away when he abandoned her in London.

This trip to Italy was a game changer. It proved to be spiritually and emotionally deeper than he had ever imagined it could be. Life had truly unfolded before him in more ways than he ever thought possible; Avinash had been given a chance to join Ari in a new life with their unborn child. He would not waste it.

***

It didn't take much to convince Ari that it should be Avinash to accompany her to the obstetrician appointments from then on. Ari agreed, but Anjali was such a good support system and she wondered if Avinash could fill her shoes. After all, she was scared during these few months of pregnancy. The risk of losing the child was high. There could be complications, and the doctors warned her to keep stress at a minimum.

During the drive to Naples, Avinash was careful with the twists and turns of the road, hoping that Ari could physically take the stress. He couldn't help but marvel at the magnificent beauty of the mountains and the ocean below.

"I know it's really beautiful, my love, but can you keep your eyes on the road, please?" Ari said, gripping the sides of her seat.

He laughed. "It's just so amazing. The ocean is so blue. The hills are so verdant."

Verdant. Verdant. Ari repeated the word to herself. It wasn't an unusual word, but it triggered a memory in her. It was the same feeling she had when she heard the name of the cemetery where Lucia had first been buried. *I must be losing my mind,* she thought.

The ride alone convinced Avinash that the baby needed to be born somewhere with a convenient location. When they arrived, Ari was tired and agitated from trying to navigate Avinash through the narrow and complicated streets in Naples. She managed a smile as he opened the door for her, trying not to let her emotional state show.

Within minutes, the nurse called Ari in, and the ultrasound took place with the technician, the doctor, Avinash, and several young medical interns in attendance. Ari felt like a science project, breathing in and out slowly and reaching for Avinash's hand, which he quickly held in support. The doctor reported in Italian to the interns that Ari was a healthy woman, thirty-nine years old, and the child was almost at the sixth month of gestation, a crucial month for a high-risk pregnancy.

Avinash stood behind her head and leaned down as he whispered in Hindi how much he loved her, how much he adored her, that she was his life, and that this was the most beautiful gift anyone had ever given him. Seconds later, an image appeared. It was the size of a small eggplant, and the doctor pointed out the infant's head, arms, and legs. He turned up the volume, and the heartbeat sounded like a freight train. Avinash was completely enthralled, staring at the monitor as Ari watched his boyish face full of excitement.

"Everything looks good. The baby is coming along fine, Ms. Cordero," the doctor said as he congratulated her.

"When is the baby due, Doctor?" Avinash asked.

"A fair estimate would be mid-August, Mr. Batra. Hopefully we will be able to determine the sex of the baby at the next ultrasound. With any luck, it will not be bashful."

Avinash asked to speak to the doctor while Ari changed out of her hospital gown. He followed the doctor to a private lounge down the hall.

"Doctor, I trust that you are doing the best for Ari. However, I'm concerned with the distance she has to travel to be seen by your hospital staff. This may cause her some stress. As you know, this is our first child, and I want to make sure she has the best care. I would like to take her to London with me for the baby's care and birth. Do you think there is any problem with my plan?"

The doctor thought for a moment. He had heard through Anjali that she had a life in Positano but that her love was in London.

"I believe you must do what is best for your loved ones. If you think she will have better care in London, you should prepare to leave quickly. She must have follow-up care every four to six weeks, and Ms. Cordero must follow the strictest guidelines. Will you make sure that she does this, Mr Batra?"

"Yes, I will. You have my word," Avinash said.

The doctor shook his hand and wished them well. "Once you arrive in London let me know, and we will transfer all her medical records to the new facility."

Ari was waiting in the hall when Avinash and the doctor stepped out of the lounge. She smiled as he approached. She wasn't sure what was going on, but she knew that any concerns Avinash had were certainly normal for a first-time daddy.

"Everything, okay?" she asked.

"Yes, yes. It's fine, darling. Let's get you home. We have much to do." Avinash took her hand and guided her back to the car.

***

On the way back, they stopped in Sorrento to have a quick lunch. Ari took him to O'Parruchiano, the same place where she had once dined with Marcelo and Agent Baromeo.

Avinash was an avid eater and tried everything Ari put in front of him, enjoying every plate with extreme delight— seafood, grilled vegetables, pasta, and antipasta. She loved to watch him eat. Actually she enjoyed watching him do just about anything. Avinash had a boyish charm about him that was intoxicating. As she played with her pasta, Avinash asked her why she wasn't eating. Ari gave him a silly laugh.

"You're doing enough eating for me and the baby."

"I'm sorry darling. So much is happening and I haven't had time to take it all in. I'm anxious and happy. It makes me want to eat and enjoy life, enjoy being with you. I'm truly not thinking about anything else other than being with you and the baby," he said as he smiled with his eyes.

Ari leaned back in the chair and felt a sense of relaxation she hadn't felt in a long time. Finally there was nothing hovering over their heads to worry about. Akash was gone and there was no threat. Ari sensed that Avinash was up to something and wanted him to spill the beans sooner rather than than later.

"So, what are your plans, Avinash? Where is the baby to be born?"

Avinash swallowed the last piece of pasta and put down his fork. He was not one to mince words, and he knew Ari always wanted to hear the short version.

"I would like your care in the hands of someone I can trust. I would like the baby to have the best of care, in the best medical environment. It's not that I don't trust the doctors in Italy but—"

"It's just that you trust them more in London?"

Avinash took Ari's hand. "Please try to understand me. I'm not attempting to pull you away from everything you love. I too have fallen in love with this place. These last couple of days, I can truly see us living here as a family. You should have the best care, and you know that I have the finest connections in medicine, but they are all in London."

Ari sighed and took in everything Avinash had said. Though she did not want to leave her newly remodeled home which she was just getting accustomed to, Ari realized he was right and that a medical team in London would be best for their child. She squeezed his hand and smiled.

"I love you, Avinash Batra. I want to make a new life with you and our baby. I believe in you. I trust you and I know you only want the best for us. Let's go to London whenever you say."

Avinash stood from the restaurant table and hugged Ari. This was a big deal for the once traditional, don't-show-affection-in-public man, but his happiness was bigger than his customs and he wanted the world to know. This was a new beginning.

***

When they returned, Anjali, Lorraine, Claudia, and Baromeo were waiting to hear the news. They met up at Chez Black for a late dinner and spent the evening talking about their plans. It was obvious that Lorraine and Claudia were not too happy that they would be leaving, but Avinash assured them they would return home once the baby was able to take a flight. As the dinner progressed, Avinash led Anjali to the side of the restaurant for a chat. Ari had seen them conspiring about something for the last couple of days, though she had no idea what. Whatever it was, Ari thought they had managed to either hide it extremely well, or perhaps the pregnancy was making her lose her ability to have a sixth sense.

When the dinner was over at ten in the evening, they all took a taxi back to Ari's home for a nightcap. Within seconds of arriving at the house, Avinash disappeared and Anjali hustled Ari onto the terrace where there was someone waiting. The older woman dressed in a sari stood up and walked slowly toward Ari. The whole setup was strange, and though she did not know who she was, Ari was unafraid and drawn to the woman. *Could she be a family member of Avinash or Anjali visiting from India?*

Anjali brought Ari closer and whispered, "Ari, do you remember her?"

"Should I remember her?" Ari said as Avinash appeared at her side.

"Think, darling. She has come a long way to see you," he said.

Suddenly, the woman took Ari's hands and started to sing a lullabye in Hindi. Her hands were soft and warm, and Ari was filled with memories as the woman's familiar words embraced her. Ari's eyes filled with tears. She opened her mouth to speak, but no words came out. She quickly let go of the woman's hands and reached to pull the bracelet off her wrist.

"You gave me this. You're my Devyani. You have come for me." Ari hugged Devyani with such an embrace that all she could do was weep in the woman's arms.

There was not a dry eye in the house, including those of Agent Baromeo, who had heard the touching story of Devyani and Ari from Anjali but could not believe the magnitude of devotion between the two women who had not seen each other in almost thirty years.

"How did you find me?" Ari asked after several minutes.

Devyani, who spoke in English, told her that Avinash had been searching many months for her and finally found her. "He has brought me to you," she said.

Devyani had been living in Chembur, a neighborhood in Mumbai, and had retired from nursing. "He told me about you and how you needed me. I had to come to you."

Ari looked up at Avinash with love and gratitude in her eyes. "This means so much to me, Avinash, to find Devyani again after so long. It's like my life is now complete. But why now?"

Avinash, still moved from their reunion, took a step forward and sat Ari in a chair just behind her. Like a gallant king, Avinash went down on one knee in front of Ari. He took her hand and kissed it sweetly.

"I wanted to make sure everyone you love was here tonight before I asked you the most important question of my life, but we are still missing some people."

Suddenly he motioned with his hand toward the terrace entrance and in walked Diego with his wife, Madeline, and behind them, Sam. They stood next to Avinash, and Ari let out a gasp, trying to get up and hug her family and friends but Avinash did not let her.

"You can greet them later, Ari. If not, I'm afraid I'll be on my knees all night." The group let out a nervous laugh, including Ari, who was somewhere between laughter and tears.

Avinash began. "Ari, from the moment I saw you, I fell deeply in love with you. The problem was, back then I didn't know what true love was, but you slowly showed me. Your example of devotion, friendship, patience, and forgiveness created the man that I am today. I cannot live without you. You are my light and my life. There is only darkness when I don't have you. Now that you carry our child, a gift of love that words cannot express, the only life that I want is alongside you. I know Santos and Marcelo are watching us from a privileged place. I have asked them for their forgiveness, their courage, but especially for their blessing. In front of God, all of our friends, and our family, I want to ask you the most important question of my life." Avinash leaned forward and Anjali placed her hands over her mouth to squelch her excitement.

"My darling, will you take this journey with me and be my wife? Will you honor this man and marry me? Ari, *Mujhasē śādī karōgī?*"

Devyani placed her hands on Ari's shoulders and squeezed. Ari looked up at her and smiled as Devyani nodded. They both knew what this meant. Ari then scanned the faces of each of her friends and her family. The answer was clear—as clear as the day she decided to move to Positano and had first landed in London. The road that destiny chose took her there first, and unknowingly she found a love that was different than Santos's, but it was a love she could not deny and it was just as real and precious. With that, Ari leaned in closer to Avinash who was waiting and nervous.

"I will marry you, Avinash Batra. You are the man I was waiting for. You are the man I love in this new life, and now our journey is one."

Avinash pulled a ring from his trouser pocket and placed the beautiful emerald-shaped diamond on her finger, and the two lovers kissed to seal the moment.

***

After a restful night, Avinash awoke to find that Ari was not in their bed. With the beautiful night of passion they'd had, he hoped to find her in bed and wake her with a kiss. Opening the sliding glass doors to the bedroom, he found Ari on the large terrace below, speaking with Devyani. He decided to give them some time together to catch up and went to freshen up for the day ahead. Anjali and Lorraine wanted to meet with him promptly at eleven.

Twenty minutes later, Avinash joined the women on the terrace and Ari poured him some tea.

"Sit, darling. Devyani and I were just talking about you."

He gently kissed her on the cheek and told her that he needed to go to town for some errands. "Please stay and catch up. I promise I won't be long. May I have the keys to the car, darling?"

In town, Avinash met with Anjali and Lorraine at Hotel Poseidon where Lorraine worked as a wedding planner. He strolled in, dressed in jeans and a long-sleeved, lavender-colored shirt, with a coal-grey sweater wrapped around his neck. There were few hotel guests; it was the last week of March after all, not the crazy summer tourist season.

Catching sight of Avinash from a distance, Lorraine whispered to Anjali that he looked better than ever. Anjali smiled and took a sip of her gin and tonic.

"Love is in the air," she said.

Avinash hugged them both before taking a seat. "Thank you for all your support yesterday. The evening went beautifully, just the way we planned. I couldn't have done it without the two of you. Ari was exceptionally pleased with Devyani and Diego there." The waiter came and Avinash ordered an Irish coffee.

"Well, Avi-ji we thought that we should not stop the planning process." Anjali said with a smile. "Since everyone is here and we have the best wedding planner on the Amalfi Coast, why not continue this journey all the way to the nuptials?"

Avinash tilted his head as he studied them. He didn't know exactly where they were headed, but he knew they were hatching a devious plan.

"Let me see if I understand you. You want to plan a wedding?"

"No," Lorraine said in her bluntest British tone.

Avinash breathed a sigh of relief. "Oh. For a moment there I thought—"

Lorraine interrupted him. "We want to plan your wedding with Ari this weekend in Positano, at this hotel, with everyone in attendance. Oh, and by the way, everyone is here for the wedding, not only for the engagement, dear."

The coffee arrived and Avinash asked the waiter for more Irish whiskey. He figured he was going to need it.

"I don't understand," he said. "What is the rush?"

Anjali leaned in and stopped him from frantically stirring his coffee. "The rush, dear Avi-ji, is that your soon-to-be wife is pregnant. The baby is due in four, count them, four months. Not to mention that everyone she loves is in one place and in the town she loves more than any place in the world. What is there to think about, Avi-ji?"

Avinash stammered but nothing sensical came forth.

"We don't need a religious ceremony. Lorraine can find a nondenominational priest. We'll have a brief blessing, rings exchanged, a nice dinner with friends, and voila! The happy couple sails off into the sunset."

Avinash was not about to make any such decisions without Ari. "Let me discuss this with her. I don't mind it, but I want her to be in agreement. I mean, so much has happened in these last months, and we really don't need any more stress. Don't get me wrong. I agree it's a good idea. I don't want to burst your planning bubble, and I appreciate the gesture, but let me talk to her."

The ladies agreed and Avinash rushed back to the house to speak with Ari. When he arrived he found her chatting with Diego and Madeline while Devyani was writing in a notebook nearby. Avinash took a seat and gathered his thoughts.

"Is everything okay, love?" Ari asked.

"Yes, but I need to ask you something. May I pull her away from you for just a moment?" he implored, hands in prayer mode.

"Of course," Diego said as he walked out with Madeline and asked Devyani to follow them to the terrace.

Ari got up from the couch and sat next to Avinash.

"What is it?" she asked.

Avinash rubbed his hands together nervously. "I just met with Lorraine and Anjali at Poseidon, and they had an idea. Don't get me wrong. It's a good idea, but I didn't want to agree to anything without taking to you first."

Ari started to laugh hysterically.

"What's so funny?" he asked.

Ari was almost in tears. "Oh my, Avinash. You poor thing. Anjali and Lorraine were planning with you at Poseidon? That could only mean one thing. When do they want us to get married?"

Avinash laughed, amazed and relieved. "How did you know they were planning our wedding?"

Ari hugged Avinash. "Those two have become a formidable event planning team. Anjali is planning on moving here with Gianni and becoming a wedding planner with Lorraine. I knew once you put that ring on my finger they would start organizing things. It seems they literally didn't even sleep on it."

Avinash kissed Ari and told her how much he loved her. "So what do we do, love?"

CHAPTER SEVENTEEN

It was a clear, crisp day in April, and the Poseidon hotel was closed for the ceremony of Avinash Batra Puri and Ariadne Cordero Echegui. The guests, forty-two in total, sat in the covered pool area of the hotel overlooking the cliff that exposed the rocky coast of Positano that lay beneath. A white canopy covered the outdoor terrace, and the portable heaters were scattered about, though the warmth of the guests would have sufficed.

Avinash did not have too much time to think about looking fashionable on his wedding day, wearing the same suit he wore to Diego's wedding. The only difference was the pagri, a Punjabi turban and a bindi on his forehead to signify he would soon be a married man. The guests waited patiently while the bride was getting ready with Devyani and Anjali, who dressed her in a beige and gold sari covering her small bump and a pallu that hung toward the back of her shoulders to keep her warm. Devyani decorated her hands in beautiful henna *mehndi*, and from her neck hung the necklace Avinash had given her for his cousin's wedding.

There was little time to plan, aside from the marriage license in Naples. Ari didn't have time to find Avinash a ring. Claudia, the queen of "everyone owes me a favor," had a jeweler in Rome, who offered to locate the most unique band he could find.

Ari had only one request for the procession: she did not want to walk alone. Diego was chosen to take the journey with her halfway down, and then Sam would take over the second half of the journey, finally handing her over to the eager groom. At the last minute, Father Nicodemo, the priest for Marcelo's funeral, agreed to officiate the wedding without his normal priest attire but as a friend, allowing the officiality of the ceremony and the Nulla Osta in the Italian courts.

The music began to play. It was an old Hindi song that Avinash had picked, and the sound of sitars and chants resonated through the hotel and up the cliffs as the cool wind took it toward the skies.

The floor, covered in peonies, seemed like an ocean of white clouds as Ari, who radiated love, walked slowly with Diego. Then Sam met her halfway and she took his arm, kissing Diego before moving on. The Dolce Vita Club, who whispered among them how beautiful and serene she looked, could not control their emotions as Ari finally reached the handsome groom. Avinash stretched out his hand to Ari as Anjali placed garlands of flowers over them both and the officiant began to speak. The aroma of incense floated over the ceremony, and Avinash glowed with pride, unable to take his eyes off Ari. She was an angel.

They both agreed they did not want a long sermon, but they did want to say something to each other that they had each prepared. As Avinash held Ari's hands, Anjali came forward with a box and opened it. Avinash dipped his thumb inside; he rubbed a red powder onto Ari's forehead and up to her hairline. He then began his words to her in Hindi while Anjali translated them to English:

"I will stay with you always; I will not separate from you.

Fate has granted you to me, so how can I release you?

I won't ever let go of these hands.

Our destinies are now one.

You recognized my love.

You understood my value.

Now my heart has awakened, love has come to its senses.

I will stay with you always; I will not separate from you."

As he finished, Avinash placed a beautiful diamond eternity ring on Ari's finger.

"My love Ariadne, I give you this ring as a symbol of my love. As it encircles your finger, may it remind you always that you are surrounded by my enduring love forever and ever.

Ari responded. "Avinash, I accept this gift, my love. I will wear it gladly. Whenever I look at it, I will remember this day and the vows we have made."

Anjali then handed Ari the ring that Claudia had bought for her to give Avinash. She had not yet seen it before this moment, but she was pleased. It was a gold ring with a beautifully cut ruby, the perfect stone for Avinash.

As Ari prepared to say her words to Avinash, a cool breeze wafted down through the guests up toward the bride and groom. Suddenly, one of the lanterns fitted inside a wooden boat fell to the floor, shattering into pieces. There was only one like it at the Poseidon, and Lorraine had thought it would be a good piece to dress up the ceremony. Ari interpreted the boat as a sign that Marcelo and Santos were both present—Marcelo being the one who took her out to sea to give Santos his resting place in the blue waters of the Mediterranean. This gave Ari the strength she needed, and she squeezed Avinash's hands and began to speak the words she'd written for him:

"I, Ariadne Cordero, take you, Avinash Batra, to be my partner in life, loving what I know of you, and trusting what I do not yet know. I eagerly anticipate the chance to grow together, getting to know the man and the father you will become and falling in love with you more and more every day. I promise to take this road of life with you as your loving partner and to cherish you through whatever life may bring us. If we suffer, may I be your support. If we are happy and plentiful, poor or miserable, may we celebrate our gains or losses, but always may it be together. In the Bible, a woman named Ruth tells her friend what I wish to tell you now. If any words were truer about a love that is beautiful and pure, these words are meant from me to you my love.

"'Entreat me not to leave you or to return from following after you. For where you go I will go and where you stay I will stay. Your people will be my people and your

God will be my God. Where you die, I will die and there I will be buried. May the Lord do with me and more if anything but death parts you from me.'"

Avinash had tears in his eyes and could not hold his emotions any longer. Anjali handed Ari a tissue, but she did not use it. Instead, she leaned closer and kissed away his tears until there were none. Avinash ran his fingers along Ari's face and gazed into her eyes as all the guests remained silent and enthralled. Never had they seen so much love between two people. Ari then remembered the ring, and she placed it on his finger:

"My love Avinash, I give you this ring as a symbol of my love. As it encircles your finger, may it remind you always that you are surrounded by my love forever and ever."

Avinash responded. "I accept this gift, my love. I will never take it off."

The audience began to laugh, and Avinash raised an eyebrow with boyish wonder. "I mean, whenever I look at it, I will remember this day and the vows we have made to each other."

Father Nicodemo blessed them and pronounced that they were now husband and wife. "You may kiss your beautiful bride," he said.

Avinash was more than happy to oblige.

***

During the quaint reception that was held inside because of the drop in temperature, Ari went to change into something warmer, and Avinash sat with Sam, Gianni, and Diego discussing football stats. Devyani did not leave Ari's side, and she welcomed her presence at every moment. They were getting ready to walk hand in hand, like mother and daughter, down the lonely hotel lobby on their way to join the others when Devyani stopped and placed her hand on Ari's belly.

Ari smiled. "What are you feeling, Auntie?"

Devyani wrapped her arms around Ari and took her down the hall. "I feel a healthy baby is on the way and that you will be very happy with this man. You know, my sweet Ari, it was Avinash who brought me here, but I have known your life story for many years."

Ari didn't understand what she was trying to say. "How could you know?"

"You were never alone after Santos left you," Devyani said with a mysterious smile.

Tears filled Ari's eyes. She knew this was true. She had felt his presence many times before. She took Devyani's arm as they climbed the three steps up to the restaurant.

It was late and some of the guests had left, except for the diehard Dolce Vita Club members who would naturally stay until they closed the place down. Avinash rushed over to Ari and embraced her, slowly leading her onto the dance floor.

"Do you remember where we first heard this song?" he asked.

Ari was trying to keep her balance and not paying close attention to the song. Then she heard the familiar words. "Yes!" she exclaimed with delight. "In Bath, on our first outing. It was playing in the room next to ours, and we were dancing just like this."

Avinash held her close and everyone else joined in. Sam even danced with Claudia, who was happy to find a dance partner, though Marcelo would always be irreplaceable.

***

After the wedding, they decided to stay in Positano a little longer, at least until the end of spring. Positano was more beautiful than ever. The flowers bloomed and everything seemed so crisp and new. At their home, on the terrace with Anjali, Gianni, and Avinash, Ari marveled at the mountains. For some reason, they seemed new or different to her.

"They have an interesting green hue," Avinash said. "Is it the same in Italian as you say it in Spanish, *verde*?"

Ari felt the strange feeling again. "Green. *Verde*. Green. *Verde*," she repeated out loud to Gianni.

Gianni jumped in. "*Verde*. Green. Valley. *Valle*."

Their eyes met and suddenly they knew.

"Val *verde*!" they yelled in unison. "Agent Valverde! It's code for Green Valley!"

They scrambled out of the house with Baromeo reporting this new development to St. John and the team.

Now in custody with London officials, Agent Raoul Valverde, who Akash dubbed "Green Valley," had been his accomplice for years. It was how Akash always stayed one step ahead of them; the information was coming from within Interpol. Agent Valverde also confessed to the manslaughter of Santos Echegui. His intent on the rendezvous evening in Mexico was to let him go, but he feared retaliation from Akash and decided to just ram the car, retrieve the box of guns, and the microchip.

The crime lab in Rome later reported that Santos had taken pictures and had found bank slips proving the money was being funneled out of Vida Blue Tequila to offshore banks. All of the information was dumped into a tiny microchip inside a bag of dirt with blue agave seeds. It was a big find indeed. The case was closed and Santos Echequi was vindicated and honored with a plaque from the Interpol team who had worked five long years to bring the case to justice. Valverde was stripped of his badge and sent to London for processing. He would be spending a long time away from his team. For her support and relentless sleuthing skills, Anjali was recognized by the team and given an honorary plaque for her contribution to the case. Ari knew all along that Santos was the hero. Santos would always be her hero. She now had four of them, Santos, Marcelo, Avinash, and the baby.

***

Ari flew to London monthly to see the new obstetrician, Dr. Prem Kapoor, who was an excellent doctor, and because of Ari's good health, she was given a little more freedom with her pregnancy. The healthy baby boy was due sometime in August and would be named Jai Dev Batra. They bestowed upon him two middle names: Santos and Marcelo. In preparation for their journey back to London to await the birth, Ari made her plans to leave Positano.

Avinash was still head at World Bank, taking a secondary role and using much of his time as a financial business consultant to large corporations. This gave him the freedom he longed for. A new chance to be with his family. Anjali would not be returning to World Bank. She had now embarked down the entrepreneurial road with Lorraine and would wait for Avinash and Ari to return to Positano the following year. She was now happily living with Gianni, who had taken a post in Sorrento and was now the head of Interpol for the Southern Italy Command. Devyani decided she had no reason to return to India, having no family other than a sister, and vowed never to separate from Ari again. Ari and Avinash bestowed her with the honor of being the baby's nanny and auntie, and she continued to be Ari's support. Claudia and the rest of the ladies would be waiting anxiously for the birth announcement to get on the next flight to Heathrow whenever the word came.

***

On a sunny day in Positano, Ari and Avinash packed up some of their belongings and drove along Viale Pasitea. Arriving at the center of town, they walked the rest of the way to the marina. It was a beautiful, clear, crisp day, and it meant so much to Ari to walk through the streets waving goodbye to all her friends. Many of them waited at the dock, including some of the townspeople who had grown fond of Ari and Avinash and had witnessed her tribute to Marcelo and Lucia.

Their trip out of beautiful Positano with Devyani included a one-way ride by ferry to Naples and then a flight to London-Heathrow. As the engines of the ferry powered up and the seagulls circled above, Avinash pleaded with Ari to hurry.

"Come now, love," he said, extending his hand out to Ari as she said her final goodbyes. "Please, Ari, the captain is ready to go."

Ari took a deep breath and brought her hands to her lips, waving goodbye one last time. "Ciao, ciao," she said, taking her husband's hand and climbing aboard the vessel

Ari looked the part of motherhood; she was radiant and beautiful. One of the young skippers lifted the heavy ropes mooring the vessel to land and they were off. Ari took Avinash by the hand and tugged him to the back of the ferry.

"That's the view, my love. That's the city I wanted you to fall in love with."

Before them, Positano fanned out like a peacock, proudly displaying its white houses, cliffs, cascading bougainvilleas, and rolling hills. Avinash gazed across the water at the town Ari had fallen in love with so long ago. There was no doubt that Positano had captured his heart.

***

Anjali arrived back at 87 Viale Pasitea and threw herself on the couch. She needed to pick up the final pieces of her belongings to take them to Sorrento, but first she wanted time to go out to the terrace for one last look at the city. Her feelings were a strange mix of sadness and serenity. If she closed her eyes, she could almost hear Marcelo's silly jokes. *Such a crazy character*, she thought. *A cherished soul.*

Anjali had so many fond memories wrapped up in this house. Those late evenings with Claudia dancing across the terrace floor by herself were classic. These moments would never be erased. It was like a vivid Fellini movie playing in her mind. Along with the days and nights of tragic loss and sorrow, Anjali remembered how food and drink, laughter and music brought everyone who lived in this home comfort and love—the very same love that remained drenched in the spirit of this house even now.

"It's time to go," she whispered.

Before heading back inside, Anjali took one last look at the beautiful Mediterranean Sea. As she did so, something caught her eye just beyond the terrace. She looked closer to find an interesting plant growing wild and uninterrupted. It was blue and healthy-looking. The jute bag she tossed out from the window above must have fallen there. Growing ever so strong was a majestic blue agave plant.

There was Life. It was Blue. Vida Blue.

THE END

About the Author

Susie Perez Fernandez writes fun, adventurous, romantic fiction.

Despite her background in public relations and corporate event planning, Susie found that being a destination wedding planner and traveling all over the world created the best storytelling. Susie began writing, Vida Blue, her first novel, after planning several weddings in Positano, Italy.

When she's not writing, Susie enjoys cooking, traveling, and exploring different cultures. She speaks several languages.

Born and raised in South Florida, Susie lives in Miami Beach with her husband, Eddy, and her Schnauzer, Pachanga.

www.21talesmedia.com/

21tales

Printed in Great Britain
by Amazon